I0716408

BENEATH THE SURFACE

PRIVILEGED SECRETS
BOOK 2

HARPER WOODS

Copyright © 2023 Harper Woods.
All rights reserved.

No part of this book may be reproduced, or stored in a retrieval system, or transmitted in any form or by any means, electronic, mechanical, photocopying, recording, or otherwise, without express written permission of the author.
For more information about this book, please contact: info@harperwoodsauthor.com

Paperback ISBN: 978-1-7374116-2-8
Library of Congress Control Number: 201867530

Cover design: Covered By Nicole
Interior design and eBook conversion: Jennifer Eaton
Manufactured in the United States of America

DISCLAIMER

The conflicts, intrigue, twists, and turns in this book are fictional
narrative for the purpose of entertainment and wonderment. The
controversial topics expressed are those of the characters and should
not be confused with the author's. The story contains fragments of
facts experienced by many, but in no way do any of the characters
reflect, in whole or in part, any real person, but rather, reflect a
conglomerated set of issues experienced by those who have belonged
to a religious cult or abused by persons in positions of power.
This novel in no way discredits the countless individuals involved in
organization and entities, including religions, who sincerely devote
and sacrifice their efforts and resources for the good of humankind.
There is also an abyss full of accounts of corruption and abu
se in religions, cults, business, and government that have been
publicized. This story takes those factual accounts and candidly
narrates a fictional novel.

Through hard times and difficult people, we recognize and strive for higher ground. I dedicate this book to those hard times and difficult people who have taught me more about myself and have pushed me to grow into being the author I wanted to be, and the person I was meant to be.

*"Perhaps the secret of living well is not in having all the answers
but in pursuing unanswerable questions in good company."*
~ Rachel Naomi Remen

PROLOGUE: PHUGTAL MONASTERY, LADAKH, NORTHERN INDIA

Unlike most young boys who preferred sleeping in on early autumn mornings, Sundara always rose at the crack of dawn. He sprang from his bed in the Phugtal monastery, eager to head outdoors, no matter how chilly the air.

His seven-year-old curiosity was like no others his age. Sundara craved adventure and exploration—that was how he learned. The wise old monks wryly enjoyed observing how different he was from his twin sister, Ananta. Ananta absorbed knowledge and developed an intuitive understanding of the world around her through quiet observation, but Sundara learned by doing. His education required a hands-on approach—he learned zoology by dissecting dead creatures. With a steady hand and meticulous accuracy, he'd carefully dismember a beast's anatomy down to the smallest parts, with focused concentration on how each segment worked in harmony with the whole. Then he would spend hours trying to mimic the unique physiological powers each animal was endowed with.

On this particular morning, after scarfing down breakfast and impatiently enduring his mother's insistence that he wear warm outer garments, he bolted out the door of the monastery, all but vibrating with anticipation. He filled his lungs with the crisp morning air. His nose tingled with the intense early-morning aromas of the plants, the ground, and the animals who lived near his monastery home. His eyes took in the changing colors as fingers of sunlight reached the mountain peaks around him, then spread downhill, turning dull browns to reds and oranges and grays to shades of green. He loved this time of year and the changes it brought to his world, as autumn fulfilled its task of dialing back the energy of summer in preparation for the restfulness of winter in the majestic Himalayas.

Mireille, his mother, allowed Sundara to roam free, and he explored whatever part of his environment suited his fancy. Some days it was the Tsarap River and all the life forms that thrived in the high-altitude cold blue waters of the Himalayas. On other days, he headed into the scattered woodlands that framed the farmed, terraced pavilions so he could learn about the creatures who lived there.

Today, Sundara had a particular destination—he headed straight for an inconspicuous cave that was tucked behind foliage growing out of the steep precipice that surrounded the monastery. He'd never noticed it until yesterday. He'd stumbled upon it in the early evening, but it was too late in the day to explore it. With the sun's last sliver of glowing tangerine quickly fading, he knew that he had to get home. Sunset was curfew, and his mother didn't tolerate tardiness.

If he'd found the cave when he was even a few months younger, he still might have passed it by, figuring it was too dark inside to find anything interesting. Mom would never have let him handle fire at his age, so taking a torch was out of the question. Now, however, he no longer needed a torch or even a candle to see his surroundings in the dark. By dissecting and studying bats, Sundara had mastered echolocation. With his eyes closed and his mouth stretched wide open, he could engage his diaphragm to emit high frequency sounds inaudible to the human ear. The sounds would bounce off objects and return to him in mathematical patterns, providing him with a mental map of his surroundings. With his newly developed skill, he could identify objects blindly in the pitch-dark without the aid of firelight. The time it took for the sound wave to impact, the resistance of the impact itself, and the change in pitch upon its return, distinctly revealed whether it was a human, a tree, an animal, a rock, or even an insect.

With the surefootedness of a snow leopard, Sundara climbed the cliff with ease and entered the cave. He felt exhilaration rising in his soul, anticipating the discovery of life forms he'd never encountered before, including some that probably never saw the light of day. Within twelve steps, the blackness enveloped him, and he stopped to get a feeling for the environment. He was cautious, but not fearful. The last thing he wanted was to swallow a nasty winged bug, so he had to rely on all his senses to be sure it was safe to open his mouth.

After determining the coast was clear, Sundara closed his eyes and focused his entire attention on preparing his larynx and diaphragm. Slowly and carefully, he opened his jaw as far as it could possibly go, breathing in through his nose and out through his mouth. With each exhale he would consciously stretch it even further, until his mouth became a cavern of its own and his vocal ligament elongated into a tense vibration of a high-pitched sound wave. At first, the map of the cave came easily to him. He identified the location of stalactites and stalagmites. As the sound wave disturbed living beings from their rest, he recognized bats by the fluttering of their wings.

Sundara made his way deeper inside, taking delight in the twinkling lights on the ceiling, which looked like a starry night sky. *Bioluminescent glowworms*, he thought excitedly. His ears picked up the distant trickle of slow-moving water far ahead. It was to be expected in a cave like this, as rainwater and snowmelt from higher altitudes found their way downhill through the cracks and crevices in the mountain. He'd mentally charted his path and was about to close his mouth when a strange frequency bounced back to him, a frequency that made him immediately stop in his tracks. It was barely detectable—if he hadn't been paying acute attention, he would have missed it. Perhaps that's what the object was hoping for, or maybe it was testing his ability. Nothing slipped by Sundara.

The boy didn't scare easily. Although he was only seven, he was tough, confident, and courageous. He already knew he was different from all other humans, as were his parents and twin sister. He was aware that he possessed a singular collection of physical and mental abilities, and that he could outmaneuver and outsmart just about anything or anyone he encountered. Right now, however, the presence of this unexpected, unknown life form triggered his adrenaline, making his heart pound and his blood pressure spike. He became both nervous and euphoric—whatever was out there was big.

The mix of fear and excitement was so intoxicating that Sundara became immobilized. Mouth agape, he stood frozen in place, all the while knowing that the object was getting closer. Closing his mouth, his acute sense of smell picked up the damp, earthy aroma of leather— an odor that tickled his nose. He felt the heat and humidity of the creature's huge body pulsating an arm's length from him.

As if on cue, he reached out his hand just as the brute's huge palm grasped his young and fragile arm. It then wrapped its large fingers firmly but gently around Sundara's wrist as if it were a slender twig. Without resistance, Sundara allowed the giant to guide him deeper into the cave.

CHAPTER 1
GERMANY

Ruth stood over Heinrich's grave in a private cemetery in Quedlinburg, where generations of Müller family ancestors had been laid to rest. She focused intently on the three blue forget-me-nots she'd just planted in front of his headstone. Meanwhile, her mind replayed the fond memories they had made together.

Until Heinrich's funeral, Ruth had never met her family. Her mother had twelve brothers and sisters, but Ruth had been taught by her parents from a very early age that anyone outside the Society of Truth—even blood relatives—was to be considered "worldly," bad association. As a result, Ruth was kept isolated from them. Now, she was meeting her cousins for the first time, and hearing their stories was both overwhelming and delightful. She was even more thrilled to meet her last living aunt—her mom's sister—a ninety-three-year-old woman who eagerly reminisced about what Ruth's mother had been like as a kid. There was humor in the stories she told, but there was also heartbreak. Ruth's mother had cut all ties with her Sibylline family when she had joined the Society of Truth. She never saw any of her siblings again.

Jacob Hoffman, Ruth's driver and protector, waited patiently in the car while she planted the flowers. Handsome and blond, with a masculine rectangular face, ice-blue eyes, and a chiseled, square jaw, he looked like he'd stepped out of an Aryan poster from the 1930s. Tall and powerfully built, he had the ideal physique for a bodyguard. From

Glocks to knives to ninja throwing stars, he'd had extensive weapons training, and was an expert in taekwondo, hapkido, and kung fu. His encyclopedic lethal skills were an odd juxtaposition to his gentle nature—Jacob was a staunch defender of the Way of Kyndeness, which made him the perfect candidate to protect Ruth. Ruth was spry and energetic for a woman in her seventies, but there was no way she'd be able to defend the coveted artifact that had been entrusted to her care.

Having planted the forget-me-nots, Ruth wiped the dirt from her hands, bid one last farewell to Heinrich, and then walked toward the car. Jacob had already opened the door for her. Once she eased herself into the passenger seat of the Mercedes, the soft patter of light spring rain, coupled with the metronomic back-and-forth of the windshield wipers, lulled her to sleep almost immediately. It had been an eventful few days, and she was exhausted. After she saw the love of her life, her dear Heinrich, take a fatal USF bullet to his forehead, Ruth's friends had quickly arranged private air transport. Sibylline pilot Min Yunghui had flown them both from New York to Germany so Heinrich could be buried in the family plot in Quedlinburg.

Ruth didn't wake up until the car stopped moving and Jacob had pulled up to the Bavarian-style chalet that she would now call home. The cottage sat on land that was part of her family's estate. The acreage was adjacent to a large lush forest that surrounded the Weisshotel Castle. Ruth hadn't had a chance to research her new home, but she didn't have to. As she reconnected with her family and Heinrich's family, her relatives educated her about the area. A son of one of Ruth's cousins, a man her family referred to as "Little Henry," even though he was six foot five, was a gifted botanist who eloquently expounded upon the special scientific properties of the soil surrounding Quedlinburg.

She opened the car door and breathed in the fresh alpine air. After fifty-some years of dutiful obedience at the headquarters of the Society of Truth in Brooklyn, New York, she'd become accustomed to urban aromas—the local pizzeria, hot dogs and sauerkraut from street vendors, and the smell of fabric softener wafting out of Laundromats.

She'd also become inured to the mercurial changes in city weather —how quickly winter reverted to spring each April, catching everyone in shirtsleeves and unprepared for the sudden chill. Throughout their half century of marriage, Heinrich had always made a priority of protecting Ruth, and that included keeping her out of bad weather—or trying to. He would plead with her to take the subterranean walking tunnels that connected the properties the Society owned at the end of the Brooklyn Bridge, but Ruth always insisted on using the streets and sidewalks. She told him she preferred it, never confessing the darker reason for her refusal. The tunnels brought back frightening childhood memories of hiding underground from the Stasi, the East German secret police. The trauma of it had left her with lifelong claustrophobia —she often trembled at even the first steps into a cellar or basement. Sometimes she could overcome it, sometimes not, but she preferred not having to deal with it at all—trudging through a snowstorm or sweltering in the August heat was so much easier.

The aroma of the trees and foliage in Quedlinburg had a rich scent —better than fresh. Almost...ambrosial or divine. She wondered whether local *Heilpraktikers* were still using regional plants to treat common maladies. Even the forget-me-nots that adorned Heinrich's grave had medicinal value. Healers crushed the plants leaves and stems and applied the mash as a poultice to stanch the flow of blood from a cut. Heilpraktiker was the German term for wellness practi-tioner, or naturopath, and it had been an honored healing profession for centuries. As a child, Ruth had dreamed of becoming one, but it was always out of the question—growing up in the Society of Truth had made it impossible. The religion abhorred botanical potions, and cautioned their members that using them bordered on witchcraft or demonism.

Ruth would have been shunned for pursuing any education in naturopathy, but for women in the Society of Truth, it wasn't just learning about medicine or healthcare that was forbidden. Higher education of any kind was frowned upon. Although there were women in the Society with advanced degrees, they'd earned them before joining the religion. The Society deliberately made no use of their educational achievements—Donna Chandler, whose husband was a member of the Elder Board, held a PhD, which qualified her for a desk job in the marketing department, where her intelligence and creativity languished.

Ruth, however, became the exception. After Heinrich began his tenure on the Elder Board, Ruth found herself with a singular niche job. She had a sharp eye for detail, and could spot typos and grammatical errors that others had missed. As a result, she became the Society's proofreader—hers were the last eyes on every piece of Society religious propaganda before it went to print.

Because many of the pamphlets and tracts she was asked to review had been poorly written, Ruth's position evolved from proofreading to editing to writing. Eventually, she became the primary author/ghostwriter of most of the Society's literature. No one could ever know, of course—for her to have told anyone that she was the actual author would be an indication of a nonsubmissive and independent attitude not befitting a godly woman. It was recognition enough, she was told, just to be given a small office on the tenth floor—the nerve center of headquarters. She was the only woman there, except for the cleaning lady.

Ruth Müller's position in the Society was unique, but the demand that she keep her competence a secret was not. From the top of its hierarchy to the bottom, the Society of Truth was a quintessential patriarchy that relied on an army of cowed, subservient women—an army whose skills and contributions could never be acknowledged. To do so would shake the Society to its foundations—its belief system and its power structure were grounded in a doctrine of pervasive and unchallenged male superiority.

It had never occurred to Ruth that she was taking part in a huge misogynistic lie. She'd been trained from childhood to believe that the Society of Truth was the one true religion of the one true God. All nine million members of the organization had the same unshakeable understanding—that God inspires only men to write, teach, and lead. Its all-male writing committee, overseen by the all-male Elder Board, wrote all the study materials printed and published by the Society of Truth.

Who's doing all the writing now? Ruth wondered as she admired the charming Quedlinburg cottage.

"Ruth...Ruth...Earth to Ruth," Jacob joked.

"Oh! I'm sorry, Jacob," Ruth said, giggling. "I was daydreaming. The chalet is delightful. I'm sure I'll be happy here."

"Go on in and put some tea on the stove. You'll see the kettle, and..."

"Don't you worry, young man," Ruth assured him. "I know my way around a kitchen. And...thank you for taking such good care of me and my"—Ruth paused, then put her finger up to her mouth in mock "shhh" secrecy—"my you-know-what."

"It's my pleasure, Ruth," Jacob replied.

After tea, Ruth headed for her bedroom and began to unpack, then stopped. Nothing was getting put away until the you-know-what was safely hidden away. Casing the bedroom and finding no hiding spot that measured up to the security Ruth felt the relic deserved, she looped the drawstring around her neck so that the small black velvet bag nestled in her cleavage.

"Over my dead body," she mumbled to herself as she began putting away her belongings. "They'll have to take me down first before I give up this precious cargo."

After unpacking, Ruth moved a few things around to satisfy her artistic eye. Because of Heinrich's position on the Elder Board, he and Ruth had lived in a penthouse apartment atop one of the Society's buildings. Her flair for interior design was apparent in her furnishing choices and color palette—simple but elegant midcentury modern furniture, upholstered in tones of blush and charcoal. It was the perfect foreground for their breathtaking views of Manhattan, the East River, and New York Harbor.

Ruth had loved their penthouse home, but in a heartbeat, that penthouse no longer mattered. Erica Pfeiffer, the tenth-floor cleaning lady and the only other woman allowed on the Society's executive floor, had revealed to Ruth that the Society was secretly involved in pedophilia, and had been conspiring for decades to cover it up. Erica had spent fifteen years ingratiating herself into the Society, and she'd been remarkably successful. Having become engaged to Devon Nelson, the youngest member of the Elder Board, she had been waiting for the right time to expose its corruption. Had it not been for Erica, Ruth and Heinrich would still be in Brooklyn, working diligently but unknowingly to support the Society's evil secret agenda.

Ruth had steadfastly refused to believe the allegations until Erica had insisted that she could prove them and had challenged Ruth to see for herself. The proof, she had said, was locked inside the Society's research library. After Erica had obtained the door code, the two had accessed the room. Erica had showed Ruth a bank of filing cabinets that held decades of case files on boys and girls who had been violated by Society members. More recent cases had been computerized, but they were all there, documented and neatly organized by date. The files also showed that the Society had aggressively ensured that each case had been settled out of court, with little or no penalty for the pedophile, even if the man was a repeat offender. Often that resolution was achieved by smearing the young victims, alleging that they had brought the molestation on themselves by deliberately inciting the behavior. They were at fault because they had lured the elders into sin.

As soon as Ruth saw the files, she knew that she and Heinrich would have to leave the Society—the view from their penthouse and Heinrich's prestigious position on the Elder Board couldn't compensate for being complicit in the sexual violation of children. She had also felt an obligation to assist Erica in exposing the Society's dark secret—she very much wanted to hold the Society accountable for its long history of misdeeds.

To coincide with the Müllers' escape from the Society, Erica had engineered a daring raid on the research library. The heist included not just duplicating the child molestation files, but also removing an ancient scroll and an artifact that dated back to the Garden of Eden. That artifact looked like obsidian, but was actually a piece of petrified tar containing the last remaining seeds of the Tree of Life. The seeds had been entrapped in the tar thousands of years ago, but over the centuries, that tar had hardened and compressed. When Ruth left for Germany with Heinrich's body, friends had given her a black velvet drawstring bag as a parting gift. Only later did she discover that the petrified tar and seeds were inside it. That bag that now dangled between her breasts.

The sun was setting and the orange sky appeared to have moved in the uneven lattice glass of Ruth's bedroom window. Lattice glass was a common architectural feature in old buildings in Germany. The diamond-shaped leaded glass panes made everything outside seem a little distorted, but this was more than distortion. Ruth quickly realized that there was something orange moving up and down just outside her window.

"Well, well...could you be the same orange-bellied kingfisher who greeted me at Heinrich's gravesite?" she asked the bird. "Did you follow me here? Why are you hopping so frantically, my little one?" On closer examination, she began to understand that the bird was trying to tell her something—something urgent.

At that moment, Jacob burst into Ruth's room. "I've got to get you out of here!" he exclaimed, breathing heavily. "Now! They are coming. I left a false trail. Grab the seeds and follow me." Ruth patted her chest to let Jacob know that the little black drawstring bag was already on her person, then followed him out the back door.

Not again, she thought. She'd had more adrenaline rush in the last few days than she'd had since she was a child hiding from the secret police. On the run once more, this time with her bodyguard, her heart was pounding in her ears.

She couldn't help but notice the same little bird hopping and squawking on a patch of nearby blue forget-me-nots growing on the side of an old cobblestone wall. The early-evening air had enhanced their sachet scent, and it didn't take long for Ruth's eyes to well up with tears. She was thinking about Heinrich—her own forget-me-not —the love of her life who had been cold-bloodedly murdered just days before. Things had happened so fast that she hadn't had a chance to mourn or grieve, but neither Jacob nor the kingfisher had any patience for that now. Jacob grabbed Ruth's hand and hurriedly pulled her down the length of the wall toward some cobblestone steps that had been set down centuries ago. They ascended the medieval stairway into a green meadow. As the bird hopped ahead toward the forest, Jacob and Ruth followed it, just as if they were in an animated children's feature film, but this was no cartoon—this was real.

All too soon, they could hear the roar of heavy vehicles racing up the drive to the chalet. Ruth paused to look back, but Jacob forcefully pulled her down behind some nearby brush. "If the bad guys are in sight, so are you," he whispered.

Ruth's eyes registered panic. "Where do we go now?"

"The Weisshotel Castle," Jacob replied.

"Why would that be safer than my chalet?" Ruth asked.

"The castle is a tourist hotel, and it is also heavily guarded Sibylline property—it's a harder target, and we'll have more people ready to protect you," said Jacob. "Out here, all you have is me, and I'm afraid that's not gonna be enough."

The Sibyllines, as Ruth had learned from Erica Pfeiffer, were an organization that dated from the dawn of human history. They were led by powerful, badass women who advocated for gender equality, critical thinking, free will, and the Way of Kyndeness—a benevolent and proactive way of relating to others.

The Sibylline mission was in direct conflict with the male-dominated United Soponium Fellowship. The USF was just as old as the Sibyllines—but their goal was entirely different. The USF sought absolute power over people and resources through dark manipulation of politics, commerce, and religion. One of those religions was the Society of Truth.

Ruth knew that there was a lot more to it than that, but she also knew that the Sibyllines had come through for her—and for Heinrich—when she had needed them most. And for now, she had only one choice—to trust her Sibylline knight in shining armor until she found safety...or until she woke up from this godforsaken hallucination. Throughout her life, she'd often had nightmares about hiding from the Stasi, and Heinrich had always cuddled and reassured her when she was terrified. Now, however, she was trapped in the instant replay of that same bad dream, except this time it was real. She had never imagined that she would find herself in this situation again, running headlong through a dense forest to save her life, just as she had when she was six years old. At least this time she was wearing shoes. At least this time, she had the Sibyllines to support and protect her.

Ruth was in shape for her age, thanks to her insistence on climbing ten flights of stairs at the Society headquarters on a daily basis. She'd done it for decades, telling everyone that it was good for her heart, but there was a deeper psychological reason as well. The elevator at Society of Truth headquarters was an antiquated windowless box that was prone to breakdowns. Like the underground passageways, it made her claustrophobia kick in. The idea of getting stuck between floors was terrifying, so she always took the stairs. Now, her efficient heart and sturdy legs gave her the energy she needed to keep pace with Jacob.

Jacob had no doubt that they were being pursued by pros—the elite tactical troops of the USF were all specially trained, not only in picking up trails, but also in sensing the energetic frequencies of intense emotions, like fear. This was about to become a huge problem because they would surely be able to pick up on Ruth's fright.

Jacob's job was not only to protect Ruth and the seeds, but also to calm her down so that her pheromones didn't give away their position. He heard shattering wood and glass in the distance as the USF squad burst into the chalet and proceeded to turn the place upside down. "Sie ist nicht hier!" Commander Schultz shouted to his second-in-command, Greg Blunt. "The relic is not here, and neither is she. That *alte Fotze* is onto us, and I'll be damned if she gets away!"

"Out here...!" Blunt called back from outside the chalet. "They left a trail. There are fresh bicycle tracks."

"Forget the trail!" Schultz commanded. "It's a decoy. We know they're headed to the castle. Take the Audi and head northwest, then cut them off on foot. I'll follow with the canine. The old dame can't get far. Now, go!" Schultz ordered.

Through the trees in the distance, Ruth could barely make out an arched dark shadow on the side of a bluff covered in vines. The sun had already set, and darkness would soon envelop the landscape. They had already hiked about three miles, and although Ruth would never complain, the headlong flight from the chalet had aggravated a childhood injury to her foot. The ball of her foot was burning with pain, and she was limping badly.

They were about fifty meters from the arched black metal door that accessed one of the castle's many underground tunnels when Jacob heard the crackling of twigs approaching from behind. He threw Ruth over his shoulder in what he knew had become a life-or-death race to safety.

The gunshot was aimed strategically. Intended to wound, not to kill, the bullet entered and exited Ruth's right shoulder, then lodged into Jacob's back. Ruth cried out, then went limp. Jacob staggered and fell to his knees, but he knew he had to reach the door. With Ruth's deadweight draped around him, he willed himself back onto his feet. A second shot ricocheted off one of the rocks that formed the bluff. A third was fired from above, but whizzed overhead as Jacob took cover under the ancient brick portico above the door.

Jacob's vision was growing dim and he knew he would soon lose consciousness. He reached out and shakily placed his fingertip on the electronic lock. The device read his print, and the creaky metal door opened for them to enter, then quickly closed behind them. Jacob gently lowered Ruth to the ground, then passed out.

CHAPTER 2
PHUGTAL MONASTERY

Anguish lay heavy in the air—it was palpable, a living presence. The monastery had ceased to be a place of serenity and quiet reflection. The monks felt the intense energy coming from the inner hall and main sanctuary, where fiery passion entwined with complicated love between twin siblings had erupted in physical combat, with lethal consequences. One person was dead, and another had been gravely wounded. This tragic outcome was overlain by a mother's sorrow and sense of loss, and by her daughter's profound anguish over a dead lover.

The monks collectively sensed these deep emotional frequencies and sought out one another in the corridor. As they made their way toward the scene of the battle, a low grief-stricken moan vibrated under their feet and reverberated along the stone hallway. It was as if the earth itself was lamenting the massive damage to life, the shattering of precious relationships, and the violation of this place of peace.

Once the monks reached the entrance to the main sanctuary where the struggle had occurred, they reverently parted, making a path for Saji, their eldest, to make her way to the front. The years had shrunk her body, but not her aura or her feminine wisdom. Her luxuriant gray hair was pulled away from her face in a thick braid that trailed down her back. With utmost respect, she silently entered the chamber and walked toward Mireille, on whom the effects of the battle were immediately visible. Mireille's long wavy auburn hair, which usually flowed over her shoulders in elegant silken waves, was disheveled, knotted, and messy, and her clothing was askew. She sat cross-legged on the floor, rocking as she pressed her son's head to her bosom. Saji's kind and gentle hand on her shoulder immediately filled Mireille's body with comfort. Her dark-indigo eyes could no longer hold the heartbreak as her grief poured out in a flood of uncontrollable tears.

"He's not dead, Saji," Mireille said through her sobs. "I don't know if he can hear me or sense that I'm here. I don't even know if he'd *want* me to be here." She paused, then continued, "Oh, Saji! Out of all the skills I have—I can read auras, feel emotional frequencies, and even transport my body small distances, but this...this..."

Mireille spoke haltingly. Her speech came in short intermittent bursts, and was punctuated by sharp but shallow intakes of breath, as tears and words fought one another for her oxygen supply. "I don't know how to do this—how to love someone so much that it hurts, yet despise what he does."

"I know," Saji replied empathetically.

"My son is different—Sundara is not like other people. An imperfect human would have died from that blow."

"Yes, milady," said Saji. Saji surely knew how different Sundara was from almost every other human being, except for his mother and his twin sister, but Mireille needed to talk.

"He's paralyzed from his neck down, and he may or may not recover." Mireille gazed off into the distance as her tears fell onto her son's face. She continued rocking as Saji carefully lowered herself to the floor and settled herself against Mireille's right shoulder—this was going to take a while.

"The twins...Sundara and Ananta...they were inseparable," Mireille continued. "In the early mornings, when they were little, Sundara would get up at the crack of dawn and go on his little adventure walks all by himself. I never worried about him—maybe I should have—but he always seemed so capable of taking care of himself, even as a young boy. He'd be so excited about the discoveries he would find in nature and bring home to show me."

The memory of her young children brought a smile through her tears as she went on. "He loved telling his sister, Ananta, about all the creatures he found, and Ananta was always so captivated by his stories. There was such goodness in him."

Mireille's smile quickly faded. "One day…" She paused while fingering Sundara's sweaty hair away from his face. "He was around seven…He came home with a look in his eye that I couldn't define, which was odd. I could usually sense the goings-on with the twins, but all I could feel was that a morsel of his goodness had been shaved from his core. After that, his stories became darker, and they were fewer and farther between, until he had no more stories to tell. It was as if he had discovered something that day that changed his vibration—and he was determined to keep it to himself."

"Did you ever find out what it was that changed him, milady?" Saji asked.

"Yes." Mireille shook her head. "It was when I visited Eleusis, a city in Greece."

"I've never heard of Eleusis," Saji replied.

"That's because it was 'Christianized,' just like most of the scrolls and books in the library in Alexandra were also 'Christianized.' In other words, destroyed because they didn't fit the patriarchy's agenda."

"It's a good thing your manuscript wasn't stored there. It would have ended up in the fire with all the other historical journals that women wrote," Saji interjected. "Tell me about what happened when you visited Eleusis."

"Like most people who journeyed to Eleusis for spiritual revelations, I, too, had a vision, only mine wasn't pleasant—not at all. I asked for it. I pleaded for my eyes to be opened to the truth of what happened to my little boy, and the truth is what I got."

Saji waited in anxious anticipation. Mireille had told her many stories over the years, but this was new.

"Do you remember the story I told you of the giants that once roamed the area we now call the Black Sea?"

"Oh, yes, milady. You named them the Nephilim. It means 'the fallen.' How could I forget?"

"Well, the vision I was given while I was in Eleusis was horrific. I saw one of the Nephilim sodomizing my son—my young Sundara! It was so clear it was like it was happening right in front of me!" Mireille sobbed.

Saji put her arm around her. Tears formed in her own eyes and trickled down her face. "I'm so sorry, milady. How awful!"

"He's been mind-controlled ever since," Mireille bawled. "That half-angel, half-human—huge, evil, crossbred—creature didn't drown in the flood! For the longest time, I believed that all of them had died in that massive deluge. I was stowed away on a large boat, and watched with my own eyes as the water kept rising and the Nephilim giants kept moving to higher ground. It was easy for them—they were sure-footed climbers, but the water rose faster than they could run, and the one thing they couldn't do very well was swim—most likely due to the density of their bodies. To this day, I still have nightmares of them flailing, trying desperately to stay above water, gasping for air. As horrible as they were, I felt bad for them on that day, watching them struggle and drown."

"How could the one have survived?" Saji asked.

"I can only guess that it found an air pocket in some underwater cave where it waited out the flood. There's evidence that there's more than one."

Saji got chills just thinking about the implications of what this could mean.

The two women sat shoulder to shoulder for some time. Saji said nothing—the best thing she could offer Mireille now was her compassionate, reassuring presence. The two had been friends for almost a century. Saji had met Mireille when she joined the monastery as a young woman—they had laughed together because they both looked to be about the same age at the time, even though Mireille was already thousands of years old.

"The Nephilim stole Sundara's innocence," Mireille declared. "My son was a victim of child sexual abuse, and the world has been paying the price ever since."

Saji gently eased her palms under Sundara's head as it rested in his mother's lap, a loving sign that it was time for Mireille to release him into the monks' care. Mireille acquiesced by moving slightly and allowing Saji to cradle Sundara's head in her caring, frail hands.

Saji looked toward the entrance and nodded to the group that had gathered in the hall, a signal to her fellow monks to enter and carry out Sundara's body. The ritual for transporting an unconscious or deceased body was as old as the monastery itself. The monks divided into two groups and lined up on either side of Sundara. The monks on one side reached under the body with their right arms, while the monks on the other side reached under with their left. After firmly locking arms under the body, they lifted Sundara and carried him out with practiced gentle but confident movements.

The monks chanted, "Om...May spiritual light remove all obstacles that Sundara may be enlightened...Om." The sound echoed off the walls of the cavernous chamber.

Mireille watched numbly, still rocking, until Saji, once again, put her arm around her. She then melted into the old monk's embrace. Once Sundara's body was out of sight and the room was quiet, Saji stood, then offered her weathered hand to Mireille. She took it and rose unsteadily to her feet.

"There is nothing but love here for Sundara, your precious firstborn of the twins," said Saji. "Please allow us to care for him now."

"My old friend," Mireille replied, "the real Sundara was lost a long time ago. He was born into this world with goodness and innocence, and as a child, he allowed the Source within his inner being to guide him. But slowly he shifted, escaping my notice for far too long, and then it was too late."

"Please do not blame yourself for that," said Saji.

"His body is still handsome and perfectly formed," Mireille continued, "but over the centuries it became a hard shell made up of layers of ego and pride, layers that smothered and suffocated his beautiful inner being. The Nephilim made sure of that."

"Were it not for the Nephilim..." Saji began.

"Yes," said Mireille, gazing off blankly and thinking of the world that could have been. "But, Saji, you should know that it wasn't me who administered the blow that paralyzed him. It was Sundara's father, Easa, from the spiritual realm. Easa did it through me—I was just the delivery system. If it had been left to me, there would surely have been a nanosecond of pause—a mother's loving hesitation...enough time for it to have ended badly for Ananta and for me, just as it did for John Matthews."

Sundara had faced John Matthews before doing battle with his mother. John had rushed to Ananta's defense as soon as he heard

Sundara vow to rape and impregnate her, but quickly found himself badly overmatched. After lifting John by the neck with just one hand, Sundara had hurled John across the corridor. Still airborne, John's body had slammed headfirst into the monastery's rock wall, some twenty feet away. By the time he crumpled to the floor, he was already dead.

"I know that Easa instigated the strike that paralyzed Sundara," said Saji, "but even as the 'delivery system,' causing that much deliberate harm to your own son must have given you great pain."

Mireille nodded. "Striking Sundara was traumatic. Having done so, I needed time to sit with him and remember the boy who, like his sister, had once been the pure expression of love between his father and me. I needed time to reflect on the man he had become. Thank you, Saji, for being patient and sitting with me."

"Milady, I am honored that our friendship allowed you to share those moments with me. I deeply believe the good spirit of that boy, however atrophied, is still within Sundara," said Saji. She chose to leave unsaid what she was also thinking: *It remains to be seen whether our treatments can penetrate all those armored layers of evil and violence that have grown over that innocent core.*

Mireille, of course, read Saji's thoughts, even though they were unspoken. "Sundara will be incapacitated long enough to reflect on the meaning of real beauty, long enough to feel remorse for having tried to kill his sister, long enough for us to get through to that little boy who still resides within. At least that is my hope. I know this is the reason why Easa, from the spiritual realm, allowed him to survive. He must know that Sundara's inner being is still there—buried deep beneath all of those centuries of perverted identity. We'll soon find out whether enough remains of that beautiful inner being to thrive once more. Now, Saji, please take me to my daughter. I need to see Ananta."

Saji placed her palms together, bowed, then led Mireille to the room where Ananta and John Matthews, her dead lover, had been laid out. As Mireille opened the door, memories of the defining event of Ananta's childhood came flooding back.

Ananta had fallen to her death from the monastery's outer wall when she was just ten months old. Mireille had been utterly despondent as Easa carried their daughter's tiny lifeless body into this chamber. Lying with her, he had miraculously transferred his energy into her corpse and brought her back to life.

Mireille stepped into the chamber and fought back tears as her memories of Ananta's resurrection overcame her. She inhaled deeply —it was as if the scent of the room had been frozen in time. John and Ananta were now lying skin to skin under the same ancient cloth mantle, on top of the same bed that Easa had used, and for the same purpose. Ananta was deeply engaged in a desperate attempt to replicate the miracle that had brought her back to life as a toddler. Only time would tell whether she'd succeed.

The soft, silken blanket was a true work of art. It had been made in South India during the Mauryan Empire by a concubine named Lydia, a woman whose beauty was unsurpassed. Lydia was a skilled weaver, and had fashioned its intricate pattern from a mix of white bark, linen, and cotton. The cloth, like Lydia herself, was praised by all who'd seen it as the loveliest in the land.

But Lydia's story was not a happy one. She was being kept in bondage by one of the Mauryan prime ministers. He used her artistic talent for monetary gain, and used her body to satisfy the sexual desires of his colleagues as well as his own. On one of Easa's many treks through the mountains and valleys of India, he'd come upon her plight. When he freed Lydia and offered to bring her back with him to Phugtal, she had insisted that this special cloth come with them. Its delicately interlaced threads of green, blue, and gold told the symbolic story of her life as a sex slave, and her vision of release. Lydia had imbued each delicate knot with a special energy, blessing it with acknowledgement of her own self-worth and eventual personal power and freedom. The cloth had been treasured and preserved by the monks ever since—there was both tragedy and triumph in every stitch.

Saji gave Mireille a silent nod, indicating she was going to quietly depart.

Mireille didn't make a sound as she approached the bed where her daughter and John lay. Drawing near, she could see the subtle rise and fall of the cloth from Ananta's slow and deliberate trancelike breaths. *You are definitely your father's daughter*, Mireille thought to herself. She lovingly reached out her hand toward her child, as a mother would do, then paused. It was pure maternal instinct to want to offer a comforting touch, but she pulled her hand back instead. Mireille did not want to disturb the deep hypnotic state required to perform this kind of miracle. It had taken two days for Easa to bring Ananta back to life. Mireille wondered how long it would take Ananta to bring John back to life—if she could do it at all.

As she turned to leave, she noticed a backpack on a hard wooden chair, along with neatly folded clothing. *These must be John and Ananta's belongings*, Mireille realized. She picked up the backpack as she left, leaving the clothing behind and closing the ornately carved, over-sized wooden door behind her.

According to the first entry in Mireille's manuscript, Mireille was the first child of Adán and Eva. It told of how she was born before her parents ate the forbidden fruit from the Tree of Knowledge in the Garden of Eden. Mireille was perfect in every way. She had written the true journal of humankind's history, even as she safeguarded the seeds of the Tree of Life. She had also kept the Way of Kyndeness alive through the Sibyllines, despite unrelenting global adversity—much of which had been fomented by her own son.

With a flawless physique and ideal health, she never seemed to physically age. She didn't look a day over thirty-five, but even though everlasting life was in her DNA, she was still a physical, mortal human. Like other humans, she got tired, and oh, how tired she was now!

After the momentous events that had left her son in a coma and her daughter striving to resurrect her lover, Mireille was both physically and emotionally spent. The shoulders of her lithe body sagged as she walked slowly upstairs to her living quarters.

Her room was spartan, not at all what one might expect of a woman who had access to every known invention and every kind of esthetic embellishment. Thousands of years earlier, when she resided in Shangri-la for a time, she had filled her environment with baubles and ornate décor. Eventually, she rid herself of almost all of it—she found that the unnecessary clutter was counterproductive to maintaining calmness and tranquility in her sanctuary. Now her quarters looked rather similar to those of the Phugtal monks.

She collapsed into her favorite oversized reading chair and began unzipping John's backpack. The water bottle...the manuscript that had been spirited away from the secret library inside the Society of Truth. The ancient pages had been rolled up into a scroll, but she immediately recognized that something was different. Tape had been carefully stuck to all the edges, and then folded over, like a clear laminate border. There was no way she'd be able to remove it and keep the old parchment intact. It was now a permanent addition to the pages, with subtle traces of fingerprints, a few fine hairs, some oil, and faint skin markings.

It must have been the only way Ananta and John could keep it protected and hidden until they could safely return it to me, Mireille concluded. She pressed her old journal to her heart, closed her eyes, and allowed the gratitude for its return to pour over her like the warm aromatic anointing oil that was used to bless a new monk.

One day, when I finally tell them that the history in these pages isn't true, Ananta is going to be very cross with me, Mireille thought. *And who could blame her? I'd sent them to risk their lives for a decoy. Once I explain that it was a needed diversion to keep the USF away from the real manuscript that chronicles the true history of humankind, I know she will understand. So will John...Poor John...Fully aware of Sundara's great strength and metaphysical power, John had rushed to fight him anyway, to defend Ananta. Even as a Sibylline protector, this was far beyond what was expected of him when he was watching over her as "Erica Pfeiffer" at the Society of Truth. His love for her must be great indeed.*

While Mireille was in deep reflection in her aerie on the highest floor of Phugtal, the monks were settling Sundara into his temporary quarters, many feet below. They'd carried him down several flights of stairs to the deepest part of the monastery, where there were no windows or doors to the outside. Part prison cell, part ICU, the room had been carved out of the hillside—solid rock abutted each exterior wall, and the only way out was up.

By the time Saji arrived, the monks had already secured Sundara's arms and legs to the side rails of the adjustable hospital bed that was anchored to the floor. She looked at the cuffs and shackles, looked at the other monks, then doubled over in gales of laughter. The others were puzzled until they realized what Saji instantly understood—there were no restraints strong enough to keep Sundara from escaping—unless he remained paralyzed and comatose, in which case he was in no need of restraints.

As the laughter of the monks died down, Saji turned to Yara, her chief assistant and protégée. Although still in her twenties, Yara had already shown great promise in the healing arts. In due time, as the years took their toll and Saji's powers finally declined, Yara would take her place. "Tell me, what have you decided to use as his IV cocktail?"

"To support his body, mind, and spirit," Yara began, "we're using a simple adaptogenic three-in-one punch to start. We've prepared a cannabis blend to light up receptors in his physical body—enough to begin healing, but not enough to bring him out of paralysis just yet. We're also using *Entada rheedii*, the African dream bean, to stimulate epiphanies, and fly agaric mushroom—*Amanita muscaria*—to connect him with his father, Easa, in the spiritual world. We'll start there, watch how he reacts, then decide how to progress his treatment."

"Very good," said Saji. "No doubt he'll have quite the dream to talk about when he wakes."

On the other side of a glass partition in the treatment was a control panel on a far wall. The panel tracked Sundara's vital signs—it emitted the usual blinking lights and beeping noises one would expect from an ICU monitoring unit. Saji entered the control room to examine the detectors, scanners, and recorders. All of Sundara's systems were being documented—neurological, circulatory, digestive, musculoskeletal, endocrine, lymphatic, and Kirlian. Right now, the Kirlian camera image was showing a mostly black aura, with small patches of gray and brown. Looking more closely, however, Saji detected an almost imperceptible sliver of red.

A smile played at the corners of her mouth. "Surprise, surprise," she whispered. "At least we have a tiny fragment of something to work with."

When the monks had finished hooking up the equipment and had made sure that all of it was functioning properly, especially the IV and oxygen, they departed, leaving Yara to join Saji in the control room. "Looks like our boy will be resting comfortably for a while," Yara said, "but you never know how this guy is going to respond. Would you like me to stay with you for a bit?"

"That won't be necessary, Yara. Please go attend to Mireille. This ordeal has taxed her emotionally and physically, and she is exhausted. See if she is in need of anything. I'll stay here and observe."

"Goodnight, then." Yara bowed in namaste style, then turned and left.

Saji dimmed the lights, took a seat in the black office chair, leaned back, and sighed. It had been quite the unprecedented day, and although her daily regimen of meditation, Qigong, and heavy chores had kept her strong and healthy, even at the age of 107, the events had taken their toll on her energy level. Although Mireille was resting and Sundara's treatment had begun, Saji still felt a sense of foreboding. Among the monks, she was known for her ability to pick up energetic patterns, and she could tell that something was off.

After fifteen minutes of motionless anticipation, the earth began to lurch so violently that it sent her chair rolling into the rock wall behind her. When the shaking stopped, she peered through the glass to check on Sundara. He was still motionless in his bed, but the IV cart had skidded across the room.

The cart looked to be trailing a multitude of snakes behind it—the force of the earthquake had pulled the tubing from Sundara's body. Only after Saji was sure there weren't going to be any aftershocks did she enter the treatment room to reattach them. After wiping the connectors with alcohol and checking for air bubbles, she reached for Sundara's arm and reconnected the IV. When she stood up to reach for the second IV line, she was astonished to see that his eyes were wide open.

Sundara was unable to speak, but his eyes followed her every move. He started blinking dramatically and emphatically, as if his eyes were shouting at her. When Saji realized that eye blinking was all he was capable of, her fear subsided. Nevertheless, the unexpected entry of Mireille made her jump.

"A little on edge, Saji?" Mireille asked.

"On edge!?" Saji answered. "That's an understatement! Did you feel the quake? The violent lurching was enough to wake Sundara. Look at his eyes."

Mireille leaned over her son. His blinking stopped as he stared intently at his mother. If there had ever been a moment in time when the two shared a telepathic conversation, it was now, and Mireille held the upper hand. Sundara knew what was coming, and for the first time in his life, he was utterly powerless. He was at the mercy of his mother, whether he liked it or not—and he didn't like it...not one bit.

Mireille stroked Sundara's thick dark-auburn hair. Then, for the first time in many, many years, she kissed his forehead, just as she had when he was a boy.

CHAPTER 3
SLIPSTREAMING

Devon Nelson, an elder of the Society of Truth and a rising star in the United Soponium Fellowship, had done everything possible to make sure that his ex-wife, Gabby, and the rest of her whole-wheat, do-gooder accomplices had stayed locked up. Together with Ken Kreighton, the director of the Drug Enforcement Agency and a powerful fellow USF member, he had closely examined all the plant materials they'd confiscated from Gabby's Compassion Garden. They had also analyzed the extracts and remedies that had been removed from her underground lab. Although they had identified exotic plants and extracts that were banned by the federal government for consumption as a food or supplement, there was no evidence to prove they'd been ingested.

This was no accident—Gabby had long anticipated a raid like this, and had been meticulously clever about how she stored and categorized the compounds she formulated. Some had been marked "Skincare Only. Apply Topically." Others were cleared labeled "Exclusively for Research Purposes. Not for Human Consumption." Even the Epithalon—although it hadn't been regulated yet for injection to lengthen life span, Gabby had labeled it "For analysis Only."

Devon had no doubt that everything confiscated in the raid had been either ingested or administered intravenously, but he couldn't prove it—Gabby, that bitch, had covered her tracks perfectly. She'd made sure that the quantities of all compounds and extracts were within legal limits for possession, and that they had been labeled for a use consistent with government regulations. Even a substance like delta-8 THC, a psychoactive cannabinoid, was clearly identified as being extracted from hemp and not from marijuana—but no one would ever know, because the molecular structure of delta-8 was the same, no matter what source it came from.

Nelson was bummed out—he'd been gleefully looking forward to jail time for Gabby, but because the cannabis plants and medicinal potions from her lab and garden didn't contain unlawful levels of Schedule 1 drugs, no charges could be brought against her. Together with her son, Zach, the two had been the keepers of both the Compassion Garden and secret underground laboratory, but if Kreighton's DEA couldn't make charges stick against those two, everyone else was off the hook as well. Legally, at least, the rest of them were just accessories, and besides, even Ken Kreighton didn't dare bring charges against Sadie Dixon, a highly respected NYPD detective.

Kreighton had no choice but to let them go. That said, he told his officers to make no effort to return them to Hudson, New York, where they'd been taken into custody. Cameron; Zach; and Gabby, together with her brother, Rocky; Jen Strauss and her daughter, Debra; and Detective Sadie Dixon were paraded out of their cells. Nelson personally unlocked Gabby's cell door, which gave him the opportunity to drop one last delicious piece of revenge.

"You're free to go. There will be no federal charges," he began with a demonic smirk. "This is one of those times when fire is the solution."

Gabby's eyes widened. "You didn't!" she hissed as she lunged at him.

As the officers whisked the group down the corridor and into the elevator, no one realized that Cameron had slipped behind an office door. Once the group had been half escorted, half propelled out onto the sidewalk, their wallets and cell phones together with Sadie's service revolver were rudely tossed in a heap in front of them. Only when everything had been picked up from the pavement did Gabby realize that Cameron's wallet and phone were still on the ground.

"Okay, where's Cameron?" Rocky asked.

"Shit!" Gabby exclaimed. "This is not good. They must have figured out that Cam had betrayed the USF—no one does that and survives. Now they're going to torture him to tell what he knows! I have to do something—I'm going back inside!"

"No, you're not!" Jen insisted, firmly grabbing Gabby's sleeve. "You'd never get past the front desk. Cameron can take care of himself, and besides, whatever's going on in there, you can't do anything about it. Our job is to get the hell out of here."

"And just how is that supposed to happen?" Zach asked petulantly.

At that moment, a pearlescent ivory Cadillac Escalade screeched up to the curb. As the passenger window lowered, the red-haired driver leaned over and yelled in a Scottish accent, "Did anyone call for a r-r-r-ride?"

"*That's* how!" exclaimed Gabby as she jumped into the shotgun seat.

Gabby was overjoyed to see Cameron alive and well, and wrapped her arms tightly around his neck as she planted a kiss on his mouth. The Scotsman's already ruddy complexion began turning scarlet, then burgundy—Gabby's exuberant grasp had cut off his oxygen supply. Meanwhile, the others climbed in the back.

When Gabby finally released Cameron from her boa constrictor embrace, she took her right hand and slapped him across the face. Stunned and blindsided by the move, he just sat there, speechless.

"That's what you get, Cameron R-r-reid!" Gabby exclaimed in an excellent imitation of his Scottish burr. "That's what you get for making me worry about you! I thought they were gonna torture you, and...and..." She couldn't finish. The stress that had been building up exploded, and Gabriela Abbott—the gal who always had it together—buried her face in her hands and cried.

Cameron pulled her close. "Hey, hey, hey. It's okay. I got you, Gabby. We got this—together. I'm here now. I'll always be here to protect you from now on."

"Uh...Cam?" Rocky hated to interrupt the tender moment from the back seat, but he had no choice. "I think you better *go!*"

Cameron glanced in his rearview mirror and saw police vehicles speeding toward them. Their lights and sirens were blazing, and they were closing fast.

"How did you disappear, and what did you do?" Sadie cried out from the wayback.

"I, ah, *bor-r-r-owed* this SUV. Had to have room for seven," Cam replied calmly as he floored it and peeled out. "Best buckle up," he added as everyone slammed backward into their seats.

With a sharp left turn onto South Eads Street, he sped up the Interstate 395 North on-ramp. "Those aren't cops—they're USF. All I have to do is dodge them for about five hours till we get back to Hudson."

"I don't know what's still going to be standing when we get there," said Gabby ruefully. Nelson's final arrow had found its mark, and she was obsessing over his parting words: *This is one of those times when fire is the solution.* She was all too familiar with his obsession with pyromania. Based on what he'd said, she assumed that he'd torched her garden and her underground lab—the lab that had taken years of travel to exotic places to obtain rare healing plants, and even more blood, sweat, and tears to become a state-of-the-art scientific research and testing facility. But Devon was nothing if not cruel and vindictive —it was all too possible that he'd set fire to the house and restaurant as well. *Even if that happened*, she told herself, *at least nobody found out that Devon is really Zach's father.*

"You make five hours of dodging the bad guys sound like no sweat," said Rocky.

"Piece o' cake…" Cameron replied. "Or maybe not. Holy fuck!"

Cameron had spotted a low-flying black helicopter coming right at them. "That chopper isn't the police, either. They're my former colleagues from the Cell—the black ops specialists of the USF—and they want me dead. And please don't take this the wrong way, but if the rest of you get killed in the process, they won't have a problem with that. You're all just collateral damage."

"This is getting better by the minute!" Rocky gasped.

"But why?" Debra asked. "If all they wanted were the seeds, they're gone. As far as they know, the seeds were flushed down the toilet and are doing the backstroke down the Potomac."

"If I were them, I'd be assuming there's more where they came from—and that they were probably somewhere near Gabby's restaurant," Sadie answered. Sadie's sixth sense had picked up on Gabby's worries that returning to the Gabby Abbey might not be a safe option.

"Cam," she said cautiously, "we need to rethink where we're going. I'm not sure heading back to Hudson is what we want to do."

"Okay," he replied. "Survival first. Lose the tail. Destination later."

About eight cars ahead, Cam spotted an eighteen-wheeler in the right lane. Weaving in and out of traffic, he pulled in directly behind the big rig. It was a move he accomplished without braking, so everyone else in the car was screaming. They surely believed that Cameron was about to deliberately drive into the ass end of the Old Dominion freightliner, and that they all would perish in the collision and fireball that followed. The crash never came. Cam maneuvered the Escalade within inches of the Mansfield bar at the rear of the trailer, then hit the brakes just enough to match the truck's speed as he took his other foot off the gas. It was if they'd invisibly hitched themselves onto the semi.

"Awesome!" Debra exclaimed with new admiration. "That was dope! Will you teach me how to do that?"

"Aye, lassie, that I will," Cam replied, "but I think it would be better if ye learned to dr-r-r-ive first."

Hearing the banter between Cam and Debra, Gabby figured it was safe to open her eyes. She instantly regretted it. Seeing how close they still were to the truck's rear, she screamed, then braced for impact by placing her hands on the dashboard and locking her elbows.

"You can do that if it makes you feel better, my love," Cam said with a smile, "but it's not going to put any more distance between us and the truck."

My love…he called me "my love!" she thought to herself before realizing that she was still terrified.

"I'd feel a lot better…my dearest…" Gabby replied, her voice dripping with sarcasm, "if I knew what you were doing, and that you were doing it on purpose."

"Now, now," Sadie chimed in from the back seat. "Stop fighting, you lovebirds."

"It's called 'slipstreaming,' " Cam said. "With precise timing, you pull up behind a semi as fast as you can, getting ahead of their tailwind. Then the air pressure sucks you into their pocket, pulling you along as if you're connected. It's dangerous though, and I…"

"You're damned right it's dangerous!" Rocky interrupted with alarm. "What if...what if...the...the...geez! I can't even talk! What if the operator of this massive vehicle in front of us decides to stop?"

"Don't worry, Rocky. Mr. Old Dominion won't stop," Cam assured him. "He knows I'm here and what I'm doing, and it's in his best interest not to stop. Trust me. He's not too happy about the situation, but he's gonna cooperate—for his own good."

Everyone cheered as the USF chopper peeled away from the pursuit. With the tractor-trailer blocking its line of sight, getting a clear shot at the Escalade was impossible.

"One down. That leaves the cop behind us," said Zach.

"Cops? What cops?" asked Cameron.

Zach turned around and saw nothing. "Huh? Where'd they go? They're gone, too!"

"They're USF, not cops, and they're still there, but they're hanging back—waaaaaay back—a quarter mile behind us at least," Cam declared. "If they did anything to cause us to swerve, even a little, it could disrupt the tailwind. No telling how the trailer unit would respond. Probably depends on the cargo inside, but a rollover and fire-ball would be a distinct possibility."

"Wouldn't that be just peachy," said Rocky.

"A jackknife might be the most benign outcome," Cameron contin-ued, "and even that would be catastrophic. With Old Dominion's cab and cargo suddenly sprawled at right angles to each other across four lanes of traffic, everyone would hit the brakes simultaneously, creating a chain reaction of rear-end collisions at speed. It could easily become a mass casualty event. Although the USF doesn't care about killing us, they certainly don't want to be among the victims themselves—and they don't want all that media attention, either. They have no choice but to hang back and wait it out, at least for now."

"Wait *what* out?" Gabby inquired with exasperation.

"Wait until either the truck driver decides to slow down and stop, or until we decide to ease off his rear—and that's not an option for us. The trucker won't slow down and stop on I-395 through DC, so this means we have"—Cam looked at the dashboard clock—"about thirty minutes—depending on which route he takes—to come up with a plan."

"Who says the truck driver is a '*he*'?" Debra interjected.

"Seriously, Debs?" Rocky was about to have a meltdown. "Is this really the right moment for militant feminism? Do you really wanna spend our last thirty minutes—our last breaths—arguing about whether the person who's driving that monster has a schlong or an ax wound?"

"Ax wound!" Debra countered, insulted. "Are you serious? Did you just refer to my flower as an ax wound? That was downright rude! Let's at least keep it Yiddish, shall we, and call it a…a *schmirsky!*"

"Focus, people!" Cam shouted. "Let's keep our attention on the problem at hand. Sadie, you've been in vehicular hot pursuits before… any ideas?" He waited for Sadie to answer, but she didn't respond. She was too mesmerized by Cam's slipstreaming to speak.

"*Sadie!*" they all shouted in unison.

To everyone's surprise, it wasn't Sadie who answered. Jen had been listening, watching, and analyzing, and now it was her turn to weigh in on the problem. "Believe it or not, I've done this before," she began.

"What? *You?*" Debra was in disbelief. Her mom had been raised as a "good girl" in a devout Society of Truth family. Slipstreaming was a part of her mother's past she knew nothing about.

"When I was seventeen…in a van…from Nebraska to California. I'll tell you the story later, Debra, but for now, just hear me out because we're a little time-challenged here. We can use the tailwind to our advantage, but we'll have to brace ourselves. Cam will stop as quick as he can—on a dime. The Old Dominion driver will feel the trailer swerve slightly, and will attempt to steady it before the truck jackknifes or starts to fishtail. *She*"—Jen emphasized a female truck driver—"will hopefully gain control of her cargo trailer. But in the meantime, the Escalade will spin out."

"And that's a good thing?" Rocky asked.

"It is, and it's brilliant!" Cam exclaimed. "There's only one glitch. I need about ten car spaces behind me and a wide shoulder."

"Gonna be a bit tough for a bit," said Sadie as she rejoined the conversation. "We're about to go over the Potomac and the Washington Channel. It's a good thing evening rush hour is over, but just like in New York, there's traffic 24-7 here. Best bet is that our eighteen-wheeled benefactor is going to continue on I-395, then connect with I-695. I-695 magically turns into I-295 once we hit the south bank of the Anacostia River—go figure. Crossing our fingers that this is *her* plan, and that we don't come upon any traffic jams."

Cam could feel the panic among his passengers. Other than Jen, and possibly Sadie, no one else in the car understood why this maneuver wasn't suicidal, but he no longer had time to explain. The best comfort he could offer was a play-by-play of what to expect. "Don't worry. I'll get control of the spin, then turn around. That will put us on the shoulder, facing into oncoming traffic—which will be quite the surprise to those USF pseudocops. They'll have no choice but to blow right by us. Sadie, what are the exits after Pennsylvania Avenue?"

"There aren't any," she said flatly. "Not until Benning Road, and that's a left-hand off-ramp from the fast lane, which won't help at all. The best you can do is veer off into the woods about a quarter of a mile past Penn. There's a small patch of highway there that doesn't have a guardrail. We can't miss it—*you* can't miss it, Cam, or..."

Sadie wisely chose not to go into detail about the consequences, or why she was so familiar with these roads—at least not now. "I can't tell from my vantage point here back in the cheap seats," she continued, "but does this overpriced hip-hop status symbol have four-wheel drive?"

"Aye, Sadie, that it does," Cameron replied.

"Kick it in as you pull out of the spin. Judging from the pavement, it looks like it rained not too long ago—the shoulder will likely be soft, and you'll want the extra traction. Once we start going through the woods, it's gonna get bumpy, but not for long. You'll end up in a residential subdivision."

Sadie's memory drifted back to her childhood. She was eight when her Bulgarian psychic mother was referred to DC homicide by the NYPD, and asked to help solve a brutal murder in Georgetown. The case deeply affected her mom—the killer had a fetish for handicapped children, and the murders were especially grisly. Eventually, he was traced to Pope Branch Park, the exact location where they would end up when—and if—Cameron could wrangle the Escalade to safety.

The sign for the upcoming Pennsylvania Avenue exit jolted Sadie out of her reverie. "Hang on, guys," she warned. "Cam, watch the odometer! In point two five miles—exactly—hit those brakes like you're smashing the head of your worst enemy!"

"Now!" Cam shouted and stomped on the brake pedal. Everyone but Zach and Debra shut their eyes as the car spun out. Seconds later, Cam got control and brought the Escalade onto the shoulder, then drove directly into the woods. Sadie was right—it wasn't just bumpy, it was as if the earth itself was heaving up and down. Even the Escalade's high clearance didn't seem to help. As Cam kept his firm grasp on the steering wheel, everyone else had one hand on their seatbelt, and the other braced against the roof.

Cam soon found the way into a quiet residential subdivision near Pope Branch Park. He pulled into a wooded area and turned off the engine. Stunned silence overtook the group as each of them attempted to process what had just happened. Individually and collectively, they were astonished at finding themselves alive and intact.

Cam broke the silence. "Jen...Sadie...do you know how to contact any Sibylline supporters in this area?"

"I don't know anyone nearby," Sadie replied, "but I know who does." Without waiting for feedback, she scrolled through the contacts on her phone and placed a call.

"Two very ordinary sedans will arrive shortly," Sadie said as she hung up. "When they get here, we'll split up. Jen and Debra—you come with me. Gabby, Rocky, Cam, and Zach—you need to quickly climb into the other vehicle. The cars will take two different routes, but we'll all end up at the same destination."

"Where's that?" Cam asked.

"Can't say," Sadie responded. "Need-to-know basis. It's crucial that the location not be compromised. I don't think we'll be intercepted, but if that happens, we won't be able to give away what we don't know. And one more thing: as soon as you get into the car, you'll be handed a blindfold. Don't resist. Don't kvetch. Just put the damn thing on. It's for the protection of other Sibylline supporters, but it's for our own protection as well."

"What about you, Sadie? Do *you* know where we're going?" Rocky asked.

"Nope," she responded, "and I'll be wearing a blindfold just like everyone else."

Within ten minutes, two sedans pulled up. Without a word, Gabby, Cam, Zach, and Rocky piled into the silver Mitsubishi Lancer, while Jen, Debra, and Sadie climbed into a black Volkswagen Jetta. Seconds later, everyone was blindfolding themselves as the cars took off in opposite directions.

CHAPTER 4
MATRIX

Milton Chandler opened his eyes and winced. The brilliant sun had found the one-inch gap between the panels of the custom matelassé room-darkening drapes that his wife had bought for their penthouse, and was now sending an unrelenting beam straight at his face. The pain was intense—it felt like a laser cutting through his eyeballs.

"What the hell just happened to my life?" he mumbled.

Just forty-eight hours earlier, he had the world by the tail. His fellow members of the Elder Board had elected him president of the Society of Truth—the first Black man to hold that office. And then it had all imploded.

He wasn't sure whether he was hung over or still drunk, but either way, he felt like shit. Milton hadn't consumed this much alcohol since college, years before converting to the Society of Truth. His pounding head and physical misery were relentless reminders that his wife had walked out on him and that, under duress, he'd resigned his position as president less than a day after being elected. It would be just a matter of days before he was thrown out of the penthouse.

He felt like he was peering up from the bottom of a well from which there was no escape. Hopelessness was a new feeling for Milton. Over the years, he had counseled many Society members suffering from depression or suicidal ideation, but his heart was never really in it. He'd done it because it was expected of a man in his position.

Milton thought back on the list of Bible passages he'd used to advise and encourage those in the congregation who were despondent or anxious. Donna had put that list together for him—his wife Donna —who just yesterday had been captured on Society surveillance cameras kissing another man. That kiss had set the collapse of his life in motion. Even as she confessed her infidelity to the Elder Board, she'd brazenly accused one of the other elders, Devon Nelson, of fornicating with his fiancée in the tenth-floor corridor—just a few feet away from where they were meeting. And Donna wasn't the least bit penitent about any of it.

When she had walked out the door—out of their life together—it wasn't that useless collection of Bible quotes he reached for to ease his own feeling of deep despair. It was wine, specifically his favorite chardonnay from his college years. Once it sunk in that Donna wasn't just gone, but *gone*...Milton headed for the historic Hotel St. George at the corner of Clark and Henry Streets. Tucked into the Clark Street façade was Michael-Towne Wines & Spirits. He was delighted to discover that they carried his college favorite, Kendall-Jackson chardonnay, and bought out their entire inventory—all four bottles of it.

And now he felt wretched, inside and out. Opening his eyes with great difficulty, Milton looked around the bed and saw four pale-green bottles. All bore the K-J logo, and all four of them were empty. "Oh no..." he groaned to himself. That explained why his lips and tongue were bone dry, and also why he felt saliva rising in his throat. The spit was soon accompanied by the bitter taste of bile, coupled with a pressing urge to gag. He was already heaving when he threw back the covers and ran for the bathroom. He knelt down in front of the toilet just in time. After vomiting his guts out, he pulled himself up and snatched the bottle of aspirin from the medicine cabinet. He chewed four—filling a glass with water to swallow them required more hand-eye coordination than he could muster.

Milton barely recognized himself in the bathroom mirror. He had always prided himself on his appearance—it was important to him to look like an executive. He was tall, fifty-something, and well-groomed. He liked to think that the "salt" in his close-cut wiry black hair made him look distinguished. Now his skin looked gray—ashen, even—and his eyes were bloodshot. With aspirin grit lingering on his teeth and tongue, he stumbled back into bed, only to find that he must have already thrown up in his sleep. His pillow was covered in damp, putrid smelling vomit. He tentatively touched the back of his head, then put his fingers to his nose and recoiled. There was no doubt what had happened.

Not caring, Milton laid his head back, then reached for Donna's pillow. He buried his nose in it and inhaled her scent. *How did this happen?* he wondered. *How could I have lost everything, and how did it happen so fast? I don't get it. Things were going just fine. No...they were better than fine. They were perfect. I had just become the first Black president of the Elder Board. I had a devoted wife who was doing everything she could to advance my career. We lived in this beautiful penthouse in the dorm building at Society world headquarters—for free—and now it's gone. Why?*

As an adult man, Milton had never shed a tear. He'd always credited himself with having a great inner reserve of emotional strength, but that too was gone. Instead, something in the moment overcame him, a force so fierce and powerful that it was beyond his ability to control. Milton began sobbing uncontrollably. Sweat beaded upon his forehead and upper lip. Mucus started running out his nose. He felt dizzy, as if the floor was moving, but he concluded it was his half-drunk state. He didn't care. He clutched Donna's pillow to his chest, then curled up in the fetal position and cried himself back to sleep.

After paying the Sikh cabbie who drove her across the bridge into Manhattan, Donna Martin Chandler barely had enough cash for one night at the Hilton Garden Inn in the Financial District. She was grateful when the desk clerk told her the hotel was running a special promotion—a complimentary breakfast was included in the price of her room. Her plan was to enjoy one brief interlude of alone time and a little personal pleasure—she'd face the unpleasant task of calling her parents in the morning.

Once she told them what had happened, she knew that it would be a good news, bad news conversation. As happy as they'd be to hear that she'd ditched both Milton and the Society of Truth, they'd undoubtedly be miffed at being asked to pay for her flight home. They were a couple of modest means, and their daughter was a woman whose husband—now estranged husband—had been at the top of the heap, or so they thought, and yet...and yet...how was it possible that his wife couldn't scrape together the price of a plane ticket to Lincoln, Nebraska? They'd do it, of course, and Donna knew that they'd also grudgingly agree to support her until she found a job and got back on her feet.

Even so, the news of her ignominious return would spread quickly among friends and family. She cringed at the prospect of the endless I-told-you-so's that were surely coming her way. Going through school, Donna had taken great pride in what she had accomplished. She'd been clever about putting together grants and scholarships to get her BA at Spelman College, and then through grad school at Emory, where she'd earned her PhD. Donna was both inventive and resourceful—to get her doctorate, she'd had to "make a way out of no way," as pioneers of the civil rights movement often described it, and that approach to problem-solving became second nature to her. She had thrown away a bright future when she married Milton and joined the Society of Truth, but her advanced education remained an integral part of her sense of self-worth. She hadn't meant it for it to come across as arrogant or conceited, but some people who "knew her when" took it that way. Now she was looking at months or perhaps years of people gleefully rubbing her nose in her failure.

Imagined jeers of "Oh how the mighty have fallen" rang in Donna's ears as she checked into the Hilton, but as she walked through the lobby, she couldn't help noticing a crowd of well-dressed attractive women. They all appeared to be in their late thirties to late fifties, and they were mingling and laughing. Most held glasses of wine, but there were two other things that drew her to the group. The first was their poise and self-assurance—whatever it was they did in life, they were good at it, and they knew it. That confidence was coupled with an undeniable camaraderie. This was a true sisterhood—each of them gave off a "got your back" support vibe for the others in the room.

The women of this sisterhood were of every race and ethnicity, and they were all shapes and sizes. They were decked out in colorful attire that was both elegant and sexy—they were proud of their bodies and their brains. Donna could tell they took care of themselves inside and out, which made her both envious and self-conscious. She'd been strikingly beautiful as a younger woman, and was still attractive—she had her mother's high cheekbones, large brown eyes, and perfectly shaped brows. She still had a good figure, but no one knew that except Milton. She also carried a few more pounds than she would have liked because Milton loved her perfectly formed, bootylicious ass, and without a bit of extra weight, it would have been too scrawny. Her curves were completely obscured by her shapeless clothing. As an elder's wife, she'd been expected to set a properly reserved example in her personal appearance. Arriving at the Hilton, she was dressed in a brown knee-length skirt, a blouse buttoned up to the neck, thick pantyhose, and low-heeled, sensible shoes. Women at Society of Truth headquarters were supposed to be inconspicuous, and this outfit was one approved version of the modest "Christian" clothing that they were expected to wear.

Donna's attire made her look like a sparrow at a peacock convention, but she didn't care. All that mattered was that these women—whoever they were—were her new tribe. "Excuse me," she said politely to a woman getting a refill at the bar just off the lobby, "I was wondering about your group. You all seem so excited to be here. Is this a college reunion? Are you here for a conference?"

The woman turned and looked directly into Donna's eyes. She was stunning, with a radiant glow and a kind smile. Her exquisite curly black mane glistened with subtle copper highlights. It was more than just a healthy, bouncy Afro—it was an attitude. Almost reflexively, Donna touched her own straightened hair, which she blow-dried and flat-ironed at Milton's insistence. Afros, cornrows, and other "ethnic" Black coiffures were inappropriate for the wife of a member of the Elder Board, he'd declared. "The other elders and their wives would find it too extreme and too threatening," he told her. "Wear your hair like a White woman."

"I'm Keisha," the woman replied as she held out her right hand. "Keisha Brown."

"Oh, I'm so sorry," Donna apologized as she stopped fiddling with her hair and shook Keisha's hand. "My name is Donna...Donna Ch... Donna Martin." Donna had stammered for a second before making the deliberate choice to start calling herself by her maiden name. It was, in a way, her official declaration of independence. "I just couldn't help but notice all of the happy faces in your group. I just have to know what everyone is so happy about!"

Keisha laughed while looking her up and down. "My intuition tells me that you could use a little laughter yourself right about now..." she said as she pivoted toward the bartender. "Jimmy!" she called out. "Could we get another Merlot over here, please? This woman is in desperate need of liquid mood elevation!"

Turning back to Donna, Keisha wasted no time. "We are the Matrix of Women Leaders, and our mission is to lead with fierce kindness. Our work brings us great joy. We are all entrepreneurs, medical or legal professionals, or C-suite executives. Do you own a business, Donna?"

"Shall I start a tab for you, ma'am?" Jimmy asked as he placed Donna's Merlot on a cocktail napkin.

Keisha answered before Donna could speak. "This one's on me, Jimmy. So is her next one, if she wants another."

"You got it, Ms. Brown!"

"Why, thank you!" Donna responded gratefully. She was actually even more grateful to the bartender, whose question about paying for the wine had rescued her from having to answer Keisha's question about whether she owned a business. Her mind raced through a truthful scenario of how she might have responded: *Actually, Keisha, I have a PhD from Emory University, but instead of making something of myself, I chose to join a religious sect so that my husband could lead a global membership that includes five million Stepford wives who believe women should obey men as if they were gods.*

"Cheers!" said Keisha, smiling warmly as she touched her glass to Donna's.

"Cheers!" Donna responded enthusiastically. The merry clink struck her as musical, and it felt good to look into someone's eyes with an exchange of heartfelt good wishes.

Donna hadn't clinked glasses with anyone since she celebrated her PhD with her fellow grad students at Emory. Toasting was strictly forbidden by the Society of Truth—it had been denounced as a satanic ritual. She never understood the logic or the theology behind that condemnation, but she'd gone along with it—just as she had with so much else in the Society that seemed to make no sense whatsoever.

That first sip of Merlot never reached Donna's lips. Instead, she found herself fighting to remain upright as she lurched into Keisha—the floor was heaving under her feet. Their glasses clanked together loudly as wine sloshed to the floor.

The two women grabbed for the bar to stabilize themselves. "Was that a...?" Donna started.

"...an earthquake? Damn straight it was!" Jimmy replied. "Are you ladies okay?"

"Yes, thanks, just a little shook up," Keisha replied.

"Maybe more than a little," Donna admitted.

"Looks like your vino was the quake's biggest casualty," Jimmy observed as he poured two more glasses of Merlot. "No worries—trade those in for new ones."

Everyone in the bar was now receiving texts and phone calls as friends and family checked it to make sure they were all right. Keisha's phone went off as well. "Donna, you'll have to excuse me," she said. "This is a call I have to take."

Donna's shoulders sagged as a feeling of self-pity washed her. *Of course, no one would be calling me*, she thought. *I have no cell phone for anyone to call, and soon enough, no one will want to—I'll be shunned by my so-called friends who are still stuck in that damn religion.*

"Wait!" Keisha called after Donna as she reached for the bartender's pen and a fresh napkin. "Write your name and digits on here, and we'll hook up before I leave."

Donna was too embarrassed to admit that she didn't have a cell phone, so she wrote down a made-up number on the napkin and handed it to Keisha. She felt bad about doing it, but she made a mental note to look up both Keisha and the Matrix of Women Leaders at a later date. She looked forward to heading up to her room for a long bubble bath and a restful night's sleep—without Milton's snoring or worse, his clumsy attempts at intimacy.

Keisha stuffed the napkin with Donna's info into her shoulder bag as she pulled out her cell phone and walked toward a quiet corner of the lobby. "You're speaking with Keisha Brown," she said. "How can I help?"

"Keisha, this is Sadie Dixon. Would you be able to pick up my kids at seven and take them to Sam Henry's? I'm running late."

Keisha immediately understood that Sadie was speaking in code. "Sam Henry" meant Safe House, and she had seven people who needed immediate transport and protection. "Running late" meant it was potentially a life-or-death situation.

"No problem, Sadie," Keisha replied as she merged Sibylline central dispatch into the call. The operator quickly contacted two of her on-call rovers in the DC area and sent them to the confirmed pickup location at Dupont Park.

"We'll rendezvous at Sam Henry's at about midnight," Keisha said. "That'll give you time to settle in. Meanwhile, I'll finish up my business here in Manhattan."

After Keisha hung up, she stood there for a moment observing Donna, who was still hovering near the bar looking very awkward and alone. Keisha sensed Donna's dejection from across the room, but she was getting another feeling about her as well. She walked over to the bar and tapped her on the shoulder.

"Miss Donna," Keisha started, "I have a proposal. Come sit in on our workshop this evening—I'll get you in as a VIP. If you like what you hear...well"—Keisha paused—"first things first. Let's see if you like what you hear."

"I would be honored," Donna said, "but I have to confess that I'm not a professional or an executive or a business owner."

"No worries," Keisha replied. "I got you, girl."

Keisha quickly had a name tag printed up and handed it to Donna, who grinned as she peeled off the backing and affixed it to her blouse. It read *Donna Martin: Sponsor*.

"I have to go for a bit," said Keisha. "These women will show you to your seat. You'll be at table two. I'll come find you a little later on."

Shortly thereafter, the lights dimmed as the image of a petite Asian woman in her early forties appeared on the large screen behind the stage. Donna could see Keisha standing off to the side as the woman on the screen began speaking. "Welcome all of you, Matrix of Women Leaders. I am Min Yunghui, and I'm coming to you live from Germany, where Sibyllines have been standing up for the Way of Kyndeness for many generations."

The audience gave Min a warm round of applause. "As many of you know," Min continued, "I have spent much of my career flying Sibyllines around the world, but what you don't know is that I have a secret passion…"

Min paused just long enough for her audience to get the wrong idea about what kind of passion she was talking about. "No, not passion like that," she continued with a twinkle, "although that's good, too. My real passion is a gift handed down to me from my father. It's been in the family for a very long time."

Min hoisted a large ancient book toward the camera. "This book contains closely guarded formulas for growing, extracting, and blending herbs and other natural substances that create and sustain health and longevity. For centuries, these secrets were kept within the Korean royal family—my father's ancestors. Although there hasn't been an emperor on the Korean throne for many generations, the family kept these life-affirming secrets to themselves."

Keisha looked around the room to see how the audience was reacting to Min—everyone was focused on the video screen. Min took a deep breath before continuing. "That secrecy ends with me. I'm sure you all share my belief that it's wrong to be selfish about health and wellness. A commitment to help others has motivated me…no, a commitment to help others has *obligated* me to share these ancient secrets with all people of the earth. That is why I am coming to you live from the Weisshotel Castle here in Quedlinburg, Germany. This is the beginning of a new era of kindness and well-being for all."

The audience stood and applauded, then settled back into their seats. "As most of you know, it won't be easy—kindness and well-being have powerful enemies. The United Soponium Fellowship and the entities it controls would have you believe that, as deeply flawed individuals, we humans are incapable of changing the world for the better," Min continued. "They insist that we obediently bow to powers beyond ourselves—powers that control our medicine, our governments, our commerce, and our faith—especially our faith. They have artfully used their greatest weapon—religion—to shape humanity's perception of our Source—our own Higher Power—as an angry, judgmental male god."

Keisha surveyed the room once more—all the women were

nodding. Donna, eyes wide, was leaning forward in her seat, peering intently at Min. "This almighty guy—let's call him Superdude—not only withholds blessing, but also wants us to believe that he will sic *his* adversary the Devil—another male deity—on anyone who crosses him," Min declared. "And for millennia, the powers that have controlled our lives hoodwinked us all into submission—they got away with it. Meanwhile they plundered the Earth's soil, atmosphere, and water—and they did it for power and profit. When we look around at the environmental devastation they've inflicted on our planet, not to mention the ruined lives of generations of human beings, kindness and well-being seem hopeless...*or do they?*"

Min paused, then repeated with emphasis, "*Or do they...*Let's look at it from a different perspective. Could it be that we humans are innately wired to cooperate, collaborate, and compromise? Haven't radical individuals throughout history—our fellow Sibyllines, mostly women, but many men, who put forth 'dangerous' ideas like individual liberty, women's rights, and equality—proven that progress in the name of kindness is embedded in our DNA? Today, we are making great strides to prove that wellness and kindness can be a global way of life. We are spreading a new message that our inner, individual power is stronger than any power outside of ourselves. People all over the world have jumpstarted the Way of Kyndeness by shedding the burden of conformity and fear. It's time we—as citizens of the cosmos—insist on our right to make our own choices because this is the answer for life on our planet. I made my choice, so have you, and so has one of our kindest trailblazers, Keisha Brown. It's my pleasure to introduce her to the stage."

The audience laughed and applauded as the Carole King song "I Feel the Earth Move" played while Keisha made her way to the podium.

"Apropos, right?" she began. " 'I Feel the Earth Move' is one of my favorite songs, written by one of our greatest songwriters, Carole King. We've always assumed that the lyrics refer to earthshaking romantic chemistry between two people, but could she have had something else—something deeper—in mind? A love so transformative that it not only shakes the ground underneath us, but tumbles the sky above us? We of the Matrix of Women Leaders are the movers and shakers. We are the sorcerers who will reshape the world."

There was some low mumbling in the audience, and many women shifted awkwardly in their seats. "Sorcerer..." Keisha repeated. "Not a word you're comfortable with, is it? How about if we spell it a little differently?" The word SOURCE appeared on the white screen behind her in large black letters. A couple of seconds later, the letters R-E-R popped up, then skidded right to attach themselves to the end of the word SOURCE.

"Sourcerer..." Keisha said again. "That's better, right?" The audience immediately grasped the point she was making. "When we align with the Source energy that exists within us, our beauty shines, and our inner gifts and talents brighten the world—we live as source-erers. Sit with yourself, in quiet, and ask not 'What do I think?' Instead, ask yourself 'How do I *feel*?' If you love what you do—if you feel joy and gratitude even through tough times, you're radiating your own inner Kynde power. You're in alignment with our Source. You are a sourcerer. You're bringing about change, and you as an individual are far more powerful than you can imagine. All it takes is one person at a time, and soon we will feel the beating heart of the Universe as a collective group of sourcerers. Do you feel it? Can you feel it in this room, right now?"

The audience's applause flooded the room and began to sync into united rhythmic clapping. The big screen behind Keisha changed to a black background as white letters appeared. It spelled out: THE WAY OF KYNDENESS.

Keisha motioned for the crowd to settle. "Doesn't kindness make everything seem more beautiful, including yourself, in your own eyes?" she asked. "The glow that emanates from a kind sourcerer is expansive. So expansive that people may even say, 'What are you doing lately? Girl, you look so good! Did you get a facelift? Botox?' "

The audience laughed.

"I want to challenge you," said Keisha. "It's time to take kindness beyond teaching our kids manners. Beyond allowing a car to move into our lane ahead of us, or picking up a piece of trash, or helping an elderly person carry their groceries. That's polite and all that, but we need to take kindness further."

"But how?" asked a woman in the back of the room.

"So glad you asked," said Keisha. "We must—without a speck of fear or hesitation—be the influencers—the sourcerers—who elevate the energy of the room as we enter. When we speak before our boards of directors—which are still overly male, and we must do something about that, but that's a topic for another time—and when we rise to address them, we will command attention—not because of what we say, but because of how the power of kindness glows on our faces and fills the room."

"What about the home front?" another woman called out.

"This can be where it's hardest to be a sourcerer," Keisha replied. "When we gather with our loved ones who insist that we conform to their religious or political beliefs, they go speechless because there is no counterargument to the kindhearted joy radiating from our bodies. We lead through *feeling*—the feeling of kindness, joy, and love. And all of you women business leaders out there, if you have an employee who has dug their heels in prideful or selfish defiance...well...that's when your fierce kindness has to let them know not to let the door hit them in their unkind ass on their way out!"

Everyone began to laugh.

The workshop continued, with Keisha giving up the microphone to various women speaking about their personal journeys of shifting to kind leadership—to sourcerership—and relating the challenges and successes they've experienced along the way. While they were speaking, Keisha took Donna quietly by the hand and led her out of the meeting.

"Well, what do you think?" Keisha asked.

"Wow!" Donna answered. "It feels so good—so different from what I'm used to hearing...at least lately. It makes such intuitive sense—it *feels* right! My soul feels nourished! I think it's been waiting on the rest of me to become a mover and shaker—in a kind way—all my life!"

"Then come with me," Keisha suggested.

"I'm there!" Donna agreed. The bubble bath would have to wait, she told herself—this was *so* much better.

Keisha and Donna jumped into the first cab in line in front of the hotel. "Where to, ladies?" inquired the taxi driver.

"Brooklyn Bridge—Brooklyn side, please," said Keisha. "Just drop us at Luke's Lobster in the park."

"Keisha, I do have some questions about the presentation by the woman in Germany," said Donna.

"Min Yunghui? She's a pilot and a health practitioner and a botanical expert—a multitasking marvel," Keisha replied.

"But what was all that stuff about Sibyllines and the United Soponium Fellowship?" Donna asked.

"I don't mean to put you off, Donna," said Keisha, "because those are important questions and you surely are entitled to the answers, but that involves a much longer conversation than we can have in this cab ride."

To Keisha's surprise, they sped across the bridge, which was rarely without traffic. Nevertheless, she still had time to appreciate this venerable New York landmark. In its own way, the Brooklyn Bridge was as much a symbol of the city as the Empire State Building or the Statue of Liberty. Keisha smiled as she admired the reflection of its graceful garlands of lights twinkling on the East River below.

As the Brooklyn waterfront came into view, both women took note of the fifteen-foot sign atop the structure at 30 Columbia Heights—the one that said *The Truth* in blood-red Art Deco neon lettering. That building was Society of Truth headquarters, and the sign had been greeting bridge traffic headed into Brooklyn for almost fifty years.

For a long time, just seeing that sign had triggered Keisha—it was enough to send her spiraling into a pit of emotional darkness. It had taken a lot of therapy, but she eventually came to accept the time she spent as a Society missionary graduate student was part of her journey —a phase that was finally behind her. Now Keisha looked at the sign like the relic from her past that it was—it had no power over her, and she no longer feared it.

Donna had a different reaction. To her, the sign seemed to be reaching out to pull her back—back to Milton, and back into the unsatisfying life she'd fled. She'd been feeling elevated—buoyant, even —after the presentations at the Matrix workshop. Now the sign felt like doom, an evil shadow encroaching on her bright, shiny new future. Just looking at it gave her the creeps, making her muscles tense and her breathing shallow, but she said nothing.

"Thanks for the tip!" the driver called out as Keisha and Donna exited the taxi. The two women headed toward Old Fulton Street and took a left, with Keisha taking the lead. There it was, Mario's Market. She was counting on Mario and André keeping their same late-night baking schedule. He'd always told her that it was the only way to make sure that the breads and pastries were as fresh as possible for their morning customers. If the market was dark, she wouldn't be able to connect with Sadie till morning.

"Yessss!" said Keisha as she triumphantly pumped her fist in the air. "They're here!" The Closed sign was on the front door and the dining and retail areas were dark, but she spied a light coming through the small window in the rear door marked Employees Only—someone was in the kitchen. She knocked aggressively several times before hearing footsteps. Then a tall Jamaican peeked through the window.

"Is Mario here?" Keisha yelled from outside.

"Who be asking, ma'am?"

"Keisha Brown is who be asking, André," Keisha replied with a grin on her face.

André pushed the door open to see the face attached to the familiar voice. "Mi Raah!" he exclaimed. "Keisha Brown in the flesh!"

André rushed to open the door and wrap his arms around his old friend. "Wah gwaan?" he wanted to know.

"Same as always, André. Advocating for love and kindness—you know me! And I have a fellow advocate here with me. Her name is Donna."

Donna reached out her hand. "Pleasure to meet you, André."

"Ya, likewise," André replied.

"I see you're all right, too—it's almost midnight and you're still up baking!"

"Oh yeah. Mi doing fine here," said André. "Wouldn't change anything—nope! You be runnin' for president one day, missy!"

"I would love to talk and catch up, but I must talk to Mario about an urgent matter. Is he...?"

"Yah, Keisha!" André said. "I fetch him for you."

Seconds later, using his left hand, Mario pushed the kitchen door open. His heavily bandaged right hand was cocooned in a sling. "Keisha Brown!" he exclaimed. "*Cara mia*, I think I know what brings you into my market at this time of night, and it's not that you've missed me and my…cannoli!"

"You know I dream about both, Mario," Keisha said, giggling flirtatiously. Her smile faded as she took note of his bruises and his injured hand. "What happened to you?" she asked, then added, "That's your cue to say, 'You should see the other guy!' "

"Let's just say that the *stronzo* who chopped off my 'up yours' will be surprised when I shove it up his *culo* the next time I see him!" Mario bragged.

"That's my Mario!" Keisha exclaimed. "You haven't changed a bit. Listen…we don't have much time, I'm afraid. My friend Donna and I have urgent business."

"Follow me, *ragazzas*," Mario instructed.

Mario led the women toward the back of the market, but instead of heading into the kitchen, he stopped in front of what appeared to be a closet door under the staircase. "Your seven blindfolded friends arrived about an hour ago," he said. "Watch your step and be careful."

"Always," Keisha replied. "How did they seem to you?"

"Happy to be rescued in DC, but the long drive to Brooklyn was a lot. And then there was the hairy escape from the DEA that got them to Dupont Park. In other words, they're exhausted and they're crabby."

"The DEA?" Keisha asked.

"That's as much as I know," Mario said. "I escorted them to the main chamber, where they're unwinding. I pulled out the chests of clean clothing, but they could all use a hot shower. Mostly they're in need of solid information, and I told them that's exactly what you'd provide. Is there anything else you need from me?"

"Food," Keisha said simply. "Food helps everything. Do you think you and André could whip up a big pan of your amazing butternut squash ravioli with brown butter sage sauce and bring it downstairs?"

Mario's face softened. Years earlier, this had been Keisha's favorite meal with him. He was flattered that she still remembered it. "Of course. If I recall correctly, we paired it with a roasted beet and goat cheese salad, crusty garlic bread, and a memorable Chianti. It would be my pleasure, *tesoro*," Mario agreed. "For you, I can pull that off even one-handed!"

After Mario returned to the kitchen, Donna followed Keisha down the staircase. At the bottom of the stairs was a long corridor. Battery-operated light fixtures anchored to the tiled walls offered a soft glow, as well as a bit of warmth that took the edge off what otherwise would have been a dank and musty chill. The passageway was lined with ornately framed paintings, all of which depicted women.

Donna was in a state of utter astonishment. The only tunnels she'd ever seen in New York were the ones that connected the buildings of the Society of Truth, just blocks from where they were standing. As she observed the artwork, she couldn't help asking, "Who are these women?"

"You heard Min mention Sibyllines," Keisha said. "The women in these paintings are Sibyllines—female prophets."

Donna stopped in front of one to give it a closer look. The inscription plate affixed to the gilt frame identified the subject as Amalthea. "Amalthea is the Cumaean Sibylline," Keisha explained. "She lived in ancient Italy in a cave near Naples, and when I say 'ancient,' I mean several hundred years BC. Daniel, as in Daniel and the lions' den in the Old Testament, was her contemporary. Daniel was a prophet, and although male-dominated religions have worked very hard to convince us that only guys can be prophets, we know that's not true. There have been just as many women prophetesses, and Amalthea was one of them. Michelangelo was well aware of women's wisdom, power, and psychic abilities, and wanted to make sure that these Sibyllines were properly acknowledged. He placed them prominently in the ceiling of the Sistine Chapel, right alongside their male counterparts from the Bible. Have you ever seen the Sistine Chapel, Donna?"

"Only in photographs," Donna admitted ruefully. "I'm not well-traveled, not very *worldly*." She thought back to her dinner with real estate agent Bozz Kruger. Ordinarily, dining alone with a man who was not your spouse was frowned upon by the Society of Truth, but since she'd been asked to give him a tour of the Society's Brooklyn property holdings, it was all part of her assignment. At least that was a defensible way of looking at it. Nevertheless, she remembered the sexual electricity she felt from him, and how he'd made her understand how starved she was for the good things in life. "I'm just starting to realize that I've been missing out on a lot," she admitted.

"Oh, honey...get ready," Keisha said. "As long as you're hanging out with me, you're not going to be missing out on much of anything. C'mon, we have urgent business to take care of."

At the end of the Sibylline corridor was a door. Keisha punched her PIN number into the lock and the two women entered the underground safe house.

CHAPTER 5
BROOKLYN HEADQUARTERS

"What the hell was that tremor?" Nelson barked as he entered the tenth-floor conference room with his nostrils flaring. "I'm shocked—but grateful—that the old elevator didn't break down with me in it. That would've been the icing on the cake."

Nelson had a lot to be angry about. Michael Wright, the new USF "elder," had vanished as quickly as he had arrived. After deploying the DEA to arrest his ex-wife, Gabby, and her crew and haul them to DC, they'd been turned loose for lack of evidence. Once they were released, some of the USF's best black ops teams had pursued them—both by car and by helicopter—only to have them completely disappear. Speaking of disappearing, Heinrich and Ruth Müller, along with John Matthews and Erica Pfeiffer, his erstwhile fiancée, had all taken a powder. No one knew where they were. Worst of all, the Society's child sexual abuse scandal was generating toxic headline news both here and around the globe. For Nelson, the only bright spot in the last few days had been getting to torch Gabby's lab. Angrily walking into this meeting of what was left of the Elder Board, he was seething.

Sam Silverman, the Society of Truth's attorney, was already in the conference room. Expecting to lead the meeting, he had seated himself at the head of the table. The three other surviving members of the Elder Board were also present. The geriatric trio was not exactly brimming with vitality: Thomas Schmidt had Parkinson's, Ronald

Theadeau refused to allow anyone to label his forgetfulness as the onset of Alzheimer's, and Paul Fitzgerald stubbornly continued to use a cane, even though he really needed a walker or a wheelchair.

"Get up, Hebe!" Nelson directed Silverman. "You're in my seat."

Sam Silverman rolled his eyes. "Look, Nelson, just because you pay..."

"That's right, Silverman. We pay you, and handsomely at that. Your obscene retainers are an ungodly drain on this godly organization. So shut up and get your kike ass out of my chair!"

Schmidt, Theadeau, and Fitzgerald gasped in unison. Language like that had never been spoken in any Elder Board meeting. These were men who fully embraced the teachings of the Society of Truth. They weren't members of the USF, like Nelson was—they had no idea that this ancient male-dominated organization existed.

That didn't mean their hands were clean. As elders, they'd been informed about repeated instances of child sexual abuse and other debased acts that had been committed by male members of the Society. They knew of offshore accounts and hidden slush funds. They had approved budgets that included hush money payments and settlements to keep corrupt acts from becoming public knowledge, knowing full well that they were deliberately evading accountability for the grievous damage done to innocent lives over many decades.

Paul Fitzgerald attempted to restore some civility to the room. "Brothers," he began in a tone of disapproval, "before we begin this meeting, I suggest we throw the burden of our tensions and animosity up to God with a word of prayer. We are all in need of the Holy Spirit to maintain Christlike behavior and clean speech." Fitzgerald then bowed his head. "Dear Heavenly Father..." he began.

Nelson made no effort to feign submission to the Lord, but he didn't interrupt, either. He looked at Fitzgerald, Theadeau, and Schmidt with disdain, knowing it was only a matter of time before the three old farts were terminated from their Elder Board positions and replaced with men who owed their allegiance to the USF. Hopefully, whoever the lord consul sent him would stay longer than Michael Wright.

"...and please guide our decision-making today as we strive to do your holy work, all to the glory of Your great name. Amen," Fitzgerald concluded.

Even before the other elders could utter their responsive "amen," Nelson launched abruptly into the meeting. "Silverman, show me the inspection reports, including estimates of costs we will incur to repair the Brooklyn properties. Have there been appraisals?"

"Yes, but…" Silverman began.

"But nothing!" Nelson erupted. "Let's be a little smart about how we deal with these sexual abuse cases! Our first priority is to sell off our holdings. Divestiture will give us the liquidity we need to settle those goddamn lawsuits out of court."

As Nelson fumed, the other elders looked furtively at one another, and then at Sam Silverman. "The good news," Silverman began, "is that there are only a couple of items that need to be brought up to code, but there's even better news—we won't have to take care of any of it! Because"—Silverman paused for drama, as if awaiting a drumroll —"because the appraisal came in at $320 million—for just the two city block–sized buildings and the three neighboring Columbia Heights properties. And best of all, we already have an offer from Josh Krushing for $340 mil. That's $20 million over the appraisal!"

"The same Yid who's the son-in-law of that New York billionaire?" Nelson asked.

"Yes, that is Mr. Krushing," replied Silverman, choosing to ignore yet another anti-Semitic insult. "He wants to purchase the properties as is—*and* it's an all-cash offer. My recommendation is to snag the deal right now, with two contingencies. First, we fill in the tunnels. There's already too much speculation and urban myth about what goes on down there, and the last thing you need is some sensationalist news article about them—something that makes the Society of Truth look more…"

…more corrupt than it already does, thought Fitzgerald.

Few New Yorkers were aware of the Society's underground passageways, a series of tunnels that connected its Brooklyn properties with one another. The first had been created in the 1920s by a prior owner, a giant pharmaceutical company. When the property was sold to the Society of Truth, the tunnel was included. As the Society acquired more real estate, it soon became clear that the ability to access each building without having to deal with inclement weather was ideal. Three more tunnels were excavated, linking all eight of the Society's holdings.

Whoever preceded Silverman as the Society's attorney had been really good at his job. Although the tunnels ran under public streets, technically making them public property, the lawyer had negotiated an agreement with the Department of Transportation giving Society members exclusive use of the passageways.

"Secondly," said Silverman, "the Krushing Organization won't take possession until the Society has moved into its new headquarters. They're willing to wait up to a year for you to do that, but they want to see good-faith efforts toward that end. Construction on your future HQ needs to begin ASAP."

"We don't even have a site yet," said Fitzgerald.

"Actually, you do," Silverman replied. "I've already found the perfect property about sixty miles northwest of here. Take a look."

Silverman passed his android to Nelson for him to scroll through images of a lush 300-acre parcel. "It's in a very rural area," he said, "two and a half hours from the city, but worlds away, as it were."

As Nelson swiped the images, he had one thing in mind...building a new headquarters from scratch would allow him to create an underground USF conference center that would be completely within the Society campus—and protected by it as well. He'd be able to take sole credit for that accomplishment, and it would make him look good with the powers that be at the USF—whoever they were.

Schmidt, Theadeau, and Fitzgerald waited eagerly for their chance to see the photos, but Nelson passed the phone back to Silverman instead. "Great job, Silverman," Nelson said. "This meeting is adjourned. Silverman, meet me in my office."

"The meeting is most assuredly *not* adjourned, my young Brother Nelson," said Schmidt firmly. "Not until we address the child sexual abuse scandal. Our brothers are being criminally accused from coast to coast. Settling these matters out of court is the correct approach, but we have a greater issue here."

"And what might that be?" Nelson demanded. There was an

acerbic edge of condescension in his voice—surely Schmidt had nothing to say that would be worthwhile.

"We're not just hemorrhaging money to settle with these accusers, we are hemorrhaging membership as well," Schmidt began. "The Society is nothing without our believers. While you are rightly concerned about our serious financial challenges, we must stop the skid in our membership. We used to brag about having nine million members—now we're closer to eight and a half, and the numbers are continuing to drop. To halt the decline, we must mount a vigorous defense of the Society—otherwise our members will surely be deceived by what they see and hear in the news, and will continue to abandon their faith."

Nelson stared at Schmidt. The old geezer had an excellent point. "What do you suggest, Schmidt?" Nelson inquired.

"I suggest we create a formal video—an official statement of policy—and ask every member to see it. It will encourage the flock of God to be skeptical of the news, and to be even more distrustful of the legal system. If an elder is criminally charged with child sexual abuse, we should admonish our faithful not to believe the court—we already know that judges and juries do not deal fairly with the Society and its members. We must also remind them that when we do settle out of court, it is not an admission of guilt. To the contrary, it's the godly thing to do. We are following Jesus's advice in Matthew 5:25, where he says…"

Schmidt picked up his Bible, but Parkinson's made his hands too shaky to find the page.

"Allow me, Brother Schmidt," Paul Fitzgerald offered, taking the Bible from Schmidt's hands. "Jesus tells us: 'Settle matters quickly with your adversary who is taking you to court. Do it while you are still together on the way, or your adversary may hand you over to the judge, and the judge may hand you over to the officer, and you may be thrown into prison.' "

"Yes," Schmidt said. "It's from the Sermon on the Mount. Jesus commands us to settle out of court."

"Wow," said Nelson, surprisingly impressed. "That's quite brilliant of you, Brother Schmidt. Since it seems that our writing team, Ruth

Müller and her accomplices, have abandoned us, how about you draft the script?"

"It would be my honor to do so," Schmidt replied.

Schmidt and Theadeau got up and left. Paul Fitzgerald, however, was too unsettled. He wasn't about to go home and silently brood like he had so many times in the past. Over the years, there had been some pretty shady conversations in that conference room, and he'd kept silent about all of them, but this...this was getting too bizarre, and Nelson was acting very strangely.

"Don't wait up for me, Brothers," Fitzgerald called to Theadeau and Schmidt. "I am going to grab my suit coat from my desk chair for these chilly old bones."

Theadeau and Schmidt assisted each other to the elevator and departed. As soon as Nelson and Silverman entered Nelson's office, Fitzgerald silently made his way around the corner, allowing him to overhear their conversation.

"Nelson, you may be underestimating the threat this child abuse scandal poses to the Society. I don't think you understand how bad some of these cases are," Silverman declared. "How could an entire body of elders in a Michigan congregation be so twisted that they could repeatedly molest each others' children? Worse yet, how could they get away with it for so long? The evidence was so overwhelming that we had no choice but to dissolve the entire congregation and redistribute the members to nearby worship centers. We barely managed to keep the elders out of jail, but now this email drip campaign threatens to undo everything and expose what we've done to keep the lid on the story—actually, on this story and so many more."

"What do you mean...'email drip campaign'?" Nelson asked.

"Where do you think the impetus for continuing news coverage is coming from? Five emails per day are being sent to individuals in the Society who were sexually abused as children, or who were the parents of kids molested by leaders in the religion. Reports seem to confirm that the emails included copies of Society files—files that document both the accusations and what the Society had done to make them go away. It's all out there—the blackmail, the bribery, the shaming and shunning of the victims and their parents. The inescapable conclusion is that someone accessed the Society's confidential records and downloaded them. That someone is now sending victims the entire contents of their files—five a day, every day. These victims—most are adults now—are outraged and are lawyering up. In fact, an attorney in San Diego has completely shifted her business model, and is now focusing exclusively on child sexual abuse lawsuits against the Society of Truth!"

"Five emails a day. Shut down the server," Nelson said. "Problem solved."

"We can't find it," Silverman replied, "and believe me, we've tried. Every time we've attempted to trace the dispatches, they've ricocheted off servers all over the world until..."

"Until what?" Nelson demanded angrily.

"Until they end up at a single computer in Rome," Silverman replied.

"Whose?" Nelson.

"It belongs to one Joseph Aloisius Ratzinger," said Silverman.

"Who?"

"You probably know him better as Benedict XVI, the retired ex-pope. While he was pontiff, he became somewhat notorious for using the power of the Catholic Church to shield child-abusing priests, a reputation that dated back to his time as an archbishop in Germany. Whoever set up this email drip system knew what he—or she—was doing, *and* they had a wicked sense of humor."

"I'm *not* laughing!" Nelson exploded.

"Nobody's afraid of Society retaliation anymore," Silverman continued. "Emotional blackmail isn't working, either. This stuff is all over social media, and the press has picked up on it. Camera crews are camped out in front of our worship centers, using them as backdrops for their stand-up broadcasts. They're careful to remain on public property so we can't kick them out. I suspect that it's just a matter of time before they start sticking microphones in the faces of our members and asking for comments."

"And what are *you* doing about that?" Nelson asked.

"What *can* I do?" Silverman responded curtly.

Nelson frowned, nodding as he rubbed his upper lip with his index finger, then brightened as he spoke. "You're right, Silverman," he finally replied in a falsely agreeable tone. "What *can* you do when people shed themselves of fear, embrace courage, and can't be controlled? No control equals no power."

"Precisely!" Silverman replied, thinking he'd won Nelson over to his side.

"Retaining power is what it's all about," Nelson continued. "It's the only game in town, and if that's a game you can't win, I'm going to find a Rottweiler of a lawyer who can. So you can stick your law degree where the sun don't shine. And PS: You're fired!"

"What?!" Silverman exclaimed. "You can't fire me! Do you have any idea how much I know about what goes on here? By the time I'm done with you, that fifteen-foot red sign will be the laughingstock of the universe. And PS: Kiss your real estate deal with Krushing good-bye. We kikes stick together."

Fitzgerald, still listening, was shocked at both the foul language and the content of the discussion, but what surprised him most were the threats Silverman was making. Whether it was brave or reckless only time would tell.

"Three words," Nelson answered. "Attorney. Client. Privilege."

Fitzgerald had no doubt that one of the two was going to storm out the office at any moment, and his money was on Silverman. It would be awkward—or worse—if either of them knew he'd been eavesdropping, so he hid behind the wall at the top of the stairs. He could still hear the heated words as Silverman stomped out of Nelson's office.

"Correction!" Silverman barked back. "*Four* words, and make it the headline of tomorrow's *New York Times*...Attorney Exposes Privileged Secrets. And by the way, any presumption of attorney-client privilege evaporates—poof—if it's been deployed to cover up evidence of a crime. And if you don't think I can get immunity from the DA's office for bringing you down, think again."

Silverman steamed toward the elevator and punched the Down button. He stepped inside, but the closing doors were halted by a hand—Devon Nelson's hand—as he joined Silverman in the elevator.

After the doors closed, Fitzgerald approached the elevator and waited. He wasn't about to push the Down button until he was sure that Nelson and Silverman had reached the lobby—the last thing he wanted was for the ancient elevator to creak back up to the tenth floor, obligating him to ride all the way down with two very angry men. He watched with interest as the elevator stopped at the ninth floor. He waited for it to continue its descent, but it never did. After ten minutes went by, he took a chance and pressed the Down button. When the elevator arrived and the doors opened, there was no sign of either Nelson or Silverman.

CHAPTER 6
OBEAH POWER

Growing up in the birthplace of Bob Marley may sound hip, but in late 1970s, the Trench Town neighborhood of Kingston, Jamaica, was a dangerous place to be. Two opposing gangs fought for control, and Seventh Street was the Mason-Dixon line. Bloody street brawls were a regular occurrence.

André Ellis was born in Trench Town, and was surrounded by turf warfare and political unrest for most of his childhood. The violence around him was in stark contrast to his family's long devotion to the healing arts—generations of women in his family had developed a deep understanding of botanical medicine. They also had a singular connection with quantum physics—knowledge they internalized hundreds of years before the modern scientific discovery of the atomic world. They could make objects move through the air using the power of their thoughts alone.

This expertise in telekinesis—the ability to manipulate matter using laser-focused observation and unwavering intention—plus their uncanny skill with curative leaf broths, bark teas, and other unconventional remedies, made other Jamaicans leery of them. Their abilities were condemned as black magic, but it was a bad rap. Obeah women were keenly aware of how special their gifts were and deployed them benignly.

Over many generations, André's Obeah ancestors had passed down their masteries through a carefully selected chain of their female descendants—women who not only displayed evidence of the inherited gift, but who also showed deep reverence for it. When André demonstrated these attributes as a young boy—the first male in his family line to do so—his mother and grandmother taught him the Obeah skills that were usually imparted only to the women of the family. André's skills as an Obeah practitioner grew, but what interested him as least as much as metaphysical power were his mother and grandmother's abilities to blend and combine spices. He learned to cook as a boy—his family had wisely kept him indoors to keep him safe—and he loved it. After learning how to prepare his great-grandmother's jerk marinade, he improved on it, deepening the complexity of flavors, and making it his own. As a result, he'd become famous all over Kingston for his vegan Triple J—Jamaican Jerk Jackfruit.

On a visit to New York, a cousin who lived in Flatbush took André to Mario's Market, and Mario and André soon bonded over their common enthusiasm for food—and their shared love of inherited family recipes. André was never afraid to disagree with Mario about cooking. A spirited conversation about the relative merits of French vs. English thyme in André's jerk marinade segued into a passionate discussion on whether Myers's or Appleton Estate was the better dark rum to use in tiramisu. It was at that moment that Mario offered André a position as sous-chef in his kitchen. André accepted on the spot—he enjoyed bantering with Mario, and his position as a cook would give him the opportunity to apply for his green card.

Since that time, they'd become the odd couple of the neighborhood. Seeing them together made people smile—the short, chubby older Italian and the lanky young Rasta with his dreads. On the surface, they looked like the unlikeliest of friends, but everyone could sense their deep camaraderie—they were almost like father and son. Beyond his inspired use of cinnamon and nutmeg (which he touted as an aphrodisiac), André proved he was a true asset to Mario's business. He had a personable and generous manner with the clientele, most of whom he greeted by name as they walked in the door.

He understood the power of food to make people feel better, even on their darkest days. Whenever she came in looking glum, Keisha, like many other customers, often found an extra zeppole or cannoli had been slipped in with her order. The first time André was caught doing this, he was afraid he'd be fired for giving away merchandise, but Mario had another idea. After closing the shop at the end of the day, he brought the young man upstairs into his office. He thanked André for helping people in need of comfort, and told him about Kyndeness and about the Sibyllines. André knew then and there that the women in his family had been Sibyllines—even if that hadn't been what they called themselves. Mario then showed him the surveillance he maintained on the Society of Truth as he was helping to protect Ananta, one of the foremost Sibyllines, who was then known as Erica Pfeiffer, the tenth-floor cleaning lady.

In the kitchen, André had just finished putting the last finishing touches of freshly grated Romano on the pan of butternut squash ravioli. As Mario was packing it into a large tote bag, along with the beet salad, two bottles of Chianti, bread, plates, and utensils, he glanced out through the small window of the kitchen swinging door. His eyes were not as sharp as they once were, but he thought he glimpsed a shadowy figure moving stealthily through the main area of the market.

"André," Mario inquired quietly, "did you remember to lock the front door after you let Keisha in?"

"Ah, no. Me soon go," André answered as he started toward the door.

"No!" Mario whispered insistently. "I think someone's already inside."

André may have been a peaceable man, but you didn't survive childhood in Trench Town without learning the basics of street fighting. He was also very conscious of his role as Mario's protector. After Mario had been brutally attacked by Michael Wright—who he now knew to be a USF agent—André had vowed to make sure that no further harm would come to his friend and mentor.

Both men soon heard creaks coming from overhead. André pointed to the ceiling and made an uphill walking motion with his index and middle fingers—the intruder was headed for Mario's second-story office. They both assumed it was a USF operative assigned to come back and finish off Mario, along with anyone else suspected of supporting the Sibyllines.

Mario looked at his heavily bandaged right hand and sighed. "I'm afraid you'll have to take care of this on your own, André," he whispered. "I'd be a liability with this thing, and I really need to get this food to the bunker without being followed. If this *cornuto*, whoever he is, is already upstairs, I can leave without him seeing me."

André nodded. "You go now. Take care of Miss Keisha. And take care of yourself—maybe stay down in the bunker for a while. Me mash up da bumbaclot. Bless up."

Mario took the bag of food and rushed toward the door under the staircase that led underground. As he started downstairs, he was thrown off balance and had to quickly reach for the handrail, lest he tumble down the steps, leaving a trail of salad and ravioli behind him.

André had already grabbed his Gokujo boning knife when the pastry tables began to wobble and the pans hanging on the pot rack started clanking together. Their noise covered the sound of his footsteps as he crept out of the kitchen and started up the stairs to confront the intruder.

With his back to the staircase, Bozz Kruger steadied himself in the doorway of Mario's second-floor office, waiting for the tremors to stop. The room still bore the telltale signs of the grisly encounter that had taken place a few days earlier. There was a crusted dark-brown puddle of dried blood on the carpet beneath the desk where Michael Wright had amputated the middle finger of Mario's right hand. There were also blood smears on the window pane leading to the fire escape, where Mario had tried unsuccessfully to get away. Looking around, Bozz noticed an iPad sitting face down in a wire bin on Mario's desk. He picked it up and found that he was looking at live video surveillance from six hidden camera locations at the Society of Truth. He watched as a meeting in the tenth-floor conference room at the Society of Truth was already in session, with Devon Nelson leading the conversation...

Silverman, show me the inspection reports, including estimates of costs we will incur to repair the Brooklyn properties. Have there been appraisals?

Kruger continued to watch and listen to their conversation about the sale of the Brooklyn properties and the acquisition of the new property until the meeting ended.

Great job, Silverman, Nelson said, *This meeting is adjourned. Silverman, meet me in my office.*

Bozz Kruger had been peering so intently at the iPad and listening to the conversation in the headquarters conference room that he had no idea André had crept up behind him.

"Hmm…" said André, "so dey gwaan fill in all the tunnels, huh?"

Startled, Kruger swung around, but after looking André up and down, he immediately relaxed. As an elite USF Cell operative, the powerful, muscular Black man had been highly trained in advanced martial arts. He had no doubt that in a physical contest, he could easily overpower the slender Jamaican. "Let me guess…from your Rasta cap, you must be a…what's that Jamaican term for a streetwise tough guy? Oh yeah—a ragamuffin. You seriously think you can overtake me with that kitchen knife you're holding—*ragamuffin?*"

"You mean *dis* knife?" André asked. He held it out at arm's length, then released his grip on the handle.

André's Obeah doctress forebears had taught him well—Bozz Kruger's eyes opened very wide as the knife remained suspended in midair.

The knife didn't move while André focused singularly on Kruger's left hand—the one holding the iPad. Kruger felt his wrist slowly bend downward as his fingers spread open. He tried to maintain a grip on the device, but he had no control over what his hand was doing. The iPad dropped to the floor.

"Caribbean black magic!" Kruger said. "I should have figured."

"Try quantum double slit," André responded. "That's the interaction between the observer—that would be me—and the asshole being observed—that would be you! But that's the difference between USF assholes and the Sibyllines. The elite of the USF will always try to keep the secrets of the universe from…let's see—how did you put it?— 'streetwise, tough-guy ragamuffins.' "

Bozz Kruger didn't like the tables being turned on him, let alone by a mere pastry chef, but in the nanosecond that it took for his body to lunge toward André, the levitating knife spiraled toward him and froze in space, with its point barely touching his right eyeball. Kruger grabbed it by the handle to pull it away, but it wouldn't budge. He tried to let go of his grip on it, but it was as if his palm had been Gorilla Glued to the handle. The blade began to get hot…red-hot, until both his eye and his hand began to burn. Tears started streaming down his cheek. He squirmed. He tried to pull it away with his other hand, but the force binding his hand to the knife was too strong.

"Stop!" Kruger cried out. "Stop, I tell you!"

"Say 'I'm a ragamuffin,' " André commanded like a fifth grader in a wrestling match.

"Are you fucking kidding?" Kruger snapped.

"Say it!"

"Okay, okay! I'm a ragamuffin! Now get this knife…"

Just then, Kruger's grip on the knife loosened and the weapon fell to the floor. Kruger jumped back, then ran for the window and raced down the fire escape.

André laughed. "Mi see yuh likkle more den…*ragamuffin*," he said as he picked up his knife and the iPad. The iPad's video surveillance was still on the tenth-floor conference room, but the room was empty —everyone had left. André then clicked on the live stream inside the president's office. Milton Chandler had barely had a chance to move in before being forced to resign, and now it had a new occupant—Devon Nelson. The screen was black, but the audio was still working. André figured that the video camera had been destroyed, but no one had bothered to check for a separate microphone.

Nelson and Sam Silverman were obviously in the middle of a heated conversation…

So you can stick your law degree where the sun don't shine. And PS: You're fired!

You can't fire me! Do you have any idea how much I know about what goes on here? By the time I'm done with you, that fifteen-foot red sign will be the laughingstock of the universe. And PS: Kiss your real estate deal with Krushing goodbye. We kikes stick together.

Three words. Attorney. Client. Privilege.

Correction! Four words, and make it the headline of tomorrow's New York Times…*Attorney Exposes Privileged Secrets…And if you don't think I can get immunity from the DA's office for bringing you down, think again.*

Listening intently from Mario's loft office, André knew that threatening to expose Nelson and the Society was inherently dangerous. "Oh dis no good," André said aloud. "That lawyer, if he nuh careful, he gwaan be dead."

CHAPTER 7
THE CASTLE

"Ruth...Ruth...can you hear me?"

Ruth's right index finger moved, a sign that she was coming to. Her eyes slowly squinted open—just a small crack at first. She felt as if she was swimming out of a deep, dark coldness up to a whiteness of daylight that was blinding. Like a deep-sea diver whose ears are plugged, she heard muffled voices—near, yet far away. Half-dreaming and half-awake, she realized something bad had happened. A terrifying memory engulfed her and she started shaking uncontrollably. She knew she had to fully wake up, but she didn't know how.

"Ruth, it's okay. You're going to be okay," the soothing voice said as a warm hand eased itself into her chilly palm.

Out of Ruth's peripheral vision, she caught sight of an IV bag of dark-red fluid hanging at her bedside. The Biblical command to abstain from blood (Acts 15:20, 28, 29) had been drummed into her from infancy by the Society of Truth, so the idea that someone else's blood was now coursing through her body caused her to panic. Her body began to convulse as tears streamed from the corners of both eyes.

"Nurse, the Sooji Chim hand needles—now!" The same soothing voice, now suddenly authoritative, was coming from a petite Asian woman in her early forties. Her long shiny straight black hair was gathered up into a ponytail, and her kind eyes were set off by naturally long lashes. She wore almost no makeup.

As her eyes opened, Ruth recognized whose voice she was hearing. The woman was Min Yunghui, the pilot who'd flown her to Germany so Heinrich could be buried with his ancestors. Min was a descendant of Korean emperors, and the youngest in a long line of Korean herbal medicine practitioners. Min, who had expanded her knowledge of the healing arts by obtaining a prestigious degree in five-element acupuncture, now inserted a fine Sooji Chim needle into Ruth's left hand at the pisiform point—the bone at the base of the palm that protrudes above the inner wrist. Ruth didn't feel the needle, but she immediately felt a tranquilizing calmness overtake her.

"Breathe, Ruth, breathe," Min said softly. "Breathe in slowly and deeply through your nose. Feel your ribs and chest expand as the air fills your lungs. Good, very good. Then exhale slowly and completely." Min pushed down on Ruth's sternum to help her expel all the leftover air. "Wonderful," she said encouragingly. "Now do it again."

Ruth felt a deep, cellular peace wash over her body.

Min continued speaking in a soft and gentle voice. "Ruth, do not be disturbed by the red bag. I understand your fear of blood transfusions, and I know why it affects you so deeply. I want you to think of this blood in another way. Think of it as a great kindness that has been offered to you. Many loving and kind donors gave their blood to save you. People of all races, spiritual beliefs, genders, ages—people whose lives look nothing like yours—rolled up their sleeves and donated this life-giving gift. It was their way of casting their vote for you. People you never met voted for you to live—you—a complete stranger. It's the ultimate act of kindness—and it's something to feel grateful for."

It took everything in Ruth's power to respond—but she just had to. "Well, if I start talking in tongues or singing like Dolly Parton," she said in a raspy voice, "it's not me—I'm just the ventriloquist for everyone else who's taken up residence in these old arteries of mine."

Min broke out in laughter. During the flight from New York to Germany, Ruth had remained solemn. She was bringing Heinrich's body home, and she was still in shock from having watched the USF gunman put a bullet into his forehead. This was the first time Min had been on the receiving end of Ruth's cheeky sense of humor.

"How long have I been unconscious?" Ruth asked.

"It's been thirty-six hours," Min answered.

Ruth tried to grope for the black drawstring bag around her neck, but winced in pain because of her shoulder wound.

"Is this what you're looking for?" Min asked as she held up the small velvet bag. "Don't worry, Ruth. The seeds are safe, and you are safe as well."

"Where am I?" Ruth asked.

"You are in the underground treatment center beneath the Weisshotel Castle," said Min, "a hotel owned, operated, and protected by your Sibylline family on your mother's side."

Ruth settled back into her pillow with a bit of regret. Her maiden name was Weiss, but she'd never known about this castle—or anything else associated with mother's family. Growing up in the Society of Truth and being indoctrinated with its dogma, she'd been taught from birth that the Society was her one, true family—her blood relatives didn't count. It had never occurred to her to research her ancestors on her mother's side, but she'd been happily surprised by how warmly she had been received by the relatives she'd met at Heinrich's funeral. These wonderful people were the family she never knew she had, and they accepted her instantly. They should have been part of her life from childhood—and would have been, but for the Society.

"While you were unconscious," Min continued, "we extracted the seeds from the tar. It was quite the challenge, as we knew it would be. Phase 1 was easy—evaporating the last remaining amount of moisture. We had to do that first so that we could find its melting point, but not before converting the oxygen and other volatiles into gas. Then, after devolatilization..."

"Whoa! You lost me at volatiles!" Ruth exclaimed. "Maybe you can stick me with another one of those needles that will help me understand what you're saying. Or maybe somebody whose blood I'm recycling can explain it to me!"

"Sorry, Ruth," Min said, laughing. "I get carried away sometimes. We're now undertaking a thorough examination of the petrified tar that the seeds were trapped in. The mineral content and molecular structure will reveal a lot, and should help us adjust the micronutrients in the soil and create the optimal growing environment for the seeds. In the meantime, we placed them back in the bag. Would you like to see them?"

"Yes! Yes, of course!"

Min adjusted Ruth's bed, raising her head and rolling the bedside table in front of her. She then opened the bag, picked out the six seeds, and placed them on the table.

Ruth touched them gently, then rolled them around with her finger. "They seem so *ordinary*," she said.

"Underwhelming, I know," said Jacob from the doorway. "Did you think they were going to glow and that you'd hear angels sing?"

"My dear Jacob! Please come here so I can see you," Ruth pleaded with tears in her eyes.

Jacob came near Ruth's bedside and placed his hand on her arm. "They managed to remove the bullet and stitch me up good as new," he said.

"*Ich verdanke dir mein leben*, my Jacob," Ruth sputtered in German through tears.

"No, Ruth, *we* owe our lives to *you*. All of us do," Jacob countered. "You're the one who risked your life to retrieve the seeds, leaving everything you knew and loved behind. You've been chased, hunted, shot at—and that's just since you got to Quedlinburg. You did it because you understood what real truth, love, and kindness are. You did it for humanity."

"Stop!" Ruth urged modestly. "My dear Jacob, we have more important things to focus on than praising this old woman."

"I don't want to argue with you, Ruth," Min said as she placed her hand somewhat possessively on top of Jacob's, "but this guy is *my* dear Jacob. I'm perfectly willing to share him with you, but only because he has faithfully served the Sibyllines here in Germany since before I came to the castle."

Jacob looked at Min affectionately. "And...this is *my* dear Min—my superhero woman. I'm sharing her with you, Ruth, but only because I don't have a choice. She's not only a doctor—"

"But also a pilot," Ruth interrupted, "and a very good one!"

"Thanks, guys," Min started, "but how about we put this precious little bag of seeds back where we know they'll be safe?"

"I would love that," Ruth said. "I got so used to wearing that bag that I feel naked without it!"

Min placed the seeds back into the little black velvet pouch and carefully laced the string around Ruth's neck. "Ananta trusted you with the seeds," said Min. "That says a great deal about who you are."

"My friends trusted you to fly Heinrich and me here," said Ruth. "That says a great deal about you as well." The two women hugged awkwardly—a full embrace was impossible because of Ruth's injury, but there was no question about the respect and affection they had for one another.

As any good practitioner would do, Min took the stethoscope from around her own neck and listened to Ruth's heart and gut, checking her oxygen and temperature as well. She also checked the IV connection in Ruth's arm. "Everything looks good," she said. "Now...you need rest and nutrition. Your first meal is on its way. I'll be back to check on you soon. In the meantime, my Jacob—*our* Jacob—will sit with you."

The USF operative whose bullet had hit both Jacob and Ruth as they ran for the arched black metal door had been apprehended at one of the Sibylline watch posts near the castle. He'd been slightly wounded as he was captured, and was being held down the hall from Ruth's treatment room. After leaving Ruth, Min stopped at the restroom before checking on him. As she was washing her hands, she looked into the mirror above the sink and saw his reflection. He was standing right behind her, and he was armed.

"I thought you were a prisoner," Min said with more calm in her voice than she felt in her heart.

"I was," he replied.

"But..." Min said.

"But I have something you want," he replied.

Slowly, his hand lowered the weapon, barely brushing the skin on her ear. After skimming the barrel of the gun along her arm, he gently dropped it into the sink. Min grabbed it and spun around, pointing the pistol at the man's face.

"You're not going to shoot me," he declared. "You're going to want what I can give you."

"Perhaps," she replied, "but you'll find that we Sibyllines don't take well to being forced to negotiate in the girls' room, and we *really* hate men who hurt people we care about." Min quickly used a two-handed uppercut to smash the pistol into his left temple. The blow buckled the knees of the would-be assassin, and he crumpled to the floor.

"You're right. I wasn't going to shoot you," Min said, but the assassin couldn't hear her. He was out cold.

Only then did she check out his weapon, a Walther PPK—the safety catch was on. "And it would appear that you weren't going to shoot me, either," she said to the unconscious man at her feet.

Min stepped over the body and called for Jacob to take him back to his holding cell. Then she made her way up the spiral stone staircase and stepped out into the open air. She needed to clear her mind. *What could he possibly have that I might want?* she wondered.

A short path led to a grand rose garden, where the first flush of blooms was just starting to show color. She stopped in front of a ruined wall laced with ivy, where the castle's ancient aviary used to be. There was a stone tablet embedded in the wall, with an inscription that dated from the summer of 1824. It had been written by one of the sweet-hearts of the famous German poet Johann Wolfgang von Goethe.

Seventy-five-year-old Goethe, after having recovered from a near fatal heart illness, fell for fourteen-year-old Elsa Clementine. He wanted to marry her, but her parents strictly forbade it. The word pedophile hadn't been invented yet, but they knew that his proposal was based in lust, not love. He'd made no secret of his own sexual thirst for children, and unapologetically wrote about it in his poems. He wasn't just attracted to underage girls. Goethe also wrote about pederasty—sex between a man and a young boy—as a topic worthy of poetic and artistic depiction.

As Min was lost in thought, Jacob silently came up behind her. "He's awake," he said.

Min jumped. "Geez, Jacob!" Min said in exasperation. "You know better than to sneak up behind me like that!"

Jacob laughed. There was no romantic attraction between the two of them—they were more like siblings, and as is the case with all siblings, there was rivalry. Jacob got a sophomoric thrill from trying to scare her every chance he could. Leaping out from behind a door, sneaking up on her, or hiding in a closet were his favorites. Most of the time she ended it with a punch in the gut or a cuff on the ear, but Jacob enjoyed that, too. Min groused every time he pulled one of these stunts, but it was all for show. There was no doubt about the affection, respect, and camaraderie underlying them.

"And Ruth's asleep. I thought you'd want to know," Jacob added.

"Thanks," Min said. "Let's go see our Houdini."

When Jacob unlocked the cell door, the USF assassin was sitting upright on a cot, pressing a cold pack to the side of his head. "Am I supposed to think this ice pack is your *kind* way to atone for bashing me in the temple?" he asked.

"If it had been up to me, I wouldn't have given you an ice pack at all—you can thank *kind* Jacob here for that. As far as I'm concerned, there's no amount of ice that can make the brain of yours any colder," Min declared. "So, what is it that you want? It's obvious that you're not going to lift a finger to help the Sibyllines without something in return."

"You can't possibly think that Ruth is alive because I failed my assignment," he said with a mix of arrogance and bravado. "I'm the best of the best...I shot Ruth in the shoulder—at that angle, at that exact location—on purpose. It went right through her with very little damage. And then I *let* myself get caught."

Min folded her arms in front of her and stared at him. "I'm listening," she said. "Go on."

CHAPTER 8
TRANSCENDENCE AND PSYCHEDELICS

Ananta was in a trance. Thirty-six hours ago, she'd embraced John underneath the ancient woven cloth that Easa had brought back with him to Phugtal, and she hadn't moved since. Her consciousness of the physical world around her was completely absent—even the feeling of John's cold, naked lifeless body next to her skin.

Ananta had mastered acute awareness of the feeling of Source energy channeling through every part of her being. As she was growing up in the monastery, the wise monks had instilled this mindfulness in her, beginning when she was a young girl. They called it "channel consciousness," and she had become highly proficient at it. She surrendered to its force daily. Remaining spiritually connected in this way, Ananta enjoyed fulfilling her passions and the purpose she was meant to live, but what was now happening under this blanket was very different. As she lay on top of her dead lover, John, something she had never experienced before was taking over her consciousness underneath this beautifully woven miraculous fabric.

She felt that the power of divine love in each delicately looped knot had come alive. That power was speaking to her, but not in verbal language, or even in defined thought. It was more of a collective concept emanating from the heart of the universe. As soon as she yielded to this power, the familiar feeling of Source energy flowing through her began to morph into something much deeper. Rather than feeling herself to be a carrier of that energy, Ananta became one with it. She felt as if the Source was happening *as* her. Time and space dissolved. The dimensions of everything physical departed.

If Ananta had ever thought of kindness as too generic and simple to change the world—even for a fleeting second—she was wrong. In her hypnotic state, she saw it all—the infinity of all that was past and all that was present flashed in front of her in a fraction of a second. And then a vision of the future came to her. A vision of a future world whose inhabitants use their free will to choose Kyndeness began trickling into her consciousness like water from a free-flowing well. It dripped slowly at first, but as the stream became ever stronger, Ananta began to sob.

Overwhelming gratitude for the decision made by her grandmother, Eva, to eat of the Tree of Knowledge as a symbol of her choice in choosing independent free will soon flooded her like a deluge. She was also filled with appreciation for her mother, Mireille, for choosing to accept the opportunity to preserve the seeds of the Tree of Life. Ananta also understood the true nature of her father, Easa, when he lived as a man in a physical body, and how both she and her twin brother, Sundara, inherited a sliver of Easa's mortal genetic code that originated from his earthly mother, Maryam.

"Ananta," whispered a deep voice.

She heard it, and before she could even wonder where the voice was coming from, he said, "I am to be sensed, not seen. Feel me."

A sudden rush of sheer, warm sensual bliss engulfed her. The night she had spent inside the tent with John on the way to Phugtal, sheltered together from the hard late-winter rain and nestled in each other's bodies inside the sleeping bag, had been extraordinary, to say the least. But even that moment paled in comparison to the feelings she was experiencing in this encounter with John on a mutual spiritual dimension. She didn't think it was possible, yet here they were, in the invisible world of infinity, feeling erotic in the presence of each other, yet without physical body parts. She could sense him, as if he was saying, "Come to me."

While Ananta was experiencing a heightened sensual awareness in this transcendent space, her body in the physical realm began to respond sexually. Underneath the blanket, her form began to twist from one side to another, quivering, consumed by passionate desire as if by fire. She began moaning as the fingers of her right hand sank into the skin on John's body—a body that was beginning to feel a little less cold—while her left hand twisted the sheet underneath them. Her body arched with orgasm as her breath caught, and a muffled cry could be heard emanating from her opened mouth.

She knew at that moment that they had intimately become one in spirit in a nonmaterial expanse, while united in cells and molecules in a physical reality. A feeling of familiarity melted over her as she began to transition her consciousness back to her material body.

No! I'm not ready to go back! Please...! she wanted to cry out, but her voice wouldn't work.

Aware of the sweat on her skin, she felt John's body next to her and began to sob uncontrollably,

"John, my love, please come back...please. I'll do anything... anything. You have to come back! I know you are alive in there. Wake up!"

As she was easing herself out of her trance, she heard John's voice. "We are eternally connected now," he said.

In the depths of the Phugtal monastery, there had been an unmistakable fury in Sundara's eyes as Mireille leaned in to kiss him on the forehead. To him, it felt like a violation—even a rape, of sorts.

"I remember the last time I tried to hug Sundara," Mireille said to Saji. "He was in his early twenties, all packed to leave the monastery and travel. He was ready for a journey, and I wanted to hug my son goodbye, but when I reached out to him, he recoiled from me. 'Please, Mom, don't!' he said."

"Where was he going?" Saji asked.

"He told me he was going to explore the world with a friend," Mireille replied. "When I asked where they were going to start, he said the mountains of Turkey near the Black Sea. A shiver went down my spine, but I couldn't stop him from going."

Mireille's ability to influence her son's behavior began eroding when he was seven. After his encounter with the being who lived in the dark cave, no matter what his mother did—and she'd done everything she could think of—she could not counteract or undo what happened that day when the goodness was sucked out of him as a child...

...Until now. Now, when Sundara was lying helpless and immobile in the bowels of the monastery, and Saji and Yara were monitoring his every bodily function. After the battle upstairs and through the intervention of Easa, Mireille had been provided this miraculous opportunity, and she was not going to waste it. She intended to do everything she could to restore the goodness her son had been born with. Sundara was about to embark on a different kind of journey—a journey back into himself, or so she hoped. In its own way, Mireille's unwelcome kiss in the Phugtal treatment room had been a kiss goodbye to the man who'd come to personify everything she opposed.

As Saji listened to Mireille, she remained focused on Sundara. It was essential to precisely calibrate the amount of therapeutic treatment that was to drip intravenously into Sundara's bloodstream. The quantities she was administering to him might have struck some healers as audacious or irresponsible. They were far higher than even the most advanced shamans would utilize, but Saji's ability, experience, and intuitive understanding of the needs of the patient were second only to the skills of Mireille herself. She could ascertain the exact amount that a person's psyche needed for neurogenesis—the rebirth of the mind.

In Sundara's case, initiating that rebirth posed a unique challenge. Sundara was thousands of years old. Over the centuries, he had been effectively brainwashed—relentlessly programmed to embrace a worldview that became increasingly male-biased and increasingly rigid with the passage of time. It was this toxic closed circuit that nourished and fortified his conviction that male humans were the epitome of creation —and therefore were to be held in higher esteem than women and all other living things. For Sundara, the bedrock of this dogma was his unwavering belief in his own physical and mental superiority.

Within Sundara's distorted mindset, it followed as a matter of course that men were rightfully entitled to world domination. This had led him to his position as the lord consul of the United Soponium Fellowship. Using the USF as a base, he had been able to incite and coordinate a myriad of activities around the globe, all of which were designed to advance male supremacy in every area of endeavor—politics, finance, the arts, science, medicine, and religion.

Through religion—their most effective tool—the USF had convinced both men and women that their dominant and subservient roles had been ordained by God. Strict obedience to this patriarchal dogma would ensure a favored reward—blessings in this life and an eternal, blissful afterlife. Those who defied what was touted as God's natural law were condemned to misery and worse—both in this life and on the other side of the grave.

As it turned out, not everyone took "God's natural law" at face value. Generation after generation of philosophers, scientists, artists, and critical thinkers challenged it, arguing instead for a society based on reason, tolerance, freedom, and gender equality. Despite the efforts of the USF, and Sundara in particular, these skeptics were never completely snuffed out. Over the course of history, Mireille had marshaled the Sibyllines to thwart him wherever possible. Clinging to the slender hope that Sundara might see the light on his own and abandon his allegiance to the USF and his quest for power, she had long shied away from personally confronting him face-to-face—until the showdown in the great hall of the monastery. When he tried to rape and then decapitate his twin sister, she could not ignore the fact that her son had become all but completely detached from the Source. To save her daughter, Mireille had no choice but to intervene against her son, and now his psyche would be completely rewired on a deep, neurological level.

Sundara lay inert on the table. The naturopathic extracts that Saji had so carefully measured began coursing through his system. The mix had been formulated to stimulate the momentum needed to bring him back into alignment, and to restore his connection to the Source. Even Saji herself did not know whether it was possible to vanquish the malevolent forces that were feeding and reinforcing his oversized ego, but the high concentrations of mind-altering botanicals she was giving him represented the best—and only—chance of success.

What was taking place in the depths of the Phugtal monastery was nothing less than a pitched battle for the essence of Sundara's being—for his very soul. If he had been able to verbally articulate the dynamically alive trip he was taking in his mind while his physical body lay lifeless, he might have described it like this:

After my mother removed her golden veil, I heard a noise that reminded me of my childhood. It was a cracking noise I'd heard often in the monastery kitchen when I was a boy, as the monks who were preparing the evening meal broke the tops off bunches of carrots. Now, however, the sound I heard was made by the bones in my neck snapping —and then I went limp and lost consciousness.

Suddenly I felt nothing. I was in a coma, and I knew it. It was as if my senses had become separated from my physical body. From a point outside myself, I could see and hear what was happening to me. I heard my mother's words to Saji, and felt her finger stroking my hair. I wanted to recoil from her touch, but I couldn't. I sensed the warm, wet tear that fell from her eye onto my cheek. I felt the hands of the monks under me, lifting me and carrying me in a procession down to the lowest level of the monastery. I tried to rebel against being handled in this way, but I was powerless.

They strapped me to a bed with side rails so I could be monitored from an adjacent room. Unable to move, I could not fight off the fluids they sent flooding into my body through intravenous tubing, but I did prepare myself mentally to resist in the only way I could.

After hundreds of years of orchestrating the most masterly crafted world plan to separate humans from their Source, I refused to be compelled to face the Divine in my own mind through the use of sacred plants. Not me. I was Sundara, the Strong and the Beautiful. I held power and control over my consciousness. By force of will, I would withstand the change they were trying to induce.

That's not how it played out.

The psychedelic trip began in the ocular region of my brain. The first thing I saw was a geometric zigzag line in the shape of a half circle, full of flashing neon colors. It grew so large in my vision that it blocked my view of anything beyond it. I wanted to close my eyes so that I didn't have to see it, but my eyes were already closed. I had no choice but to keep looking at it. The image was accompanied by a tension and stiffness that gripped every part of me. It wasn't just that I couldn't move—it felt as if my entire body was clenched in an unrelenting muscle cramp—a head-to-toe persistent spasm. My muscles were so tightly contracted that I thought they were going to implode. Eventually, these bright pulsating colors stopped flashing and began to change into hues of beige, tan, and brown. Then the zigzag shape evolved into the silhouette of a three-dimensional body. It was walking toward me, ugly—terrifyingly hideous.

I was forced to look at this gruesome being that took up my entire field of vision. As it became three-dimensional, I had no choice but to look it in the eye. There was no blinking, no glancing away, and it was then that I realized I was looking at myself—the most repulsive, grotesque version of me. With my body in total paralysis, for the first time in my life, I had no control, no power over my physical being. Something was in charge, and it wasn't me. It was the sacred plants.

The full body cramp and its sustained, dynamic rigidity generated an all-encompassing nausea that engulfed my entire being. This was no ordinary biliousness whose discomfort was localized in the belly. Every organ—every one of the forty trillion cells in my body—was trying to vomit. Even the hairs on my head wanted to throw up at the sight of my loathsome holographic self. I began to gag, then retch.

The disgusting hologram of myself gradually transitioned back to the geometric prism of neon colors, then morphed into various mandalas and vortices. For hours, these hypnotic kaleidoscopes steadily eased away my tension.

Then the memories started flooding in. I saw myself playing with my twin, Ananta, both of us ten months old as I began to walk my first steps. I was headed for the monastery's ledge. I saw Ananta stand, wobbly at first but then steadying herself as she, too, took her first steps to save me from lunging over the ledge. She pushed me back, only to fall to her own death as a result of her backward momentum. It was both devastating to see my sister die and exhilarating to be rescued. How could she have known? Was it our connection as twins?

The visual recollections began coming faster and faster. The tsunami of memories picked up speed until they were crashing in on me almost on top of one another, and yet I recognized each incident with crystal clarity. Every glimpse into the past held the power to either seize me with devastation or release me with exhilaration. My senses became electrically acute.

That's when the giant beast came into view in the distance.

"That should do it," Saji assured.

"Nicely done, Saji. I couldn't have formulated it better myself,"

Mireille said. "Sundara should be well on his way to a trip he will never forget—only this time, it's not to the Black Sea. Watch him closely, wise one. He's no doubt got a lot to purge, and we don't want him choking on his own vomit. Be ready for anything he may say, and alert me if—or, I should say 'when'—he starts talking about Nephilim."

"Of course. I will alert you immediately. You taught me all I know. You can count on me to be here by his side every moment through his experience."

Just then, Ananta came bursting through the treatment room door. "Āmā! Āmā!" she called out in utter glee. "He's alive...John's alive!"

Ananta wrapped her arms around her mother and melted into her, weeping with gratitude.

"What!?" Mireille exclaimed. "Are you sure?"

"It's true!" Ananta cried. "I refused to let him go, and he came back! At first, I wondered whether the warmth from his body might have been just my imagination, but then I felt his chest expand as his lungs filled and he gasped for air. He's alive!"

Just then, Ananta's excited expression crumpled and disappeared as she got a glimpse of her twin brother handcuffed to the metal railing of the bed. She scanned the IV and the monitors on the other side of the glass partition. Saji and Mireille stayed silent and watched. Emotionless, acting as if her brother was dead to her, Ananta grabbed her mother's hand and led her up the stone staircases to the floor where John was lying. The door was open.

"What took you so long?" John joked while stuffing a piece of bread into his mouth. "I gotta say, the monks here really know how to bake a kick-ass loaf of bread!"

The young male monk standing next to John was grinning from ear to ear, then broke into hearty laughter. It was he who had baked the bread.

Mireille dropped to her knees, placed her palms together in front of her heart, and cast her eyes toward the heavens. "Thank you, my love. Thank you, my Easa," she whispered softly but fervently.

In that very moment, Mireille's expression changed—she had received an answer to her heartfelt prayer of gratitude. It was an urgent message she had to deliver to Ananta and John—a message that would change their lives forever. Its contents amazed and thrilled Mireille, but she would have to keep to herself for now.

"Ananta," Mireille called to her daughter.

Ananta didn't hear her mother's voice at first. She was joyfully giggling with John and the monk.

"*Ananta!*" Mireille said a little more insistently.

"Yes, Mother," Ananta replied while still laughing.

"I'm going to Shangri-la, and I need to take you and John with me. Don't argue—it's imperative, and we need to go now. We only have two horses at the moment, so we'll need to take turns walking."

"I don't understand." Ananta's face turned instantly serious. "What's going on?"

"I'll explain on the way, but you need to trust me right now. Do you trust me?"

"I trust her!" John called out exuberantly, feeling his energy at an all-time high. "Actually, we don't have a horse problem. Before trekking on foot to the guesthouse near the stupas, Ananta and I left two horses with a solitary monk at the last tiny monastery. I'm sure they'll still be there."

"Wonderful!" Mireille exclaimed. "You don't need to pack. Shangri-la is equipped with everything we would ever need, and we can gear up for travel once we reach Padum. Let's go!"

[illegible] world change [illegible] own [illegible] maybe a little

[illegible] enough [illegible] financial [illegible] to keep a piece of [illegible]

[illegible] mortgage [illegible] must be read [illegible] months [illegible]

Andy did [illegible] meet her properly [illegible]

[illegible] their [illegible] knew and [illegible] touch [illegible]

[illegible] College [illegible] Alison [illegible]

Nobody [illegible] highlighted patch of silver in [illegible]

[illegible] she had [illegible] to let things [illegible] done [illegible]

[illegible] there might be [illegible] matter what [illegible]

[illegible] when we could systematically change things to [illegible]

[illegible] her middle-class values [illegible]

[illegible] begin from a place that is humble and out [illegible]

[illegible] two or so [illegible] senator, from one [illegible] for all the [illegible]. That [illegible] it still be there.

[illegible] "Who? What? When? Where?" You can't even begin to think [illegible]

[illegible] accepted whatever thought [illegible] without [illegible] had once [illegible]

[illegible] forward once we reach that stage [illegible]

CHAPTER 9
THE BUNKER

Donna followed Keisha into the main chamber of the bunker—a large room that had been carved out of the bedrock under the East River. Because it was a refuge for those fleeing danger, the Sibyllines had expended considerable effort to make it comforting and homey. It was furnished with two large sofas, as well as several over-sized chairs, ottomans, and various tables. The floors were covered with thick Persian rugs, which served to take the edge off the cave-like dampness and soften the echoey acoustics. Scented frangipani and sandalwood candles, together with mechanical light fixtures that generated their own electricity, gave the room a warm glow and a calming scent. To help people pass the time, there were exercise bikes that also generated electricity, as well as assorted accessories and play-things on the tables—a levitating moon, a globe, a Newton's cradle, and a Euler's Disk, as well as other techno toys, gadgets, playing cards, and games. The Sibyllines had also installed wall art, pillows, and table décor, all of which carried images with particular significance to the movement. A dove, a kingfisher, a lotus flower, and other peaceful symbols carried messages of love, joy, and Kyndeness.

The environment had been designed to foster a tranquil vibe among those taking shelter for their safety, but at least one individual was anything but. Young Debra had been sitting with her arms crossed defensively across her chest since they'd removed her blindfold, and now looked for all the world like an angry hostage. When Keisha and

Donna arrived, she propelled herself out of the cushy sofa and spoke up loudly. "Where the fuck are we, and what the hell was that earthquake all about?" she demanded.

Jen was sitting next to Debra and placed her hand on her daughter's arm. "Deb, honey, please sit back down. Let's allow…"

Sadie attempted to create a diversion by jumping to her feet and throwing her arms around Keisha. "Keisha!" she exclaimed. "Thank God you answered your phone and were able to send transportation! We were quite desperate."

"Shove it, Detective Sadie!" Debra exploded. "No niceties. Explanations!"

Jen continued trying to calm her down, but her daughter was not to be placated. "Look at this place! It's like we've been teleported into some *Game of Thrones* episode!" Debra ranted. "We couldn't get out of this place if we wanted to—and believe me, I want to! And where is the fuckin' bathroom? Zach's eyes are crossed because he's had to take a shit since we took Mr. Toad's Wild Ride off I-295, and at any moment the goddamn seeds of the Tree of Life may be starting to sprout in his turd!"

The group was momentarily stunned into silence by Debra's profane candor, but they quickly burst into laughter.

Rocky pinched his nose in a mock stinky gesture. "And we wouldn't want those 'goddamn seeds' to be shat just anywhere, now, would we?" he said, looking at Zach. "Keisha, can you help this young fella out and get him a plastic bag to put his shit in?"

"This way," Keisha said as she led him to the kitchen for a sturdy plastic bag, and then on to the restroom.

On the way down the hall, Zach regaled her with the story of being arrested and thrown into a DEA van for the trip to DC. He'd hidden the seeds in his mouth, but when the van came to a sudden stop, he'd swallowed them. He was talking too fast for her to grasp all of it, but she didn't dare ask for details. From the loud, odoriferous farts Zach was letting out, she knew she had better get him to the bathroom quickly.

"My apologies, Debra," Keisha began as soon as she returned to the main chamber, "…that is your name, correct? After the day you've had, I'm sure *everyone* needs to use the bathroom. At least we have plumbing down here."

After everyone had relieved themselves and Zach had safely stored his bag o' poop in a sealed plastic container and placed it in a far corner, Keisha invited the group to have a seat back in the main room.

"Everyone good now?" Keisha asked. "Okay, I owe you all explanations, and I'm happy to stay here till I've answered all your questions. Debra, as to 'where the fuck are we,' we're under the Brooklyn terminus of the Brooklyn Bridge, in a bunker that dates back to the Cold War. When the Sibyllines took it over, we found that it was still fully stocked with postapocalyptic survival supplies."

"No way," said Rocky.

"Way," said Keisha. "Planners knew that in the aftermath of a Russian A-bomb attack, the ensuing radiation and nuclear fallout would persist for months, maybe years. They anticipated that the survivors of Doomsday—or Armageddon, if you prefer—would need meds, clothing, water, blankets, and a nutritionally dense food supply —in this case, some of the worst-tasting crackers you ever put in your mouth. And all that crap is still here!" she said, laughing.

Rocky, Jen, Gabby, and Debra were paying rapt attention, but Donna, Cameron, and Sadie were not. Donna kept staring at Gabby— she couldn't quite put her finger on it, but she was sure she knew her from somewhere. Cameron was focused on Donna, knowing full well that she had been targeted by Bozz Kruger, his former USF colleague. Then there was Sadie. Like Cameron, she too had zeroed in on Donna, but for a completely different reason—she was trying to figure out why Keisha had brought her into the safe house.

"Hundreds of thousands of people cross the Brooklyn Bridge every day, and they have no idea this is here," Keisha continued, "and we're determined to keep it that way. Everything about this bunker is off the grid—no cell service, no computers, no gas lines...nothing. The only modern luxury is running water, which we borrow from the East River, which is flowing directly above us."

"Eeew!" the gang responded in unison.

"Don't worry, it's treated—somewhat—for flushing toilets, showers and washing hands; it's just not potable. Like the water in an airplane lavatory, you wouldn't want to drink it—I *hope* none of you drank it! Staying off the grid is our only safe method of remaining unnoticed, and that's what will keep all of you safe as well."

"C'mon!" Rocky scoffed. "You're just messin' with us."

"I can vouch for the fact that we're at the end of the Brooklyn Bridge," said Donna. "Keisha and I crossed it to get here."

"Maybe you did," said Rocky, "but there's no such thing as a bunker under it. People would have found out—you're talking about New York, where everyone knows everything."

"And what is your name, kind sir?" Keisha questioned.

"My birth name is Peter, but please call me Rocky," he replied.

"But Peter is a lovely name," Keisha insisted. "Why call yourself Rocky?"

"Because my last name is Abbott, and I was about twelve years old when I figured out that I sure as shit didn't want to spend my entire life listening to people ask why I wasn't hopping down the bunny trail."

Sadie snorted, then guffawed—she couldn't help herself.

"Completely understandable," said Keisha diplomatically.

"And this is Gabby, my sister, and..." Rocky began introducing everyone, but was quickly interrupted.

"That's it!" Donna realized. "You're Gabby. Gabby Nel—"

"Abbott!" Gabby quickly interrupted. "I'm Gabby Abbott, and I remember you, too." Gabby hoped that Zach didn't catch on. She had to keep talking, steering Donna away from making a big deal about her previous married surname. "You're Donna Chandler, the wife of an Elder Board member, aren't you?"

"Donna Martin Chandler—soon to become Donna Martin—dropping the 'Chandler,' " Donna replied.

"Wait...what?" Keisha addressed Donna. "You're ex-Society too?"

Gabby breathed a sigh of relief that Donna had become the focus of the conversation. She'd been born Gabriela Abbott, then married Devon Nelson when she was still a member of the Society of Truth. The marriage went south pretty quickly, but Gabby tried to stick it out, despite Devon's haranguing and abuse and quirky sex habits. As soon as she learned she was pregnant, however, she filed for divorce and left the Society. She knew she'd never be able to protect her child from her husband.

Devon's vindictive nature came to the fore during divorce proceedings—he dragged them out by changing lawyers, always at the last minute before they were due to appear in court. His goal was twofold

—to make her angry and cost her money—and he was successful on both counts. The divorce—which should have been simple because Gabby wanted nothing from him or from their life together—went on for months. By the time the decree was final, Gabby could hardly conceal her pregnancy. That made her superstressed—she knew that Devon would have no interest in the child, but that he'd insist on shared custody, just for spite. In a desperate effort to keep Nelson from finding out that he was Zach's biological father, she'd told her son that he was adopted. She'd been able to keep the truth from both of them until now, but it had almost come out at DEA headquarters in DC.

"How long ago did you escape, Donna?" Keisha asked.

Donna looked at her watch. "Lemme see…approximately twelve hours ago, give or take. I walked out of our apartment and took a taxi to the hotel, and that's where I met you."

"No way!" Keisha exclaimed.

"Way," said Donna with a nod and a smile.

"Excuse me," Rocky interrupted, "as I was saying…" He tried to continue introducing everyone in the group, but was once again interrupted, this time by Sadie.

"Sorry, Rocky," she apologized, "but there's something bothering me, and I need to get it out in the open. Donna, I'm happy for you that you left that misogynistic tax-exempt grab bag of perverts and crackpots, but what the hell are you doing *here*?"

Donna shifted uneasily in her seat—she wasn't easily intimidated, but she didn't like being put on the spot, either. "I…I…I came with Keisha," she replied uncomfortably.

Sadie rotated toward Keisha and shook her head in disapproval. "Keisha, I'm more than a little shocked that you brought a complete stranger into our safe haven. What you did wasn't just bad judgment— it was reckless and potentially dangerous. The rest of us are here because we're running for our lives. This is a woman you just met, a woman you obviously knew nothing about—not even that she was a refugee from the Society of Truth."

Keisha paused before responding. "Sadie, I would never jeopardize our mission by bringing a threat into our midst. On a very deep level, you already know this. Your mother—in her beautiful soul—passed on her intuitive abilities to you—it's in your DNA. There's nothing I could say that would completely reassure you, but you have the ability to do that for yourself. Get a reading on Donna—move closer to her if you have to—and tell me whether you can sense anything menacing about her."

Sadie paused as she peered at Donna, and then closed her eyes. Her shoulders began to soften as she mingled her frequency patterns with Donna's. There was definitely a strong energy field that streamed from Donna's consciousness, but it was coupled with colors and feelings of freedom and justice. "You're correct," Sadie replied. "I apologize. I should have done that sooner, but…"

"Whoa!" Donna responded. "I've never been examined in quite that way—ever. It's almost as if I was naked—not on the outside, but on the inside! Glad you think I passed, Sadie. What would you have done with me if I hadn't…throw me into the East River?"

Everyone was silent for an uncomfortable moment. Then they all laughed, except for Cameron, who remained solemn.

"Um…I, I," Cameron began with hesitation. "I…I…I have something to say."

Gabby cringed. "Oh boy, here it comes," she said. "The last time you opened a conversation that way, it was quite something."

"Donna," he started, "my name is Cameron R-r-reid. I used to be an operative in the USF's special ops unit called "The Cell." You probably don't even know what the USF is, but because you're here, you will eventually. My most recent assignment was to find this beautiful lass, Gabby Abbott, and to snatch a relic she had in her possession—the petrified tar in which the seeds from the Tree of Life were encased. There were three of us on the seed retrieval team. The mission we were given was simple: 'Get the seeds. No prisoners.' "

"Grim," said Keisha.

"We were ordered to take out anyone who got in the way, anyone who had anything to do with the seeds," Cameron continued. "As it turned out, that included all of you—Gabby, Zach, Jen, Sadie, Rocky, and Debra—as well as Ruth and Heinrich Müller. I could go into my life history and how I ended up in the Cell, but the short version of how I left is that I found myself liking my targets a lot more than my colleagues. When I realized that I couldn't bring myself to become a mass murderer, I became a wholehearted Sibylline supporter instead."

"So glad you saw the light, dearest Cam," said Gabby.

"I did, and then some, but that's not the end of the story. The second member of my team was a man named Guy Maloof," Cam said.

"Who pretended he loved me," Rocky lamented, "and I believed him."

"And who was also a coldblooded killer, the best hit man in the USF," Cameron declared. "He's the one who put a bullet into Heinrich Müller's forehead. Heinrich died instantly."

"Oh no!" Donna gasped. "I was so very fond of Ruth and Heinrich."

"Sadie took down Guy Maloof, but not before he had badly wounded both Jen and me," Cameron continued. "The two of us are alive and healthy only because of the quick thinking and naturopathic expertise of Gabby and Zach."

"You're welcome," Zach said.

"Donna, you should know that the third member of that USF seed retrieval team is someone you already know. His name is…Bozz Kruger."

"The real estate dude?" Donna asked incredulously.

"That was Kruger's cover story," replied Cameron, "but the handsome man from Cape Town with the charming accent and rock-hard muscles has all the skills of a United Soponium Fellowship mixed martial arts fighter, and then some. He's completely lethal—he could snap your neck like a twig, and do it with a smile. And, yes, you were set up for that on-camera kiss. Since there is still an active link between the USF and the Society of Truth—that link being Devon Nelson, the man responsible for our arrest—I have to guess that Kruger is still here in Brooklyn."

Donna's eyes widened. "Wait a minute. Wait—just—one—minute! All of you!" She pointed her finger at everyone around the room, as if outlining the letter "Z." "You're talking crazy talk, and I'm the only one playing catch-up. First of all, you're right, Cameron. I first heard of the United Soponium Fellowship earlier this evening, and still have no clear idea what it is. Ditto the Sibyllines, although I gather the two groups don't like each other very much."

"We'll get to that," said Keisha.

"I left the Society just as strange things started happening. First, two men on the Elder Board, Carlisle and Angostino, kicked the bucket

—bam-bam—one after the other. I know you're not supposed to speak ill of the dead, but there was always something creepy about both of them. Then Ruth Müller manipulated me into watching raunchy videos that would make your toes curl…"

"I can't imagine Ruth showing you porn," said Gabby.

"It was at my welcoming lunch as the Society's new First Lady, and it was on a video with a bunch of other stuff that was streaming on her laptop," Donna declared. "And yes, it included indecent sex acts being performed right here in Brooklyn, in buildings owned by the Society. Margie Angostino was there, too, bless her heart—if you don't believe me, you can ask her about it."

"That was my laptop!" Jen exclaimed. "I loaned it to Ruth because Ananta asked me to."

"Who's Ananta?" Donna asked.

"We'll get to that," Keisha replied.

Sadie's detective instincts were aroused. "What else was on the video feed, Donna?" she asked.

"Devon Nelson moving file cabinets out of the tenth-floor research library and down into a secret room off the underground passageway —cabinets that supposedly contained files on victims of child sexual abuse. I told the elders about it when I got called on the carpet after they saw the footage of Kruger kissing me…" Donna said.

Sadie understood the implications immediately. "Keisha, I owe you an apology. Since Donna has seen evidence of Nelson's involvement in hiding the abuse files—and since he is aware of that knowledge—she's in just as much danger as the rest of us. You didn't know it when you brought her to the safe house—at least not on an intellectual level— but you did the right thing. She needs protection, too."

"Oh that's just great!" Donna declared. "I'll add that to my 'are you for real?' list. The Society's Brooklyn properties are being appraised to sell. And now you're telling me that the man I was assigned to show those properties to was some kind of deadly James Bond bad guy? I hear that y'all just escaped from the DEA…Oh…and let's not forget we're all sittin' in a secret bunker located under the Brooklyn Bridge operated by some ancient group of…of…"

"Sibyllines," said Rocky, finishing her sentence.

"Sibyl…whatever!" Donna repeated. "Did I miss anything?"

Everyone in the room gave a reluctant "nope" or "nah" or "that about sums it up."

"Keisha, what the hell did you get me into?" Donna demanded. "And who's Ananta, and what are the Sibyllines, and what is the United Soponium Fellowship? When I asked before, you said, 'We'll get to that.' Get to it now, please."

"Girl!" Keisha laughed. "I know! I know it sounds crazy! I don't know where to start!"

"You!" Donna said, pointing directly at Sadie. "You sized me up. You tell me what's going on. And don't you leave anything out. I don't care how long it takes. Ain't nobody leaving this bunker till I know everything!"

If there had been a momentary feeling of intimidation, it was gone now. Donna was back to being herself—taking charge. Keisha shook her head and smiled. "That's the spirit I sensed in you when I first met you in the lobby of the Hilton Garden Inn earlier today. I'm delighted it finally emerged," she said. "Detective Sadie, you have the floor."

Everyone sat and listened to Sadie as if they were at story hour in the children's section of Barnes & Noble. She explained about the seeds of the Tree of Life, and how they had been preserved throughout all of history, and how the whole Garden of Eden story had been altered and falsified by male-dominated traditional religion. She talked about Mireille, the daughter of Adán and Eva, and how her love affair with Easa resulted in her giving birth to the twins, Ananta and Sundara. She described in detail how, millennia ago, these twins, raised to be loving siblings, grew apart and became antagonists who started rival organizations.

"Donna, these groups are what we now know as the Sibyllines and the United Soponium Fellowship—the USF. And by the way," Sadie added, "Adán and Eva were the first couple—Adam and Eve in the Bible—and Easa is another name for Jesus."

Seeing that Donna's jaw had dropped, Keisha gently placed a hand under Donna's chin to close her mouth.

"And there's more," Sadie continued. "You should know that the Society of Truth tenth-floor cleaning lady, Erica Pfeiffer, is actually Ananta—daughter of Mireille and Easa—and that she'd been spying on the Society of Truth for fifteen years. Even though she's thousands of years old, she looks like she's thirty-five. And John Matthews, the secretary of the Elder Board…he looks thirty-five, and actually *is* thirty-five, but he's a Sibylline spy, too. They disappeared with Ruth and Heinrich Müller after breaking into the tenth-floor research library and duplicating the Society's child abuse files. Those were the files that you saw Devon Nelson moving into a room off one of the underground passageways. Ananta, John, and the Müllers also made off with the petrified tar containing the seeds from the Tree of Life. Oh…and I need to warn you…do you remember the story of the flood of Noah?"

Donna frowned and didn't answer.

"Yeah…of course, you do," Sadie said. "Well, legend has it that some of the Nephilim—you know…the giant offspring of the material-ized angels and human mothers—survived the global deluge and became the secret leaders of the USF. We have reason to believe that they're alive to this very day."

Donna shifted her glance and glowered at Keisha. "Told ya it would be a wild ride," Keisha said.

"About Sundara's organization, the USF," Sadie continued. "Their members have infiltrated the highest echelons of religious, govern-mental, medical, and financial organizations around the world—including the Society of Truth and the DEA. That's why we were detained. High-level USF operatives within the DEA thought the seeds of the Tree of Life—the ones that were in the tar that Ananta, John Matthews, and the Müllers had smuggled out of the Society's tenth-floor research library—were in our possession."

"Were they?" Donna asked.

"Of course, they were!" Zach shouted. "They were hidden in my mouth, but I accidentally swallowed them. That's why I have to shit in a bag and watch to see if anything sprouts!"

The room cracked up in hysterics. Debra and Rocky belly-laughed so hard they cried and had to hold their stomachs in agony.

In the midst of all the merriment, only Gabby was serious. "Listen," she began. "You should know that in addition to the seeds making their way through Zach's large intestine, there are more seeds, and they're with Ruth Müller. I packed some of the petrified tar in a small velvet drawstring pouch, and slipped it into her bag as a parting gift when she left for Germany. Until she unpacks, she won't know she has them."

"Fonzie and I personally drove Ruth to Gabreski Airport on Long Island," said Sadie.

"Who's Fonzie?" Donna asked.

"'55 T-Bird. Torch Red," said Jen. "Pristine condition, but his starter is wonky."

"I don't have kids, but Fonzie is my baby," said Sadie. "The two of us drove Ruth to Gabreski and put her on a Sibylline jet with Heinrich's body. The pilot, Min Yunghui, flew them to Germany so that Heinrich could be buried in Quedlinburg, his hometown. We haven't heard from her since."

"Min Yunghui! The woman in the Matrix presentation?" Donna exclaimed.

"Bingo," said Keisha.

"We also have no idea how Erica...I mean Ananta...and John are doing now, since they boarded a flight to...wherever they were going," said Sadie.

"There's a lot to process here, and I'm sure there's more to discuss," Keisha said. "But first things first. Hot showers for all, and clean clothes—get that leftover DEA stench off you. You'll find new duds in the trunks over there—keep rummaging till you find something that fits. A good meal is on its way. You must be famished! After you're showered and changed, we can talk over good food, and good wine, too!"

"I'm a cook, and I take 'a good meal' personally," Rocky shot back. "Please tell me you're not going to give us those ancient, stale Cold War crackers, please, please, please!"

"I wouldn't think of defiling your taste buds that way, Rocky," said Keisha with a laugh. "You'll be pleased, I'm sure."

"Where's the shower?" Gabby chimed in. "I'll go first."

"Follow me," Keisha replied.

As the two started off, Cameron rose to follow them. "Double showers save time and hot water," he said, grinning.

Gabby turned around and pushed Cam back down into his chair. "Not so fast, Casanova," she said.

"Dude!" Rocky exclaimed. "You do realize her brother and son are sitting right here, don't you?"

Gabby glared at Rocky. "Put a sock in it, *Peter!*" she declared forcefully. "It's time for you to shut up now. It's also time for you to get past being grossed out by whatever pornographic images parade through your little gay brain every time you think I might start dating again."

Gabby beckoned suggestively to Cameron with her index finger. "C'mon, Romeo," she cooed as she took hold of his hand. "Let's save hot water together."

"Your-r-r wish is my command, bonnie lass!" Cameron declared while flipping Rocky the bird in jest as he followed Gabby to the shower.

As soon as they got out of earshot of the main room, Gabby turned to Cameron and said, "I hope you don't think that I actually meant we're taking a shower together. I just did that because I'm tired of always having to put up with Rocky's talk about his own love life, but I never get to talk about the kind of love life I'd like to have one day."

"Good ole sibling rivalry. I kinda figured that, but I hoped that there was at least a glimmer of possibility of r-r-r-rubbing soap all over your naked body," Cam teased.

Gabby rolled her eyes as the two followed Keisha toward the shower. Keisha held a half smile on her face, knowing that even if it wasn't today, these two would hook up soon. As they neared the shower, a voice came booming out from the main room.

"Ciao, my friends! Mangia! Mangia! Come...let's eat!"

It could've only been one person. "Mario!" everyone cried in unison.

"That means our food has arrived," Keisha said. "You'll see fresh towels in the basket. Everything else you'll need is in the cabinet, including shampoo, soap, toothbrushes, and razors. I'm following my nose to the butternut squash pasta. Cam, it sounds like you're not gonna get lucky today, but dude...please take a shower and brush your teeth. You may be cute, but your stress-breath isn't! Oh, and by the way, double showers may be a good idea. The water tank is small and everyone else wants to get clean, too. Just sayin'..."

She was still giggling as she left.

The bathroom was large and dimly lit. It had been built to accommodate several people at once, almost like you'd find in a high school locker room—there were multiple sinks and toilet stalls, and one roomy shower lined with white subway tile.

Gabby didn't waste any time. She stepped into the shower, pulled the plastic curtain closed, and started throwing her clothes over the shower rail as she peeled them off her body. The hot water felt like heaven on her skin. It helped her let go of the built-up tension in her tight muscles, but she caught herself by surprise when she started to weep. The warm cascade released all her suppressed emotions in the wake of the recent violent loss of life she'd witnessed firsthand. She hadn't dared cry until now, not just for Heinrich, but even for Guy Maloof—the true love that Rocky thought he'd finally found. She also mourned the loss of the Compassion Garden and the underground lab. They had been her life's work—she'd poured her heart and soul into both of them for so many years. Knowing they'd gone up in flames was like a death in the family, and she was grieving.

Mostly, however, Gabby's tears were for what *didn't* happen—Devon Nelson had not discovered that Zach was his son, and Zach remained unaware that Nelson was his biological father. After being transported from the Gabby Abbey in Hudson to DEA headquarters in DC, Nelson had drawn blood from all three of them, expecting that DNA would prove his paternity. It didn't, but only because Devon had been sucking on the petrified tar from the seeds, which had temporarily warped his DNA and telomeres. But that didn't change the truth. The fact remained that Nelson was Zach's father. The close call made Gabby scared for the future—she was sure that Zach would inevitably find out and hate her—both for sleeping with such a toxic bozo, and for hiding it from him.

Listening from outside the curtain, Cam could tell that Gabby was trying to stifle her cries. He felt the protective urge to hug her...to console and soothe her, but he was a gentleman, and the last thing he wanted was for Gabby to misunderstand his actions for wanting to "get lucky"—as Keisha had so romantically put it. But when Gabby's whimpers turned into full-blown sobs, it was too much for him to ignore.

Gabby saw his forearm slowly reach into the shower. He was still wearing his shirt with rolled-up sleeves. He paused, giving her time to say no. When she didn't, he took that as an invitation, and joined her in the shower, fully clothed. Then he wrapped his strong arms around her waist. The hot water drenched them both as clouds of steam billowed out of the shower, fogging the mirrors over the sink. Gabby reached her arms around Cam's neck and buried her head in his shoulder.

"Let the tears flow," Cam said gently as he pulled her even closer.

"Cam?" she whispered.

"Yes, Gabby…"

"Keisha's right. You have stress-breath," she said as she turned around.

Cam now stood behind Gabby, embracing her from behind. Slowly, and ever-so-respectfully, he moved his hand upwards toward the bottom of her breasts, then softly kissed the sides and back of her neck. Gabby took his hands and moved them onto her breasts—her way of letting him know he could go further. He slowly lowered himself to the tile floor facing her soft, squeezable ass, and turned her around. He was about to go down on her, but she took his face into her hands and gently urged him back to his feet. They locked eyes as she started unbuttoning his shirt, then removed his pants and boxers. Gabby reached down and eased him inside of her. His stress-breath didn't matter anymore. Even though the shower water was now cool, they were making their own heat.

Keisha followed her nose and walked in on the gang throwing their arms around Mario, taking care to avoid his heavily bandaged hand.

"Keisha! My Keisha! Come here; come here! Let's feed these hungry warriors. Help your one-armed ole *tesoro maschio* with this special menu item you requested! I bet our Sibylline friends here would enjoy a hot, lusty story while indulging in my luscious butternut squash ravioli, dripping with brown butter sage sauce!" Mario declared with a twinkle in his eye.

Years ago, it had been a running gag between them—Mario loved pretending that he and Keisha had been hot lovers, and he knew people got a kick out of imagining what the unlikely couple had looked like in bed together.

"Ooooh…!" and "Ooooh-la-la!" the gang cooed.

Rocky couldn't help but lend a hand. Not only was it automatic for him to assist with gourmet food preparation, but he also couldn't wait to hear this sexy story. "Move aside, fellow foodies and old sweethearts! Allow me to turn the contents of these bags into a feast for the eyes and for the taste buds while you tell it all, Mario—every ardent tidbit. Don't leave anything out—the devil's in the details!"

Donna was uncomfortable and blushed in spite of herself. The idea that anyone would shamelessly tell stories about...about *fornicating* was way beyond her Society of Truth comfort zone. "Well..." she began primly, "between the hanky-panky in the shower and the X-rated story that Mario is about to tell us, I can only imagine that we're all definitely on our way to Hades in a handbasket!"

"One handbasket coming up!" chirped Debra. "Or do we each need our own?"

"Whatever. This ought to lubricate our journey most excellently," Sadie added as she uncorked the first bottle of Chianti. "Cheers!"

Rocky artfully filled everyone's paper plates with an esthetically pleasing array of ravioli, beet, and goat cheese salad and a fresh slice of Italian bread, drizzled with aged balsamic vinegar and a splash of olive oil. No one said a word for the first few minutes while savoring the delectable and rich flavors that paired so well together. Even Rocky temporarily forgot about the hot love story between Keisha and Mario.

Cameron entered with his wet hair combed back, freshly shaven, wearing a pair of unfashionable dad jeans and an untucked tan paisley shirt.

"Was it as good for you as it was for her?" Debra blurted out.

"Debra!" Jen scolded, then added, "Soooo...was it?"

Cam's face turned quite pink as the gang broke out in laughter. "Ask her," he replied. "Gentlemen don't tell."

"You're just the man I need right now, Cam," Mario said. "I had to leave André back at the market to deal with an intruder as I snuck down the stairs. I'm sure the prowler is a USF agent sent to finish me off."

"What did he look like?" asked Cameron.

"Dunno—André and I heard him heading for the second floor, but I didn't see him." Mario waved his bandaged hand in the air. "With this thing, I knew I wasn't going to be much help to André in a fight. The most important thing I could do was to get this food down here to all of you, so I skedaddled."

"I'm sure he's a member of the Cell," said Cameron, "and odds are I've worked with him before. These men are deadly good at what they do. I'm betting that your intruder was the last man of our seed retrieval team, Bozz Kruger, which means that André is in grave danger."

"André has some, ah, *unusual* skills," Mario replied. "If your former colleague underestimates him, he's going to be quite surprised."

"A Cell operative won't let this be a fair fight," said Cam grimly. "For him, there can be only one outcome—failure is not an option. I must go help André! Detective Sadie—you coming?"

"Really? Now?" she complained, waving her forkful of ravioli in midair.

"Signora, finish your meal. Drink your wine," Mario insisted. "Cameron, sit...mangia...My Kingston friend is quite capable. And besides, if he was going to die, he'd be dead already."

Gabby sorted through the clothing in the trunks, then chose a pair of bell-bottoms and a brightly embroidered peasant blouse. Her wet hair formed long brown tendrils that curled down her back, and she exuded the scent of shampoo and body wash. As she walked into the gathering, her face was clean and glowing.

Rocky placed his hands over Zach's ears. "Well, if that's not the look of someone who just got laid, I don't know what is," he declared.

"I'm not an infant, Uncle Rocky," Zach insisted. "I could hear what you said, and I know what you meant...Cam's a good guy. I'd rather my mom 'get some' from him than from idiots like that creep at the DEA—what was his name again?—Nelson...something?"

Gabby's face went pale as she shot a look at Rocky. "Hey, Mario!" Rocky quickly interjected. "Didn't you have a story to tell?"

CHAPTER 10
WINGMAN

Milton Chandler lay in bed, awake and miserable, ignoring the insistent knocking on his penthouse door. It was probably Devon Nelson—or one of his minions—coming to demand that he pack up and move out. As the disgraced ex-president, he'd already assumed that he wouldn't be offered the opportunity to accept a lesser position at Society headquarters—Nelson would never allow it. The best he could hope for was to become an elder at a congregation wherever he could find a job—except that he had no idea how to begin looking for work. Without his PhD wife to help him figure things out, the idea of rebuilding his life seemed overwhelming. Milton knew he was looking at the wall. As a Black man in his early fifties, with no resumé and no savings, he was not only unemployed, but also pretty much unemployable.

"All right! All right!" Milton called out. "I'm coming! Just stop knocking—it's killing my head!"

Milton lurched out of bed and tried to stand, but the room wobbled under his feet, messing with his balance and jostling his already woozy head. In a futile attempt to stop his brain from spinning, he pressed his hands to his temples. "Shouldn't have yelled," he murmured to himself as he stumbled to answer the door.

Milton was surprised to see Paul Fitzgerald, another member of the Elder Board, standing there. Fitzgerald was equally astonished—he was alarmed by the sight of the disheveled and bleary-eyed man swaying in the doorway before him. He'd never seen Milton Chandler anything but well-dressed and impeccably groomed. "Did you feel...? Oh my! Milton...Pew!" Paul said as he wrinkled his nose and waved his hand in front of his face. Milton reeked of a combination of wine and vomit, and the stench was overpowering. "What happened to you, Brother Chandler? You look awful, and you smell worse."

"Well, hello to you too, Brother Fitzgerald," Milton replied. "To what do I owe the honor of your presence?"

"My brother, I fear that you've had too much to drink," Paul continued as he hobbled his way past Milton into the apartment, leaning heavily on his cane for support.

"Be my...burrrp...guest," Milton said, belching. He gestured theatrically for Paul to enter, even though Paul was already inside.

"Go clean yourself up, man, for God's sake, while I put on a pot of coffee," Paul said.

"Sure, sure..." Milton said as he careened uncertainly into the master bathroom. He stared at the face looking back at him in the bathroom mirror, and was dismayed by what he saw—he'd seen healthier looking crack addicts panhandling in front of the subway entrance at York and Jay.

More than anything, he needed to get rid of the vomit smell. He stuck his head under the faucet, then blindly grabbed for the lavender-scented CurlMix Pure Aloe Vera shampoo. His hand came up empty—the bottle was gone. "Well, that's just fine and dandy," he said out loud. "She took it. Damn you, woman!"

As an alternative, he scooped some shea butter from a jar and slathered it all over his hair, using a brush to massage it into his scalp. Then he dampened a towel with hot water and rubbed his head vigorously. Milton was both relieved and dismayed to see how much dried barf came away with the excess shea. After giving his hair a good combing, washing his face, and brushing his teeth, he managed to put on some clean clothes. Milton took a moment to look himself square in the mirror. He no longer looked like a derelict, but his insides were still upside down.

"Now that's the Milton I know!" Paul said when he reentered the living room. "Drink this," he insisted, handing Milton a large mug of black coffee. "And sit down. I need your undivided—and sober —attention."

"Listen, Paul, I'm sure you came here with the best of intentions, but save your breath. I'm in no mood for any inspirational Biblical passages right now. In fact, if you dare open that book, both it and you will leave this room airborne."

"Hey, hey...I'm not here to preach. I'm here to ask you one question."

"Yeah? What's that?"

"Do you know where the Müllers are?" Paul asked.

"Nope," Milton replied. "Didn't Nelson tell us that they were attending a convention in Houston?"

"You believe that?" Paul asked skeptically.

"I'm not sure what I believe anymore," Milton replied ruefully.

"I did some checking—the Houston convention isn't for another week," Paul said.

"Maybe he and Ruth went early to visit some friends."

"Then why does Heinrich's cell phone go straight to voicemail?" Paul asked. "It's not like Heinrich to remain out of touch. Besides, I've called just about every elder I know in the Houston area, and none of them are aware of the Müllers being in town. They have no family here in the States—all the relatives are in Germany. And there's no way they could afford to stay at a hotel. As members of the Elder Board, when- ever we travel, our wealthier members put us up in a guesthouse or spare bedroom."

"So the Müllers have vanished. What do you want from me?" Milton asked.

"Don't get testy," Paul fired back. "I just figured you'd be as curious as I am. Frankly, I want to know not just out of curiosity, but out of sheer self-preservation. There have been a ton of mysterious disappear- ances lately. First Carlisle passes away from a heart condition he never had; then Angostino dies and his body is speedily cremated—without his wife's knowledge or consent. And now the Müllers are missing. All in all, it's hard to escape the conclusion that being on the Society's Elder Board has suddenly become more life-threatening than going over Niagara Falls in a barrel."

Milton frowned. Because everything had happened so quickly after

Donna's brazen infidelity—after she got caught kissing Bozz Kruger in front of the building—he'd never tried to connect the dots. In hindsight, even suffering from the mother of all hangovers, it was obvious that Paul was onto something. He may have needed a cane to get around, but there was nothing wrong with his mind.

"Or perhaps it's just being on the tenth floor that's dangerous," Paul speculated. "The Müllers aren't the only ones missing. Our quiet secretary, John Matthews, is not at his desk. Now that I think of it, I haven't seen Sister Erica Pfeiffer, the tenth-floor cleaning lady and Brother Nelson's fiancée, either."

Milton nodded in agreement. "And while we're on the subject of sudden disappearances, where did Michael Wright, our newest Elder Board member, disappear to?"

"Another good question, Brother Chandler," Paul replied.

As the questions mounted and the caffeine kicked in, Milton's energy and mood began to shift. His head was throbbing, but there were important mysteries to be solved. "How should we proceed, Paul?"

"I propose that we keep this between ourselves—business as usual on the surface, investigation behind the scenes," he replied. "The easiest place to begin is where we're at—we can search the penthouses of our deceased fellow elders without leaving this very floor."

"Excellent idea," Milton replied.

"Let's start by checking out the Müllers' place," said Paul. "Heinrich and I swapped spare keys ages ago, to be used in case of an emergency."

"Brother Fitzgerald, I think this officially qualifies as an emergency," Milton stated firmly.

The two men headed down the corridor. When they stopped in front of the Müllers' door, Paul began fumbling in his pockets for his copy of Heinrich's key. Meanwhile, Milton took the direct approach instead. There was a loud click as he turned the handle—the apartment was unlocked.

Once they entered, they were taken aback by what they found. Ruth was notorious for being compulsively tidy, but they walked into a mess—the place had been ransacked. The sofa cushions were askew, and the drawers were ajar. Paul used his cane to gesture toward a small pile of crumpled paper on the floor. "Milton, what do you suppose that little heap of notes is all about?"

Milton picked them up and began unfolding them. Three of the notes had been written in a graceful, feminine cursive that he didn't recognize.

Put your keys quietly in your pocket and follow me out the door. Ruth won't be waking up for quite a while.

Wait for my next instruction. I will slip a note under your door when it's time.

Mario's Market. 10 p.m.

Two of the others were in Ruth's handwriting. Paul recognized her tiny, precise penmanship from the proofreading notes she left him in the margins of the articles he wrote.

I want you to know, my love, that no matter what happens, no matter how many years of our life we spent inside of this organization that we believed was the truth but was really a pack of lies, that I don't regret any of it because every moment of it I spent with you. Being by your side forever was the best decision I ever made.

Get ready. We have to leave here at 9:40.

The last note undoubtedly had been written by Heinrich, whose block lettering had distinctively Teutonic flourishes. Both Paul and Milton had seen it many times.

Don't forget to put your orthotics in your shoes!

"The Müllers are not in Houston," said Milton decisively. "And they're not just gone from the apartment, but also they've deserted the Society. And they had an accomplice! Who could it have been?"

"The identity of the accomplice is one question," replied Paul, "but I have a bigger one. If whoever tossed this apartment didn't need these notes, what *were* they looking for?"

"And did they find it?" Milton added. "Let's check Carlisle's and Angostino's apartments. Maybe we'll discover some additional clues there."

After closing the Müllers' door as softly as possible, the two men retraced their steps down the corridor. As they were passing Milton's doorway, they nearly collided with Devon Nelson, who was headed straight for them.

"Brother Chandler! Brother Fitzgerald!" Nelson exclaimed. "Where are you two off to looking so dapper?"

Busted! Milton thought.

Paul was the first to speak. "Dapper?" he inquired of Nelson, arching an eyebrow for effect. "Dapper?? Is that what we're calling attire befitting a Christian man these days?"

"Isn't it past bedtime for men of your age?" Nelson shot back.

"Well, maybe for Milton—he's an old geezer, you know..." Paul jested.

Steady now, don't panic. What would Donna do? Milton asked himself. *That's it!* he thought, answering his own question. *She'd brazen it out!*

"Hey...speak for yourself!" Milton said jovially. "I may be dapper, but at least I don't have ketchup on my shirt. Looks like you may need a bib with your next hamburger, Brother Nelson. Come to think of it, why not change your shirt right now and come with us—I would like to invite you to join Brother Fitzgerald and me on a shepherding visit to one of our most dedicated members. LaShonda Tubbs, one of our retired full-time missionary sisters, is suffering from severe depression, and she's at an all-time low. Dontrelle Tubbs, her husband, is very concerned, and has asked us to come to their home so that we might pray with her and lift her spirits. They're in Bed-Stuy, and we'd be honored if you'd come with us."

Paul managed to keep a straight face, but barely—it took all the self-control he had not to guffaw at the audacity of it all. If Nelson had accepted the offer, he would have called Milton's bluff, but Milton knew him all too well. With his ascension to the presidency, Nelson's already bloated ego had become even more swollen, and was now so overinflated that it resembled a balloon in the Macy's Thanksgiving Day parade.

Devon warily eyed them both, then shook his head. "I have an urgent administrative matter to take care of," he replied haughtily. "Thank you for the invitation, but I'm sure you brothers can handle it."

Milton had calculated correctly that Nelson would consider this kind of pastoral visit to be beneath him—ministering personally to an older female would be a waste of his executive leadership expertise.

Worse yet, by his choice of names, Milton made it easy for Nelson to assume that these were African American members of the Society. Worst of all, the wife was struggling with her mental health. Nelson would never squander his valuable time spouting Bible verses at some batty, suicidal old crone.

Paul and Milton continued walking toward the elevator. "May God be with you, Brother Nelson," Paul called over his shoulder as he pushed the Down button. Neither of them spoke until they were walking down Columbia Heights Road toward headquarters. Milton was most considerate of Paul's limited mobility, and slowed his usual brisk pace to one that Paul could manage with his cane.

"LaShonda? Dontrelle??" Paul hooted. "Milton, your invitation for Nelson to join us was a stroke of genius. Bravo!"

"Thank you," Milton replied, "but I'm not sure he was entirely convinced. When we get to headquarters, let's ask David at the front desk to call us a taxi—we'll give him a bogus address in Bedford-Stuyvesant as our destination. Just in case Nelson comes snooping, we'll have David's word to back us up."

"Great plan," said Paul. "Meanwhile, I need to catch you up on what happened at the Elder Board meeting this morning. Sam Silverman has identified what he believes is a suitable property for our new headquarters, and we are moving toward acquisition. It's in a remote part of Orange County, right near the New York–New Jersey border. Since the news spotlight is all over us about allegedly protecting pedophiles, Nelson, Schmidt, and Theadeau are on board with selling the Brooklyn properties as quickly as possible, not only to have money to defend ourselves in court and to underwrite the damage settlements we'll be paying, but also to get out of the media limelight here in the city until this scandal blows over."

Milton stopped walking and raised an eyebrow. "C'mon, Paul...Do you honestly believe that this scandal is going to 'blow over'? As elders, we've looked the other way—and worse—for far too long, shielding molesters and abusers from the consequences of their behavior, and we did so for obscene acts we *know* they committed. Generations of children have grown up scarred and damaged, both emotionally and physically—and that's on us."

"I know; I know," Paul replied, looking down in shame and shaking his head.

"You are as aware as I am that even before these stories leaked out and became public, the issue had already gotten out of hand," Milton continued. "Why else would we have had to tell our elders worldwide that they were to send us their child sexual abuse cases in blue envelopes? Why else would we have had to set up a special department here at headquarters to deal with them?" Somewhere in his heart, he hoped Donna would have been pleased that he had finally acknowledged the problem.

"And when those blue envelopes started flooding in…" Paul said.

"We kept finding new and better ways to exonerate the perpetrators than just leaning on the Biblical 'two-witness rule,' " Milton declared. "And we congratulated ourselves on our cleverness in doing so. It's long past time for us to stop blaming—and slandering—the victim for every case that comes in. I should have spoken up about this a long time ago."

"The elders *are* going to speak up, Milton, but not in the way you might hope," said Paul. "This morning, Nelson assigned Schmidt to write the script for an official video that will be broadcast to our nine mil…no, closer to eight and a half million followers—membership has been plummeting. The video will urge everyone to be skeptical of what gets reported in the news, and to remind them that Satan controls the criminal justice system. The gist of the message will be that if one of our elders is charged with child sexual abuse, it's because the system is prejudiced against our faith."

"In other words, we're going to say that the allegations are all 'fake news,' " Milton said flatly.

"Pretty much," Paul admitted.

"These are dangerous times," said Milton. "It sounds like you and I can trust one another, but no one else. As we look into this, I'll be your wingman, and you'll be mine. And by the way," he added, "Orange County isn't just 'remote.' It's the middle of nowhere."

"Indeed," replied Paul, "but that's exactly the point. Here in the city, it's impossible to escape the media's sensationalist focus. Broadcasters know that any sex scandal is a ratings magnet, and ours is that much more, ah, titillating because kids are involved. Silverman told

Nelson that there were TV reporters doing live stand-ups in front of our worship centers, but as long as they don't trespass and remain on public property, there's nothing we can do about it. And that's not all—we are aware that documentaries are in the works that will include interviews with adult survivors and their attorneys. There are even some newly published crime thrillers based on secrets that the Society has kept hidden all these years—not unlike the way Dan Brown's *DaVinci Code* hung out the dirty laundry of the Catholic Church."

"Opus Dei," said Milton.

"Precisely," Paul replied.

"And that's why it's time for the Society to get out of Dodge?" Milton asked.

"Yes. Nelson and Sam Silverman have fast-tracked the liquidation of our entire real estate portfolio here in Brooklyn so we can hightail it into the sticks as soon as possible. The new facility will be heavily guarded and enclosed in barbed wire."

"Sounds more like a high-security prison," said Milton.

"One more thing," Paul added as they approached the front door of headquarters. "I stayed long enough after to the board meeting to overhear a really nasty argument between Nelson and Silverman. They didn't know I was there, but the upshot was that Nelson fired Silverman, and Silverman threatened to go public with everything he knew about the Society. Then the strangest thing happened."

"Tell me more," Milton said.

"I watched as they got into the elevator together. After what I'd just heard, there was no way I was going to ride down with them. My plan was to stay out of sight and wait till they got to the lobby before summoning the elevator back up to the tenth floor, but..."

"But what?" Milton asked.

"But they never got there," Paul replied.

"Excuse me?"

"I had my eye on the floor indicator," Paul declared. "The elevator stopped on the ninth floor—and just stayed there—it never went the rest of the way down to the lobby. I waited a long time, but I got tired of standing and finally gave up and pushed the button. The elevator arrived empty. From what I can tell, Nelson and Silverman never made it down to the first floor."

"Now that's odd!" Milton said, just before they entered the head-quarters building.

Milton greeted the building concierge. "So good to see you, David!" he began. "Would you be kind enough to call a taxi for Brother Fitzgerald and me? We're going to call on one of our fellow worship-pers who is greatly in need of prayer and comfort."

"Of course!" David responded.

"One more question, David," Paul added. "The Elder Board met in conference today with the Society's attorney, Sam Silverman. Did Mr. Silverman give any indication of where he was headed after our meeting?"

David thought for a moment, then shook his head. "Come to think of it, I saw Brother Schmidt and Brother Theadeau leave, followed by you, Brother Fitzgerald. It was quite a bit later when Brother Nelson finally came down, but I never saw Mr. Silverman leave." He paused, then got up and took a peek out the front door. "His car is still here—it's that silver Tesla parked over there. This means that Mr. Silverman is alone upstairs—that's simply not proper! I must go investigate!"

"No, no, David," Milton replied. "Please remain at your post. Honor your duty to guard our front door. Brother Fitzgerald and I will check it out. I'm sure Mr. Silverman is just using the conference room to finish up some legal paperwork."

"Thank you, Brothers," said David.

Milton and Paul entered the elevator, and headed straight for the ninth floor.

Bozz Kruger was enraged, and his ego was bruised. He was a USF master assassin and a member of the Cell—no one could know he'd been bested by a Rastafarian toothpick who'd used voodoo to defeat him. After fleeing Mario's loft via the fire escape, he'd received an urgent message from Devon Nelson to meet him on the ninth floor of Society of Truth headquarters.

Kruger burst through the front door and blew by David at the front desk. His burnt and blistered hand hurt like hell. So did his right eyeball. "Sir..." David began.

Kruger headed for the elevator and pressed the Up button. "Sir!" David called again.

"Goddammit!" Kruger fumed as he punched the button repeatedly. "This is the slowest elevator known to man!"

"Sir, please sign in!" David begged.

"You bloody well know who I am!" Kruger shouted with irritation. "Or at least you should. I'm the realtor working with your Elder Board —the man who's about to sell this old eyesore of a building out from under you...Screw this! The stairs will be quicker."

The ninth floor of the Society of Truth was where the artists worked, creating elaborate illustrations for Bible stories and fanciful depictions of what the apocalypse and paradise would look like. Milton and Paul had just walked past a large drawing board stocked with all kinds of art supplies when they heard loud footsteps echoing in the stairwell.

The two men exchanged glances of alarm—this was no place for them to be found. While Paul headed for the men's room as fast as his cane would allow, Milton dove under an artist's desk. From his hiding place, he soon heard Bozz Kruger's familiar baritone.

"Quantum physics, my ass..." Kruger roared, addressing no one in particular. "Who does he think he is, with his dreads all tucked up in that stupid Rasta cap? And there's no way that Jamaican reggae motherfucker did what he did without channeling the devil himself."

Milton knew of only one person who fit that description—the friendly barista at the Italian coffee shop. The narrow slit between the desk and the small file cabinet allowed him to observe Kruger's movements. Milton saw his own fearful heart pounding through his shirt, but remained perfectly still as Bozz headed straight for a back office, only to quickly reemerge as his cell phone went off.

"Kruger here—but you're not, Nelson!" Kruger sarcastically answered. "I'm here on the ninth floor, like you texted. Where the fuck are you?"

Just then, the file cabinet that Milton was leaning against shifted slightly, widening the sliver of space between itself and the desk.

Kruger was just six feet away. He'd heard the noise and was about to investigate when Nelson arrived.

"Took a while to find what we needed," said Devon without apology. "No point in showing up without it."

"Roger that," Kruger replied.

"Let's get this done," said Nelson as the two walked toward the men's room.

Milton didn't dare move or make a noise. *Poor Paul!* he thought.

Minutes later, Kruger and Nelson came out of the restroom. As the two men headed for the stairwell, Milton noticed that Kruger's right hand was bandaged, and that he had a large black bag slung over his shoulder. As soon as he heard their footsteps going downstairs, he dashed for the men's room.

"Paul? Paul?" Milton called out, fearing the worst.

"In here," Paul answered weakly from the second stall.

Milton pushed open the door to see Paul Fitzgerald crouched on top of the toilet seat. He appeared to be frozen in place—he was perspiring heavily, and his face was ghostly white. For a man with severely limited mobility, the squat must have been excruciating to maintain. One elbow was dug into his knee, while his other hand was brandishing his cane aloft, ready for what would have been a pathetic attempt to defend himself.

As Milton helped him unfold his limbs and get off the toilet, Paul began to retch. Milton turned Paul around and held him steady as he violently spewed forth everything in his stomach. Then he assisted Paul to a standing position and flushed the commode.

"Thanks, Wingman," said Paul gratefully.

"You're alive!" Milton exclaimed joyfully.

"I am," Paul replied shakily, "but Silverman isn't."

"What?!"

"When I came into the restroom, his body was on the floor. Stabbed is my guess—there was blood on his shirt, and you can still see a little on the floor there. When I heard people coming, I didn't want to risk getting discovered, so I hid in here, making sure they couldn't see my feet. I watched as Kruger and Nelson stuffed Silverman's body into a black plastic bag. Kruger kept stopping to run his hand under cold water—said it got burned—then he went into the stall right next to this one. I thought I was going to get discovered for sure, but he pulled a ton of TP off the roll and wrapped his hand in it. And all this time, Nelson kept yelling at him to hurry up because rigor mortis was starting to set in. Milton! What the hell is going on?"

"I don't know, but I do know one thing...I should've listened to my wife," Milton replied as his own knees started to buckle.

The loathing and disgust that should have shaken his conscience much earlier now rained down on him—it was a toxic deluge of guilt. Donna may have been a tad full of herself at times, but she had a healthy sense of righteous indignation. She could tell the good guys from the bad guys, and she wasn't afraid to say who was who. As soon as Donna had learned about the extent of child sexual abuse within the Society, and about the Elder Board's deliberate choice to ignore and condone it, she'd become irate. There was no way she could make allowances for hurting kids just because of Milton's prominent position in the Society hierarchy. Why hadn't he been as outraged as she was?

Why had he chosen to protect his position as the Society's first Black president, instead of feeling compassion for the victims? For children? What did that say about him? What did that say about the Society of Truth? He winced as he remembered her words: *Or has this religion, like every other male-dominated religion, swept corruption, deceit, lies, and abuse of power under the rug, putting on a holier-than-thou pretense of having the Truth?*

Milton blinked back tears as he tried to get himself back into the moment. "How are you feeling, Paul?" he asked.

"Every inch of me hurts," Paul replied. "Body, mind, and soul."

"Listen," Milton said awkwardly, "I need to—"

"I know what you're going to say," Paul interrupted. "You're not supposed to leave your wingman, but we've got to get to the bottom of this, and I'm in no shape to keep up with you. Go on ahead—I'll take the elevator and make my way back to the dorm. We'll stay in touch by text."

"That we will," said Milton. "And if I didn't say it before, thanks for putting me back together."

Milton took the stairs, then went out the rear door. Paul took the elevator and quietly exited the same way. He was about fifty feet past the barbed-wire enclosure at the back of headquarters when he heard the metal-on-metal screech of the security gate as it rolled open, allowing a black Dodge Ram pickup to enter the loading area.

Paul watched as Kruger and Nelson wheeled a laundry cart out to the loading dock—Silverman's body bag was sticking out of it. Paul snapped cell phone photos as the two men lifted the bag and tossed it into the truck bed, then sent the images to Milton.

As he was looking into the cell phone camera lens to take another photo, Paul saw Nelson pointing in his direction. He quickly texted Milton: *I've been seen. Hide!*

Milton scurried out of sight as his phone began pinging with incoming photos from Fitzgerald. The first was of a high-ground-clearance black Dodge Ram 3500 pickup. The second was of Kruger and Nelson pushing a rolling cart out onto the loading dock. The last stop-action series showed them tossing the black body bag into the truck bed.

As Paul saw Nelson heading toward him, he realized there was no point in trying to run. He sent one last message to Milton, then threw his cell phone into the storm drain. "Good afternoon again, Brother Fitzgerald," Nelson said.

"Good afternoon, Brother Nel—"

Paul never got out the last syllable—one of Bozz Kruger's muscular arms had encircled Paul's neck. The other was applying pressure at the back of Paul's head, rendering him unconscious in less than ten seconds. Once Paul had gone limp, Kruger shifted his hold. His large, powerful hands grasped Paul's jaw and the top of his head, then torqued his chin up and diagonally.

Devon Nelson heard Paul's neck bones break. The sound was not unpleasant, he thought, and he made himself a mental note to ask Kruger to teach him how to do that—Silverman had put up too much of a fight in the bathroom, and it had gotten messy. Devon Nelson had gone back to his penthouse not only to retrieve the body bag, but also to change his shirt. Happily, Milton Chandler had assumed that the blood spatter was ketchup.

Kruger slammed Fitzgerald's body to the pavement, making sure that the edge of the curb aligned with his broken neck. "They'll think he keeled over in the quake and landed this way," he declared.

Milton stayed out of sight as his phone pinged again with one last text from Paul: *Tell Lucy I love her.* Sneaking back to Furman Street and staying out of sight until the coast was clear, he found Fitzgerald lying on the sidewalk, his head at an odd angle to his body, exactly as Kruger had arranged him. His cane was in the gutter. Milton felt for a pulse. There was none. His wingman was dead.

CHAPTER 11
PURGED

Saji knew what was coming and knew it wasn't going to be pleasant, either for Sundara or for herself. She called for Yara, her assistant, and together they laid plastic sheeting on the floor around Sundara's bed. After placing a bucket near his head, they unlocked the restraint that bound Sundara's left wrist to the side rail of the bed, then rolled his body onto its right side. Their preparations were completed just in time—Saji motioned to Yara to stand back as she listened to Sundara retch and gurgle with increasing urgency. As his gag reflex became stronger, she repositioned the bucket directly below his mouth to catch as much of the vomit as possible.

"Blaarghhh!!" The fluids spewed from his mouth in an unrelenting torrent. They splattered forcefully, some in the bucket, some on the floor, and some against the wall, many feet away. For most humans, vomiting tends to come in waves, allowing some respite after each episode, but Sundara threw up nonstop for what seemed like hours. His IV barely kept him hydrated.

Even after there was nothing left, his dry heaves continued, so Saji rubbed chamomile and peppermint on his pressure points, and placed her calming, healing palms on his abdomen. She and Yara then rotated Sundara onto his back once again. Now it was time to adjust his IV. Saji added scopolamine, extracted from nightshade, henbane, and jimson-weed, and blended it with a microdose of LSD—an all-natural truth serum.

After Yara checked Sundara's vitals and gave a thumbs-up, Saji took a seat across from him and began the guided hallucination:

Saji: *What's your name?*

Sundara laughed: *Which one?*

Saji: *Your birth name.*

Sundara: *Sundara.*

Saji: *What organization do you work for?*

Sundara: *I don't work for an organization.*

Saji realized she was going to have to craft her questions more narrowly, or this would go on for hours.

Saji: *When you were seven years old, you discovered something—or someone—very special that had a profound effect upon your life. What was that discovery?*

Sundara answered in the voice of a school-age boy: *I met Helzar.*

Saji: *Who is Helzar?*

Sundara: *S-h-h-h...Helzar is my secret friend who makes my whole body tingle.*

Sundara's pulse became rapid, and his blood pressure began rising. It appeared that he was getting an erection under the sheet.

Saji: *Where does Helzar live?*

Sundara: *He lives in the dark cave by where the trees are pretty.*

Saji: *Can you describe what Helzar looks like?*

Sundara: *He has super smooth skin. He's a giant with huge hands and fingers and a really big head...Wait! Helzar's telling me something!*

Saji: *What is he telling you?*

Sundara: *"Hurt beings hurt beings," he says.*

Saji knew she had to alert Mireille as soon as Sundara began talking about Helzar—the obvious Nephilim giant—and hoped she was still at the stables, tacking up the horses with Ananta and John, but now was not the time to leave Sundara's side.

Sundara: *Helzar's finger is big.*

Sundara tried to pick up his knees and spread his legs, but the restraints on his ankles prevented him. It seemed that Sundara was having a vision of someone masturbating him.

Sundara: *Ah...! O-o-o...! Oh! OH! OH!*

He vigorously thrust his hips under the sheet, but soon began groaning in pain—his penis wouldn't stop pulsating, even after the cum had ended. It relentlessly kept pumping in a dry orgasm as his breathing changed. Sundara started making sounds like muffled hiccups, as if forcing himself not to cry. He appeared parched. Yara refreshed the IV with a full bag of Ringer's lactate, then hooked it up to the port on his arm and opened it to a full-speed drip.

Knowing that Sundara's entire system had been severely taxed, Yara kept her eye on the heart monitor. After the barfing marathon, the hallucination, and the protracted orgasm, cardiac arrest was a possibility, even for someone as robustly healthy as Sundara. She watched as he flatlined—asystole. Following protocol, she rolled the crash cart to Sundara's bed and grabbed the defibrillator. After rubbing the paddles together, she placed them on Sundara's chest. "Clear!" she said loudly.

In response to the shock, Sundara's body bounced on the bed, but there was no change to the flatline on the monitor.

"No, no, no..." Saji said. "This can't happen. Again!"

"Clear!" Yara shouted as she applied the paddles once more, then sadly shook her head from side to side when there was no result.

"One more time," Saji instructed.

Beep...beep...beep. Yara and Saji breathed twin sighs of relief, then put their palms together and bowed to one another.

The two women then looked at Sundara. The rehydrating fluids that had been flowing from the IV bag were not staying in his body. Instead, they were pouring out like a river of tears from the corners of his eyes. They ran down his face, over his lips, and onto the bed.

"Could it be remorse?" Yara asked. "Could each tear be a teaspoon of penitence, a drop of contrition for all the destruction he's wrought?"

"Perhaps..." Saji began. "Perhaps the thoroughness of the purge emptied him out so completely that he has been scoured clean, making him a fresh vessel, open to receive and hold the light of a higher vibration."

"Dad!" Sundara suddenly called out, even though he was still unconscious. His voice was that of a terrified little boy. His body then relaxed and settled into the bed.

Saji and Yara looked at each other in wonder. "Did you hear that?" Saji asked.

Yara nodded. "I'm quite sure Sundara called out for Easa, his dad," she said.

"The volume of botanical purging compounds I gave him would have killed anyone else," Saji declared. "But for one dreadful moment, I thought I'd miscalculated."

"For one dreadful moment, so did I," said Yara grimly.

"That didn't happen, but I never anticipated that his cleansing would be so thorough that he'd be able to resonate and connect with his father," said Saji. "Not after just one treatment. Easa vibrates at a highly ascended level."

The two women cleared the plastic sheeting from around the bed. Then Saji sat by him as Sundara's body fell into deep relaxation. His bottom lip trembled, his chin began to quiver, and one last tear made its way out of the corner of his eye. It occurred to her that Sundara hadn't cried like that in hundreds of years, if ever. He'd lived a narcissist's life, devoid of emotional response—no sadness, no joy. He'd experienced none of the feelings that prompted tears in other humans.

Unexpectedly, his free arm reached over and forcefully grabbed Saji's wrist. "What is happening to me? What are you doing to me?"

Yara gasped, fearing Sundara would harm Saji, but the old monk replied calmly, "I now know exactly what happened to you, starting on that day when you were seven years old."

Sundara turned to Yara. "Please leave the room," he said in a broken, jagged whisper. "I need to speak to Saji—alone."

Yara left, taking the empty IV bag with her. She took up her post in the monitor room—a safe place to watch from behind the soundproof, shatterproof glass.

The treatment had changed Sundara's appearance markedly. He usually carried himself with an air of supreme confidence, and why not—he was handsome, intelligent, powerful, and well-connected. There was no earthly indulgence he could desire that he could not make his own. His very name meant "beautiful," but lying on this bed, he looked nothing like the man he'd been. His eyes were sunken, and his skin was ashen and pale. Traces of dried snot and salty tears were crusted to his face. His lips lacked color, and he struggled to speak— the ordeal he'd experienced over the last few hours made it all but impossible.

Saji observed him without lending a hand or saying a word. She waited for the fluids to refuel his system, all the while peering at him intently. If he was no longer the man he used to be, who was he now?

Sundara knew that something within him had profoundly changed, and quickly became overwhelmed as waves of memory washed over him. There was no justification he could offer for what he'd done as the lord consul of the USF. There were no words that could ever convey his utter remorse and bottomless regret for his appalling crimes against humanity—none. How could he possibly atone for it all?

"Look...I have done some things," Sundara admitted as he awkwardly groped for how to begin.

Saji arched an eyebrow. "*Some* things?" she repeated.

Sundara's eyes widened and welled up with tears as his face contorted and his free hand covered his mouth. "How did it come to this?" he asked Saji.

"I was a young monk when I learned how it started," she replied. "I was in my midtwenties...I was skinny-dipping in the swimming hole, and I saw you watching. After I got dressed, you were gone, so I walked through the woods to find you. I knew who you were—your mom had told endless stories about you. There could only be one man as beautiful as your mom described, with your wavy dark-auburn hair and indigo eyes—eyes that were just like hers. I wasn't afraid of you. That's probably why you didn't pick up on me when I went looking for you. I followed you to the cave—through the 'trees that are pretty,' and that's when I saw the creature."

Sundara gulped and tried to sit up. "So, you know about the cave and the...?"

"The...colossal bogeyman with the head of an ogre? Yes. I told your mother about what I saw, and today I learned his name: Helzar," she answered.

"Did she already know, or was this news to her?" Sundara probed.

"She knew they had existed thousands of years ago. She called them Nephilim—you know the story. But she thought they had all died when the waters of the Atlantic Ocean rose and the Mediterranean roared into the dried-up Black Sea, where they'd been living. The surge drowned all of them over seven millennia ago...or so she assumed," Saji answered.

"What did she say when you told her that you saw one still alive? Did she believe you?"

"She wasn't shocked, quite frankly," Saji replied. "She'd been in the midst of it as it unfolded—to her, the flood and the existence of these massive humanoids isn't some nightmare fairytale. The Nephilim occupy a unique place where history, folklore, and science collide. If the global deluge never happened and the Nephilim never existed, why would every ancient culture be imbued with stories and legends about both of them?"

"And the science?" Sundara asked.

"Science was slow to catch up, but by examining sediment layers in and around the Black Sea, they've been able to prove that the region experienced a catastrophic flood, one that rose to the highest mountain peaks. And now archaeologists have been discovering giant humanoid skeletons—they've been found all the way from China to some Podunk town in North America. There is excellent evidence of a great flood that drowned these freakish giants, carrying them who-knows-where with the current."

"So, I guess it's not surprising that a couple of them would have survived," Sundara said.

Saji arched her eyebrow once more. "A couple of them?" she questioned. "As in...two?"

Sundara nodded.

"More than two?" Saji asked.

Sundara shook his head.

"You said the giant's name is Helzar. What's the name of the second one?"

"Abysses," Sundara answered.

Saji couldn't help it—she burst out laughing. "Helzar and Abysses? Really? They sound like evil characters in a children's cartoon!"

Sundara smiled, and then, he too began to laugh. "They kind of are," he said. "I named them both when I was just a kid, and thought they were supercool!"

They laughed even harder together.

"Oh, Sundara..." Saji sighed. "I can only imagine the laughter and joy you once brought your mother when you were a child before that horrific day you met Helzar. By the time she found out about him, you were an adult. At first—right after you left—she tried repeatedly to reach out to you, to bring you back into the way of the Sibyllines, but she was never successful. The only reason she interfered now is simple —you actually showed up. You were here at Phugtal, and you were a mortal threat. You were about to take her daughter—your sister—down and rape her, so she had to step in. And now I know…”

“Know *what?*”

“Now I know the mechanism that set it all in motion—I learned how Helzar gained control over you at such a young age, and you confirmed it today,” said Saji. “He attacked the base of your spine—your first and second chakras—muladhara and svadhisthana. They were wounded by repeated sexual anal penetration when you were just a boy—before your body was ready. You were programmed through trauma. This, along with other traumatic programming techniques, caused a neurological alteration in your brain.”

“What do you mean?” he asked.

“Love, kindness, and goodness were hardwired into your inner being, and those natural instincts had been reinforced on a daily basis by your parents, and by the monks here at Phugtal,” Saji explained. “But a direct consequence of repeated sexual trauma was that your capacity for self-reflection was stolen from you, overridden by a new program downloaded into you that rewarded humankind’s worst impulses. An exaggerated sense of your own self-importance, coupled with unquestioned obedience to Helzar, began ruling your primitive, animal self. Testosterone nourished your newly installed, self-centered ego, and fueled your robotic obedience to Helzar’s agenda. Greed, revenge, and hatred ruled both head and heart—you craved sexual gratification, power, and control. Over the course of your very long life, you acted ruthlessly and relentlessly to satisfy those desires—to the detriment of generations of humans around the globe.”

“This wasn’t something I chose—or was it?” he asked.

“It was not,” Saji replied. “All of that wasn’t really you. It was because of Helzar—the giant that would touch you, the giant that you’ve obeyed since you were a boy. In essence, you’ve been Helzar’s puppet since you were seven years old. The bottom line is that none of this was your fault.”

“So why don’t I feel like a victim, Saji?” Sundara asked.

"Because you're no longer the person the abuse happened to. Not anymore," Saji replied. "When you were still under Helzar's control, you were a victim. That's behind you now—you're a *survivor*."

Saji unlocked the rest of Sundara's restraints. Yara was watching through the window from the monitor room, but she couldn't hear a word that was being said.

"No, no, no, no!" Yara shouted behind the glass. "What are you doing, Saji? We can't trust him, at least not yet."

As Saji freed Sundara, the earth beneath Phugtal began to lurch violently. The monastery had been built into the rock—it was one with the mountain that surrounded it, and had withstood many quakes over the centuries. This one was different. The sharp tremors sheared off the bolts that anchored Sundara's bed to the floor, sending it sliding across the room. As the bed sped away from the monitoring equipment, Sundara's electrodes were pulled from his skin, and the IV was yanked out of his arm. The monitors began beeping loud, high-pitched warning signals, indicating they had lost contact with their patient, but they went silent when the room went black.

The earthquake knocked Saji off her feet. She found herself sitting on the floor as the lights flickered, then went out. Then she heard a low grief-stricken moan that vibrated under her feet. It was the same sound she had heard days earlier, when Mireille had struck Sundara.

It took about five minutes for the Phugtal emergency generator to kick in. As the lights sputtered back on, Saji glanced at Sundara's bed. He was gone.

CHAPTER 12
THE SONS AND DAUGHTERS OF PILATE AND PROCULA

Min Yunghui didn't like to hurry, but she felt a genuine sense of urgency about her mission. Her team had already painstakingly melted the petrified tar and extracted the seeds of the Tree of Life. Her goal now was to prepare the seeds and the soil that would receive them, and to create the ideal environmental conditions in which they would flourish. The seeds, she knew, would germinate on their own schedule. They possessed an internal timetable for their own sprouting, but the unfolding of recent events was clear evidence that all the essential preconditions were falling into place.

The clock was ticking, and Min wasn't about to ruin this pivotal moment in history by allowing herself to be conned by a cocky USF operative who'd been dumb enough to throw his weapon into a sink. "I don't have all day," she said impatiently. "Tell me what you have that you think is so worthwhile, or I'm leaving you here with Jacob, and this time there will be no ice pack. Taking out your heartless ass will be an act of kindness for the rest of humanity."

"Here's the deal," the USF agent said. "I'll tell you what I know. If you think that information is valuable enough to use, give me your word that you'll allow me to stay here. I don't care if I stay in this cell for years. Just promise me I won't be killed or harmed, and that I'll be just as protected from the USF as the Sibyllines are."

"And if your information isn't useful, then what?" Min asked.

"Then you kill me," he said matter-of-factly, "but you can't have both. You can't use the information and then kill me. You'll have to choose one or the other."

"How do you know I won't use it behind your back?"

"Because you're a Sibylline. Kindness may give you the right to withhold truth, but kindness won't allow you to lie and intentionally falsify an agreement."

Min stared at him. He was right. "We have a deal," Min agreed, "but just because I may keep you alive doesn't mean your life will be comfortable."

The USF operative reached out his hand toward Min. She hesitated, then reluctantly shook it. "My name is Garth, by the way."

"Garth? As in the American country singer?"

"No. As in the name of the pesky fly with a death wish, the one that wouldn't leave the inside of your car, no matter how many windows were open."

Min froze. There was only one person in the whole world who knew about the fly named Garth—Greg Blunt. When they were in their early twenties, Greg had been her fellow student at the Institute of Five-Element Acupuncture in Santa Monica. His family had emigrated from Slovakia to Canada when he was a baby—you could hear a touch of Canada in his voice.

On the last day of class, his car wouldn't start, so she had offered him a ride. A huge black horsefly shared the drive with them, madly buzzing around the car and hurling itself frantically against the windows. "That fly has a death wish," Greg had remarked at the time.

Min had opened all the windows, but even with the wind blowing as she drove down Santa Monica Boulevard, the damned fly couldn't figure out how to escape. Only when Greg opened the door after Min had pulled up in front of his house did the fly finally depart. She vividly remembered saying, *Too bad. I was kinda getting used to the little fella. In fact, I was going to name him Garth.* That was the last time she'd seen Greg—surprisingly, he hadn't attended their graduation.

"Greg Blunt?" Min said.

"That's me," he said.

"Say the word 'about,' " Min demanded.

"Aboot," he replied with a grin.

Down the hall in the recovery room, Ruth had fallen back into a deep sleep. Her body started to twitch as her brain began replaying the same terrifying dream she'd had since childhood, but she no longer had Heinrich to wake her from it. She didn't have her loving best friend to stop the bad dream and wrap his comforting arms around her as they spooned.

"You've got five minutes to give me that useful information you talked about," said Min.

"Don't you want to know how I knew her name?" Greg inquired.

"Whose name?"

"Ruth's name. I told you I deliberately didn't kill Ruth, but you never asked me how I knew that Ruth was her name," Greg said.

"Okay...How did you know her name?" Min asked.

"I only got five minutes?"

"Nope," said Min. "Now it's four because you wasted a minute answering a question with a question."

"Wow, you're a hard-ass!" he complained.

"You already knew that," she said.

In her nightmare, Ruth saw herself as a fearful six-year-old child, shivering, dirty, and clammy, and trying to ignore the searing pain in her wounded foot. As she cowered in a hollow made by a fallen tree, it was all she could do to keep from crying out in pain—she knew the Stasi were out there with their dogs. Only when she heard the dogs' cries grow fainter did she allow herself to whimper as she exhaled. Even so, she stayed perfectly still, camouflaged by her mantle of bark and leaves as the worms, spiders, centipedes, and other inhabitants of the decaying forest floor explored her skin. And then she blacked out.

Ruth awoke to the sound of snapping twigs as they parted to let the light stream onto her face. The arms of a familiar man tunneled into the mulch to lift her out of her hiding place. He carried her back to the small bunker where her parents and other members of the Society of Truth had taken refuge from the Stasi. She heard her mom and dad crying tears of joy as they thanked the man who had found her.

Ruth was crying as well, but for an entirely different reason. Her parents had no idea that their "hero"—Ruth's rescuer—was also her rapist. She had been too ashamed to tell her mother about how often he'd roughly fingered her vulva under her clothing, and besides, he'd made her promise that she'd keep their "special little secret." She couldn't tell anyone how badly it hurt each time he thrust himself inside her, or how much she hated the rank smell of his pubic hair, or how awful it felt to be gagging when his penis was halfway down her throat. Hours earlier, after wiping away the cold goo of his cum, she'd run away from her tormentor, even though she was barefoot and still in her nightclothes. Now that he'd found her, she was sobbing uncontrollably because she once again would be prey.

———✦———

Down the hall in the prison cell, Greg was still talking. "As you know, this ancient castle was built by Sibyllines, but it was eventually overrun by a USF German count. He cleared the entire area and used the lumber to build luxurious private hunting lodges for noblemen. Some hunted foxes. Others hunted schoolgirls. In the heyday of the Third Reich, it was a playground for officers of the SS."

"Yes, I know all that," said Min. "After World War II, the Weisshotel Castle—and indeed all of Quedlinburg—was controlled by the East Germans and, by extension, by the Soviets until 1990. I'm also aware that the Sibyllines eventually took back the castle after *Mauerfall*—the fall of the Berlin Wall—and the collapse of the Iron Curtain. After that, it took a long time to restore the forest and set the stage for development of the underground terrarium where the seeds of the Tree of Life would be planted. Yadda yadda. You're running out of time, Garth. Tell me something I don't know."

"Cut-to-the-chase kind of girl," Greg said. "I like that."

Min rolled her eyes and looked at her watch.

"Anyway..." Greg continued, "a stone plaque of a poem hangs on the outer garden wall of this castle. It was written by Elsa Clementine."

"I know all about that, too," said Min. "I was just out there looking at it a few minutes ago. Ticktock."

"You may know all about the plaque, but I bet you don't know anything about Elsa herself. History says she was one of Goethe's sweethearts, but the truth is that he raped her when she was only fourteen."

Min tried hard not to look surprised, but this was a story she'd never heard before.

"And here's something else," Greg continued. "Goethe was descended from a long line of USF men—dating back to Pontius Pilate."

"As in the Pontius Pilate in the Bible, the one who ordered the death of Jesus?" Min asked.

"Is there another?" Greg replied. "Don't answer that. Here's the kicker. Procula, Pilate's wife, defied the law and illegally entered her husband's court, holding their baby in her arms—Pilate's firstborn son. She launched into an impassioned plea—in public—begging him to release Jesus. She even wrote a letter to Jewish leaders, claiming that Jesus was the son of God."

"And you know all this...how?" Jacob asked.

"In the book of Matthew, it says Procula told Pilate she had a dream about Jesus—that he's a righteous man, and that Pilate should have nothing to do with his death," said Greg. "Of course, Jewish and Christian theologians have had a field day with that ever since. Christians allege that the dream was sent by the devil, because they're sure that Christ's crucifixion *had* to happen for salvation. Jews say that Jesus himself used sorcery to send the dream. Why? Because they're sure that Jesus was not the Messiah, of course."

"What a mess!" said Min.

"Pilate chose to ignore the pleadings of his wife, but we now believe that Procula was a Sibylline...and guess who probably is the one unnamed Sibylline prophetess that Michelangelo painted on the ceiling of the Sistine Chapel?"

"The wife of Pontius Pilate?" Min offered.

"How'd ya guess? As we've all been taught, Pilate ended up

sentencing Jesus for crucifixion…"

"And you have to have a gruesome ritual murder if we're all going to get to heaven. Because nothing motivates you to pray for the hereafter like the macabre image of a bleeding, dying man. Hallelujah for Christian salvation," Min said.

Greg shook his head—same old Min. It was just like her to insert a wisecrack like that. She'd done it all the time in acupuncture college. It was one of the many qualities that he found attractive about her.

"Yes," Greg went on, "Christ was crucified or, more accurately, impaled, if you want to get technical about it. And afterward, Pontius Pilate went insane and committed suicide."

"Serves him right. He should have taken the advice of his Sibylline wife," Min replied.

"Absolutely, but after Pilate offed himself, Procula didn't waste any time. She had another child—a daughter—by another man, a Sibylline man. To make a long story short…"

"Too late for that," Min interjected.

"As I was saying," Greg continued, "Elsa Clementine—she of the poem and the plaque—was descended from that Sibylline lineage. Goethe, on the other hand, could trace his ancestry back to the firstborn son of Pilate and Procula. That guy turned out to be bad news—a ruthless officer in the Roman legions. His nastiness was hereditary—his male descendants were just like him, including Goethe, whose USF assignment was to impregnate fourteen-year-old Elsa. Why? To defile the oldest Sibylline bloodline—the one that began with Procula and her second husband—and corrupt it with the oldest USF line that began with Pontius Pilate."

"But what does that have to do with what's going on right now?" Jacob asked.

"The rape of Elsa Clementine by Goethe resulted in a pregnancy, which seemed like a USF victory at the time. Nevertheless, Elsa's parents protected her child and raised her in the Sibylline tradition."

"And so?"

"And so…" Greg continued, "Ruth's mother was a direct descendant of Elsa Clementine's child of rape. She turned her back on her large Sibylline family when she married into the Society of Truth. This made her the only one in Procula's lineage of females who actually chose to abandon the Sibylline way. Her relatives were devastated, but held onto the hope that one day she would return. She never did, so they placed their hope in her only child, Ruth. You can imagine their despair when Ruth, who'd been born and raised in the Society, married Heinrich, another Society member. When the couple deliberately chose to remain childless, it snuffed out this Sibylline bloodline, finalizing the USF victory."

"That can't be the end of the story," said Jacob.

"It isn't," Greg continued. "You see, Ananta didn't become a spy in the Society of Truth just to retrieve the manuscript and the seeds…"

"She was there to help Ruth awaken as well," Min said, completing his sentence. "In a sense, Ananta was going to save her," Min added.

"Not exactly," Greg said. "A better way to think of it is that she was going to help Ruth save herself. As Erica Pfeiffer, Ananta could lead Ruth to the information that would help her make that choice, but Ruth would have to begin to think critically on her own. She'd have to make the choice to challenge Society 'truths' and draw conclusions that would lead her to reject the male-dominated religion. Ruth would have to figure out that all the Society dogma and hypocrisy that had been drummed into her skull since childhood was a bunch of crap, but she'd have to do so of her own free will."

"What you're saying is that Ruth would have to unbrainwash herself," declared Jacob.

"And that would take time," Min added.

"Which is exactly what Ananta knew she did not have," said Greg. "As the clock was winding down, she pushed the envelope, so to speak, and took a chance. That was when she challenged Ruth to meet her in the middle of the night at the Society library, and when she showed her the drawers and drawers of case files—all the child abuse records that the Society had hushed up—including Ruth's own."

"Wait…what?" Min interrupted. "Ruth was a survivor of child sexual abuse by someone in the religion?"

"Oooh yeah. When Ruth was a kid, hiding from the Stasi with her parents and other Society of Truth members, she was raped by Elias Eberhard, a USF spy posing as a Society elder."

Jacob couldn't help but laugh. "Did you say his name was 'Eberhard'?"

"Yes...*Eberhard*," Greg replied, "and Eberhard was a direct descendant of..."

Min finished his sentence, "...of that literary titan and world-class child abuser, Johann Wolfgang von Goethe."

"Bingo!" Greg said.

"Which also made him a descendant of Pontius Pilate and his first-born son," said Min.

"Eberhard wanted to eventually impregnate Ruth, just as Goethe had wanted to impregnate Elsa Clementine," said Greg. "But Eberhard died before Ruth got old enough to bear children. And then she married Heinrich, and they both vowed to remain childless so they would be accepted as volunteers at Society of Truth headquarters in Brooklyn."

"That must have looked like a huge win for the USF," said Jacob.

"It did, but that victory was fleeting," said Greg. "With Ananta's help, Ruth returned to her true family tradition, the Sibylline Way of Kyndeness, and even brought her beloved husband, Heinrich, with her. The USF had wanted to write that Ruth—the very last descendant of Procula the Sibylline—died as a loyal member of a USF-led religion, but now they can't."

"And that's why Ananta wanted Ruth to be the seed-bearer," Min said.

Ruth tossed and turned in the midst of her nightmare. As her sense memory of Brother Eberhard's naked body towered over her, she knew that being back in the underground bunker meant he would impose himself on her as often as he pleased. She wanted to escape, but there was no way out, and instead of waking up, the dream morphed into the present day. She saw herself on the bed as Eberhard, very much alive, stroked himself as he walked toward her. She couldn't move. She felt him put one arm under her knees and the other behind her neck, just as he did when he lifted her out of her hiding place.

Her eyes shot open as she woke abruptly. She tried to flee, but the pain in her shoulder prevented it. "He found me!" Ruth screamed. "He found me!"

Min heard Ruth from down the hall and went running to her room. "It's okay, Ruth," she said. "You're okay. You're safe."

"He's gonna find me again!" Ruth exclaimed.

"No, Ruth. He's not," Min declared. "It was just a bad dream. No one is going to hurt you. You're safe now."

Jacob remained in the cell with Greg, glaring at him, wondering if everything that had just come out of his mouth was bullshit.

"You want us to think you're a double agent," Jacob said. "Why should we believe a word you said, and why would any of it help us?" Jacob asked.

"Look..." Greg answered. "The USF believes that Ruth is dead. Before I *allowed* myself to be captured, I sent a message to my commander, informing him that Ruth had fallen to her death as she reached the threshold of the entrance to the tunnel, and that my partner was taken out by a Sibylline guard. Truth is, I shot him. Now that I'm MIA, my commander doesn't know whether I got caught and I'm being interrogated, in which case they're worried about what I'm telling you. Or maybe I've got the seeds and I'm hiding out—from both the Sibyllines *and* the USF. One way or another, they're coming for me *and* the seeds, which means they're getting ready to storm the castle. If I were you, I'd put everybody on alert—your underground 'Eden Project' will be under attack very soon—sorry, dude!"

"Maybe yes, maybe no," said Jacob. "And maybe you really *are* a double agent, but you're going to stay in handcuffs under my armed supervision until we get some proof."

Ruth's heart rate was decreasing, and she started to shiver as Min changed Ruth's sweat-soaked gown. While offering her water, Min gave her the news. "We have to leave here, Ruth," she began.

"Running? Again?" she asked.

"Not running," Min assured her with a smile. "Just staying a couple of steps ahead. That's all."

[illegible]

CHAPTER 13
STAR

The stable at the foot of the Phugtal monastery accommodated up to six horses, but for the past nine years, there had been only two. These were purebred Zaniskaris, one black and white, the other chestnut, and they were ideally suited to the local terrain. They were strong and surefooted, with sturdy legs and plenty of stamina to handle the steep and rugged trails of the Himalayas. The pair in residence had been carefully trained. They did not get spooked by loud noises, by other animals, or by sudden movements. To keep them in excellent condition, the monks who cared for them rode them regularly along the network of narrow paths that surrounded Phugtal. The horses knew the routine and would get excited as the outing neared its end because it meant a fresh bath and brushing, as well as an equine pedicure—trimming, balancing, and conditioning their hooves with aromatic pine tar and a little beeswax.

"Stay here," Mireille instructed John and Ananta. "I'll get the horses saddled up and bring them out."

"Let me help," John offered.

"No," Mireille replied. "Both of you have just been through exhausting energy depletion, and John...you may have been miraculously resurrected, but your body still needs time to recover from the trauma it suffered. Please have a seat while I go reintroduce myself to the horses and gentle them into accepting the journey we're about to begin."

Ananta and John found a block of hay to sit on and listened to the nocturnal serenade, a veritable choir of chirping, buzzing, whirring, and croaking. Ananta, however, seemed withdrawn into herself. She was unusually quiet, and John decided not to intrude.

Mireille entered the stable. After briefly greeting Bella, the chestnut horse, she made her way toward Zee's stall. She could hear the happy swishing of his tail as she drew near. "Hey there, my friend," she said as she placed the back of her hand in front of Zee's nose. "Oh, you're *so* handsome!"

In Zee's case, it was not an exaggeration. His black-and-white coat was almost pinto-like, which was extremely rare for a Zaniskari. Even more unusual was the rare silver outlining of each patch of black hair. "It's been a while since you honored me with a ride on your majestic back," she whispered softly. Zee's ears were forward and alert. He nudged Mireille's hand, a signal that he was happy to see her and wanted more attention. As she rubbed his neck and shoulders, then his ears—his favorite spot—Zee whinnied with sheer pleasure.

"Feels good, huh?" Mireille smiled. "Listen, my friend, I have a very special task for you. My girl is here. Her name is Ananta. She's a lot like me, so I know you two will love each other. I'm counting on you to give her a smooth ride. Can you do that, Zee? Can you be her first ride on our journey to Shangri-la? I promise I'll be right alongside you."

Mireille closed her eyes as Zee pressed his nose to her face and snuffled gently—she had her answer. Then he rested his head on her shoulder. She put her arms around him and nuzzled her face into his long black mane. "Thank you, Zee," she whispered.

As John and Ananta waited outside the barn, John couldn't take Ananta's silence any longer. "What are you thinking?" he asked.

"I just don't understand..." she started, as if she had been waiting for the invitation to speak.

"Understand what?"

"I've often asked to go with my mother to Shangri-la, but her answer was always the same—not just no, but absolutely not. She always told me it's too sacred and that only the custodians, like Cosma, are allowed there. Why is it okay now? Why the rush, and why...?"

"...why me?" John finished her sentence.

"Yes, why you? I mean...no offense, but if her perfect daughter has had to wait all these years to be invited, how come you suddenly get to go? She doesn't even know you."

Before John could speculate on an answer, Mireille emerged from the stable with Zee's reins in one hand and Bella's reins in the other. If she'd stayed even a minute longer, she would have heard the phone ring in the stable office. As it was, however, she missed Saji's call, telling her what Sundara had said about Helzar, about his transformation, and about his escape.

Both horses were equipped with pommel bags carrying snacks, water, fire starter, and a lightweight tent. Mireille had wanted to be prepared—it was still rainy season, and a storm could roll in quickly and unexpectedly. She insisted that John and Ananta ride first, while she took to foot. They mounted the horses and Mireille adjusted their stirrups. The silver outlines in Zee's coat glistened in the moonlight.

It was only two hours by horseback to the tiny monastery in Cha, where Ananta and John had left their horses before hiking on foot to Phugtal. Both Mireille and Ananta had keen eyesight and knew the landscape well, but Mireille brought a flashlight anyway. She wanted to illuminate the trail as they walked, not just to avoid the dips, holes, and hollows in the uneven terrain, but also to avoid disturbing any Himalayan pit vipers that might be out for their nightly feast of centipedes. The bite from these high-altitude snakes wasn't deadly, but their venom could cause intense local pain and swelling that would last several days—a chance that Mireille was unwilling to take.

"You're upset, Ananta," said Mireille. "Am I reading you right?"

"You've always read me right, Mom," Ananta responded.

"Not true, my dear. You've learned to hide your emotions well, mostly from others, but even from me. You slipped right into character at the Society of Truth. In all those years, no one ever suspected you were anything other than a devoted follower and an obedient, diligent cleaning lady."

"*Aaaannd* fiancée to a woman-hating, buttfucking asshole, whose thirst for power and comically overinflated opinion of himself permitted him to believe that Ananta might be even remotely attracted to him," John ranted.

Mireille and Ananta began laughing. "Don't hold back, John. Tell us how you *really* feel about Devon Nelson," Mireille teased.

"You left out racist and pyromaniac," Ananta added with a grin.

John's face suddenly became serious. "May I change the subject, Mireille? Your daughter is upset because she doesn't understand why we are suddenly in a hurry to get to Shangri-la, and why I've been invited to tag along for the ride. Why me? Why now?"

"I get it, Ananta," Mireille began. "After all these years of turning you down, you're now wondering why the rush, and why take John with us. I want you to trust me that there's a very good reason for this journey—I *need* you to trust me. All will be made clear once we reach our destination, I promise you."

Ananta stopped to look at her beautiful mother in the light of the moon and stars. She took a breath, and a flood of memories overtook her. Mireille reached out her arms. "Come here, my daughter," she said. Ananta dismounted and fell into her mother's embrace.

"I've missed you so much, Mom." Ananta cried softly. She did trust her mother—unconditionally—but she couldn't stand not knowing the reason for this emergency trip to Shangri-la.

Mireille stroked Ananta's black hair, then pulled herself away to look at her face. "Look," she said as she placed her hands on Ananta's shoulders and gently turned her around. She then pointed to the sky.

All three remained still, gazing at the brilliant, starry expanse overhead. "Every once in a while, when I long for him," Mireille began as she pulled Ananta closer to her, "I call to him in my heart, and a gold shooting star streaks across the universe—and I know it's him. It's your father—my Easa."

As John studied the sky, he suddenly realized that everything seemed more...well...beautiful. There was more beauty in the world in that moment than he had ever seen before. More potential, more love. He felt a deep sense of calm, but there was more to it than that. He was completely at peace in the moment, without any pressing worries, and it allowed him to truly appreciate this amazing gift called life. As he scanned the heavens, he just wanted to weep at its sheer grandeur, and also at the profound gratitude he felt to be in the company of these two astonishing women.

"There's an ancient African saying," Mireille continued, "that it takes a village to raise a child. You see all those stars? The emptiness between them is not empty at all. In that emptiness is our village, my dearest Ananta, a consciousness that we are one with. If that collective consciousness were here right now—and in a way, it is—it would tell you how proud it is of you, and how stunningly beautiful you are—in part because you take after your physical father, Easa..."

"No offense, Mireille," said John, "but the rest of humanity will have to take your word for it."

Mireille laughed softly. She loved that John was not the least bit intimidated by her. "Dearest Ananta, if Easa were here to recall the day he and I met you in your physical form—the day you were born—he'd laugh about how you came bursting forth from my womb just seconds after your brother, crying as soon as you took your first breath. It was as if you were shouting your arrival to the whole world: 'I'm here! I'm here!' " Mireille stopped before her voice cracked—she felt herself getting choked up. "You are surely your father's daughter. Your midnight-black hair and big brown eyes are just like his, and I see his face in yours every time I look at you."

Mireille paused and gently turned Ananta so the two were face-to-face, then looked deeply into her eyes. "In the moment of your birth, I dreamed of all the adventures we would have together," she said. "I've certainly lived all of those adventures with you—and more. I saw life more fully through your eyes than I ever could have with mine alone. Your zest for life, for the Way of Kyndeness, for healing. I loved and lived more deeply because of you. I'm so grateful that Easa gave you to me—a gift that made me a better person. Both of us are so proud of the woman you've become—as is all consciousness—and now, we're also very proud of this man you've chosen to share your journey with."

"Look!" John exclaimed as he pointed to the sky.

A golden flash streaked across heavens. Mireille wrapped her arms around Ananta and they stood there together. Mother and daughter—and father.

John watched these two timeless—in every sense of the word—women. The life experiences they shared as mother and daughter were something no other humans had ever enjoyed, and of course, Mireille had already had an extraordinary life before Ananta was born. She knew all the ancient prophets—both men and women. She made friends with philosophers, sages, and gurus from all over the world. She worked hand in hand with the world's greatest shamans and healers. She had lived through the entirety of the earth's tumultuous history and survived—even the massive deluge around the Black Sea. She knew the history of languages, when religion got invented, and how the major world political powers rose and fell...the Babylonians, the Persians, the Greeks, and the Romans. And she'd done it all without ever revealing her true identity as the daughter of Adán and Eva.

Mireille loosened the rolled-up blanket from one of the saddles, and after inspecting the ground with her flashlight, she spread it out. She took a seat, then motioned to John to dismount from Bella. The three sat together, with Mireille in the middle. Her right hand gently reached for John's, and her left took hold of Ananta's.

"What if..." Mireille speculated to them both, "all the tumult was gone? What then? What if only kind, loving people existed in a world where everyone was peaceful, and all desires had been satisfied? What would the endgame be?"

John had just experienced the real endgame upon his physical death. He knew exactly what was waiting on the other side of death... the ultimate endgame. But that wasn't what Mireille was asking. She was talking about *this* world...*this* planet...all physical life...*this* endgame, and he didn't have the answer.

Mireille focused on John and broadened her question. "In this life, you've been trained and educated in something that would change the world. Here you are fulfilling that goal. You're now traveling the world, protecting the most precious commodity on the planet, and in so doing, you're meeting wonderful people, finding true love, experiencing thrilling adventures...a colorful life, indeed. If we were to add wealth, family, health, happiness, everything you ever wanted...then what? What would you want next?"

"I don't know" was the only thing John could think to say, then added, "But I can guess I would still want to wake up the next morning."

"That's the right answer," Mireille said. "When you say 'I don't know, but I want to keep living to find out,' all it really means is that you still desire the struggle."

"No, I don't. I hate struggle," John replied.

"You sure about that?" Mireille said. "You just returned from the afterlife...a place of unconditional love shared by mass consciousness. It was like nothing you had ever experienced before, and it was bliss, correct?"

"Yes, it was..." John tried to think of the perfect word to describe it, but "bliss" was the best definition.

"And yet, instead of choosing that, you would choose to wake up here tomorrow morning—here, where you struggle as a human. Every desire and every goal that you've attained in your life—you have achieved through struggle. The reason you are here in the Himalayas, is because of struggle. Struggle is all you've known. And yet, when you have nothing else left to desire, because you have it all, you would still want to get up to another day—*here*."

"Look at where I am. Look at who I'm with, Mireille," John replied. "How could I *not* choose *here*?"

"How is it, then, that you can insist that you hate struggle?" Mireille said. "What do you think the next day has in store for you, if not some kind of struggle? Struggle is exactly what you want, or you wouldn't want to wake up *here*. You'd want to wake up"—Mireille let go of John's hand and gestured toward the heavens—"*out there*."

John sighed as his shoulders sank. Mireille was right. If all he'd ever known and enjoyed here, in this physical life, included struggle, the only thing to expect tomorrow would be more of the same...more struggle. And yet...and yet he wouldn't want to miss it. He'd want to wake up and live another day—*here*. "How could I want another day of struggle, but loathe struggle at the same time?" he asked.

"A paradox, isn't it?" Mireille replied.

"You would think so, but if I remember correctly," John said, "that's what chapter one of your manuscript explains in quite a bit of detail. Ananta read the first chapter to a few of us. Apparently, your mom and dad, the first human couple—Adán and Eva—deliberately chose free will, knowing it would mean struggling through the conse- quences of the choices they made."

"Which leads us back to my initial question," Mireille said. "What's the endgame—*here*?"

"Heck if I know! Do you?" John asked. "Do you know what the ultimate outcome is for this planet and all life on it?"

"The answer can only be found in hindsight," Mireille began, "but hindsight is tricky business. It can be an exact science—but only if the hindsight is true. If recorded accurately, hindsight will give you a glimpse into the past—everything that took place because of freewill choices. Then, life's meaning on this planet—the endgame—becomes crystal clear. But…"

"But what?" John asked.

"But the irony of free will is that it includes the freedom to tell stories and write history however the writer chooses," said Mireille. "As a result, mankind's 'hindsight' is skewed—and I use the word 'mankind' quite deliberately, since most historical records have been written by men."

"With predictable results," said Ananta.

"I half smile, half cry at how humans have recorded their own history," Mireille continued. "Some historians take 'poetic license,' making events sound more dramatic—and making participants more noble and more valiant—than they really were. Like a West African proverb said: 'The lion's story will never be told, if the hunter is the only one to tell it.'"

" 'History is written by the victors,' " said John. "It's a quote commonly attributed to Winston Churchill, but versions of it were already in common use at least a hundred years earlier."

"The narratives written merely to embellish events and glorify heroes are relatively benign," Mireille declared. "That's how legends are born. Too much of what passes for history, however, is outright deceitful. It was written to bolster the authority and confirm the 'superiority' of those already at the top of the food chain. To accomplish these aims, those accounts deliberately obscure and underplay the contributions of women and other disadvantaged groups, giving the wealthy and powerful credit for them instead."

"The history of India as set down by the British, who ruled it as a colony from the mid-1800s to just after World War II, is what most European and North American children grew up learning," said Ananta. "And it bears no resemblance to the history of India as written by its own people."

"Sometimes the truth comes out, but it can take a while," said Mireille. "Look how long the work of NASA's Black female mathematicians was concealed rather than celebrated—that didn't happen by accident. And if contemporaneous accounts are lost or destroyed, what really happened may never be known—that's one reason why I've been keeping track."

"I get why you've kept a truthful account of human history," said John, "but why haven't you revealed it?"

"Because part of free will is having the courage to challenge written history—the flawed hindsight that is presented as the truth. But most people don't do that. A book that is bound and typeset carries its own moral imperative. Most people accept the premise that because an account of past events appears in black-and-white and claims to be true—or claims to be inspired by God—it *must* be accurate."

"But there's always somebody..." John said.

"Oh, there sure is," Mireille agreed. "There's always that one kid in the class—the rebel, the nonconformist..."

"That was me," said John with a slight smile.

"That one critical thinker who annoys teachers and classmates alike—but keeps asking questions anyway," Mireille continued. "The one who demands answers that make sense, and refuses to be placated with platitudes such as 'God works in mysterious ways' or 'if it's in the Bible, it must be so.' "

"The one who calls out inconsistencies and injustices. The one who takes a leap and, because of it, expands understanding and wisdom," added Ananta.

"These are truly unsung heroes," said Mireille. "We don't treasure them nearly enough. Hopefully, my manuscript honors them properly."

"But why write the true version of human history if you're never going to share it with the world?" John asked.

"I never said 'never,' " Mireille replied. "When the cloth of the *Mireille Manuscript* is untied, humankind will be ready for it. Unveiled prematurely, it would be disparaged as a hoax because it's so different from recorded history as we've come to accept it. Until then, the complete manuscript will remain safe at Shangri-la."

"Not to be technical," John said, "but what's at Shangri-la is not a 'complete manuscript.' "

"What do you mean?" Mireille asked.

"What do you mean by 'What do you mean?'?" Ananta scoffed.

"We risked our lives to retrieve the first chapter of your manuscript from the secret library at the Society of Truth. Against all odds, we brought it to Phugtal. It was taped to the skin on John's back the entire trip!"

"Oh...oh, yes...of course!" Mireille stammered, realizing why the edges of the paper she found in John's backpack had been bound with clear tape.

There was an awkward silence for a moment, and John and Ananta shared glances of concern. It was obvious to both of them that Mireille was withholding something about the manuscript.

"We must make it to the Cha monastery tonight," Mireille said, changing the subject as quickly as she could. Ananta wasn't ready to hear the truth about the manuscript—not yet. Besides, there was a presence Mireille was picking up, and caution was needed.

John and Ananta didn't press the issue, but instead took the cue that they needed to get going. The blanket was rolled back up and placed back in the saddle, only this time, John insisted on walking. Ananta stayed on Zee, while Mireille mounted Bella.

The old monk at Cha was happy to see Ananta and John once again, and thrilled at the opportunity to see Mireille as well. After a brief visit, he helped saddle up one of the horses that had been entrusted to his care, and sent all three on their way to Poonam's home.

CHAPTER 14
SHIT

Mario's butternut squash ravioli, beet and goat cheese salad, crusty bread, and good Chianti were the remedies that soothed the souls and unruffled the feathers of everyone inside the Sibylline bunker—even those of Debra, who'd been on the verge of open rebellion. Reflecting on their shared harrowing experience, each member of the group contributed to the animated conversation. The laughter, tears, and good-natured banter cheered almost everyone, but Gabby's focus was on her son, Zach. He'd remained quiet all through the meal, but his knee had been bouncing up and down and his fingers had been wiggling ever since he sat down to eat. She could tell that he was about to jump out of his skin.

"What's going on, Zach?" Gabby asked. "Spit it out," she said.

"We need a freezer," he declared. "If the seeds are in my"—he paused—"my goddamn turd, *and* if there's any chance that they haven't already been destroyed by my amylase, protease, and lipase—in other words, if they haven't already been digested by my gut enzymes—*and* if we want to have any chance of them germinating, we're going to have to freeze my bag o' poop. Otherwise, the digestive process will continue. The seeds will keep decomposing because they're sitting in too much moisture. Eventually, I'll have to freeze-dry them to preserve them, but if we don't freeze them now, they'll be ruined forever."

The merry mood in the bunker dissipated instantly. "You're serious," Jen said flatly.

"Dead serious," Zach replied. "Those seeds will be no good to anybody if we don't act quickly."

"Well then, let's get going," said Mario. "There's only one available freezer, and it's upstairs in my kitchen."

There was a low rumble coming from deep in the earth as everyone stood. The silverware and plates began to vibrate. Then the table itself started to shake.

"Another earthquake!" Donna cried. "Not again!"

Chunks of mortar fell to the ground, and cracks began to appear in the walls. Large portions of the stone ceiling began raining down on the group.

"Out of here! Back upstairs. Now!" barked Sadie.

Everyone bolted for the tunnel door that led to the staircase to Mario's Market. Everyone except Gabby, who darted instead toward the farthest corner of the sitting area, where the plastic bag with Zach's feces had been tucked away.

"Leave it!" Cameron shouted. "The ceiling is about to cave in!"

"I must get the seeds," Gabby insisted. "It's why we're here. Take Zach. Go!"

Cameron began pulling him toward the door to the tunnel, but Zach dragged his feet as he kept peering back over his shoulder. "Mom!" he cried out.

Only when Gabby's silhouette came into view was Cameron able to propel him through the door and into the underground passage that led toward the staircase to Mario's.

Gabby had almost reached the doorway when there was one last tremor. The sharp jolt knocked her face-first to the ground, and also dislodged the rocks overhead, burying her lower body beneath a pile of stone.

As Zach doubled back from the tunnel, he saw Cam desperately trying to move the mountain of debris that covered his mother. He immediately bent down and checked her pulse. Gabby was alive, but barely.

Cam kept digging, but he knew his efforts would likely be futile.

And even if he was successful, he feared that she'd soon succumb to her internal injuries.

Gabby was astute enough in the healing arts to have a good idea of how gravely she was hurt, and could already feel her life force ebbing. "Stop," she said as she labored to breathe. "It's no use."

"Nooooo!" screamed Zach. "I'm not leaving you here!"

Cameron took hold of Zach's arm. "Son…"

"Don't call me son!" Zach shrieked as he pushed Cam away and started pawing furiously at the pile.

Gabby mustered the last of her energy to speak. "Stop, Zach," she said softly. "My physical time with you is over now. You and Cam must take each other's hands and promise me you'll stay on this journey—together—until I can hold both of you again."

Cameron gently moved the curly brown locks of hair away from Gabby's face so he and Zach could see her. A single tear left a damp trail down her dusty cheek as she labored to say what she needed them to hear. "Zach, honey…I'm so grateful, lucky, and privileged that you chose me to be your mom," she whispered. "I hope I made you proud. Cam, promise me you'll guide him and teach him to be the kind warrior he was meant to be. Promise me."

"I promise, my love," Cam assured her.

"Now take these seeds and change the world." Then her body went limp.

Cam felt for a pulse. There was none. "Zach," he urged gently, "we have to go, and we have to go *now*. Your mom is gone and the whole ceiling is about to cave in."

As rocks continued to fall around them, Cam helped the boy to his feet and firmly grasped both of his hands. "I made a solemn promise to your mom, Zach, and I now make the same promise to you," he said. "I will be with you and take care of you always. We both deeply loved your mother, and we both know that she wouldn't want you to die down here with her. She needs you to live on and continue her dream. Come."

Cam eased the bag from Gabby's fingers and handed it to Zach, who walked like a zombie toward the stairway to Mario's Market.

The rest of the group was a couple of minutes ahead of them. They'd entered the shop to find André bracing himself under the doorway to the kitchen. He was unhurt, but Mario's Market was a shambles. The huge window facing Old Fulton Street had shattered. Shelving had rattled from the walls, sending bottles of wine and jars of Italian specialty foods crashing down. The floor was now covered with an aromatic sauce comprised of aged balsamic vinegar, Calabrian chiles, GranFruttato extra virgin olive oil, organic passata di pomodoro, and several bottles of excellent Brunello di Montalcino. Shards of glass floated atop the mix and glinted in the light.

When Cam and Zach emerged covered in dust, everyone expected to see Gabby right behind them. Sadie locked eyes with Cam as he all but imperceptibly shook his head from side to side. She knew immediately what had happened.

Rocky was in Cam's face instantly. "Where's my sister?" he shouted. Before Cam could answer, Rocky began pummeling Cam's chest, repeating, "Where's my sister!!!? You were supposed to protect us! You were supposed to protect *her*!"

Zach was in shock and swayed unsteadily on his feet. Rocky stepped back from Cam and caught Zach just his knees buckled. Their shoulders then slumped together in an emotional embrace. The two, brother and son, held each other up, wailing in shared grief.

Donna was shocked at Gabby's death, but she had one thing on her mind—she had to know if Milton was okay. Although she was very upset with him, she still cared about him. Despite his adherence to the teachings of the Society of Truth, despite his clinging to their doctrine of male superiority, and despite how boring he'd become in the bedroom, she loved him. She worried that he'd been injured in the quake, and had to find out.

"Where are you going?" Keisha asked.

"Don't fuss about me," Donna answered as she rushed out onto the sidewalk. She started walking toward the Society of Truth dormitory, weaving her way through the crowds of panicky people who had spilled out of nearby shops and apartments. As she turned the corner onto Columbia Heights, she saw Milton standing there, dazed and lethargic.

"Milton?! Are you okay?" she shouted.

"Donna?" he questioned as he turned. "Donna! Oh my God! You came back!"

He ran to Donna and embraced her, then joyfully lifted her off the ground and twirled her around, just as he had when they were dating.

"Put me down, mister," Donna ordered. "I'm not coming back."

Milton looked dejected as he lowered her feet to the pavement. "Let's get something straight right now," she declared firmly. "I am not coming back. Period. I'm not *looking* back, I'm not *coming* back...I'm not *backing up*. I'm not allowing you or the Society to contain and restrain me anymore. I'm *moving forward*. The only reason I'm here is because I still care about you. I was coming to check on you, to make sure you were okay after the quake. That's all."

"You still love me enough to want to know if I was okay. That's good enough for now. I'll take it—I'll take anything. Where did you go? Who were you with?"

"Goddammit, Milton! You're doing it again!" Donna exploded. "I come to see whether you're alive and unhurt, and the first thing you're concerned about is where I've been? You feel obligated—no, *entitled*—to demand that I account for my whereabouts and who was with me?"

Milton's shoulders slumped. "You're right..." he said. "*And* you were right all along. I...I...I have so much to tell you. There's something awful going on."

"What happened?"

Milton hesitated as his Society of Truth patriarchal autopilot kicked in. All members of the Elder Board had been issued a confidential manual on the policies and regulations they were to follow. In it was a specific mandate that elders were not to discuss weighty or confidential policy matters with their wives—ever. Women were not bright enough or enlightened enough to be privy to that information. Milton had bent that rule several times to get Donna's creative thoughts on various potential projects. That had worked well for him—by representing her ideas as his own, he'd earned an undeserved reputation for ingenuity with other members of the Elder Board. Nevertheless, for more than twenty years, he'd kept the Elder Board's most serious matters from her—including all the discussions about the Elder Board's struggle to suppress allegations of child abuse.

Milton stammered. "I...I...I..."

Realizing that Milton was censoring himself, Donna turned on her heel to leave. "I give up, Milton," she said. "You'll never change. The

Society still has you by the cojones. Don't talk to me until you take them back."

"Wait!" he called after her.

Donna turned back toward him and raised a skeptical eyebrow. "I'm listening," she said.

Milton took a deep breath. "I'm still a captive of my old bad habits —I know that—and I also know I'm going to have to work on that."

"And..."

"And you should know that Paul Fitzgerald was murdered."

Donna's eyes widened. "As in...you were present at the homicide of Paul Fitzgerald?"

"I didn't see it in person, but I have proof—it's on my cell phone," Milton replied. "Do you remember Sam Silverman, the Society attorney? He too was murdered. Devon Nelson is responsible, along with that Kruger dude—the one who kissed you."

"I have it on excellent authority that that was a setup," Donna said icily, "but that's a story for another time."

"Paul came upon Silverman—dead—in the men's room on the ninth floor of headquarters," Milton said.

"That's where the artists work—what was he doing there?" Donna asked.

"That, too, is a story for another time," said Milton. "Paul managed to get out of the building without being seen. Then he watched as they dumped Silverman's body bag into the back of a pickup. Paul took pictures with his cell phone and sent the photos to me, along with a goodbye text saying that Nelson and Kruger were onto him."

"This is so much worse than I thought!" Donna exclaimed. "As soon as I saw the pornographic videos that Ruth made me watch at my welcoming luncheon, I realized that the Society was not a religion but a *cult*." She all but spat out the word, then paused for effect. "From what you're telling me, the cult—and all holy claptrap about how men should be in charge of everything—is just a front. The Society of Truth is actually a ruthless criminal enterprise."

"Everything I've seen in the last couple of days tells me you're correct," Milton admitted.

Milton collapsed as his body was wracked with sobs. Donna was right—again. His view of the world was skewed, and his priorities were wrong. Everything he'd done to get ahead in the Society had been done in service to a lie—and an evil one at that.

"I...I...I have to start over. But how?"

"You don't have to do it alone, Milton. Come with me."

Milton stood there looking at his beautiful and spirited wife. He never loved her as much as he did at that moment. He reached out his hand without saying a word. Donna took hold of it and began leading him back to Mario's Market.

CHAPTER 15
CHA

Sundara stood outside the monastery—the quake-induced blackout had given him the opportunity to slip away unnoticed. Now he took stock of his physical well-being. Other than bruises at the sites where the electrodes and IV connector had been ripped away from his body by the force of the tremor, he was uninjured. Nevertheless, the purging marathon had taken his stamina.

Perhaps worse, his insides were upside down. He was aware that he had started seeing things in a way he never had before, and he was tormented by the powerful clash of emotions he was experiencing. Tender, heartwarming thoughts of his mother were flooding into his consciousness, entangled with heartbreaking grief, anger, and resentment.

He felt hopeful...but was unable to define what he was hoping for. For Sundara, hope was an unfamiliar and uncomfortable feeling—it implied that he was lacking something in the present. In all his time as the lord consul of the USF, there had never been a need or desire he could not fulfill. What did he lack now?

He felt fearful...but what did he fear? Before the purge, he was afraid of nothing. To the contrary, he instilled fear in others, then exploited it so he could feed off their anxiety and panic. Now, however, he was the one who was afraid. Sundara was filled with dark, dripping fear—and for him, fear was as unfamiliar as hope.

...Hopeful, but for what?...Fearful, but of what? He did not know.

Another unfamiliar feeling began rising within him, as if it was trying to allay the fear and boost the hope. Could it be trust...or faith? But trust and faith in what? The emotions at war within him were unbearable. He wanted to scream, but didn't dare call attention to himself. *What is happening to me?* he thought.

He needed time to sort it all out, but if he tried to do that here, in the shadow of Phugtal, he risked being recaptured. Activity near the monastery stables caught his eye. He crept in closer to get a better look, and saw his mother leading two horses. Ananta was on one, and a blond geekish man was on the other. Sundara did a double take when he realized that it was John Matthews, the guy who had been brave enough—and foolhardy enough—to challenge him in an effort to defend Ananta. *It can't be*, Sundara said to himself. *I threw him. I saw him hit the wall, and I saw him collapse to the floor. No way he survived. How is it possible he's sitting on a horse next to my sister? And where are they going?*

Sundara stayed out of sight as he followed them, hiding himself behind a boulder when they dismounted and looked at the sky. His keen sense of hearing allowed him to hear every word his mother spoke to Ananta.

In the moment of your birth, I dreamed of all the adventures we would have together...I saw life more fully through your eyes than I ever could have with mine alone. Your zest for life, for the Way of Kyndeness, for healing. I loved and lived more deeply because of you. I'm so grateful that Easa gave you to me—a gift that made me a better person. Both of us are so proud of the woman you've become...

His mother's words to his sister made Sundara's melancholy even more acute—he was all too aware that neither of his parents could possibly be proud of the man he'd become. When he saw the golden star shoot across the sky, he quickly cast his eyes downward. Seeing this reminder of his father was far too painful.

As he followed the trio from a distance, he was quite sure his mother had sensed his presence, but if she had, she hadn't let it on to Ananta or John. He hung back as they arrived at the humble monastery at Cha. After a brief visit, they picked up the third horse they needed for their journey, then departed.

Sundara watched as the elderly monk sent them on their way and retreated into the simple structure. There was something calming and reassuring about him, and about the monastery itself—something that told Sundara he could find refuge and respite there.

"Come in, my son. I know you are there," the monk called out.

Sundara entered through the thick ornately carved door to find the monk seated on the stone floor, legs folded, eyes closed, and hands on his knees, palms up. Once Sundara was inside, the monk opened his eyes and rose effortlessly to his feet. Sundara was impressed— the monk had unfolded his legs and stood without using his hands. He was tall—for some reason that surprised Sundara. The monk bowed, and Sundara bowed in return.

The smell of incense permeated the one, open room. White candles with burned black wicks were everywhere. A fireplace kept the room warm. There was no plumbing and no electricity, just an outdoor well with a hand pump, and an outhouse. The room was sparsely furnished and held a small square table and four chairs. To the side was a counter with fresh greens, utensils, a pitcher, and a bowl. A storage cabinet was tucked underneath it. In the far corner was a desk flanked by bookshelves supported by large rocks that had been foraged from the local area and hauled or dragged indoors. In another corner was a mat, pillow, and thick blanket, as well as a freestanding cupboard. The furniture was old but well cared for, and was made of solid wood that had darkened from years of being oiled.

"You may stay as long as you need to," said the monk, "but while you are here, there will be an exchange. Our first exchange is this...you will add logs to the fire, fill the kettle with water and boil it, chop the greens, and make us a soup. For my part of the exchange, I am providing the greens that will sustain us, water that will hydrate us, a room that will protect us, and a mat for you to sleep on. Do you understand?"

"I do," Sundara answered. An unfamiliar feeling accompanied his acknowledgement of this simple cooperative arrangement, a feeling he couldn't define.

"Just..." the monk said in almost a whisper.

"Just what?" Sundara asked.

The monk said nothing further. Instead, he quietly and gracefully resumed his seated position, legs folded and palms up.

Sundara finally realized that the monk would say nothing further, and that the sentence was complete in itself. "Just" was only one word, but it was enough, and it was also the perfect descriptor for the comforting feeling that Sundara was experiencing. The simple exchange felt...*just*.

Once Ananta, John, and Mireille were miles away from the monastery at Cha, and Mireille sensed that the presence in their midst was gone, she felt safe answering her daughter's question.

"I know you've been wondering...why John?" Mireille began. "Why now? After all these years of fiercely protecting the sacred secrets at Shangri-la, and you begging me to take you there, why am I finally bringing you now—*insisting* that you come with me on this urgent trip...and why John?"

"Whoa!" Ananta said to Zee as she brought him to a halt. Mireille and John followed suit, and all three horses pulled up side by side.

"You're with child, my child," Mireille said.

There was a long, silent pause.

Ananta giggled. "Very funny, Mother, but if you're talking about that night when John and I had sex in a tent during a rainstorm, you're quite wrong. I know my body quite well, I assure you, and I was not ovulating. I even reassured John at the time, and told him not to worry."

John exhaled in relief to realize it was a joke between mother and daughter, but as soon as his shoulders had relaxed from the shock, Mireille had more to say.

"That's not when the conception occurred," Mireille declared.

Ananta frowned.

Mireille went on, "The baby was conceived yesterday."

"That's impossible; I was—my body was—dead yesterday," John declared, casting a judgmental side-eye at Ananta.

"Hey, Romeo! Don't look at me like I whored myself out somehow —in between battling my twin brother and raising you from the dead!"

"You are correct, John," said Mireille. "Your physical body was quite dead. But hers was not. In order to come to her, you had to be in the same dimension she was in—you had to return to a *near*-death dimension. You were truly in limbo—your life force partly returned to your body, even as it remained partly in the spiritual realm. It was in that domain that you made love. A spark of life was initiated, and it remained inside Ananta once both of you fully returned to your physical bodies. You both are with child—a child who is incubating in Ananta's belly as we speak."

"I've never heard of such a thing!" Ananta replied in astonishment. "How could that…"

"This is insane!" John chimed in. "There's no way…I mean…how in the world…"

"That's just it," Mireille continued. "It's not of this world, and it's not of *that* world, either. When Ananta partially departed her physical body to find you in the spiritual realm and bring you back, you found each other in a portal of transition, and connected as one in the time you spent there together. Never in history has this ever happened!"

Mireille watched as Ananta placed her palms over her belly and looked down at it, shaking her head.

After eating a bowl of lemongrass soup, Sundara fell asleep on the bare floor of the monastery. The old monk compassionately laid a blanket over him, then folded another and placed it under his head. Sundara's dreams were a troubling jumble. Childhood memories and strange and illogical scenes with unrecognizable people were interspersed with horrendous scenes of unimaginable suffering. He awoke saturated with sweat.

"Your nap was restless," the old monk said softly. "My name is Bodhin. It means 'awakening.' "

"Yes, I know," Sundara replied. "My name is Sundara."

"Meaning 'beautiful,' " Bodhin responded. "Aptly named, young Sundara."

"I'm not as young as I look, and certainly not as beautiful as my name indicates, either."

The monk sensed a heavy, painful sadness in Sundara. "A time of great pain is a time of great transformation," he said.

"Transformation—I don't feel much like a work in progress," said Sundara dejectedly.

"I know who you are, Sundara," said Bodhin. "I heard tales of you when I traveled to Phugtal, or to neighboring villages and farms for necessities. So…my question to you is this: Should I be afraid of you?"

"No," Sundara replied, "at least not anymore. If you'd asked me a few days ago, I would have been obliged to give you a different answer."

"Very well, I'm not afraid. I can't say the same about you, though. You should be very scared of this big bad monk!" Bodhin laughed, revealing the gap where his front teeth used to be.

"You live here all alone. Why did you choose this life?" Sundara asked.

"I was born a Birla," said Bodhin.

"It's like being born a Rothschild," Sundara said.

"And then some," said Bodhin. "For centuries, a conglomerate of interconnected Birla family enterprises has controlled one of India's largest and most profitable business empires. Somehow I didn't inherit the family finance gene, or the greed gene. I wanted a much simpler life. I saw through the corruption of big business and commerce, and its entanglement with politics and religion, and I wanted no part of it."

Sundara thought grimly about the USF—the meshing of big business with politics and religion was its raison d'etre.

"When I was twenty-three, I was paralyzed in an automobile accident," Bodhin continued.

"I know how that is," said Sundara. "I was recently paralyzed from the neck down as well."

Bodhin's eyebrows elevated in surprise. "What happened?" he asked.

"Let's just say I got in a fight with my mother, well actually, with my father—and came out second best," Sundara replied. "How is it that you are now healed, Bodhin?"

"As is their custom, my family threw money at the problem—tons of it," he replied. "The Birla Foundation endowed chairs at the best universities in India, and state-of-the-art Birla neurospinal research facilities sprang up all over the country. I suppose those places might do somebody some good eventually, but even the latest innovations in conventional medicine didn't help me at all. I couldn't walk. I couldn't feed myself. I had to wear a diaper. That's when I turned inward and began to meditate on my spinal cord—and only on my spinal cord. I pictured it in my mind, rebuilding it axon by axon, dendrite by dendrite, synapse by synapse, all with the goal of regenerating the pieces of the spinal cord that would reconnect at the C1 or Atlas vertebra, where it had been severed."

"Like a cellular construction crew!" Sundara exclaimed.

Bodhin nodded and laughed. "Despite all the naysayers telling me I was crazy, I eventually began to regain some movement. I started by being able move my toe, then my foot, then my ankle. When I focused my meditation on intentionally rebuilding my body, it responded, and this was an astonishing thing, even to doctors—perhaps *especially* to doctors."

"Intentional healing is a natural scientific law," Sundara said. He was very familiar with the concept. When he was at the Society of Truth posing as new Elder Board member Michael Wright, he'd had an encounter with Jen Benson and Detective Sadie Dixon in Jen's condo. After Sadie had shot him and Jen had stabbed him with her kitchen knife, he'd removed the bullet and sewed up the knife wound with a turkey basting kit he had found in the cupboard. But that was just DIY first aid. Once he'd stabilized himself, he had purposefully willed his body to deal with his injuries, and healed very quickly.

"As I was starting to have some success," Bodhin continued, "I broadened my scope, and then the most astonishing thing happened."

"What do you mean, 'broadened your scope'?" Sundara asked.

"I expanded my healing intention to include other beings on the planet who had damaged bodies, envisioning and intending the rebuilding of their internal structures. That's when the healing of my own body accelerated," said Bodhin. "There was obviously a connection between one and the other, but when I told this exciting news to my family and my doctors, they didn't pay attention."

Sundara nodded. "I'm not surprised," he said. "And I suspect that their lack of reaction was quite deliberate. The powerful forces of establishment medicine and religion have worked for centuries to debunk intentional healing and naturopathy. Doctors and clergymen are still trying to make people believe that practices like applied kinesiology—some call it muscle testing—and energy medicine are demonic. Physicians, hospitals, and pharmaceutical companies don't want you to pursue wellness on your own, and they sure as hell don't want you to be successful. They make money when people are sick or injured. The system has been deliberately set up this way. I should know. They'd be out of business if everyone could heal themselves as you did."

Bodhin looked at Sundara with surprise. He hadn't expected his visitor to be so perceptive.

"Critical thinkers like you figured it out," Sundara continued. "Let me guess—that's why you decided to live a life of concentration, tranquility, and mindfulness, meditating on healing the world. Am I right?"

"Yes, but not because it would benefit me," Bodhin insisted. "I truly believe it benefits others—remotely, energetically. This is very satisfying to me."

Sundara listened intently, and with a large dose of remorse. Bodhin had spent his entire life intentionally meditating on healing other living things, and Sundara had done exactly the opposite for thousands of years. As the lord consul of the USF, he always put himself first. His ego had been all-consuming—the idea of directing his formidable healing powers toward anyone other than himself had never occurred to him.

"That's the missing piece," Sundara declared sadly, "doing it for others. No one teaches that. Spiritual gurus and motivational life coaches make millions of dollars teaching people to look inward, meditating on themselves, *their* passions, *their* vision boards, *their* healing. When has anyone ever made a vision board for the world—for the planet? This New Age phase is still steeped in a self-interest mindset. People are so sure they're being spiritual when they're actually being selfish. Once again, it's been set up this way—I should know."

Sundara turned solemn again, thinking back on his memories of the Phugtal monks when he was a little boy—before he turned seven, before his first sexual encounter with Helzar. He remembered playing hide and seek with them, and laughing himself silly until he couldn't breathe. He also thought back on how they had spent so many hours in meditation, and how they did only one thing at a time—slowly, deliberately, and completely. Looking at Bodhin's toothless grin, he remembered how they always smiled, no matter what. Above all, he remembered feeling loved by them.

"You know, Sundara, transitioning can be very simple," Bodhin said softly.

"Yeah right," Sundara scoffed. "I know you believe that it's that simple, and maybe it is for most people, but I'm *not* 'most people.' I'm carrying a lot more baggage than any other human being on the planet. The abuse, torture, betrayals, exploitation, acts of hatred...the bloodshed, the genocides. The unspeakable. And I know that I'm responsible—for all of it."

"You say to me, 'I know you *believe* that it's that simple,' " Bodhin began. "And I say to you, 'I know you *believe* it's complicated.' Whether it is simple or complicated is only in the belief of it. If you *can* believe it is simple, then...it *will* be simple."

Sundara hung his head in shame. He wished Bodhin would stop looking at him. "You really don't understand," he insisted. "For almost two thousand years, I was derailed. I killed, I maimed, I raped, I stole. I instigated and committed crimes too horrible to describe. I became the world's number one villain."

"Derailed...you make yourself sound like a trainwreck," said Bodhin.

"That's not wrong," Sundara replied.

"You say to me, 'I was derailed,' but I say to you, 'You were launched,' " said Bodhin. "Whether you were derailed or launched is only in the belief of it."

Sundara felt frustrated. "These are nothing more than word games," he said. "No matter what I say about my past, old monk, you're going to minimize it. Any attempt I make to describe what I've done will pale by comparison with the ghastly reality of it. And all you'll do is gloss over how horrible it was with some inscrutable aphorism."

"You sell me short, Sundara," Bodhin replied softly. "I do not invalidate your past at all. Exactly the opposite. I honor it because I know that the only reason you are here is because everywhere you have been —everything you have experienced—and yes, everything you have done, no matter how awful—has brought you to this place. If it weren't for all of it, you wouldn't be here. Your past was not a derailment, Sundara. It was a launching pad. And you landed here, with me."

Sundara looked at Bodhin. He felt that same kind of love and concern coming from him that he had felt from the Phugtal monks when he was a little boy.

"During transformation, you will first feel agony," Bodhin continued. "I suspect that's where you are now on your journey. That feeling will cause you to long for something different. Longing can feel empty because you long for what you do not know. I think you're experiencing that as well. But then, all of a sudden, in your longing, you will be launched into something new. It could be sudden clarity through an inspirational thought, a song, or the words from a friend...like me!" Bodhin grinned from ear to ear. "Agony, longing, and clarity—it's a process that is ancient and powerful, and it is the result of free will."

Sundara shook his head. "I never had free will, Bodhin," he said. "That's my problem. It was stolen from me when I was seven. This ancient and powerful process of free will is all new to me. I feel like I'm a seven-year-old kid all over again, imprisoned in this one thousand nine hundred and ninety-year-old body. And all of that body's tragic past is trapped within me—I'm stuck carrying a dreadful history that I can't get rid of, one that I had no freewill choice in making."

"The lightness and darkness of free will move together," Bodhin declared. "The old Hebrew word for 'longing' comes from the same root word as 'passion.' The place within where you feel dark heartbreak is exactly the same place that inspires you—the place where you vibrate with beauty. Don't think that your dark days of feeling agony and heartbreak are over. They will come again, but now, when the longing follows—and it will—free will is going to move you to ask yourself what you are longing for. And when clarity follows the longing—and it will—you can trust that you are being launched toward something sacred."

Sundara waited, hoping Bodhin had more wise and soothing words to say. Bodhin picked up on it and continued talking. "This world is one of immense contrasts," he said. "And now is both the best of times and the worst of times because free will has almost come full circle. Humanity's dark, daunting ability to inflict horrendous, unthinkable, and unspeakable pain and harm on others now perfectly mirrors its luminous, uplifting capacity to show love and compassion, harmony and kindness. It's a faceoff between two forces of equal strength and proportion."

"Is that what you mean by lightness and darkness of free will moving together?" asked Sundara.

"Just so," said Bodhin. "Throughout history, both the good and the bad, the black and the white, the sacred and profane have been humanity's freewill choices, collectively and individually. To be sure, powerful forces such as religion, politics, and business have tried to tip the scales of the choices we make. Religion has stripped people of critical thought, brainwashing them into believing that suffering is inflicted by a vengeful cosmic male god that demands penitence and absolute obedience as his price for a blessing. Politics has long goaded people into toxic nationalism, spawning territorial disputes, genocides, and hatred of "the other," instead of stimulating our freewill tendency to cooperate, negotiate, compromise, and seek peace. Commerce and the never-ending drive for success demands that people toil at work they hate. Why? Because they've been told that this is the tradeoff they must make to acquire the creature comforts they crave. They buy more and spend more, hoping their cars and homes and jewelry will insulate themselves from suffering and emptiness."

"Religion, politics and commerce...you got that right..." Sundara murmured while shaking his head.

Sundara felt his body soften for the first time since leaving the Phugtal treatment room. He trusted Bodhin with a pure, childlike trust that was foreign to him. He felt a very strong compulsion to tell Bodhin about the USF and his involvement in it—the religion, politics, and commerce—and how it launched him here to Cha, on this day.

Bodhin sensed that Sundara needed to unburden himself—it was his turn to talk. "Time for another exchange," he declared. "Let's put a kettle on. You fetch the water. I'll get the honey and herbs."

CHAPTER 16
AURA

When Yara saw that Sundara was gone, she came racing out of the monitor room and into the treatment room. "Impossible!" she cried. "He couldn't have just disappeared! And his clothes are gone!"

"Not impossible at all," Saji replied calmly. "His strength returned, as did his other abilities—abilities that are beyond most humans. But don't fret."

"Why not, Saji?" Yara replied. "Why shouldn't I be worried, not just for myself, but for Ananta and Mireille, and for humanity at large?"

Saji reached for Yara's hand. "Come with me," she instructed.

Yara kept talking as they returned to the monitor room. "There's nothing to see in here, Saji. His electrodes were torn off during the quake. Either that, or he ripped them off himself—but either way, there's nothing to monitor anymore."

Using generator power, Saji turned the Kirlian camera back on. After the monks had carried Sundara downstairs for treatment, the camera had been programmed to capture a photo of his aura every five minutes.

"Look," Saji said. "This first photo captured Sundara's aura immediately after he arrived, before any treatments were administered. What do you see?"

"I see black," Yara said flatly.

"Is that all?" asked Saji. She clearly was using this as a teaching moment for her young assistant.

"Looking closely, I also see a very small, very thin red line," Yara replied.

"Excellent. It was that tiny red sliver—the red of fiery passion—that gave me hope, because fiery passion can be guided. It can be shaped and expanded into something worthwhile. You should also know that the mightiness of a black aura is not necessarily negative—it can also indicate power for good. That was not the case with Sundara, of course, at least not when we began treatment. You can see that his aura shows no other caring, kind, loving, or healing colors—no blue, green, or purple—and definitely no gold."

Saji said nothing as she began scrolling through the photos. "Oh my God!" Yara gasped as she watched the colors change. "The red...it became dark pink!"

"The fact that it was changing was just the beginning. Look here..." Saji pointed to the next few images.

"Wow!" Yara exclaimed. "The black turned to indigo. The red sliver that turned cerise then changed to a glowing, radiant gold—and it's much larger!"

"Yes, and yet, he still has a lot of black," Saji added. "Sundara is still powerful, but now it's balanced, and can be used for good. Check the time stamp on this final photo. It corresponds exactly with the moment when Sundara called out 'Dad!' That's when the gold appeared. Do you know what this means?"

"I believe gold means he has divine entities protecting him, and that he's being guided to reach beyond himself. Is it possible that Easa, his father, is now guiding him?"

"I have no doubt," Saji replied.

"Then why did he run?"

"Because there's nothing else he could do, Yara," Saji answered. "That golden presence in his aura tells the entire story. With the treatments we gave him, Sundara was profoundly changed. It became impossible for him to go back to the man he'd been, the man who tried to decapitate his sister."

"So Sundara has become a Sibylline?" Yara asked.

Saji nodded. "In essence, yes," she said.

The astonished look on Yara's face brought Saji both delight and satisfaction. Guiding and inspiring the young monks had become one of her main duties, and it brought her great joy. "Only two paths remain for him," Saji continued. "Sundara can either fool the USF into believing that he's still on their side and take the organization down from within, or he can join forces with us and take it down from the outside."

"A double agent or a double-crosser," Yara replied. "Either choice is extremely dangerous."

Poonam was thrilled to see Ananta and John coming down the dirt road on horseback, together with another woman she did not recognize. She assumed they were returning to her home in Padum to give back the horses they had borrowed. Her children recognized Ananta and John right away, and ran out to greet them. Poonam watched and listened to the joyful reunion, but her children were fascinated by the beautiful woman who accompanied them. As soon as Mireille dismounted, the three young girls didn't hesitate to run their fingers through her long, silky dark-auburn hair and stare into her mesmerizing indigo-colored eyes.

"You are so beautiful," said the fourteen-year-old.

"Why thank you!" Mireille responded. "You are beautiful too, my *chhotee bahan*. What are all your names?"

All six children respectfully recited their names, beginning with Ved, the oldest son. Ved was a handsome twenty-year-old young man. He would have won the hearts of every teenage girl at the small village school, but because Poonam and her family were farmer-guardians—protectors of remote Sibylline territory and cultivators of the land—neither he nor his siblings attended there. That didn't mean they were ignorant. All were highly intelligent and sharp-witted, and Poonam and her husband made sure they received an excellent home-schooled education, using a curriculum developed by the monks at Phugtal.

"My name is Meree. What is your name?" the cute six-year-old girl asked.

"My name is Mireille," Ananta's mother responded warmly. "Our names sound very much alike, don't they!"

When Poonam heard Mireille say her name, she fainted.

"Oh my goodness!" Ananta exclaimed. She quickly ran to Poonam's side, tapping her cheeks with the palms of her hands and calling to her, "Poonam...Poonam..."

Poonam's eyes opened. "Ananta, is...is...is that your mother?"

"Yes, Poonam, it is Mireille—but please don't pass out again!" Ananta said with a smile.

As Poonam got to her feet and curtsied to Mireille, the children led the horses to the stable.

"Mireille, it is an honor to welcome you to my home," she said. "Ananta and I have been friends for a long time. That has been a great privilege for me...but now to meet you, the daughter of Adán and Eva! I only wish my husband could be here, but he's on duty at a Sibylline outpost, guarding the territory." Poonam stopped to catch her breath, then clasped her hands together in supplication. "Please forgive me, milady. I am so flustered and overwhelmed that I am being a poor host. May I offer you tea, yogurt, and bread? I have some excellent oil for the bread—and wine as well. This is a very special occasion."

Mireille knew the custom, and knew how important her visit was to Poonam. Although she very much wanted to hurry on toward the portal to Shangri-la, there was no way she would refuse this lovely Sibylline woman's hospitality. After the children had placed all three horses in their stalls and fed and watered them, they joined in the feast, asking Mireille question after question.

"So...how old are you really?"

"How come you don't look old?"

"What was it like when you were a little girl?"

Poonam and her husband had already taught the children most of the answers, but they sat enraptured as Mireille engaged them with her storytelling.

John looked at his watch. "I hate to break up this party, but we really should be taking off for Khalsi. It's a nine-hour drive—the Jeep is still here, I hope!" Mireille and Ananta looked at John with gratitude —neither of them had wanted to be the one to tell Poonam that it was time to leave.

"Oh yes!" Poonam replied. "It was stocked and fueled the evening you dropped it off so that it would be ready should you return. And look—you *did* return...with Mireille!"

Ved barely remembered Ananta—he was five when she had left for Brooklyn to infiltrate the Society of Truth. Now, however, he was old enough to drive, and he scurried off to retrieve the Jeep.

"Poonam, may I bother you for a few more supplies?" Mireille asked.

"Anything, milady."

"We're about to travel to cold weather, and—"

"The gateway to Shangri-la?" Poonam interrupted. "Oh my goodness! Yes, of course! Let's see...you'll need..."

Poonam ticked off all the outerwear the trio would need to endure the frigid weather high atop the glaciers on Belukha Mountain. She had just stored away the family's winter gear, but she instructed her children to bring the box up from the cellar.

Ved hopped out of the Jeep, then handed John the keys and a package wrapped in brown paper. "I made these for myself, but I want you to have them," he said with pride.

John was charmed by the young man's thoughtfulness. "Thank you, Ved," he replied. "I am honored to receive something you made for yourself."

John managed to keep a straight face as he opened the package, but it wasn't easy. Ved's gift was a pair of grotesque-looking oversized socks with chains sewn onto them in a web of crisscross patterns. The chains covered the entire sole and toe areas.

"I wear them when I go ice fishing. I hope they will help you, too. Pull them over the outside of your boots. They clank when you're walking, but they'll keep your feet from sliding," Ved explained.

"I'm sure they'll come in handy," said John with as much grace as he could muster. "Thank you again."

"I'm afraid we are leaving you with a horse problem," said Ananta. "Two of these horses need to be returned to Phugtal, and one of your horses is still at the monastery at Cha."

"We'll take care of it," Ved replied, sounding very much like the man of the house.

Goodbyes were accompanied by hugs and kisses. Poonam's hug

was interrupted by a ringing telephone. She ran into the house to answer, then quickly came running out of the house.

"John!" she called out as he turned the key in the ignition. "It's for you."

CHAPTER 17
DELIVERY TRUCK

Quedlinburg's Weisshotel Castle was a major tourist draw all year long, and one of the main attractions was its world-renowned restaurant, owned and operated by the Sibyllines. The chef changed the menu frequently to feature whatever was fresh and available in local markets. Between employees and staff, delivery trucks, and tourists, there was a daily bustle of traffic entering and leaving the grounds.

Beneath the castle, however, was a world that well-heeled restaurant diners and hotel guests never saw. Access points leading to ancient tunnels, catacombs, and subterranean parking beneath the castle were staffed by Sibylline guards, and were strictly off-limits to visitors. After recapturing it from the USF, Sibylline renovations included construction of a state-of-the-art laboratory and a computer nerve center, as well as secure bedroom suites for overnight Sibylline guests.

Other than those facilities, however, a large part of the area under the Weisshotel was deliberately left unimproved, including a major portion of one of the larger catacombs. That area became a large, ventilated terrarium known as the Eden Project. The plan had been for conditions in the terrarium to replicate the original habitat where the ancient Tigris and Euphrates rivers converged—the ideal environment in which to germinate the seeds of the Tree of Life. When Sibylline horticulturalists began having trouble maintaining equilibrium within the closed system, however, Min Yunghui was brought in to consult on the problem and take over leadership of the Eden Project. With the generations of ancient horticultural expertise that she inherited from her royal Korean family, she rebalanced the system to keep the terrarium healthy and thriving.

Min had been looking forward to overseeing the planting of those seeds, but that was no longer possible. With the information Greg had provided, she and Jacob knew that a USF assault was imminent. To protect the seeds and Ruth, the seed-bearer, they had to abandon the Eden Project and leave the Weisshotel grounds. The first part of their mission was to ensure they were not pursued—they'd figure out where they were going once they were safely away from the hotel.

Jacob steered Greg to a restaurant supply truck parked in the castle's basement garage. On the outside, it looked just like the ones that brought fresh produce to the Weisshotel restaurant. On the inside, however, it was fitted with padded benches along each side—it was used regularly to ferry Sibylline workers in and out of the castle without attracting attention.

Jacob opened the back doors of the truck and instructed Greg to take a seat, then secured his ankle to the metal leg of the bench. "I'm going back inside to help Min with Ruth," he said. "Wait here."

"Like I have a choice!" Greg called after him as Jacob went back into the catacombs. He was alone in the truck for a half hour before he saw Min pushing Ruth in a wheelchair, heading in his direction.

"Where's Jacob?" Min asked when she approached the truck.

"You don't know?" Greg replied. "He said he was going back to help you with Ruth before the USF showed up, but that's as much as I know."

Min tried to assist Ruth up into the truck, but Ruth pushed her away, insisting that she could do it herself. "It's my shoulder that got shot, not my legs," she declared as she defiantly rose unassisted from the wheelchair. Min quickly but firmly grabbed her under the arm—in the Weisshotel treatment room, Min had given her an IV full of concentrated curcumin, vitamin C, amino acids, trace minerals, and cannabinoids, along with antibiotics. She'd also received a microdose of nano-THC to relax her for the trip, and it had made her stoned and a bit wobbly.

Min helped her lie down on one of the padded benches and placed a pillow under her head. After folding the wheelchair and stowing it to the side, she returned to check Ruth's vital signs. "Comfy?" she asked.

"Oh yes," Ruth replied as she patted the black drawstring bag around her neck. "Both of us are."

"Did everyone make it out?" Greg asked.

"Everyone down below, yes," Min answered. "There's no need to evacuate the hotel and restaurant. It's a public place with lots of tourists—there's nothing the USF wants up there."

"You're right," Greg agreed. "They'll be focused on the terrarium and locating the seeds, which they know will be underground. Besides, they won't want to call attention to themselves with a bunch of tourists who might start asking questions."

Min was beginning to text Jacob when he emerged from the tunnel into the parking area. "Where were you?" Min asked.

"I went back in to make sure everyone was evacuated safely, and to help you with Ruth," Jacob replied.

Min gave him a puzzled look. "Then why didn't I see you?" she asked as she noticed a pistol in a shoulder holster under his arm. "And why the weapon?" Min inquired. "You know how I feel about them."

"Why the interrogation, Minny?" he shot back. "This place is about to get overrun by the USF's finest. My assignment is to protect you and Ruth, and you're telling me you're creeped out by this? Here—take a better look." Jacob pulled the weapon out of its holster and waved it around in the air.

"Please put that away," said Min.

"Let's talk a little about hypocrisy," said Jacob as he pointed his pistol at Greg.

"Glock 19, I see," said Greg.

"Minny, you certainly didn't have a problem cuffing this guy upside the head with his own piece—Walther PPK, right?" Jacob began. "You Sibyllines are all about Kyndeness, but when it comes to protection, it always falls to those of us who are packing. Isn't that right, Greg? That's what I'm here to do, Minny—to fiercely protect you...and Ruth."

"What do you mean 'You Sibyllines'?" she asked. "Whose side are you on? And by the way, what's on your ear?"

Jacob brushed his left ear with his hand and brought it to his face.

"A little blood is all. I must've scratched it on something while I was rushing to help everyone out."

Rushing to help who out? Min wondered. *It wasn't me or Ruth...* "What's that noise?" she said aloud.

An insistent buzzing was coming from Jacob's pocket. "Well, well, well," Jacob said as he pulled out Greg's cell phone. "+91 international calling prefix—looks like you have a fan in India. Answer it and put it on speaker. I'm dying to know who this is..."

"This is Greg," he answered.

"This is Saji at Phugtal monastery," said the voice on the other end of the line. "And this is a three-way call. I have John Matthews on with us as well. He's in Padum with Ananta and Mireille. They are headed to Shangri-la."

Min straightened in her seat and stared at Greg. She recognized Saji's voice and not only knew who Mireille was, but also knew John Matthews and Ananta—she'd flown them from New York to Ladakh, along with duplicates of the Society's child abuse files and the first chapter of Mireille's true history of humankind. Jacob's eyes darted back and forth between Min and Greg, but he said nothing.

"Hey, Greg!" John exclaimed. "How do you rate, you filthy bastard? While I was stuck being the house mouse at a desk job in Society headquarters, you were out there being a fake ninja for the USF."

"Yeah, but the upside is that you had a beautiful woman to look at every day, and then you got to traipse through the Himalayas with her," Greg countered. "I, on the other hand, found myself cloaked in bat guts, inching my way through foul-smelling, pitch-black caverns."

"Enough, both of you," said Saji firmly. "After his battle with Mireille, we have every reason to believe that we successfully deprogrammed Sundara. Kirlian images taken before, during, and after his treatment show profound changes, and the final photo is evidence of his transformation."

"Where is he now?" Greg asked.

"I don't know," said Saji.

"Wait...what?" John exclaimed.

"He escaped during an earthquake," she replied.

"He escaped? How the hell, Saji?"

"Think about it," Saji replied calmly. "If you were Sundara, and you had transformed, what options would you have at that point?"

The line went silent for a few moments.

"She's right, John," Greg said. "We know enough about these oversized USF elite leaders to know they are telepathic. Look…I went through hell and back learning how to rewire my energetic field so that I could get close enough to get a reading on exactly what they're up to, not to mention I had to wear the dead parts of…yeah…I already told you that. I still can't believe I didn't get caught, but I never had eyes on the beings themselves. If Saji's treatments really did transform Sundara, he's figured out that he has to be the one who takes the lead in bringing down the USF—from the inside or the outside. Either way, he had to get out of Phugtal to do it."

Min was watching Jacob as his face became increasingly alarmed. She assumed her own face wore a similar expression as she raced to connect the dots. *Wow!* she thought. *Jacob didn't believe him when he said he was a double agent, but this is proof that Greg was telling the truth. I should have figured that out—the idea that this guy I went to acupuncture school with would defect to the USF never did make sense. Caverns—what caverns? And how do Greg and John know each other?*

Min grabbed the phone out of Greg's hands. "John and Saji, this is Min Yunghui, the pilot who flew John and Ananta to Ladakh. I've also transported Mireille to Belukha Mountain when she traveled to Shangri-la. I am the lead botanist of the Eden Project here at the Weisshotel Castle, where the seeds were supposed to be planted—and where we captured Greg in his double-agent mode as a USF agent."

"Hello, Min," Saji said. "You were going to be my next call. What do you mean 'supposed to be planted'?"

"Thanks to Greg, we are aware that the USF knows or strongly suspects the seeds are here—we expect an assault on the castle's underground facilities to begin anytime now," Min replied. "For the safety of our staff, all Sibyllines involved in the Eden Project have been evacuated. Only Jacob, my bodyguard, Greg, and Ruth, the seed-bearer, are still here, and we're headed out as soon as we hang up. I await your instructions."

"Mireille, Ananta, and John are on their way to Ladakh," said Saji. "They'll be flown to Tyungur from there. Since you already know the drill, meet them in Tyungur, transfer them to the ski plane, and fly them to the glacier on Belukha Mountain."

"Wait...*all* of them??" Min asked incredulously. "Mireille is taking Ananta *and* John with her to Shangri-la?"

"Yes," Saji replied without elaborating. "How quickly can you get to Tyungur?"

"We're about four hours from Frankfurt International Airport," Min said. "There's a Sibylline Dassault Falcon 8X hangared there. Fueled to the max, it should be able to handle the eleven-hour flight to Tyungur. The plane will make it just fine, but I don't know about me—it's been a while since I've had a full night's sleep."

"I can spell you," Greg offered.

"And me and my friendly Glock here will be watching!" Jacob interjected as he patted his shoulder holster. There was an uncharacteristically menacing tone in his voice.

"Jacob, really?" Min said as she rolled her eyes.

"That's fine. I'm sure Jacob sees it as part of his patented 'fierce protection plan' for you and Ruth," Greg said mockingly. "I have no problem flying at gunpoint, but do the math, Jake."

"It's Jacob, not Jake," Jacob said brusquely.

"As I said, do the math, dude," Greg continued. "If a weapon is discharged inside an aircraft and the target is the pilot, whatever happens to one person pretty much happens to everyone."

"Good, then we have a plan," Saji said.

"Yes, it's settled," said Min. "Greg and I will spell one another in the cockpit during the marathon flight to Tyungur. I'll handle the ski plane trip to Belukha Mountain, but what do I do with my passengers...and what do we do with the seeds? Wouldn't they be safer in Shangri-la?"

"Not possible," Saji replied. "The USF has long believed we wanted to get the seeds to safety in Shangri-la. We've been happy to let them think that, but it was never the plan. The seeds must be subject to humankind's free will, including the struggle for ownership. Shangri-la is not the place for them."

"Whatever we do, I suggest we do it fast," Greg said. "When the USF overruns the castle and doesn't find me or the seeds, they'll know something's up."

"Surely you're not suggesting that you get to go to Shangri-la!" Jacob said.

"Surely I'm not," Greg said quickly. "Look, big guy...I know we didn't start out on a good footing, and yes, I fired the bullet that winged you in the shoulder, but you gotta let it go, dude! I'm not the enemy. I never was. We're on the same team."

"Okay...yeah...sure. Same team," Jacob snorted.

"And you can take your hand off your holster now, Jacob," Min added.

Saji took charge. "Min, we don't have time to arrange for protection of any drop-offs in Frankfurt, so you'll need to take everyone with you to Tyungur. When you arrive, bring Ruth, Jacob, and Greg to the Sibylline lodge—I'll have accommodations prepared for them. Then return to the hangar and rendezvous with Mireille, Ananta, and John. The ski plane will be waiting for you. Land on the Belukha Mountain glacier and drop them near the stealth gateway to Shangri-la. Then return to Tyungur as quickly as possible."

"Stealth gateway?" Ruth piped up. "Sounds mys-teeeer-ious!" she added with a giggle. She was clearly still stoned from the THC.

"You're right, Ruth," said Saji without mocking her. "It is mysterious, and it's the energetic bridge that leads to Shangri-la."

"I'd like to accompany Minny..." Greg began, "ah, I mean Min...on the flight to Belukha Mountain. I won't be needed at the lodge in Tyungur—Jacob will be protecting Ruth. Flying Mireille, John, and Ananta to the glacier is potentially dangerous—not just for our three travelers, but for the gateway itself. Shangri-la is our last, best Sibylline sanctuary. If anyone followed them or tipped off the USF about the location of the portal, it could be overrun and lost forever. I'd like to volunteer to protect Mireille, John, and Ananta—and Min, of course. All of them are quite capable of defending themselves, but if there's some kind of emergency en route, I think it would be wise to have another pilot on the ski plane."

"Good call, Greg," Saji agreed.

"Then that's a wrap," John replied as everyone hung up.

Min and Greg looked at one another and nodded, then looked at Jacob. He was grim and nervous. "You need either a nap or an attitude adjustment, Jacob. Pick one," said Min. "I think your shoulder injury and that ear wound are getting the best of you. We all have a lot to process, and we're gonna be busy."

"You're right, Min," Jacob replied. "A nap sounds great. If you don't mind, I think I'd like to sit up front with the driver."

Jacob stood up to leave, but Min stopped him.

"You're not leaving Greg attached to the bench," she insisted. "Unlock him. Now." Jacob begrudgingly set Greg's ankle free and then reached for the roll-up rear door.

"Unh-uh," Min said. "Wallet, too."

Jacob tossed the wallet onto Greg's lap.

"How about my cell phone?" Greg said. "You never know when I'm gonna get the urge to call John or Saji."

Anger flashed in Jacob's eyes as he fiercely hurled the phone at Greg. Greg reached high above his head to intercept it. Otherwise it would have banged into the side panel of the truck. "Wild pitch," he said. "I was a catcher in Little League. I don't think baseball is your sport, Jake."

Jacob stormed out the back door, slammed it shut, and climbed into the shotgun seat next to the driver. Instead of closing his eyes to rest, however, he frantically began sending text messages. The truck drove up the Deliveries Only ramp, then exited the property and made its way onto the main thoroughfare.

Back in the cargo area, Ruth had fallen asleep. Min and Greg looked at each other and giggled. Then they both started talking at once.

"You always—" Min began.

"I had a secret—" Greg said.

"You first," said Min.

"I had a secret crush on you," Greg said softly, "but I was too shy, and you were too beautiful and intelligent. I was so completely flustered and intimidated that I blew off graduation. I returned to my family in Canada, and then we all moved back to Slovakia—my grandparents were getting on in years and needed help. My mother took care of them, and I started Sibylline training. That's where John and I met —both of our families are descendants of Slovakian Sibyllines."

"That explains how you and John bonded and become such good friends," Min said.

"Your turn," said Greg.

"I remember in college, I loved your voice," she said.

"That's weird, because I hardly ever said anything," Greg replied.

"True, but when you *did* speak, your voice drew me in. It not only had calmness and warmth, but the words you said mattered. They were always well-chosen and meaningful," Min recalled. "I found myself wishing that you spoke up more often."

"Really? Like what?" Greg asked.

"Well…for example…Remember that one class we had that taught how acupuncture treats disorders by direct acupoints to organs? You raised your hand—to everyone's surprise—and suggested a theory that the acupoint first activates the corresponding brain cortex, changing the chemicals released to the sick body part, affecting pH, etc. It was a whole new paradigm."

"Yeah, I remember that."

"I should have recognized your voice when we captured you…I'm mean, when you *allowed* yourself to be captured, but your appearance had changed so much since our acupuncture days that I didn't make the connection…"

"That's me, Greg Blunt, master of disguises," he said with a grin.

"Wait!" Min exclaimed. "Did you just say that you had a secret crush on me?"

"I was wondering how long it would take you to pick up on that," Greg said as he checked the time on his cell phone. "Two minutes and thirteen seconds." He felt his face getting warm as he watched her gaze at his face—first his eyes, then his mouth, then back to his eyes. *Does this mean she wants me to kiss her?* he asked himself.

CHAPTER 18
DELUGE

Once they poured themselves a cup of the sweetened herbal hyssop tea, Sundara began his story.

"Many cultures have a great flood legend," he began, "but the earth did not experience just one episode. Deglaciation—the melting of the polar ice cap—caused multiple inundations across the globe, but the one that first comes to mind is the one described in the Bible. It occurred about seven millennia ago. It wasn't actually a *global* flood, but the stories describe it that way because, to the people who experienced it, the water covered their then-known world, which centered on what we now call the Black Sea."

"Hundreds if not thousands of years earlier, the earth's climate had warmed, causing the Black Sea to dry up," Sundara continued. "The Bosphorus Strait, which connects it to the Sea of Marmara and then through the Dardanelles to the Aegean, had become blocked. The newly revealed soil on what had been the seabed was abundant in nutrients. Population centers arose around the fertile fields as farmers worked the mineral-rich ground.

"All of those settlements, however, were doomed. As the polar ice cap melted, water poured into the North Atlantic, and the knock-on effect rippled through every body of water on earth. Huge volumes of water pushed through the Strait of Gibraltar, elevating the water level of the Mediterranean, which in turned raised the sea level of the Aegean and then of the Sea of Marmara. When the waters inevitably broke through the bottleneck at the Bosphorus, it wasn't gradual—they gushed through the strait and surged into the Black Sea like a tidal wave or tsunami. And there you have it—a *global* flood. Most ancient cultures have a version of this story, but the basic plot is the same: Massive flood kills all, but a few lucky people escape."

"My parents believed in a great flood," Bodhin said. "In their Hindu belief, the god Vishnu—the god who creates, protects, and transforms the universe—warns the first man, Manu, of an impending flood and advises him to build a giant boat. I guess Manu symbolizes those lucky few survivors."

"There were a couple of others who were lucky as well," said Sundara. "But they weren't fully human. They were giants—monsters, in fact. My mother named them 'Nephilim,' meaning, 'the fallen.' "

"Giants, huh?" Bodhin responded, smiling.

"I know; I know," said Sundara. "It's a stretch, right?"

"I may not be that elastic," said Bodhin skeptically.

"I get it," Sundara responded with a grin. "It sounds improbable."

"So, who are these giants, and where did they come from?" Bodhin asked.

"The science of genetics was a long way off, but these early agrarian societies had already figured out that physical beauty was a trait passed down in families," Sundara began.

"And even back then, being attractive was an asset, whether you were male or female," said Bodhin, "just like now."

"Handsome men and beautiful women became the parents of the prettiest offspring—that's just how it had always worked..." Sundara continued. "Until these baby monsters began showing up. The most attractive young women in the settlement, who should have been giving birth to gorgeous children, started giving birth to freakish-looking babies instead. They had big heads and strange hair, but no genitals. Many horrified parents and grandparents killed them at birth, thinking they were perhaps a curse, but there were some mothers who naturally bonded with their babies—grotesque or not."

"Isn't that what you'd want a mother to do?" Bodhin asked.

"Generally, yes," Sundara replied, "but allowing these infants to survive was unfortunate—they grew to be about nine feet tall as adults. They were slightly telepathic and very strong, which made matters worse. The bigger they got, the more they abused their size and brute physical strength. They terrorized entire communities—they stole, they vandalized, and they raped indiscriminately—men, women, boys, girls, animals...anything that lived and moved."

"How could they rape if they didn't have genitals?" Bodhin asked.

Sundara sipped of his tea as he recalled his own personal sexual experiences with Helzar, and pondered how much he could bring himself to explain. "A penis...a vagina...any body orifice...combined with a giant finger...some paraphernalia," Sundara replied, sparing Bodhin the graphic details.

"So, just because *they* didn't have genitals, they still had sexual cravings and could satisfy them on others' genitals?" Bodhin asked.

Sundara's shoulders sagged. "That's an understatement," he said. "Their sex acts were filled with anger and resentment because, as hybrids, they were unable reproduce. But yes...sex was very gratifying to them, not just for their own intense sexual pleasure, but also because they used it to exert power and control."

"I see," Bodhin said, knowing it was time to let the matter drop. He was very aware that Sundara knew more than he was saying, and that it was somehow both painful and very personal. *Don't push the river*, he thought to himself. *He'll tell me when he's ready.*

"As the southern reaches of the Bosphorus farmlands started getting boggy, a few wise and insightful folk took that as an omen that it was time to split. Others ignored the signs completely. Still others stayed put, unwilling to abandon their thriving crops, but they hedged their bets by building a boat, just in case."

"Thus the story of Manu in Hinduism, and Noah in the Old Testament," Bodhin said.

"Yes, as well as the epics of Gilgamesh and Atra-Hasis, and other ancient myths," Sundara replied. "When the waters came flooding into the Black Sea, most beings drowned, including the Nephilim. Although they were strong and agile, and could climb and just about pull a tree from the ground by its roots, there was one thing they couldn't do—they couldn't swim."

"Why not?" asked Bodhin.

"Their bodies were too dense, and the floodwaters overtook them before they could flee on foot. All but two of them drowned. One who survived had been roaming high in the Küre Mountains—in what is now modern-day Turkey—not far from the shore of the Black Sea. Observing the catastrophe taking place below him, he quickly took refuge in a cave and sealed the entrance, preserving a supply of oxygen and walling out the flood. He remained holed up there until the waters receded."

"And the other one?"

"The other one had long made a habit of exploring," said Sundara. "When the flood rushed into the Black Sea, he was far away in a mountainous part of India we now call Himachal Pradesh, not far from the site where the Phugtal Monastery would be built."

"So, pretty much next door," said Bodhin, pointing toward the southeast in the general direction of the monastery. "And...did anyone ever find out the reason for the grotesque births of these...these Nephilim giants?"

Sundara nodded grimly. "This is where everyone's belief systems are going to need a big adjustment, but bear with me. This is the truth as I understand it."

"I believe you, Sundara," said Bodhin. "In our time together, I have come to realize that although you may not tell me everything, what you do tell me is truthful."

"The handsome fathers of these hybrid monsters weren't human at all," Sundara continued. "They were extraterrestrials inhabiting human male bodies. During the flood, when they realized that those bodies were about to drown, they abandoned them. Their wives and their hideous offspring watched as these partly transparent avatar-ish beings emerged from their earthly skin casings—like butterflies leaving their cocoons—and..."

"And what?" Bodhin asked.

Sundara snapped his fingers. "And dematerialized. Just like that, they vanished out of sight."

"How do we know this?" asked Bodhin.

"A few of the Black Sea farmers who were riding out the flood in boats witnessed the transformation, which is why there are allusions to it in some historical writings, like the Bible," Sundara explained.

"So...the fathers were alien, not human," said Bodhin.

"Exactly," replied Sundara. "That's why their progeny were so large and grotesque. They were half-human from their mothers, and half-alien from their fathers—making them sterile hybrids without the ability to reproduce. Although the Nephilim didn't inherit their fathers' ability to dematerialize, they did get their telepathic capability, at least some of it, which is how the two survivors found one another once the floodwaters receded. When they realized that they were the only two left of their kind, they got pissed off. And they're still pissed off today—seven thousand years later."

"That's a long time to stay mad," said Bodhin. "How did they channel their anger?"

"Revenge, pure and simple," said Sundara. "They devised a plan to use their power and longevity to destroy human free will and take ownership of the planet. They've been on a rampage to exert control over humankind and over the earth's resources. They've had a lot of success, but they didn't do it alone—they had help."

"Let me guess—their alien fathers came back in human form."

"Close, very close, Bodhin," said Sundara. "The alien fathers did come back, but not as materialized humans. They realized they could manipulate people more easily if they remained invisible. They devised three mechanisms of control. The first was paid slavery—the euphemism we use is business. To stay alive and put food on the table, everyone is supposed to get a paying job and work hard—and all that effort keeps people too tired to pay attention to everything else that's going on. The second device was governance, aka politics and international relations. Once boundaries are drawn, squabbles over who rules which land and which resources are all but guaranteed to create strife—often violent strife. The third apparatus was fear of an all-knowing, all-seeing judgmental god—what we call religion."

"Business, politics, and religion..." said Bodhin. "Pretty much everything falls into one or more of those categories."

"Exactly," said Sundara. "The Nephilim and their alien fathers have used these three levers of power, together and separately, to keep humankind in chaos for thousands of years. It's not that every part of each of those systems is entirely bad—the world has expanded because of them. But perhaps it would be better to ask whether the world would have expanded in good ways anyway—without them."

"I believe that without organized religion, humans would have discovered and aligned with their Source—their Creator—on their own," said Bodhin. "It seems likely that they would have 'found god' within themselves a lot sooner."

"I have to agree, Bodhin," said Sundara. "Moreover, I suspect that you've identified the reason why many branches of Christianity find something nefarious in practices like meditation—and even in yoga."

"The empty mind is the devil's playground," replied Bodhin with a wry smile. "But tell me, Sundara, how did you yourself come to know about these surviving Nephilim?"

"That was the beginning of my derail...I mean...launching pad," Sundara sighed. "I met the first Nephilim in a cave near Phugtal. I named him Helzar."

Sundara's face clouded as he recalled that first encounter, and in that moment he decided to disclose the rest of the truth to Bodhin. "As a child, I was programmed through sexual trauma," he began.

"That must've been horrible for you, Sundara," Bodhin said softly.

"I didn't realize how horrible it was until much, much later," Sundara replied. "I was a seven-year-old boy when it started. I was a very inquisitive child—I was curious about everything, including what the giant was doing to me. Repeated child sodomy damaged the nerves at the base of my spine, and caused a neurological realignment in my brain."

"Did that make you angry?" Bodhin asked.

"No, and that's part of what was so reprehensible about it," said Sundara. "That neurological realignment colored how I viewed what was happening to me. As I was growing up, I thought of these recurring traumatic sexual experiences as something special that Helzar and I shared. To me they were bonding rituals, not abuse."

"I'm so sorry," said Bodhin.

"I have to confess that I was drawn to the idea that these beings were powerful," Sundara admitted. "By that time, the Nephilim and their alien fathers had control over much of the 'civilized' world."

"How did that happen?" asked Bodhin.

"About two hundred years after the flood, they had already sexually traumatized many carefully chosen young boys, and groomed them as future leaders of business, politics, and religion."

"Their three levers of power," said Bodhin.

"One of them was named Nimrod. He was able to convince just about everyone that they could actually achieve God's blessing and entrance into heaven. All they had to do was follow his orders as God's representative in the flesh, and build his renowned city, including an immense tower. He made himself quite the hero, and kept the Nephilim's desires fed. But then the inevitable happened."

"What was that?" Bodhin asked.

"Free will intervened. A group of people mobilized in secret to thwart Nimrod's efforts. Most, but not all, the rebels were women, and they were working under the direction of my mother, Mireille. The women were prophetesses, known as Sibyls, and they began spreading the idea that no individuals should willingly sacrifice their own free will, passions, and enjoyment of life—no matter what—but especially not for a promise as bogus as the idea that abject obedience to men buys you a first-class ticket into the afterlife."

"Sounds a lot like heresy," said Bodhin.

"More like insurrection," Sundara replied.

"Same-same," said Bodhin, "or at least that's what two of your levers, politics and religion, would tell you. And this group of rebels wasn't afraid to openly challenge Nimrod?"

"Oh, they didn't go public," said Sundara. "They stayed under the radar until they were too numerous and too powerful to ignore. They called themselves Sibyllines. Some did end up dying for the cause, but not before they reclaimed possession of their free will, took a hike from their day jobs building Nimrod's tower/stairway to heaven—a monument to the male ego if ever there was one—and scattered."

"Things went badly for Nimrod after that," Sundara continued. "He was defeated and eventually beheaded by Esau, Abraham's grandson. I wish I could say that humankind learned from this experience, but we did not. We continued trying to make our own lives better by enslaving others. After Nimrod came the Egyptians and their pharaohs, but the Nephilim and their extraterrestrial masters were still the power behind the scenes. The Egyptians deployed thousands of slaves to build the pyramids, but they used alien engineering to design them. How else would they have been able to erect those massive structures with such precise, closely fitted stonework? The Nephilim and their alien masters —or Maestros, as I now call them—also pushed the Egyptians into keeping up the practice of child sodomy, convincing them that it opened the third eye."

"The third eye is the ajna, or brow chakra," said Bodhin. "It is the gateway to higher consciousness. Whether that eye is open or closed has nothing to do with child abuse."

"The Egyptian dynasties fell—all of them—and throughout history, that's pretty much how it has gone ever since," said Sundara. "There have been kings and emperors and czars and pashas and dictators, all of whom have tried to make humans completely subservient and obedient to their command—and the Nephilim and the Maestros have been behind them all. They've often been on the brink of gaining absolute control, but they never quite got there."

"Why is that?" asked Bodhin.

"Because free will got in the way every time," said Sundara. "And the Sibyllines have had a lot to do with that."

"But the giants haven't given up," said Bodhin. "Or have they?"

"No, they haven't," said Sundara. "The battle between those using power and fear in relentless pursuit of self-aggrandizement and those using love, kindness, and goodness to expand our existence has never been more intense. One group is led by the Nephilim and the Maestros. The other group is led by Mireille, my mother, and Ananta, my sister."

"The women in your family are the leaders of the Sibyllines?" asked Bodhin.

"They are. And until yesterday, I had been doing everything in my power to stop them. Just as Mireille and Ananta mobilized the Sibyllines, the Nephilim created the United Soponium Fellowship—I was the lord consul. I helped the giants use religion, politics, and business to subvert free will. For a while, I was narcissistic enough to think I controlled the organization, but I was just the lead puppet. Over the centuries, I became very good at my job—and then I made it worse."

"How?" Bodhin asked. "How could you have possibly made it worse?"

"When I was programmed to obey the Nephilim, they knew I was a huge asset. I was the son of Mireille and Easa, with a body of knowledge no one else had. My biggest mistake—my greatest act of recklessness and one that I can never take back and never put right—was telling the giants about the seeds of the Tree of Life. Ever since then, the giants have stopped at nothing to..." Sundara stopped speaking abruptly.

"What is it, Sundara?" Bodhin inquired.

Sundara's eyes widened and his posture straightened.

"An epiphany?" Bodhin asked.

"You could say that," Sundara replied. "The USF has invented an implantable artificially intelligent microchip. This is a chip that can learn on its own, calculate the best possible options, and then make independent decisions."

"Sounds remarkable!" Bodhin responded.

"Yes," said Sundara, "but the way those chips are set up to be used suggests we humans are headed for a very dark future. The chips are programmed to weigh options and make decisions that advance specific USF agendas. I have no doubt that they've been set up to help to destroy free will."

Bodhin smiled, much to Sundara's dismay. "Why are you smiling, old monk?" he asked. "There can be no good news for human beings in the destruction of free will."

"That is true," Bodhin replied. "I am smiling because I think maybe that's the sacred place you're being launched to, Sundara. Could it be that you are the one whose task it will be to stop them?"

Sundara smiled back at his friend, then nodded as he stood to leave. "If that's my job, I'd better get started," he said.

"Your mother and sister only took one of the two horses," Bodhin replied. "Please take the other."

"Thank you, Bodhin. I'll take you up on your offer."

Bodhin brought out the saddle and reins, then helped Sundara prepare the horse for travel.

Sundara bowed and placed the palms of his hands together. "I'll never forget you, my dear friend," he said as he climbed into the saddle.

"Nor I you. Safe journeys, Sundara." Bodhin bid him farewell, and handed him an amaranth and sorghum cake wrapped in cloth for the trip.

CHAPTER 19
AFTERMATH

Nelson watched from the passenger seat as Kruger wedged himself behind the wheel of Silverman's Tesla. Silverman had been slight and about 5 foot 8, and his seat had automatically adjusted to his body as soon as the door opened. Kruger was 6 foot 2 and very muscular. After shoehorning himself into the vehicle, he groped for the control that would push the seat backward. Kruger was wearing bright-blue nitrile surgical gloves. The lumpy outline of a hastily applied rolled gauze bandage could be seen under his right glove.

The black Dodge Ram with Silverman's body bag in the truck bed drove past Nelson and Kruger and then pulled over, waiting for the Tesla to catch up. As Kruger was about to turn from Pearl Street onto High Street, heading toward the Brooklyn Bridge on-ramp, the car suddenly jumped toward the curb and sideswiped a parked car.

"Holy crap! I hope no one saw that!" Devon exclaimed. "Watch where you're going, Kruger! If your hand hurts too much to drive, say so. I'll take the wheel."

"You think *I* did that, Nelson?" Bozz shot back. "That was an earthquake! Look around, you idiot! Everything's still swaying. I'm going to pull over, in case there's an aftershock."

As they sat anticipating another tremor, Nelson fired off a text message to João Moreira, the driver of the Dodge Ram: *Do not get on the Brooklyn Bridge. Await further instructions.* Once he sent the text, a smug grin spread across his face.

"What the hell, Nelson?" Kruger asked. "We're in a stolen car with a left side that's all stove in—a car that belongs to a dead body in a truck bed that's a couple of blocks ahead of us—and we're here like sitting ducks, waiting to see if there's going to be another damned earthquake. In a few seconds, the streets are going to be swarming with cops and emergency vehicles. Our situation is nothing to smile about."

"Relax, Kruger. The earthquake has given us a tremendous opportunity," said Nelson. "The Society faithful might even call it Providential."

"What do you mean?" Bozz asked.

"I know how you're going to ditch the car," he replied.

"How *I'm* going to ditch the car?" Kruger asked.

"Rendezvous with Moreira at the Tompkins Housing Projects," Nelson ordered. "Take a couple of whacks at the Tesla, then take off. The macacas who live there will make quick work of finishing what you started."

Kruger bristled at the racial slur, but said nothing. *Macacas like me*, he thought to himself.

He'd already taken a dislike to Nelson when he'd been summoned to the ninth floor of Society headquarters to help him get Silverman's corpse out of the men's room. Killing Silverman had been completely unnecessary—and Nelson had made a mess of it. Then he'd had to break Fitzgerald's neck—in public—after Nelson saw him watching as they loaded the body into the truck. All in all, Nelson seemed to be pretty damned cavalier about making him do his dirty work—and now he was walking away?

"You make it sound like you've got other plans," said Kruger.

"I do," said Nelson as he unfastened his seatbelt and opened the passenger door.

"You're keeping your hands clean and leaving *me* to deal with Silverman's carcass?" Kruger inquired angrily. "*And* you're leaving me to take the chance that we might be seen trashing the Tesla?"

"It's the fuckin' Projects, Kruger," said Nelson with exasperation, as if he were talking to the class dunce. "You got gangs, you got drug dealing, you got five-dollar-crack whores turning tricks in the shrubbery. Trashing cars is the least of what the jungle bunnies do there."

Jungle bunnies? Bozz felt his cheeks flush with anger, but willed himself not to respond—a credit to his USF Cell training. "Where do you want me to deposit Silverman?" he asked in as neutral a voice as he could muster.

"Take Hymie to the Croton Dam and toss him," said Nelson. "It should go without saying—but I'm going to say it anyway—that you need to dump the body on the reservoir side—*above* the spillway."

"And what the fuck might you be doing that's so bloody important?" Kruger asked.

"You seem to have forgotten that there are two stiffs to deal with," Nelson replied condescendingly. "I must go console the newly widowed Lucy Fitzgerald. Part of that effort will involve making elaborate funeral arrangements for her husband, Paul." Devon slowly shook his head from side to side in a feigned expression of sorrow. "So sad. Poor man fell down and broke his neck during the earthquake. Pity."

Oh, so it's that way, is it? Kruger thought. *Nelson is a bigoted blame-shifting shitweasel. If the cops ever interrogate him about Fitzgerald's death—and why wouldn't they, since it's the third fatality on the Elder Board in a very short time—he'll finger me for the murder in a heartbeat.*

Nelson opened the door and got out. "More importantly," he continued, "I must set up a meeting with Josh Krushing's people—don't want the quake to give them an excuse to start second-guessing the deal. Text me when the Jew is taken care of."

"Ah, Nelson?" said Kruger.

"What is it now?" he replied impatiently.

"I can't do any of this shit if you walk away," said Kruger.

Nelson whirled to stare at Kruger. "Excuse me?" he said incredulously. Kruger's attitude was sounding a lot like insubordination—or outright mutiny.

"Can't go anywhere without Silverman's key fob," said Kruger.

Nelson rolled his eyes as he tossed it at Kruger, who put it in his pocket, then drove off. Nelson began walking back toward headquarters, but soon stopped and pulled out his cell phone. He tapped the Society's app—the same one used to post daily motivational Biblical passages. Members were encouraged to start their days with those holy texts, but the Society cautioned them about using the internet for anything else—they did everything possible to make the faithful fear the World Wide Web.

Nelson quickly composed an urgent memo that would go out to all members.

A message from your President:

Earthquakes are a harbinger of End Times. They are also a warning not to give credence to false stories in the media—stories that have been fabricated by those who wish to weaken your faith and destroy the Society of Truth. Do not be fooled by lawsuits initiated by ex-members who have turned their back on the Lord—for money. Now more than ever, the Society is relying on your support. We thank you in advance for your increased monthly donation—your outward, visible symbol of your dedication to God.

Nelson hit the Send button, then resumed walking toward head-quarters. As he turned onto Old Fulton Street, he saw a couple near Mario's Market. As he got closer, he realized who they were. "Milton Chandler!" he called out as he quickened his pace.

"Crap!" Milton whispered to Donna. "What do we do now?"

"Follow my lead," Donna said.

"That does it!" she exclaimed in a half shout, even though she was speaking inches from Milton's face. "Twenty-five years of marriage down the toilet because you choose loyalty to the Elder Board over your wife. Go! We're done here!"

"Donna, I'm not choosing between you and the Elder Board," Milton replied just as loudly. "*You're* the one making the choice—not me! *You're* turning your back on God and His true organization. *You're* breaking God's law by ending our marriage, not me!"

Bravo! Donna thought to herself. Milton was parroting exactly what the Society had taught its members to say to renegade spouses whose "faith had gone weak."

"Brother Chandler!" Nelson called again. "May I have a word?"

Donna thought she'd add a bit more melodrama to cement the appearance of her rebellion against God. She sashayed behind Milton as he walked toward Nelson, deliberately swinging her hips and shaking her finger at Nelson.

"Devon Nelson!" she exclaimed. "You should be ashamed of yourself. Why are you here, la-di-dahing your way down the street, when you should be rolling up your sleeves to help your brothers and sisters who've been affected by the quake? Or do you think that's women's work?"

Nelson started to reprimand Donna for her lack of deference. "Sister Chand—"

"Sista, my ass!" Donna exclaimed in a defiant tone she hadn't heard out of her own mouth since college. "We—you and I—we are not kin, Devon Nelson. Not in blood, not in culture, not in race, and certainly not in this disgusting religion!"

Milton hung his head in mock remorse. "My humble apologies, Brother Nelson. This is how far my wife has strayed far from God's flock. I'm so very sorry you had to witness this outburst. I tried to reason with her, but I think you knew—even before I did—that this woman had a predisposition toward ungodly independent thinking."

"Indeed, Brother Chandler, but seeing you here is something of a surprise," said Nelson. "And where is Brother Fitzgerald? Last we spoke, the two of you were off to call on one of our depressed older sisters."

Donna hoped Nelson didn't see her cringe. *How are you going to answer that, Milton?* she wondered. *You're on your own with this one. There's nothing I can say that will bail you out.*

"The quake caused a change in plans," said Milton smoothly. "Cabs were impossible to come by, and Brother Fitzgerald suggested we reschedule the shepherding visit for another day. As for me, I know you're supposed to shelter in place in a sturdy doorway during an earthquake. But as soon as the shaking started, I panicked. All I wanted to do was get out in the open. That's when I spotted my apostate wife. You heard the rest."

Oh, baby! Donna thought. *That was goooood!*

"It's too bad, Donna," Nelson began pompously. "You took the devil into your heart, just like Eve did when she chose independent thinking over obedience to almighty God and to her husband. Your fate will surely be worse than the wife of Lot, whose body of salt no longer exists. Your opportunity to return to the Lord will be stripped from you, and your future will be one of eternal damnation."

Nelson's pronouncement gave Donna the opportunity she was looking for. *Something to take Nelson's mind off Fitzgerald, the more outrageous the better,* she thought. She invaded Nelson's personal space

and provocatively gyrated her hips just inches from his groin. "So…
you're my judge and jury, are you now, Devon?" she asked
provocatively.

"This is what I've been dealing with," said Milton. "My profound
apologies once again, Brother Nelson."

"Apologies accepted," said Nelson. "Brother Chandler, I'd like to
take advantage of your experience and expertise as we finalize our
departure from Brooklyn. We have a lot to do in a very short period of
time."

"Fuck both of you!" Donna exclaimed as she stormed away with
her head held high. Stomping off into the sunset was the last scene of
her performance. As she powered past Mario's Market without pausing, she caught a glimpse of Milton and Devon as they crossed Old
Fulton, heading back toward headquarters. As soon as she was confident that she was in the clear, she doubled back to Mario's, and entered
to a round of applause.

"Brava, brava!" said Keisha.

"Wicked sistren!" André added.

"You were watching all that?" Donna asked.

"Not just watching," Keisha replied. "We heard everything, too. The
busted-out window has made this an open-air café—with front row
seats for whatever live soap opera is happening on the sidewalk.
Correct me if I'm wrong, but it looked to me like you and Milton were
playing that out for Nelson's benefit."

"You got that right," said Donna. "Milton has had a change of
heart. He discovered something that awakened him to the true nature
of the Society, and I was bringing him here to join our team. Nelson
was the last person we expected to see. We improvised that whole
scene!"

"What did he discover?" Keisha asked pointedly.

"Buckle up and buckle down," Donna began. "Milton didn't have
time to give me all the details, but he told me that the Society's attorney, Sam Silverman, was murdered. Paul Fitzgerald, another member
of the Elder Board, saw Bozz Kruger and Devon Nelson throwing
Silverman's dead body into the back of a pickup truck behind Society
headquarters. Apparently, it was the last thing poor Paul saw before

they killed him, too. Paul sent Milton a message asking him to tell his wife that he loved her—he knew what was coming next."

"That's horrible, but I can't say I'm shocked," Keisha said. "That religion is not what people think it is."

"Can't call it a religion anymore," declared Donna. "It's not even a cult. It's a criminal enterprise with a religious façade."

"I remember Paul," said Jen. "He was a kindly old guy. Pretty sharp, too. He and his wife...Lucy...wasn't that her name?"

"Yes," Donna answered. "Poor, sweet Lucy."

"I remember her," said Keisha. "When I would come into Mario's Market for a cappuccino to sit and study for missionary school, Lucy would be in here with the wives of the other elders. She loved Mario's espresso, and she had a sweet tooth. She'd always order an Italian cream horn. She and Paul, they always seemed a bit less holier-than-thou than the rest of them, now that I think about it."

"So, Donna, if Milton comes over to our side and what we just saw was all a charrr-ade," Cameron began, "and Nelson and Milton have just headed back to headquarters all chummy, am I supposed to understand that Milton has just enlisted himself as an undercover spy? Do you think he's aware that that's what he has done? It could mean his life, and..."

Cameron shook off a tear while remembering Gabby. "...and we've lost too many good lives already." Cameron was grief-stricken, but he had to put his own heartache aside for the good of the others. He now had to take all of his resources—every skill, every piece of knowledge, every ounce of energy and strength he had—and put them in service to breaking the USF. He held them responsible for Gabby's death—if it hadn't been for them, Gabby would never have been in the bunker when the earthquake happened.

"By cozying up to Nelson, I fear that Milton's now all in, whether he wants to be or not," said Keisha.

"I think he's down with that," said Donna. "After so many years abetting the evil that the Society has done, I think he feels obliged to do whatever he can to start putting things right."

"Well, if you ask me," young Debra chimed in, "we're gonna need to stay in touch with Milton—both for his own protection, and to make sure we're not getting played. You may trust him, Donna, but I sure don't. Who says he won't backslide and redefect to the Society and betray all of us?"

"Oh, he's not like that," said Donna. "Once Milton commits, he'll stick with it."

"I'm gonna put his number into my cell phone," Debra continued, "and I should get yours, too, Donna."

"Ummm…actually…I don't have a cell phone," Donna confessed.

"Sure you do. You gave me your number in the bar at the Hilton…" Keisha reminded her.

"It was bogus, Keisha," Donna admitted sheepishly. "I wasn't allowed a paid Society cell phone like the one Milton has, but I didn't want you to think I was a loser, and after that, everything happened so fast."

Debra pulled out her cell phone. "Okay then, I'll start with you instead, Keisha. What's your number?"

"Not so fast, young lassie!" said Cameron. "Let's be smart about this. While we were the guests of the DEA, I'm sure they went through our phones, which means that the USF knows every contact and every call and text we've made on those devices."

"He's right about that," said Sadie. "Our phones have been compromised—well, not mine because it's NYPD encrypted. But for the rest of you, they'll be tracking whoever you call from here on."

"So, what do we do?" asked Rocky.

"Burner phones," said Sadie. "Cheap, prepaid. We'll use them only for communication with one another—it'll be like our own little Sibylline network."

"On it," said Debra. "Mom, do you think the Strauss family can spring for the phones?"

"Absolutely," Jen replied as she scribbled a series of numbers on a scrap of paper, then signed her name. "Go see my boss, Ms. Staffonshire, at Citibank—don't deal with anyone else. Janet should recognize you, but you keep growing, so remind her that you're my daughter, and then give her this account number. Tell her I'll be back at my desk soon, but that I need a few more days of personal time. Pull out two thousand dollars in cash—that should be enough, right?"

"Do I need a password?" Debra asked.

"JonathanXIV," Jen replied.

"Okay, but why?"

"Where does your brother go to college?" Jen said.

"Max is at UConn—much to Dad's everlasting chagrin," Debra replied.

"Who's the UConn mascot?"

"A husky."

"And all of those pups have been named Jonathan—after Jonathan Trumbull, the first governor of the state of Connecticut. The current mascot is Jonathan the fourteenth," said Jen.

"You're so weird, Mom," said Debra.

"You already knew that, daughter mine. Get a receipt for the phones...and bring back change!" she added.

"Okay, one problem solved," said Cam. "Let's list out the rest of what we need to do." He looked around for something to write on, then spotted the blackboard on which Mario wrote his daily specials. Grabbing a small piece of chalk, he started writing. "Here's what needs to be done," he said as he enumerated tasks on the board.

#1: Burner phones—check.

#2: Freeze-dry seeds.

#3: Plant seeds.

Cameron turned to look at Zach. "These two assignments are tasks only you can take care of, Zach. Sadie put Ruth and her seeds on a plane for Germany, but that's as much as we know. For the moment, the most prudent thing we can assume is that those seeds are gone, which means that if there are any seeds left, you've got 'em."

Cameron continued to write the list:

#4: Locate Ruth Müller.

"Let me take a shot at that, once we get the burners," said Keisha. "Min Yunghui is a friend. She flew Ruth to Germany, and I think I know how to reach her. She might not know the full story, but she may be able to connect me with someone who does."

#5: Get intel from Milton.

"Donna, that's you," said Cameron, "at least at the outset. But as Debra suggested, all of us will have Milton's number in our phones—listed as someone else, of course."

#6: Break the USF–Society connection. Neutralize Bozz Kruger.

"I would like to suggest we add number seven to the list," Rocky said through his tears, "and I nominate me. My sister believed in eating well to be well. It's what our farm-to-table restaurant was all about. I want to keep her spirit alive...and besides...it's all I know how to do..." Rocky began to cry again.

Zach finally spoke. "Cook your heart out, Uncle Rocky. Cook for Mom."

The two embraced again. Cameron was the one who finally spoke up. "Good call, Rocky. Mario will need all the help in the kitchen that he can get."

"Italiano with a fresh new spin!" Mario exclaimed. "And each plate a work of art."

"Who's Art?" Debra asked with a giggle.

"I'm going to need André with me to tackle task six," said Cam. "Eventually, the goal is to neutralize the Society of Truth and take down the entire USF operation, but we have to start where we're at."

"Ya my mon!" André agreed. "'Tis me and Cam on number six. Dey USF mudda fuckas ain't no match for Obeah! And one of them—he already found dat out the hard way!"

"Are you talking about the guy we heard going upstairs?" Mario asked.

"Did you kill him?" Donna asked, not knowing whether she wanted the answer to be yes or no.

"Don't answer that!" said Sadie. "Not while I'm present. I'm still a cop, and if you're gonna confess to a crime, André, I can't be around to hear it."

"No, Detective Sadie!" André responded. "I only confess to giving him a good scare, and to burning the palm of his hand."

"How'd you do that?" Cameron asked.

"I suspended a kitchen knife in midair in front of his eyeball, and he was dumb enough to grab da handle!"

"*What???!!!*" they all said in unison.

"I told you he had some unusual skills," said Mario.

"Dat palm, I'm thinkin' it's blistered real good," said André. "Mebbe he had to bandage it up."

"Bravo," said Mario.

"One more thing," said André. "When I got upstairs, I found him looking at your iPad, Mario—the one with the multiple video feeds from the Society of Truth. The camera in the president's office was dark, but the audio still worked."

"Those must be the cameras that recorded what Ruth showed me at the luncheon," said Donna, "including the images underground."

"That would make sense," said Keisha. "The Society sure has a thing for underground."

"Well, as Cam says, we've got to start where we're at," said Donna. "And we already know of some nasty business that is going on in the Society's underground passageways. It may not be a command center, but some dark activity goes on there, for sure. Ruth showed me video of it at that luncheon. Apparently, there's a sewer-access door down in the tunnels, but what's behind the door isn't a sewer. The video showed Devon Nelson moving a bunch of black filing cabinets into the room. Ruth said they contained the Society's child sexual abuse cases."

"I think I've seen the door you're talking about," said Keisha. "A few days after I arrived at Society headquarters as a new missionary school student, I got totally lost down there—completely disoriented."

"Da tunnel—like swimmin' in da deep," André said. "Yo mind's compass get all messed up."

"Exactly!" Keisha agreed. "I found myself in front of a door with that same sign: Sewer Access."

"I know it's been a bit, Keisha, but if you were to walk the tunnels again, do you think you'd be able to find it?" Cameron asked.

"Ummm…alone?"

"I'll go with you," Donna offered. "Anyone you might run into down there still knows me as the obedient wife of an Elder Board member. I'm sure Devon Nelson hasn't spread the announcement that Donna Chandler has gone rogue. It's not in his interest to do so, at least not yet. He has bigger problems at the moment—like covering up his responsibility for two homicides."

"At least two," said Sadie. "Don't forget that men on the Elder Board have been dropping like flies. The fact that Nelson is behind the deaths of both Sam Silverman and Paul Fitzgerald suggests he could be implicated in the deaths of Barry Carlisle and Henry Angostino as well. Proving it may be a different story."

"Donna, Keisha, I strongly suggest taking André with you," Cameron advised. "You never know who might be down there. We already know that the Society has been thoroughly infiltrated by the USF, and from André's recent experience upstairs, it sounds like Bozz Kruger is still around."

"At the risk of underlining the obvious," said Jen, "André doesn't exactly look like he'd, ah, *blend in* with the rest of the Society population." With dreads tucked into his crocheted Rasta cap, his scruffy goatee, and large pendant earrings, André's appearance was distinctive, and unmistakably Jamaican.

"No sweat," Donna said. "I'll just say André and Keisha are potential buyers for our buildings. They've already seen me touring Bozz Kruger around the properties. It will appear perfectly normal for me to be showing them to somebody else."

"Good idea. André can scope out the sewer-access door and figure out how to get it open," Cameron said. "I'm quite sure there's not going to be an extra key under a doormat down there."

Sadie looked at Zach, who was having a lot of trouble quieting his legs and fingers. Because he was fidgeting so much, she could tell he was starting to lose the battle with his ADHD. "Zach, honey, you've got the most important jobs of all," she said. "To carry them out, you're gonna need a wingman—er...woman—for protection, and that would be me. I have a plan."

"It's settled then," Mario concluded. "Upstairs, all of you—except André. He and this one-armed *paisan* need to wait for the board-up service to come put plywood over the busted window. No telling when they'll show up. Pull out as many blankets and pillows as you can find. Get some shuteye so you'll be well rested. Tomorrow we begin!" Then he shooed them out of the kitchen and toward the loft staircase.

Bozz Kruger walked the half block to where the Dodge Ram had pulled over, then knocked on the driver's side window. "I'm going to drive past you in a couple of minutes," he said to his USF associate, João Moreira. "Follow me—before we can take care of Silverman, we've got to ditch the Tesla. Nelson wants us to take it to the Tompkins Projects, bash it up a little, then split."

"Got it," said Moreira as he placed his hands on the steering wheel. Like Kruger, he was wearing surgical gloves.

"We'll need to wipe the Tesla clean of prints—door handles, seats, steering wheel, and dashboard. We'll be getting rid of Silverman's prints as well as our own, but the registration will confirm that it's his vehicle, and by the time the cops find it, the locals will have stripped it of anything of value, leaving their own prints behind. The trick will be to do it without getting seen."

Kruger parked the Tesla near the corner of Tompkins Avenue and MLK Jr. Place. Moreira pulled in right behind him, then grabbed a crowbar from the truck bed. After puncturing the Tesla's right front tire, he smashed the windshield while Bozz wiped down the interior.

"Good enough," said Bozz. "Let's get out of here."

"Where to?" asked Moreira.

"Croton Dam," Kruger replied. "Take the BQE to the Major Deegan —I-87. Eventually, it turns into the Thruway. Jump off at Underhill Avenue and head west."

"You seem pissed off," said Moreira as they headed out of the city.

"I am," said Kruger. "Nelson's an arrogant, racist pig who thinks I'm his errand boy...you too, actually."

"Did he say something?" Moreira asked.

"Yeah. He talked about how the 'macacas' and 'jungle bunnies' in the Projects would finish stripping the Tesla once we got started on it."

"Ooh, that's bad!" said Moreira. "It's hard not to take that personal."

João Moreira had lived in Brooklyn since he was a teenager, but he'd been born in Salvador, Bahia, Brazil. As Portuguese settlers immigrated to their colony in the New World, they brought in African slaves to work the fields and mines—four million of them. Many of their descendants remained in Bahia, including João's Yoruba Nigerian grandparents and great-grandparents.

"That's exactly how I took it," Kruger replied.

"What did you do after he said that?" Moreira asked.

"Nothing," said Kruger. "If I got started, I'd have bashed his bigoted, patronizing brains in, and then we'd have another body to get rid of..."

Just then, traffic slowed to a crawl. "Crap. Just what we don't need," said Kruger. "Tarrytown/Route 287—what the hell is the Mario Cuomo Bridge?"

"Mario Cuomo is probably the only person who calls it that," Moreira said. "It's the Tappan Zee. Here..." Moreira pulled up the Uconnect on the Ram's navigation console.

"Actually, take the 287 for the bridge," said Kruger with a sly smile.

"That's really the long way around to get to Croton—we won't be able to get back across the river until we get to the Bear Mountain Bridge—and that's above Peekskill."

"I have a better place for Mr. Silverman than the Croton Reservoir," Bozz said. "Set the nav system for Long Meadow Road. This lawyer's going to get a change of venue."

About a half hour later, Kruger told Moreira to take a left off Long Meadow onto a dirt path that dead-ended near a small boat dock at the south end of Sterling Forest Lake. The half moon glistened on the water, providing just enough light for the two men to work without flashlights. They pulled the black bag out of the truck bed, removed the body, and undressed it. After carrying Silverman out to the end of the dock, they tied weights to his corpse.

"Wait!" whispered Kruger, just as they were about to heave the body into the water.

"Wait what?" replied Moreira nervously. "Let's get this done and get out of here!"

Silverman's head landed with a soft thump on the wooden dock as Kruger dropped it to reach into his pocket. He pulled out a small black object, pried Silverman's fingers open, then wrapped them around it.

"Now—on the count of three," he said, lifting the head once more.

After a small splash as the body hit the water, Silverman's body sank quickly into its watery grave.

"What was that about?" Moreira asked Kruger.

"Key fob," Kruger replied.

"And we dumped Silverman here rather than at Croton Dam because..."

"Let's just say it's a little surprise for Devon Nelson," said Kruger. "This is the site of the future world headquarters of the Society of Truth, and construction will start soon."

When they reached the interstate, Moreira suggested they head back via Route 17 through New Jersey. They made several stops along the way, jettisoning Silverman's shirt and pants in Mahwah, the body bag in Saddle River, his underwear in Ho-Ho-Kus, and their nitrile gloves in Paramus.

It's done, Kruger texted Nelson as they crossed the Tappan Zee Bridge.

"I still don't get it about the key fob," said Moreira as they passed Yankee Stadium.

"It'll make Silverman's body easier to identify," Kruger replied. "And..."

"And what?"

"And Nelson's fingerprints are all over it."

CHAPTER 20
CAPPUCCINO

Keisha was the first one up, and knew exactly what she wanted. Without waking anyone, she quietly tiptoed into Mario's loft kitchen and expertly began working his espresso machine. After using a tamper to press the finely ground beans into the portafilter, she placed a tiny cup under the spigot and hit the power button.

She had no idea that Mario was watching her from the doorway. He'd taught her to make the perfect cappuccino years ago, when she'd been one of the rare, unmarried female missionary students at the Society of Truth.

She'd been a quick learner because coffee was in her DNA. Her grandparents grew coffee on the mile-high plateaus of Kenya, and it had made them wealthy. Their beans had a worldwide reputation that rivaled Jamaican Blue Mountain and Kona Volcanic Estate. Keisha's father was born and raised there, but he married a woman from New York and moved to Brooklyn, where they both converted to the Society of Truth. Keisha was their only child. The family lived more than comfortably on her father's substantial monthly income from his family trust.

Keisha's grandparents doted on her as she was growing up and had set up her own trust fund that she could tap into when she turned eighteen. When she began her studies at the Society, she had more financial resources than the average impoverished Society student—enough to refuse to drink the acidic brown water that passed for coffee in the Society of Truth cafeteria. Mario's became her favorite place to study, and he tried as best he could to make sure she always had a place to sit. He often said that she had an endowed chair at the table closest to the kitchen.

The two of them would banter about how the best growers of the coffee bean were the Kenyans, and the best roasters were the Italians. They would joke about how that would make them the perfect couple, but it was all in jest. Their friendship was based on humor and intellect, not on romance—well, except for that one red-hot Chianti-fueled midsummer evening in Mario's loft that neither one of them could remember in detail.

They mostly brought out the funny in each other, but they also had their share of serious conversations. Keisha loved that no topic was off-limits with him—which surely had not been the case in her family as she was growing up. Her talks with Mario were the reason why she started doubting the doctrines of the Society of Truth. When she began actively contemplating leaving the Society, Mario had been the one who convinced her that she could make it on her own.

Female apostates often suffer financially. Alone in the world, cut off from friends and family and having few job-related talents, many who leave struggle to find work. Both Jen and Gabby had found that out when they escaped. As Keisha was debating her departure, Mario kept assuring her that with her luminous intelligence and great people skills, she'd have no trouble finding employment. And after all, he told her, she'd have her trust fund to fall back on.

That trust fund turned out to be the weapon her parents tried to use for revenge. To punish Keisha for severing her ties with the Society, they cut her off from her inheritance. Mario found himself slipping her some cash when she finally left, just so she could stay afloat. As soon as she got a job, Keisha retained a lawyer and challenged her parents in court, saying they were not legally entitled to deny her the money. She won her case easily. Without that lever of control, Keisha's mother and father renounced her as their daughter. Since she had forsaken the Lord, they said, they were forsaking her in shame. She was, in effect, dead to them. It was a heart wound that ached to this day.

Keisha opened the refrigerator, pulled out the organic whole milk, poured it into the stainless pitcher, and began steaming it. When it was just perfect, she turned it off, wiped the steamer nozzle, and poured both the espresso and hot milk into a mug, topping it off with a perfect image of a leaf made with milk froth.

"Just like I taught you," Mario said.

Keisha was so startled that she spilled her cappuccino. "Geez! How long have you been standing there, old man?"

"Now, now. Be nice. I may have lost some hair and found some love handles..."

Just then, Debra dragged herself and her tousled head of light-brown hair into the kitchen. "I. Smell. Coffee," she droned as if sleep-walking.

Jen followed shortly thereafter, followed by Sadie, Donna, Zach, and Cameron. Only Rocky and André were unaccounted for—but not for long.

"Gud mawnin!" André announced in a lilting voice full of Jamaican joyfulness. He smiled broadly as he entered the loft from the stairwell with a serving platter in his hands. "Mi bredda Rocky—he know how to cook! We have brioche French toast with homemade date syrup, fresh figs stuffed with goat cheese, spinach, and mushroom mini quiches, and..."

"Coffee?" Debra repeated with her eyes at half-mast.

"Ya mon, me come!" said Rocky in a deliberately comedic attempt to imitate André's Jamaican accent. He too had made his way up to Mario's loft from the main kitchen downstairs. He was gripping a full pot of fresh dark roast coffee in his right hand, and had threaded a clutch of colorful Italian Deruta ceramic mugs on the fingers of his left.

"Serving you first-class passengers..." he continued, this time mimicking a flight attendant on the aircraft PA system, "is André, our chief steward. Please keep the aisles clear as he makes his way through the cabin. I'll be coming through behind him with coffee, cream, and sugar."

"Coffee," said Debra as she lumbered toward Rocky, her arms held straight out in front of her, zombie style. "Need. Coffee."

André set the platter down, then pulled some plates from the cupboard.

As the gang got caffeinated and filled their plates, Keisha contemplated her assignment—going back into the Society of Truth tunnels. She was no longer fearful of the Society itself, but the thought of returning to the passageways brought back bad memories of how her mother and father had abandoned her. She had no idea where they were now, or whether her grandparents were still alive.

"It's tragic that the mass of people have been led to believe they're in need of saving," Keisha said, "when what they really need is love and understanding, not forgiveness."

"Religions are in the guilt business," said Jen. "Make you feel bad about yourself, then offer you salvation—at a price. It's great racket."

"Religions want folks to feel aligned with God through obedience —not spiritual connection," Donna declared. "I sure did. People are trained to believe that if they placate the owner of the universe, they'll cheat the nonbeingness of death—or Dante's fictional hellfire."

"Death and hellfire. Jeezy creezy!" Rocky exclaimed. "Is this really what we want to be talking about over my delicious breakfast? Let's talk about something else—anything else."

"The seeds," said Donna. "I'd like to talk about the seeds."

"What about 'em?" asked Zach.

"I think the seeds raise more questions than they answer," said Donna. "I mean, think about it. Let's say Zach gets the seeds from the Tree of Life to sprout, and let's say the trees really do give eternal life to people who partake of them. Then what? Seems to me that once word gets out, all hell's gonna break loose. Who gets to eat and live, and who dies? And who decides?"

"I've been wondering the same thing," Deb chimed in. "Let's say all 'good' people—pick whatever definition of 'good' floats your boat—get to eat from the Tree of Life and live forever...Does that also mean they'll stay kind and good forever, or do they have to keep coming back for refills from the tree, like getting a booster shot? What about free will? Will that be gone?"

"The only person who might be able to answer your question is Ananta," said Sadie, "and I suspect she's a little pushed for time right now."

"And on that cheery note, I'm outta here," said Debra. "Bank first. Then phones. Thanks, Rocky and André, for a great start to the day."

She grabbed a piece of French toast. "One for the road," she said, took one last swig of coffee, and headed for the staircase.

"Donna," said Cameron, "as soon as Deb gets back with the burners, send a crypto text to Milton to let him know how he can contact you. I'm sure in your years of marriage there's something you could say that would indicate to Milton it's you. Also—and this is super important—get him to send you the photos that Fitzgerald sent him. Then forward them on to all of us."

"Why?" Donna asked.

"Because the more people who have them, the safer Milton becomes," said Cam. "As long as the only place those images exist is on his phone, then killing him solves a really big problem for Nelson and Kruger. Better yet, as soon as you see them come through on your phone, tell Milton to delete them. His cell, after all, is Society property, and if Nelson confiscates it, game over."

"What will *you* do, Cam?" Zach asked.

He called me Cam! Cameron thought to himself. He sensed something different in Zach's tone—it was warm and affectionate. There was a connection going on—it was as if Zach had finally realized that he couldn't bear to lose someone his mom adored so soon after her death.

"I'll be fine, Zach. I'm not going anywhere just yet. Son...you have to focus on your very important task. You have a wealth of knowledge when it comes to plants. We're counting on you to carry on the work that you and your mom started."

At that moment, they shared a look that everyone else in the group noticed. Zach had never experienced anything close to a father figure before. He basically had only his mom and his Uncle Rocky—and Rocky was more like a buddy than a dad. The look they exchanged revealed that a deep, genuine connection had been forged between them.

"Well," said Sadie, "to Donna's point, we won't know whether or not hell's gonna break loose unless we get the seeds freeze-dried and then planted. You ready, Zach?"

"Yes, ma'am," he replied.

"Zach and I have our assignment," said Sadie. "We're heading out. Rocky and André, breakfast was fabulous. Thank you so much."

After grabbing his bag of frozen shit from the freezer, he followed Sadie out the door of Mario's Market.

"Yes, thank you both," said Keisha as she rose to leave. "Gratitude…a true Sibylline virtue…"

"Hey, hey, hey!" Rocky shouted. "Deb, Zach, and Sadie are excused. Everyone else, plant your fannies back in the chair. André and I didn't spend all those hours cooking so you could dine and dash. Food is fuel. Chow down and hydrate, people. Then—and only then—are you released from this gourmet chef's kung-fu grip! Hi-yah!"

Still playing the clown to paper over his grief, Rocky began to playact a slapstick gay martial arts maneuver—*The Karate Kid* meets *La Cage aux Folles*. André grabbed his wrist in midair, and stopped the chop. "Mi luv ya, funny man," he said.

"Ya mon," Rocky replied, morphing the chop into the Jamaican handshake that André had taught him, only to have the Rastafarian embrace him in a full bear hug instead.

CHAPTER 21
TRANSFORMATIONS

Debra returned to Mario's with burner phones for all, then gave Donna a quick tutorial to make sure she knew how to use hers. She also made sure each phone had everyone else's contact info. She input Milton's number as Sottocasa Pizza on Atlantic Avenue, which was owned by a friend of Mario's. The group then split up to address their individual assignments.

"As I said yesterday," Donna reminded Keisha and André, "to keep from arousing suspicion when we get into the passageways, we'll need to make you appear like wealthy prospective buyers of the Society's Brooklyn properties. Keisha, you already look the part. André...not so much."

"You mean my cap and dreadlocks don't make me look credible?" he said, laughing.

"No, they make you look, ah, in-credible," said Keisha, "but I suspect that it's not just what's going on above the neck that concerns Donna."

André looked down at his flour-sprinkled, food-stained apron. He untied it and tossed it on the table. "Problem solved!" he exclaimed.

The two women giggled. André's tie-dyed T-shirt and well-worn Jesus sandals did not suggest he was a man of means. "C'mon, my Rastafarian friend," Donna said. "We need to go shopping."

André examined his wallet. "I got three twenties; will that work?"

Donna laughed. "Well, not for Bloomingdale's, but it'll probably work at the old Plymouth Church. They have a thrift shop, and it's on our way."

Donna, Keisha, and André set out for the secondhand store, just a few blocks away. "How ironic," Donna said as they approached the church. "The Society convinced us that churches like this were the work of the devil himself, but the truth is that this church has been fighting slavery and sex trafficking since its inception."

"And its inception was quite something," said Keisha. "Lincoln spoke here before the Civil War, before he was elected to the presidency. Abolitionist Henry Ward Beecher—brother of Harriet Beecher Stowe—was Plymouth's first pastor. He made his church into a key stop on the Underground Railroad that smuggled escaped slaves out of the South. Brooklyn locals called it 'the Grand Central Depot'—and if you're looking for irony, Donna, Beecher hid the runaways in a tunnel under the sanctuary."

The trio entered the Underground Thrift Shop, and it didn't take long for the two women to find the perfect attire for André—an elegantly casual sprezzatura-style suit and silk shirt, accessorized with blingy cufflinks and a pair of Romano Martegani loafers—no socks. "You look like a guy who's made billions on marijuana, now that it's legal," Keisha said, laughing.

"Ya mon," said André, getting into character. "I be a ganja mogul—too cool for you."

"Put your earrings in your pocket," said Keisha as she corralled his dreads into a braided suede hair tie. André reluctantly left his precious Rasta cap with the cashier, who promised to hold it for safekeeping until he returned.

Donna chose to begin the "real estate tour" at 97 Columbia Heights, one of several access points to the underground tunnels that linked the Society of Truth holdings. As they reached the bottom of the staircase, Keisha put her hand to her mouth to keep from gagging. "Sorry," she said. "That's really vile!" she exclaimed.

"Oh yeah!" André agreed.

"I guess I've gone nose blind," Donna replied.

Over the years, the Society's underground corridors had sprouted utility rooms. The tunnel Donna had chosen led past the laundry, where elderly women sat on rickety metal chairs as the machines whirred, straightening out used wire hangers while they waited for their clothes to dry. Beyond the laundry were the commissary and cafeteria, and in the corridor, the cloying fragrance of cheap laundry detergent mingled with food odors from the cafeteria.

But those smells weren't what was causing Keisha to retch. Even the pungent aroma of decades of greasy scrambled eggs, overdone Salisbury steak, burnt coffee, and rancid cooking fat failed to mask the underlying stench of dirty old men and illicit liaisons. Every so often, during the late-evening hours when all activity had stopped, a tipsy soul with weak kidneys and a full bladder would unzip and take a whiz, but because the corridors were dimly lit in the night, they were also a haven for those with more lustful desires. Not all sexual activity involved couples—the passageways were also frequented by the Society's many middle-of-the-night masturbators. One of them was Devon Nelson, who found it more thrilling to jack off in the tunnels—and risk being seen—rather than in the privacy of his penthouse apartment.

Through this section of the tunnel, Keisha allowed Donna to strut her stuff as the Elder Board wife/VIP tour guide. She cordially greeted everyone they met, sometimes pausing to introduce Society members to the gorgeous jet-setting couple from Jamaica who were seriously considering buying the Society's Brooklyn buildings. As they turned a corner into a less populated area, Keisha took the lead, and eventually found her way to a short dead-end tunnel.

"Here! Over here! This is it!" Keisha exclaimed. "I recognize the sign on the door."

Sewer Access.
This Door to Remain Locked.
City Officials Only.
Safety Attire Required.

"That's what I saw in the video Ruth showed me," said Donna. "Don't get too close, Keisha. See that surveillance camera?"

André crept along the wall to stay out of the camera's line of sight. Then he reached up and broke the camera off its mount with his bare hand. Keisha and Donna stood there dumbfounded. "You mean this surveillance camera?" he asked.

"How are you going to open the door?" Donna asked.

"It looks like it uses a built-in radio frequency identification system," André said. "But it's time for you to go back to Mario's now."

"Not me, I'm staying. I want to see what's in there," Donna insisted.

"I'm curious, too, but he's right, Donna," Keisha said. "We'd be more of a liability than an asset, especially if Kruger shows up. André, you know how to find your way back out, right?"

"Ya mon!" he replied.

Zach and Sadie walked briskly toward the Brooklyn Bridge, then turned right on Front Street. Zach gingerly held his bag of poop at arm's length, trying to stay upwind of the unpleasant whiffs that wafted out from time to time.

"Gimme that, for heaven's sake!" Sadie guffawed as she took the bag on the end of Zach's fingers. The smell of human excrement didn't bother her all that much—she'd smelled far worse in her years as an NYPD detective.

"Zach, stop!" she yelled suddenly.

Her warning came too late—Zach had already stepped squarely into a large pile of dog shit that some irresponsible pet owner had left on the concrete. For Sadie, it was an everyday hazard on the sidewalks of New York, but for Zach, on top of everything else that had happened to him in the last couple of days, it was one misfortune too many.

His ability to cope went tilt—his eyes welled up with tears. Then his cheeks turned red and his hands began curling into fists—sure signs that a meltdown was imminent. "Hey, hey, hey..." Sadie said. She couldn't allow him to make a scene—drawing attention to themselves in public would be dangerous, and their mission was too important. "You've been through a lot, Zach," she continued in a tone that was equal parts compassion, calmness, and determination, "but now is..."

Zach heard Sadie's voice trail off as his perception of the woman standing in front of him changed. He no longer saw Sadie—he saw his mother instead. "...now is not the time to lose your composure," he heard Gabby say. "You miss me, I know. I miss you too, more than you could ever imagine. You're carrying all this grief—so much that I can see it whirling inside you."

"I thought…I thought…I thought…" Zach stammered as he struggled to find the right words. Meanwhile, he began hyperventilating and his fidgeting sped up—he had no control over what his hands were doing. Then he stamped his foot. "This isn't what you told me was going to happen, Mom," he pouted.

"I know, Zach, I know," Gabby replied.

"You always believed in the law of attraction. You would tell me things like '*You will attract in your life what you believe in your heart*' and shit like that," he began. "You taught me that if we follow a path we believe in, the universe will be on our side, and everything will come to us. You said that we'd attract everything we intend—everything we want."

"Yes, Zach, that's what I told you," she said.

"Well…everything you taught me was a crock—a lie! And it makes me mad. I'm pissed off—*that's* what you see coursing through my veins! This is not what I intended, Mom, not what I wanted! I didn't want everything we worked for to be destroyed! And I sure as hell didn't want you to die!"

"I didn't want to die either, my sweet boy—at least not so soon," Gabby said softly.

Zach wanted to cry, but he was too angry. Gabby rested both hands on his shoulders so they were face-to-face. "Here. Look here," she said firmly as she lifted his chin. "In my eyes. Tell me, what *do* you want?"

"I want what I can't have—what I can *never* have," he said angrily, "which is you. Here. Alive. Now. I want everything that *we* wanted —*together*. I want the two of us to discover and grow plants—*together*. I want us to extract the healing compounds from them—*together*."

"Why do you want those things?" Gabby asked.

"Why?" Zach barked irately as tears began to flow down his cheeks. "You *know* why, Mom!"

"Because you want to help humanity. Right?"

Zach nodded as he wiped the tears from his cheek.

"You see, Zach…the universe really *is* on your side," Gabby said with a warm smile. "Protecting and nurturing what you have in that bag could possibly be the most powerful thing you could ever do to help humanity."

"But it didn't keep *you* alive, Mom. It killed you instead," he insisted. Zach wiped his nose with his sleeve, then lifted the bag to her face. "If you hadn't gone back for this, Mom, you'd still be here."

"I *am* here. I'm right here in front of you," Gabby said. "My physical body may be gone, but my spirit is here, and my life is still one with yours. It's one with Sadie's, too. Bodies are simply an accumulation of physical matter—cells, organs, fluids—but the *life* that exists within those bodies—that life is all one with each other. Just because the body goes away doesn't mean life does."

"But I want your body back, too," Zach sighed.

"So do I, honey," Gabby replied. "Situations are going to happen, and you may not be able to change them, but you *can* choose how to experience them. That's always in your control—always. No one can force you to feel how they think you're supposed to feel—which doesn't keep some people from trying. Your job is to be authentic—feel the crisis of change in every fiber of your being. If you're angry, feel angry. If you're sad, feel sad."

"I feel both angry *and* sad, Mom," said Zach, "and I don't know what to do with these feelings."

"Angry is sad's bodyguard, and the two together are the essence of grief," Gabby replied. "It's perfectly natural for you to feel that way, but here's the key. Accept grief and embrace it, but don't let it consume you for too long. Take charge of it and use it as fuel—as a springboard for growth. And I know that sometimes it's *really* hard to do—like now."

Zach shook his head. "I can't, Mom."

"Yes, you can," she said.

"I hurt so much, and I feel so alone without you."

"It's a challenge, but you are my amazing son, and I have no doubt that you can rise to it—look at how many other challenges you've already met in your life!" Gabby replied. "And you have Cam and Sadie and so many other people who are ready to help you! Eventually, you'll be able to look back and see that the crisis had to happen. Why? Because it was essential for change—for growth. And you...*you, Zach*...attracted it, because you desire growth."

Gabby paused for a moment to let what she was saying sink in. "This is so much bigger than you, or me, or any one person," she continued. "We're headed for the time when the Way of Kyndeness is going to take over. Those in power don't want you to believe that. They want to keep you—all of us—off balance, whipsawed between despair and hope. They've figured out that human beings are easier to control that way. But, Zach...please believe me when I say that this is the beginning of the crisis that all of humankind needs for growth, and you are destined to play a big part in it. Take charge, honey. Take charge of the crisis of change...take charge of it for *me*... Let me take delight in watching you figure out how to meet the challenge, and how to experience it with joy—not misery. Can you do that for me..."

Zach's breathing began to slow and his fists unclenched, proof that Gabby's words were hitting their mark. Her voice and presence then trailed off, and he felt his mother's hands morph into Sadie's hands on his shoulders. "Can you do that for me, Zach?" said Sadie. "Can you be the man that I, and your mom, need right now?"

Zach remained silent, puzzled by what he'd just experienced. He squinted at the woman in front of him. Not only had Sadie sounded just like his mom, but also she'd been reasoning and making sense just like his mom.

"Say yes, Zach," Sadie pleaded. "Please say yes...It's just shit. It's just a bunch of smelly shit. That's all it is. Shit. Shit. Shit."

"Shit," Zach whispered.

"Yes!" Sadie replied. "Smelly shit—and the most precious seeds on the planet that could end humankind's suffering are in it! That's all! No biggie."

The irony turned Zach's tears into laughter, and they doubled over together. Their unrestrained shared hilarity was cathartic—exactly what both of them needed. When it subsided, Zach walked to a patch of grass and wiped the dog poop off his shoe. Then they continued on their way.

Ten minutes later, Sadie opened the door to Soulscapes, a New Age shop on Front Street. A small bell tinkled softly as they walked inside. At the back of the shop, a heavyset woman with long silver hair was dusting an ornate shelf crowded with water pipes, God's eyes, geodes, prisms, and essential oils. "Make yourself at home and let me know if you need help," she called out without turning around.

"Help," Sadie said.

The woman quickly turned to see the person whose voice she instantly recognized, then laid her feather duster down on the shelf and opened her arms. Sadie melted into the storekeeper's warm embrace.

"Aunt Phoebe. It's so good to see you—as always," she said.

"You too, my dear," Phoebe replied. "Hugging you always feels like I'm also hugging your mom. Now tell me, what do you need help with because I know you're not here to get your tea leaves read?"

"I want to introduce you to a fellow grower—if you know what I mean. This is Zach—Zach, this is my mom's sister, my Aunt Phoebe."

"Hello, young Zach. You may be a grower, but I bet you never tried this stuff," Phoebe said as she pulled an itty-bitty cardboard container from her pocket.

Zach could smell the familiar terpenes of marijuana oozing through the cardboard, but there was something different about it. Just the scent of it made him feel—well—a little more alive.

"That's my Aunt Pheebs," Sadie said. "Always concocting something amazing. Speaking of which, I have a favor to ask."

"Anything...anything at all! I have all this because of you!" said Phoebe as she gestured around the shop. "I will be forever grateful that you gave me your mother's store when she...transitioned."

"It was an easy call, Aunt Pheebs," Sadie replied. "Not only were you the right woman for the job, but also...as an NYPD detective, owning a head shop would have been an odd side gig for me, dontcha think?"

"So tell me," said Phoebe, "what do you need my help with?"

"Zach needs to plant a couple of rare seeds that have been already mixed with...with some fertilizer," Sadie said. "And he needs to oversee them, which means he'll need a place to lay his head for a while." Sadie then held up the bag for Phoebe to see.

"Oooo! Black-market shit, huh?"

"Yup...good *shit!*" Zach said as he grinned at Sadie.

"Better than black market, Aunt Pheebs," said Sadie. "Priceless and one of a kind."

"Okay then!" Phoebe replied. "I could certainly use some young companionship who knows how to grow. And I can help you look after it and give it water…"

"No!" Zach shouted. "Not yet!"

"Oh!" Phoebe exclaimed in surprise.

"We must spread the…the fertilizer…out on a sheet in a freezer to dry first! This is super important. The seeds are in the…the fertilizer, but they're super small. Once all the moisture has evaporated, then—and only then—can we mix it with a planting medium—probably a mixture of peat moss, vermiculite, and perlite. Then we'll plant it in a pot with good drainage, and *then* we can begin watering it…"

"Young Zach, I can already tell that the two of us are going to be a fabulous partnership," said Phoebe. "When we get to the planting stage, I'll make sure we give it some mycelium starter. Once it's in the ground, those seeds will easily begin communicating with the rest of the plant kingdom."

Zach cocked his head to one side and nodded, then shot a look at Sadie. "I told ya I had a good idea," she said. "You and Aunt Pheebs are going to have a *lot* to talk about! This woman knows what she's doing, and we can breathe a sigh of relief that the seeds are in good hands."

"Sounds like there's a good story here," Phoebe said. "You know how much I love stories! Sadie's mom and I made some great stories together—especially in that T-Bird of hers. Oh, if only those bucket seats could talk! Well, they could have, if Sadie hadn't taken that car totally apart and rebuilt it from the chassis on up. How *is*…? What did you name it?"

"Fonzie, Aunt Pheebs. I named the car Fonzie," Sadie replied.

Sadie handed the bag to Phoebe without going into detail about what had happened to her precious T-Bird, in part because it was still a story without an ending.

Phoebe's brow furrowed when she got a whiff of the so-called "fertilizer," then looked warily at Zach. Sadie took that as her cue to leave. "Thanks, Aunt Pheebs," she said as she hurried out the door, leaving Zach to tell the story. As she walked back toward Mario's Market, she knew that she had channeled Gabby's spirit, and that it was Gabby who had spoken to Zach.

Zach no longer felt alone. He felt as if he'd connected with his mom *and* with a new family—a strange family, to be sure, but a family nonetheless, one that "got" him, almost the way his mom did. He liked not being far from Mario's Market—where his mom's body was still in the rubble of the underground bunker. He felt the warmth of his mom encircling him, as if she was…in some strange way…more alive than ever.

CHAPTER 22
OPERANT CONDITIONING

B*am! Bam! Bam!*

Milton glanced at his bedside clock—it was 4:30 a.m. He stumbled out of bed in response to the loud pounding on his door, and Devon Nelson came barreling past him as soon as he opened it. He was freshly shaven, and his short red hair was neatly combed. He was wearing a crisp, clean black suit with a white starched collared shirt and a blue pinstripe tie.

Nelson cloaked his self-serving purpose in a Bible passage: "Scripture says Jesus got up in the morning while it was still dark and began to pray," he said sanctimoniously. "Brother Chandler, just like our Lord, we must get a head start on today's tasks. There's much work to be done!"

Milton loathed this homicidal hypocrite, but he didn't have the luxury to wallow in his hatred at the moment. His job now was to stay in character and play the part of Nelson's obsequious executive assistant—the new position of "privilege" he'd been assigned.

"Of course, Brother Nelson," Milton replied. "I just need to put on a pot of coffee."

"Umm…Chandler," Nelson said, handing him one of the two cups of coffee he was holding.

Milton looked at the cup and recoiled. He hated the cheap Styrofoam cups from the Society cafeteria almost as much as he hated the coffee itself. He pretended as best he could to graciously accept

Nelson's offering—even though he drank his coffee black, and Nelson had brought him coffee with cream and sugar—then headed for the master bathroom. After forcing himself to take one big gulp, just for the hit of caffeine, he poured the rest down the sink and jumped in the shower.

As soon as Nelson heard the water running, he began to give the place a little snoop, starting with the bedroom. He examined the framed wedding portrait of Milton and Donna—the newlyweds seemed genuinely happy and in love. After gently replacing the photo back on the bedroom dresser, he opened the top drawer and began rummaging through Donna's underwear. *Borrr-ing!* he thought...

Until he noticed another pair tucked away in the far recesses of the drawer. Nelson reached in and pulled out a hot pink lace thong. The back featured a cutout star embellished with rhinestones, right above where the ass crack would begin. "Well, well," he whispered as he held it up and looked at it. He surmised from its half-buried location in the back of the drawer that it hadn't been worn for Milton's benefit in quite a while, or maybe Donna kept it hidden for...other occasions.

Donna's thong triggered the deepest urges of his perverted imagination. He stood there imagining what her glistening dark skin might have looked like as she peeled off the lacy panty, slowly sliding it down her legs while caressing her full, plump ass. He pictured her wiggling and tantalizing him, just as she had on the street, but this time she was naked as she teased him with glimpses of her *au naturel* wooly pussy.

All women in the Society of Truth were hairy—or at least they were supposed to be, because the religion's official position was that shaving or waxing the pubic area was depraved. The fact that the religion condemned women for their lewd desire to appear "childlike," even as it condoned having sex with actual children, did not strike Devon—or another other Society elders—as paradoxical or contradictory.

As Nelson caressed Donna's thong, his arousal and erection were building. He set his cup of coffee down on the dresser and closed the drawer. Taking the pink thong with him, he went into the powder room off the living room and locked the door.

"Pink..." he said as he began rubbing his cock through his pants. "I bet it matches her cunt exactly."

Nelson pulled down his trousers and boxers, soaped up his hands, and began masturbating himself with his right hand. With Donna's thong woven through the fingers of his left hand, he brought the crotch under his nose and inhaled deeply. "Still smells like Black pussy juices," he said.

Watching himself in the vanity mirror made it that much more erotic. In less than a minute, he was groaning and pumping cum all over the sink.

"Brother Nelson!" he heard from outside the bathroom door. "Where are you?"

"I'm using the bathroom, Brother Chandler," he called back. "I'll be right out!"

He grabbed a wad of toilet paper, wiped up his cum, and flushed it down the toilet. Then he zipped up his pants and washed his hands. Nelson was halfway out the door when he saw the thong on the sink. He snatched it up quickly and stuffed it into his pocket. *Whew, that was close!* he said to himself, knowing that the risk of getting caught had amped up the intensity of his orgasm.

Milton looked at him oddly. "Here's your coffee," he said. "You left it in my bedroom."

"Thanks," said Nelson. "Now, let's get a move on."

On the walk down Columbia Heights toward headquarters, Nelson filled Milton in on his new duties and assignments. "I'll be accepting nominations for new Elder Board members, and you're in the mix. What I need you to do first, however, is build a fence."

"A fence?" Milton asked incredulously.

"A fence," Nelson repeated. "One that will surround the location of our new headquarters up in Orange County—three hundred acres adjacent to a small lake. The building will be awesome—1.5 million square feet, with a printing facility and media production center. Construction needs to start ASAP, but we can't begin until the site is enclosed. The fence will keep out the press and the riffraff."

Nelson clearly intended the new headquarters to be a fortress—or a prison. "Brother Chandler, you'll be managing the construction of a barbed-wire fence around the perimeter—ten feet high, with surveillance cameras every forty feet. A 24-hour guardhouse is to sit at the only point of entry—an electric gate allowing controlled access for concrete mixers, delivery trucks, and construction equipment and crews."

After they arrived at headquarters, Nelson strode past the front desk and headed straight for the elevator. Milton greeted David the doorkeeper as he always did, then signed in. He cheerfully added Nelson's name as well, since Nelson had been too prideful to do so himself. David nodded in gratitude.

As they walked out of the elevator onto the tenth floor, Nelson dropped a bomb. "You've got two weeks to get this done, Chandler, and we're not wasting one dime on hired workers—all labor must performed gratis by Society members. Your first task will be to recruit the workers we need and convince them to contribute their efforts for free, in the name of the Lord."

"That's a tall order, Brother Nelson," said Milton as they entered the president's office, "especially with such a tight deadline."

Nelson tossed Milton a yellow legal pad and pen—an obvious indication that he was expecting Milton to take notes. "I assure you it's feasible, Brother Chandler," Nelson replied, "and I'm about to give some tips on how to do it."

Nelson had envied Bozz Kruger's ability to snap Fitzgerald's neck, but he also knew that he possessed a skill that Kruger never would. What Nelson lacked in martial arts expertise he more than made up for with his ability to deploy weaponized spiritual opportunism on the vulnerable and the gullible. It was this talent that had fueled his rise within the Society of Truth, making him a member of the Elder Board before his fortieth birthday. Nelson had a black belt in persuasive godly jiujitsu, and he was about to give Milton his first lesson in how well it worked.

"There are two reasons why people flock to religion," Nelson began. "Number one...they don't want to die. They want some promise of life after death. It's a major factor that attracts people."

"What's the second reason?" Milton asked.

"Operant conditioning," Nelson answered. "Parents call it 'positive reinforcement,' but it's the same thing. You introduce the desired stimulus in exchange for a behavior. A trainer gives a dog a treat after the dog performs a trick. A teacher doles out gold stars to children who turn in their homework on time."

"And God bestows a blessing upon the faithful in exchange for their obedience to His one true religion," Milton added.

"Quick learner, Milton!" Nelson said.

Nelson's praise briefly made Milton feel proud of himself—until he realized that it was proof of how well operant conditioning worked.

"Would you really be here volunteering your life here at headquarters if God had nothing to offer you in return? Be honest, Chandler," Nelson urged. "Don't default to some scripted answer like, 'Even if God didn't reward me, I would still serve him because it's the best way of life.' Would you or wouldn't you?"

"Honestly?" Milton asked.

"Yes. Why are you in this religion?"

"God's honest truth is that I'm not here for some pipedream about eternal life," Milton replied.

God's honest truth, Milton thought to himself, *is that right now it's essential that I tell Devon Nelson whatever he wants to hear.*

"You're a liar," Nelson declared.

"No, Brother Nelson, I'm not. I'm here because—with or without a promise of eternal life in the hereafter—this is the best way of life —*now*—for a middle-aged Black man like me. Look...I don't know your background or where you came from, but there's no way you can possibly know what it's like to walk in my shoes. I'm here because it feels good to be the first Black man on the Elder Board, and it felt really good to bask in the glory of being the first Black president of this religion—all eighteen hours of it."

The ends of Nelson's mouth curled upward. *Chandler is even dumber than I thought*, he said to himself. *He has no bloody idea that he's the token Black man—the house nigger of the Elder Board. This... this I can work with.*

"Thank you for your honest answer," Nelson said. "It wasn't the one I was expecting, but it still proves that you're in this religion for what you can get out of it. No one would serve God in any religion if there wasn't a...a treat."

"A treat?" Milton asked.

"A treat...a reward...a prize," Nelson replied. "*That* is how you get free laborers to put up a barbed-wire fence in just two weeks."

"Can you explain a little further?" said Milton.

"Announce the expected behavior first, and do so with great fanfare. You are extending an invitation in the form of a sacred opportunity—a rare privilege accorded only to those brothers and sisters who quickly volunteer themselves in service to God," Nelson declared. "Then state the reward. Those who answer God's call will not only gain the Lord's stamp of approval and blessing in this life, but will also store up credit and treasures for use in the next life. A banker might put it in financial terms: a small investment of your time and talents today will bring huge dividends in heaven. Our followers will be compliant worker bees in the palm of your hand before you know it. The fence might even get completed in less than two weeks. You'll see."

"So, that's how it's done?" Milton said. "That's the secret of your success?!" *Might as well get in a little flattery*, he said to himself.

"It is," Nelson confirmed conceitedly. "Do the work. Build the fence. Get a cookie from Jesus Christ *and* a gold star from God the Father Almighty. Exploi-fucking-tation. The Sibyllines have it all wrong—people aren't naturally kind and supportive if there's nothing in it for them."

"Who are the Sibyllines?" Milton asked.

"Never mind," said Nelson. "It's enough for you to know that men are hardwired to be dominant, and women are hardwired to crave their dominant man. And they're both hardwired to be selfish," he continued. "That's human nature. What's in it for me?—W.I.F.M. It's how the world works. It always comes down to that."

"Sounds like the law of the jungle," said Milton.

"It would be," Nelson replied, "except we've figured out how to control it. Religion, commerce, politics…they are all inventions to keep everyone in line. Otherwise, there'd be chaos."

"Religion, commerce, and politics…" Milton parroted. "Right."

"And among those three, the most powerful is religion—specifically patriarchal religion," Nelson declared. "It's a foolproof invention that keeps people in check and under control. Think about it: a man god—an all-powerful patriarch—who dictates both correct behavior *and* consequences for incorrect behavior, aka sin. And those consequences are dire and everlasting—eternal death with no hope of life or a burning forever in the fires of hell. How does this male god know you've sinned? Big Daddy comes fully equipped with a killer surveillance system—put one toenail over the line and you'll pay for it, either in this world or the next, or both."

"I know we're not supposed to observe Christmas, Brother Nelson, but operant conditioning seems to have a lot in common with Santa Claus," Milton said. "As the song lyrics say—'He's making a list and checking it twice. Gonna find out who's naughty and nice.' "

"Precisely!" Nelson exclaimed.

" 'He knows if you've been bad or good, so be good for goodness' sake,' " Milton added.

"You've got it, Brother Chandler! Being good for Santa is like training wheels for being obedient to God. Children want presents under the tree, but if you're a bad kid, it's a slippery slope from coal in your stocking to eternal damnation. Because the penalty for sin is so extreme, fear of that penalty is hands-down the greatest tool we have for exercising control over adults. People want to please Big Daddy, and believe they'll be 'blessed' for it. Patriarchal religion—whether it's Protestant, Catholic, Jewish or the Society of Truth, is nothing more than operant conditioning."

Milton had never heard such philosophy from a member of the Elder Board before. He didn't remember any talk about operant conditioning in any of the board meetings, either. Had he closed his mind and shut his ears to all of it?

Milton took possession of Fitzgerald's office and contemplated how so much had changed so drastically in so little time. Just a week ago, the tenth floor was bustling. Every office had an Elder Board member in it. Ruth Müller was at her desk. John Matthews was managing the office, and Erica Pfeiffer was keeping everything tidy and spotless. Now...now it was a ghost town. Angostino, Carlisle, and Fitzgerald were all dead, and the Müllers, John, and Erica were gone.

Just then, Thomas Schmidt emerged from the elevator—and barely made it. He was moving so slowly that the elevator tried to close on his walker several times before he was fully clear of the doors. "Hello, Brother Chandler," he said. "Glad to see you're back in the saddle. I have a favor to ask. Brother Nelson requested I write a script for a broadcast video that will help strengthen the faith of our brothers and sisters."

Ah yes, Milton thought to himself. *This is the video that Paul Fitzgerald told me about.*

"Of course, Brother Schmidt," he replied, pretending to be clueless. "What is the subject matter?"

"Reports of child sexual abuse within the Society are being bandied about everywhere, and we are getting pilloried in the media—and in the courts," Schmidt replied. "They're all scandalous lies, of course, lies perpetrated by apostates—their revenge on us for shunning them, if you will. But they're being repeated so often that it's having a deleterious effect on our membership rolls, and on our revenue. I have the script in mind, but my hands—well—they have a mind of their own these days. Would you be so gracious as to allow me to dictate it to you?"

"It would be my pleasure," Milton responded.

As Schmidt spoke, it took everything Milton had to keep a straight face as he typed. He couldn't believe he'd bought into this bullshit for so long, and silently thanked Donna once again for opening his eyes. Schmidt's last paragraph really made him squirm:

Satan the Devil is on a rampage during the final part of the last days. He is using his earthly apostates to spread slander in one last-ditch effort to weaken our faith in the Lord. Turn your back on their lies. Turn your back on the courts that do Satan's work by convicting our elders. Remain loyal to God. Remember, dear friends, we would never want to bring reproach upon God and His true organization by discussing and perpetuating these lies.

"Is that it?" Milton asked.

"Yes. That's all I could find on our website, and I didn't want to overstep what had already been written."

"Wise move, Schmidt," said Milton. "I'll email it to the broadcasting department. Who's been appointed to do the video?"

"Didn't you know?" Schmidt asked.

"Know what?"

"You...you're going to do the video," Schmidt replied.

Milton thought he'd give operant conditioning a try. "But, Brother Schmidt, you are a much more capable public speaker than I am. You have a marvelous, deeply resonant voice, and on this very serious topic, your voice of authority is perfectly suited to the message—a message that you yourself created with the blessing of God's spirit upon you."

Milton watched as Schmidt puffed up his chest slightly.

"You raise an excellent point, Brother Chandler. I think it *would* be more appropriate for a speaker like me to deliver this timely message. But because it wouldn't do for my shakes to be seen on camera, it falls to you to be the man of the hour." Schmidt then condescendingly patted Milton on the shoulder and slowly shuffled to his office.

Milton sighed. A few days ago, he would have been genuinely peacocking at the thought of delivering an international broadcast to the Society faithful, but everything had changed, and there was no going back. He'd still have to strut his stuff on camera, acting like he was God's representative in the flesh, but it was all going to be an act—just a bit of religious melodrama.

Before emailing Schmidt's script to the video broadcasting department, he wanted Donna's opinion. He figured she was at Mario's, but he didn't dare go there because Nelson was most likely watching. And he couldn't call, either, because his cell phone was owned by the Society—if he called the market, it would show up on his call history. Milton came up with a plan and decided to pay Lucy Fitzgerald a condolence visit.

Paul's widow answered the door with a warm smile. "Well, hello, Brother Chandler. It's so loving of you to stop by. Please...come inside. I just put the kettle on."

Lucy Fitzgerald was a relentlessly pleasant woman who looked like she'd gotten stuck in a time warp. She still had the same short, tightly curled strawberry-blonde hair that she'd had the day that she and Paul had been accepted as volunteers at the Society of Truth—that was half a century ago. Her coiffure was her calling card—no matter what, she never got caught with gray roots. The Society's barber shop was located in one of the underground tunnels, and Lucy had a standing weekly appointment to get her hair washed, curled, and blown out. Once a month, her appointment would also include a trim and a color touch-up.

She greeted Milton in a neatly pressed gingham dress. Her apron and dainty Timex watch with expansion wristband made her appear like a cross between June Cleaver and Harriet Nelson.

"Sister Fitzgerald, I was so sorry when I heard about Paul," Milton said. "As I'm sure you know, he and I had plans to pay a shepherding visit to one of our retired missionary sisters when the earthquake took him from us."

"That sounds just like something he would do," Lucy said. "Always thinking of others, not himself." As the kettle began to whistle, she excused herself to the kitchen to pour the tea and arrange homemade scones on a tray.

"Sister Fitzgerald," Milton called out from the living room, "may I use your home phone to call Donna? She has my cell phone with her. She's been out proselytizing with other sisters today, and I just like to keep tabs on her, especially after the earthquake."

Milton had a fleeting pang of guilt about lying to Lucy—even for the best of reasons. She was in so many ways the ideal Society wife—unfailingly kind, and utterly incapable of believing that anyone in the Society of Truth would have an ulterior motive of any sort. *Devon Nelson would call her a triumph of operant conditioning*, Milton said to himself.

"Of course!" Lucy called back from the kitchen. "Please make yourself at home. You're a good, protective husband."

Milton pulled his cell from his pants pocket and looked up the number of Mario's Market, then dialed it from the Fitzgeralds' landline.

Mario answered, "Mario's Market. This is Mario. How may I help you today?"

"Mario, this is Milton Chandler, Donna's husband. If she's there, I need to speak with her...quickly."

Mario scurried from the kitchen into the café. Donna and Keisha had just returned from leaving André in front of the "sewer access" door in the Society's underground tunnel. "It's Milton," he said as he handed the phone to Donna.

"Milton? Are you okay? Where are you?"

"I'm in the Fitzgeralds' living room. I don't have much time. I have a lot to tell you. Where can we meet?"

"Nelson has eyes everywhere, baby," Donna replied, "but I have an idea."

She called me "baby," Milton said to himself with a smile.

"Tell Lucy you're making funeral arrangements—Paul deserves the best. Then head to the florist on Water Street, just behind Mario's Market. It's the one that the headquarters always buys its flowers from, in case you didn't know."

Milton didn't know.

"I'll meet you there, incognito, in thirty minutes," Donna said, then hung up.

Lucy emerged from the kitchen with a tray of piping hot tea and warm scones. Milton didn't have the heart to eat and run, but he didn't want to linger, either. He shared an encouraging Bible passage about Paul's unique and guaranteed resurrection into heaven as part of the Bride of Christ, based on his loyal obedience to God's true religion.

He quickly drank his tea and wolfed down the delicious vanilla-iced scone—he didn't want to keep Donna waiting. Then he remembered his wingman's last text message: *Tell Lucy I love her.* "Sister Fitzgerald, I'm sure our beloved Paul's last thoughts were of you. I have no doubt he loved you deeply. He deserves a memorial service that appropriately highlights his obedient volunteer service to God's organization, and your humble submission as his wife. Thank you so much for the tea and pastry, but I must be off to begin making plans to honor him properly. Can you think of anything he would have wanted —particular flowers, for example? Is there anything that has special meaning for the two of you that you'd like to see in his floral arrangement?"

"Oh, that is so kind, Brother Chandler. May the Lord be with you and the work you do in His name," Lucy said as she accompanied him to the door.

Next stop...the florist on Water Street. If anyone was listening or watching—namely, Nelson—a visit to the florist would appear totally normal after his visit with Lucy, and his promise to take care of her husband's funeral arrangements.

Milton entered the flower shop a bit out of breath from the brisk five-block walk. "I'm guessin' you're from that religion with the big red sign," said the young woman behind the counter. "Did someone else kick the bucket? Seems like there's been quite a few of yas lately."

Milton guessed that she was not yet twenty, but she was distinctively Goth, with jet-black hair in high pigtails, short blue bangs, and heavy eye makeup. Milton was not physically attracted to her in the slightest, but the young woman had so many tattoos and piercings on visible parts of her body that he couldn't help speculating about how many more there were in the places he couldn't see. Instead of being taken aback by her appearance, however, he was greatly relieved. *Don't have to worry about whether you're a snitch for the Society*, he thought.

"Yes, unfortunately," Milton responded. "It seems like our old-timers are leaving us all at once. I need to order flowers for another funeral."

"Ya want the same sympathy package you guys always get?"

"Yes, please."

"I'll get the paperwork."

As the girl stepped into the back office, a voice came out of nowhere. "Hi, baby," Donna said.

Milton jumped back a step. "Whoa!" he exclaimed.

Donna had dressed herself in an odd combination of clothes from Mario's closet, including a knitted beanie and faded plaid flannel shirt, topped by a voluminous navy blue windbreaker with a rip at one elbow. Her face was well hidden by a pair of oversized wraparound sunglasses. "Homeless lumberjack—it's the latest style," she said with a grin.

"If it wasn't for your voice, I wouldn't have known it was you."

"Like I said, incognito," Donna replied. "Gimme your phone. I'm adding my number in your contacts as the French Pastry Café—it's across the street. Sign for the flowers, then go there and order a box of donuts to go. Take them back to headquarters to share—especially with David at the front desk. Trust me, you must create a paper trail. Call me when you're walking back. Oh! And send me the photos that Fitzgerald sent you—the ones of Nelson and Kruger and the body bag. Then delete them from your phone."

The young saleswoman returned with a clipboard. As they were discussing the details of the deluxe sympathy funeral service package, including Lucy's wish to have blue freesias and trailing stephanotis in the display—for which there would be a surcharge—Donna slipped out the door. Before leaving, Milton asked to add yellow roses to the arrangement—another surcharge—to symbolize his friendship and respect for his wingman.

Milton followed Donna's instructions precisely. On the way back to headquarters with donuts in hand, he called the French Pastry Café, and she answered. After telling Donna about being tasked to manage construction of the barbed-wire fence around the new headquarters site, he mentioned his other assignment—to broadcast the script Schmidt had written about child sexual abuse.

"Well, if a lofty position in the Society was what you always wanted, this is your claim to fame, baby," Donna replied.

There was that term "baby" again. Milton's heart melted.

"Milton? Are you still there?"

"Yes, I'm still here," Milton sighed. "I'm still here on the phone, and I'm still in this religion, and I don't know how to get out. I need you, baby. I need you now, more than ever. I'm so lost."

"Listen," Donna started, "if you want me back, and if you've really opened your eyes to all the fucked-up shit going on in the Society, then you need to work with me. We'll be partners—equals—no more you being the lord and master and head of our marriage and me as the loyal sidekick who really does all the work."

"That's what I want, too, but I know I have a long way to go to get there. Old habits die hard, and I'm sure I'm going to slip up from time to time..." he replied.

"And whenever it happens, you can depend on me to call you out on it," Donna declared. "But as long as an equal partnership is what you want, and as long as you keep working toward letting go of the ridiculous patriarchal superiority they've drilled into your brain—you're not going to feel lost for very long."

"I believe you," Milton said.

"Okay, good, because I have an idea," she said.

[illegible] to the nature of his conduct. [illegible]
worked [illegible] his conduct [illegible]
[illegible] nature of [illegible] know the way you've been [illegible]
[illegible] the discipline that [illegible] their place or ideas, the most
soldier [illegible]

"[illegible] you [illegible] to improve [illegible] that you [illegible]
[illegible] you [illegible] some sort of plan [illegible]
[illegible] Will you stop [illegible]
[illegible]

"[illegible] what you mean," he replied. "But you make all the point [illegible]
[illegible] of it all right, and I don't know why you're so upset when
you [illegible] new experience, you're [illegible]

[illegible] with me just [illegible]
opened your eyes to all the nonsense and noise of the real [illegible]
[illegible] to put us in a worse [illegible] remain [illegible]
[illegible] the bad and plain and [illegible] of all [illegible]
[illegible]

"That is not what I want," she replied. "But I have a long way to go yet
here. Maybe this is hard, but I can't expect to return to my normal life
in time," he replied.

"Whatever it happens, you think [illegible] it would be so
[illegible] I think," he replied. "He is to a [illegible] certain point that
[illegible] on. Can't you keep [illegible] slow down to the
[illegible] because that came [illegible]. Anyway, it's wonderful to be in the
[illegible] completely [illegible] for so very long.

"[illegible] Never mind my smile.

"[illegible] good [illegible] and I have greater [illegible] still."

CHAPTER 23
TYUNGUR

The restaurant delivery truck made it to the Frankfurt International Airport in just over four hours. For Min and Greg, the time flew by as they talked about everything that had happened to them since acupuncture college. When the truck came to a stop, Jacob leapt out and knocked loudly on the side panel, then opened the rear door. Ruth tried to insist that she could walk to the plane, but Min convinced her to accept a ride in the wheelchair.

Min and Greg hustled up the airstairs of the Dassault Falcon 8X and took up their positions as pilot and copilot. Min then began going through the preflight checklist, and used it to familiarize Greg with the features of the aircraft.

Jacob helped Ruth get comfortable in her seat. With her palm pressed firmly against the little bag of seeds hanging from her neck, she relaxed into the soft leather lounger. Jacob then handed her the recliner's remote. "What's this?" she asked.

"It's so you can drive your chair," he said with a smile. He showed her the buttons that electronically eased the headrest back, adjusted the lumbar support, raised the footrest and delivered heat and gentle massage, and even allowed her to lie flat. After making sure she was fully upright and safely buckled in, he took his own seat as the aircraft began to taxi.

After takeoff, Min brought the plane up to cruising altitude, then let Greg assume control. She monitored him for a bit, but once she was satisfied that he was comfortable flying solo, she went back to check on Ruth. Like a kid with a new toy, Ruth had been busy test-driving all the many configurations of her chair, and was now lying on an angle, with her feet high in the air and her head low to the floor.

"Did you know it could do this?" she asked with childish delight.

"You look like you're on an inversion table!" Min exclaimed with a laugh. "But don't stay in that Trendelenburg position for too long. All the blood will rush to your head."

Jacob, meanwhile, was feverishly texting on his cell phone.

"What are you doing?" Min inquired.

"Making sure we don't have any problems entering Russian airspace, or after we touch down," he replied. "Pulling some strings with a friendly oligarch—Aeroflot bigwig—you know how much the Russians love red tape. By the time we land, a courier will have delivered the necessary documents to the Sibylline hangar in Tyungur. Oh, and I'll change Ruth's bandage as soon as I send this last message."

"Thank you, Jacob," she said as she headed for a recliner in the back of the aircraft. Min closed the shades and pulled a soft blanket from the overhead compartment. After using her remote to convert the seat into a bed, she was out cold before her head hit the pillow.

The plane's destination, Tyungur, was a magnet for Russian adventure tourism, and attracted serious hikers, climbers, mystics, and enlightenment seekers from all over the world. Whatever their nationality or spiritual belief, most shared the same quest—to get to Belukha Mountain. At just under 14,800 feet, Belukha was the highest peak in the Golden Altai Mountains—the spine that defined the border between Russia and Kazakhstan, and a designated UNESCO World Heritage Site.

Despite the untamed grandeur of the mountains themselves, humans had lived here since the Iron Age. Scythian burial mounds, or kurgans, were preserved in the permafrost. Many tourists, however, were less focused on prehistory or natural beauty than on searching for the gateway to Shambala, or Shangri-la, a mystical place of tranquility and happiness. All had failed, and protecting the secrecy of the access point—from tourists, and especially from the USF—had long been a Sibylline priority.

Greg made the decision not to wake Min for the landing and began the descent directly into Tyungur. The humidity was rising from the ground in the early-morning air, creating small pockets of fog which offered him intermittent glimpses of the very short runway. "Peekaboo, little runway, I see you," he said aloud as he lowered the landing gear. Coming in low and slow paralleling the Katun River, he used every inch of the paved landing strip, but put the Dassault down smoothly, then taxied to the hangar before waking Min.

"Hey," he whispered close to her ear, "we're here."

Min opened her eyes, momentarily disoriented. "Here where?" she asked groggily.

"Here Tyungur. You really conked out," Greg said.

Min's eyes widened in surprise. "You landed—without me?" she asked.

"Piece of cake," Greg replied with a grin.

"Only if that piece of cake is the size of a commemorative stamp," Min said.

"Well yeah, pretty much," he replied. "A car is taking Jacob and Ruth to the lodge. They're starving, and you're probably hungry, too. I say we tag along, get some food and a quick shower, then come back. The ski plane is supposed to show up at about the same time that Mireille, Ananta, and John arrive from Ladakh. That gives us time to eat and freshen up."

Min yawned and rubbed her eyes. "You're right. Let's go," she agreed as she flung off the blanket.

The female driver of the sedan was wearing a babushka that was tied under her chin in classic East European style. Ruth remembered thinking as a girl in Quedlinburg that babushkas made women look like old hags, but her mother never left home without one folded neatly in her handbag. The Society of Truth required it for women, and it was to be deployed like a parachute, in case of emergency only. If a prayer had to be said but a man wasn't present to lead it, a woman would have to cover her head with the kerchief before beginning the prayer. Men, of course, required no such covering. To Ruth, the babushka had become the outward manifestation of woman's inferiority, a reminder that they were second best, even when talking to God.

The travelers' lodge sat at the end of an unpaved road less than five miles from the airstrip. After parking in front of a plain two-story structure, the driver went into the house. Min, Greg, and Jacob got out of the back seat; Jacob then helped Ruth, who patted her velvet drawstring pouch for reassurance. He was carrying a small satchel containing Ruth's wound dressing and stash of meds. "You've got your little bag, dearest Ruth," he said, "and I've got mine."

The lodge exterior was simple, but the inside looked like something straight out of Russian fairytale. The great room was furnished with inviting overstuffed sofas and chairs, as well as pillows, poufs, and ottomans. The centerpiece was a wood-burning stove with an ornately tiled chimney. The place was a riot of pattern and color—there wasn't one item that wasn't embellished with Russian folkloric decoration. Although nothing matched, somehow it all seemed to work together.

The driver placed her keys in a small bowl on the far side of the room and hung her bulky overcoat on a hook. She then removed her sunglasses and scarf. The person who Ruth had pegged as a frumpy Russian peasant turned out to be an attractive, very fit, and stylish young woman whose light-brown hair had been coiffed into a wispy bob with blonde highlights. Her large dark-hazel eyes were set off by her long natural eyelashes and pearly-white skin.

"Min Yunghui!" she exclaimed as she scurried toward Min. After half embracing, half squishing her, she kissed Min three times on the cheeks, as is traditional in Russian culture. "What an honor! And you...!" She turned and lunged toward Ruth with her arms wide open.

"No!" Ruth bellowed and backed away.

The woman stopped in her tracks, startled, then realized Ruth was injured. "Oh! I'm so sorry!" she apologized. "And you must be Greg," she said.

"I am," he replied, "but who are you?"

"I am Katarina Volkov. Please call me Kat." She reached for Greg's hand and shook it energetically. "All of you must be famished after your long flight. Come, follow me into the dining room for some borscht. It's my specialty!"

Min looked at Jacob with skepticism, and wondered why Kat had introduced herself to everyone except him.

The rustic, carved dining table was already set. Kat quickly returned from the kitchen with a large tureen of hearty beet soup and a platter of fried pastries. Their aromas filled the air, reminding everyone how hungry they were. Once seated, Kat filled everyone in on her background.

"My parents have been Sibyllines in Russia for a very long time," Kat began as she ladled the soup into bowls. "Of course, they kept it well hidden when it was still the USSR."

"Authoritarian Communism and Sibylline philosophy don't go together very well," said Greg.

"Authoritarian *anything* and Sibylline philosophy don't go together at all," said Min firmly. "I can't imagine we're any more popular now that Russia has become just a garden-variety dictatorship."

"This dictatorship is basically a gas station with an army and a chip on its shoulder," Greg declared. "Behind the façade of military power, however, there's a whole lot of people who are tired of being poor, but who are too scared to do anything about it—at least for now. As the world transitions away from dinosaur juice and toward more environmentally friendly fuels, the Russian economy is going to have to make the pivot and reinvent itself in a hurry. Don't you agree, Jacob?"

"Ah...ah, yes. Yes, that's true," Jacob replied.

Kat placed a hot pastry in front of each guest. "Jacob texted me before you left Germany and asked if I was available for this last-minute assignment," she said. "He and I had never met in person, but I know many of the young Sibyllines that he mentors. I jumped at the chance to help on this most important mission, even in the smallest way."

"Don't let Kat's bubbly personality fool you into thinking she's a pushover," said Jacob. "She was my top student in combat. I wouldn't mess with her."

"Why would we?" asked Min. "She's on our side."

"On our side...right," Jacob responded tersely.

How strange, Min thought. For her, it was yet another instance of Jacob's recent odd behavior. Greg's gambit to draw him out about Russia's ability to wean itself off fossil fuels had been a good one. In the past, it was a topic that Jacob had often talked at length about, but today he'd been monosyllabic and just short of rude. And then there was what happened on the plane. She'd been too exhausted to call him on it at the time, but a Russian oligarch contact—really? Especially one with aviation connections. She'd been flying Sibyllines around the world for many years now, and she could think of several important flights where she'd had to spend extra time and fuel to avoid Russian airspace. *Having an "Aeroflot bigwig" paving the way for a more direct route would have come in handy*, she thought. *How come he never mentioned this to me before?*

Min rejoined the conversation just as the subject matter turned to the medicinal properties of plants. "When I was a girl, I told my mother that I wanted to be a *Heilpraktiker*—a healer—when I grew up," said Ruth, "but of course, that was impossible."

"But why?" Kat asked.

"The Society of Truth considers naturopathy to be a black art—the Devil's work," Ruth replied, "and in any event, I was female, so any profession was out of the question. I'm still fascinated by the subject, and it seems to me that what I saw Gabby and her son, Zach, doing in their greenhouse probably has a lot in common with what you were doing in the castle, Min. Sometimes I wonder if that fungal network... what do you call it?"

"I call it the 'Wood Wide Web,' but that's just in jest. Its real name is mycelium," Min responded.

"Yes...I wonder..." Ruth said, "since mycelium is how all the plants and trees on the planet communicate with each other, perhaps there's more communication going on than we think."

"Ruth, it's too bad we didn't have more time together with the Eden Project before we left the castle," Min said. "I can only hope that if the USF came looking for Greg and the seeds, they didn't destroy too much, and we'll have a chance to rebuild."

"I have an idea, Minny," said Greg. "If we're headed back to Quedlinburg after dropping Mireille, John, and Ananta on the Belukha glacier, seems to me that you could use an assistant to help you with the Eden Project—an apprentice, if you will."

Min smiled broadly. "Someone who's a quick study and eager to learn," she added.

"And it would make Jacob's job so much easier," said Greg, "because both of his women would be in the same place at the same time—except when you're on air-chauffeuring duty, Min."

Ruth's eyes sparkled with delight. "I'm presently unemployed," she said, "and if that position is open, I'd like to apply for the job. I have to figure that I'm pretty much fired from my last job as a writer, editor, and proofreader—I left without giving two weeks' notice."

"Consider yourself hired, dearest Ruth," said Min. "You're all mine now, and I'm going to work your fingers to the bone!"

Ruth grinned as she held up her uninjured arm and wiggled her fingers. "See? They're already bony," she said. "Doesn't scare me a bit."

There was laughter all around as Greg caught a look in Min's eye that it was time for them to get going. "Is it possible to get hot showers, warm clothes, and snow gear for Min and me before we leave?" Greg asked.

Kat nodded and gestured for Min and Greg to follow her to one of the guest rooms upstairs. "I was instructed to suit you up for your flight to the glacier," she said as she opened the bedroom closet. "The private bath is through that door."

"I can't believe I never knew about you, Kat," Min said.

"Oh...but I knew about you, Min Yunghui. You're famous among all my Sibylline friends!"

"Really? How many Sibylline friends do you have?"

"Are you kidding?" Kat answered. "We're everywhere! Look..."

Kat opened her phone and showed Min all the Sibylline social media groups she belonged to, along with numerous followers on her personal sites. She scrolled through tons of pictures, comments, memes, and videos of thousands and thousands of young people from all over the world, supporting, networking, and collaborating with each other.

"Who checks to make sure they're all Sibyllines?" Min asked.

"No idea," Kat replied. "And this is Chastity, my BFF," Kat added as she showed Min a close-up of a girl Kat's age with a big smile, a gold beret over shoulder-length brown hair, and a tiny nose ring. "She's in my economics class. And this is Hue. He's a finance and business law major. He tutors Chastity and me on things like international finance and econometrics...blah, blah...anything to do with the mighty dollar," she said with a giggle. "And all of them have heard of you, Min!"

Kat tapped her camera app and shot a selfie of the two of them. Before Min knew what Kat was doing, Kat quickly posted it. Seconds later, the dings from likes began pouring in. It was as if someone had hit the jackpot on a slot machine—it was so loud and persistent that Kat had to mute her phone.

"May I look at your cell?" Min asked.

"Sure!"

Min sat scrolling through Kat's photos while Kat began pulling warm garments from the closet and tossing them on the bed. As Min was skimming, she stopped and backtracked to a picture that caught her attention. Enlarging it to get a closer look at the people in the background, she saw Jacob amongst the young people, laughing along with them. She smiled at the happiness that seemed to radiate from him when mentoring these young, energetic Sibyllines—so different from his saturnine behavior of late. She wished he'd told her more about them, and that she could have been more personally involved in the mentorship, but between her twin responsibilities as both a horticulturalist and a pilot, she was already overextended.

"I have to get back downstairs to the dining room. Dessert awaits!" Kat declared. Min handed the phone back to Kat as she left the room.

"What's eating at you, Minny?" Greg asked.

"There's something weird going on with Jacob, but I don't know exactly what it is," she responded. "Why don't you shower first? I'll check out this garb that Kat pulled out for us."

Greg entered the bathroom and called out to Min through the closed door. "When Kat said the room had its own private *bath*, she meant it literally," he said. "There's no shower."

The walls and floor of the bathroom were covered in tiny white octagonal tiles set off with an inlaid, intricate design of eight-pointed stars executed in black. A restored white claw-foot bathtub with black feet sat at one end of the room. Immediately next to it was an electric towel warmer with large, toasty white towels ready to be wrapped around clean, wet bodies.

Greg filled the tub, then submerged his exhausted body in the hot water. Meanwhile, Min rummaged through the cold-weather gear, choosing apparel appropriate for her size, and guessing for Greg—long underwear, scarves, insulated leather gloves, and hooded jackets. She expected Greg to be finished quickly, but he seemed to be taking his sweet time. She knocked lightly on the door, but he didn't answer. The door was unlocked, so she cracked it open and quietly called his name, but he didn't respond. Opening the door, she saw him slumped in the water up to his chin. He was sound asleep.

Min couldn't help but gaze at his naked body—being a double agent meant he had to stay in shape. And yes, she was attracted to that body, and to the wit and intellect attached to it. She knew he felt the same attraction for her as she did for him. She swore there were a couple of moments while riding in the back of the restaurant supply truck on the way to Frankfurt when they almost kissed, but something held them back. Maybe they were both afraid of waking Ruth.

Ruth's not here. What's stopping you now? Min asked herself. With that thought, she decided to take a chance. She slipped out of her clothes and dropped them onto the tiled floor. She lifted one leg over the side of the tub and slowly lowered it into the water on the far side of Greg's body, and then immersed her other leg, straddling him just below the knees. Then she gradually lowered herself into the water.

Min tried not to rouse him, at least not quite yet—and miraculously, she was successful. *He had to stay hyperalert, flying for eleven hours*, she told herself. *No wonder he's still asleep.* Bracing her hands against each side of the tub to hold herself steady, she kissed him gently. Greg responded, half-asleep and half-awake, pressing his warm, soft lips to hers. He tenderly wrapped his arms around her, pulling her into himself, then slid his hands up and down the back of her smooth body, feeling every inch of her curves. Min craved him, and she could feel him responding to her as they both began to breathe more heavily. He opened his eyes, looking at her, taking in the moment.

"Do you want me to stop?" Min whispered.

"Do I look like I want you to stop?" he whispered back as his body surged with desire.

The heated towels felt amazing once the hot sexual encounter was over. "And we didn't even slosh out too much water out of the tub!" Min said proudly.

"Tsunami next time, Minny," he replied with a very satisfied smile.

After putting on all the cold weather gear, the two came downstairs to say their goodbyes, but only Kat was seated at the table. "We'll be just a minute," Jacob called over his shoulder on route to the bathroom. "Ruth's bandage needs changing."

Despite her body's contentment and relaxation, Min's antennae were up and twitching—she was still bothered by how Jacob was behaving. *He's been acting strangely ever since we left the castle*, she told herself. *Something's off, that's for sure. Should I step in?*

Min found herself embroiled in an intense internal debate. *On the one hand, Jacob has never been anything but wonderful and attentive to Ruth, and I'm sure if I butt in, he'll be offended*, she reasoned. *On the other hand, Min Yunghui, what the hell is wrong with you?! Respect your intuition. You're a Sibylline, and that's Ruth, a true heroine if ever there was one, and she's been entrusted with the seeds from the Tree of Life. Your job is to do whatever you need to do to protect them, and her. And seriously? With so much at stake, do you really care if Jacob gets pissed off?*

"Ruth, my dear, let me assist you," Min said aloud.

"I need to change her bandage," Jacob protested. "I'll take her."

"Nonsense, Jacob. I'm sure Ruth would like to use the restroom as well, and would prefer a lady to accompany her. Wouldn't you, Ruth?" Min insisted.

"Oh, it's so nice to be fought over," Ruth said with a giggle, "but Min is right. Maybe it's my leftover Society of Truth modesty, but it's much more dignified to have another woman help with personal plumbing issues. Better than revealing all my droopy delicate lady parts to a handsome young man like you."

Jacob reluctantly handed over the black doctor's bag to Min, and the two women headed off to the bathroom. After a few minutes, the women came out, and everyone said their goodbyes. Jacob chauffeured Min and Greg back to the Sibylline hangar to drop them off, while Kat and Ruth stayed behind at the lodge.

CHAPTER 24
VIDEO

Rocky already knew his way around a commercial kitchen, so all he needed was a little direction from Mario to take over from André—along with Mario's family recipes, which Mario handed over gladly. Rocky soon discovered a new love—Italian pastries. Baked desserts had never been his forte—he preferred savory offerings—but kneading the soft sweet dough was both therapeutic and sensual. Working lovingly with his hands to make something delicious—something that made people happy—was exactly what he needed to be doing to honor his sister, Gabby.

Debra and Jen also found themselves completely absorbed in helping Mario with postquake cleanup and filling customer orders. Jen worked the cash register, while Deb perfected her skill at making leaf and heart designs in the milk foam of cappuccinos and lattes. One of Mario's regulars even whispered that her espresso tasted slightly smoother than "the Jamaican's."

"Don't tell him I said that, though," the customer added with a grin. "I'll deny it."

Mario paused and looked around at his bustling market. Despite the devastation…despite all the trauma and death…and despite facing nothing but uncertainty about their own futures, these people were finding joy in the present, joy in simple tasks, and joy in working together. No hidden agenda, no ulterior motives. All they wanted at this moment was to be helpful, add a little humor, and contribute toward a collective good. It warmed Mario's heart as he watched such resilience and laughter. What was going on in his market was living testimony to the genuine cooperation and kindness that was built into all humans. These "ordinary people" weren't ordinary at all—they were true embodiments of the Sibylline way of life.

What a contrast they were with members of the Society of Truth. Mario had served them coffee for decades, and he could spot them as soon as they walked through the door. There was a self-righteous air of phoniness about almost all of them—pretending as if they had nothing to sell, when in fact they were salesmen of the first order, intent on peddling their religion to everyone, along with the distorted vision of reality that came with it. The clean-shaven men in their polyester suits and ties and cheap but well-shined shoes looked like they were playing dress-up. The women were in costume as well, but in an entirely different way. With their thick pantyhose, knee-length skirts, and dresses—never pants—they were wearing their submissive status on their bodies, no matter how they felt inside. They were also unnaturally quiet, unlike the men, who tended to enter the café bantering loudly—much louder than Mario's other customers.

Mario then reflected on their offspring, the little ones who were being raised as well-behaved Society of Truth members—he'd seen how their parents controlled them in his market. Many kids cowered or flinched if the dad raised his arm to get the attention of waitstaff— too often, that gesture meant they were about to get hit. One way or another, the children who grew up in the Society had all been damaged by the religion. They were fed a steady diet of physical abuse—often in the name of "discipline," verbal tirades, women's subservience, relentless religious indoctrination, willful disbelief in science, deliberate discouragement of higher education, and of course, sexual molestation. The Society pretended that these were happy, devout families, but it was all a charade, a bit of cheap theatre to cover the fact that the men were beating and browbeating their "loved ones," all in an effort to reassure themselves of their own male superiority.

Mario remembered one instance in particular. The father of an infant not more than six months old lost his temper because the baby couldn't stop crying. He grabbed his son from his mother's arms and retreated to the restroom, where he spanked the shit out of his child.

Mario could hear the blows from behind the pastry counter. When father and son returned, no one else in that door-to-door ministry group said a word. The mother, however, grabbed her baby and put him to her breast, covering herself with the baby's blanket as she glared at her husband with sheer hatred. That was about fifteen years ago. He wondered where that mother and son were now. *I hope they escaped*, he said to himself.

Mario had the utmost respect for the women who'd summoned up the courage to leave, both for themselves and for their children. He saw the same quiet strength in Jen that he'd seen in Keisha, whereas Donna and Deb had more of a mouthy, independent streak. All of them were phenomenal women—he couldn't imagine any of them as obedient and submissive Society members.

Donna was wiping down a table when Bozz Kruger opened the front door and entered the market. "I see you're movin' on up," he observed wryly.

Donna's heart skipped a beat. She recognized his deep voice instantly, and her first inclination was to go for his throat. In one dreadful day, this man had deliberately created a crisis that had turned her life upside down. With a single kiss that was caught by a surveillance camera, he'd made Milton look like a cuckolded, incompetent fool who couldn't control his unruly, lascivious wife. As she thought further, however, that terrible crisis had landed her exactly where she was—surrounded by new friends, and poised to begin a new era of personal growth. If it hadn't been for Kruger, she'd be spinning her wheels in the Society, and Milton would still be the token Black president of a murderous cult of pederasts.

Kruger walked to the counter and ordered two espressos and two tiramisus. "Bring them there," he told Debra, pointing to the table that Donna had been wiping down.

"Please join me, Mrs. Chandler," he said with a touch of menace as he pulled out the café chair. Jen served them each tiramisu, while Deb brought the two espressos to the table. Both felt the tension between Donna and the man opposite her, but they had no idea who he was.

Donna slowly slid both her espresso and tiramisu across the table toward Kruger. "I didn't order these. Indulge yourself," she said.

"I insist," Kruger said, pushing the cup and plate back across the table. As he did so, Donna could see that his right hand was bandaged.

"I know who you are," she declared.

"Oh really?" Kruger replied sarcastically.

"What I *also* know," Donna retorted, "is that you're a fuckin' pawn in the hands of a type of evil so dark that even you can't conjure up, and they don't give a shit about you."

She paused, looking at him with contempt. "You think you have power, but your testosterone-addled brain is deceiving you. You're nothing. You're worse than nothing," she scoffed. "You're an insignificant mite on the hair of a wart on the back of a slimy toad in a grotesque swamp. And you know what? The swamp monster that's gonna chew you up and eat you alive...is also gonna shit you out his foul asshole and not even wipe his butt."

Bozz Kruger burst out laughing, but it was all for show—he was seething inside. Donna had struck a nerve—Devon Nelson had repeatedly made Kruger feel like an underling, and he was still pissed about being summoned to clean up after Nelson's rash murder of Silverman. He was even more pissed about Nelson's racism and air of entitlement.

Donna remained impassive, staring into Kruger's eyes as his jaw clenched and a vein throbbed in his forehead. "I should break your fucking neck, and the necks of everyone in here," he said. He was furious that Donna was devoid of fear. Fear is what he drank. Fear is what he feasted on.

"Go ahead," Donna said, calling his bluff. "Oh wait...you can't... because you're not the boss of you. You can't just come storming in here like some thug in a bad gangster movie, slaughtering everyone in the place and laughing while you do it. Al Capone you're not. You're not even Clyde, of Bonnie and Clyde. Hell—you're not even Louise, of Thelma and Louise. You have to answer to a higher-up. You can't murder me in cold blood in front of all these customers in the light of day—like you did with poor Paul Fitzgerald."

Kruger's eyes widened. *How did she find out about that?* he wondered. *Nelson sure as shit didn't tell her—it had to come from her stupid husband.*

"Thought you could keep that one a secret, huh?" she taunted, then realized she may have gone too far, and perhaps even put Milton in danger. Donna had to pull back. "I see you hurt yourself," she said, changing the subject. "What happened to your hand?"

Kruger felt the blood rush to his cheeks as he compulsively pulled his sleeve over his knuckles to cover the bandage. Finding himself at the mercy of the Rastafarian was a source of ongoing shame and embarrassment. "It...it got burnt," he replied uncomfortably.

"Interesting use of the passive voice, Mr. Kruger," Donna replied. "Looks to me like you had a close encounter with a hot kitchen knife."

Jen and Debra elbowed each other when they heard the name "Kruger." This was the man Cameron had described while they were still in the bunker—the same man who André had bested upstairs in Mario's office. Jen then grabbed Debra's arm to restrain her from making any sudden moves. Donna didn't seem to be the least bit afraid of Kruger, and Jen was insightful enough to take that as a cue.

Kruger glowered and struggled to keep his temper. "Now, if you'll excuse me, I have work to do," Donna said. She stood, then turned toward the coffee counter. "Jen, honey," she called out, "I think Mr. Kruger has lost his appetite. Would you mind taking these fine desserts and espressos away?"

"Oh, and, Mr. Kruger," Donna added as she walked away, "André says he could teach you how to make a good caramel macchiato. He thinks you could have real potential as a barista."

"Good day, Mrs. Chandler," Kruger responded with extreme formality. "And by the way, better warn your tattletale I'm gonna find him."

As soon as Kruger was gone, Jen and Debra ran to Donna and quickly enveloped her in a hug—she was shaking from head to toe.

"That was Kruger?" Jen asked.

"Sure was, and I'm afraid I might have said too much while I was talking to him," Donna admitted. "By trying to be a smartass, I think I put Milton in danger. I need your help fixing this—we *have* to fix this —you know as well as I do that they'd have no compunctions about killing Milton."

"You got that right," said Deb. "No offense to Milton, but for these guys at this point, what's one more member of the Elder Board?"

"Donna, call Milton and let him know that Kruger might be onto him," said Jen. "What we need in the meantime is a red herring—

something that will demand their immediate attention and take the heat off your guy."

"I think I know what that could be," said Donna, "but it's not something I can do myself. Jen, how much do you know about IT?"

"Everything I know fits in a thimble," Jen replied. "I work with the bank's computer system because it's essential to my job, but I know how to use it in the same way that I know how to drive a car—by sticking the key in the ignition and stepping on the gas. What do I know about what's under the hood? Absolutely nothing."

"Too bad," said Donna. "My idea calls for hacking into the Society's system and making a little, ah, substitution."

"Did someone say 'hacking'?" asked Debra.

While Jen kept the customers happy, Donna took Deb aside. She described the self-serving script that Schmidt had written to justify the Society's position on the child sexual abuse scandal, and how Milton had been assigned to do the video broadcast. "But I'm afraid the subject matter is too mature for you, Debra."

Debra bristled. "I'm flattered that you want to protect what's left of my innocence, Donna, but I haven't been PG-13 for a very long time. And with all due respect, I don't like the idea that you think you can decide what I can and cannot handle."

"Neutral corners, both of you," said Jen. "Donna, I should explain that I raised my children to believe that no subject matter is taboo—we talk about everything. And when I left the Society, I made the deliberate choice to make sure they were fully informed about the birds and the bees."

Debra rolled her eyes. "We call it fucking, Mom," she said with exasperation.

"I apologize, Debra," said Donna. "Too many years in the Society almost made a prude out of me. I told Milton about an idea for an alternative script. If we can get into the system, we can snag one of Schmidt's old videos, then dub in new audio. Once they realize they've been hacked, it'll be too late."

"I'm impressed," Deb said.

"The question is…can you do it? If so, we need to do it fast."

"I can't answer that without talking to Sadie," said Deb.

As if on cue, Sadie returned from dropping Zach off at Aunt

Phoebe's. After fueling her with a cup of espresso and a cannoli, Deb explained the plan.

"Hmmm…" Sadie mumbled. She tilted her head in thought, then smiled. "Mario!" she called out to the kitchen.

Mario had Frank Sinatra playing in the background while teaching Rocky how to toss and catch dough to make calzones. He emerged from the kitchen covered with flour. "He'll get the hang of it eventually," he said. "Meanwhile, it's a blizzard in there."

"We need a computer," Sadie said.

"Upstairs," Mario responded. "It's a dinosaur, like me, but it works, and it's all yours."

"Donna, you write the script," said Sadie. "You know their style. Once you're satisfied with it, it'll be Deb's turn."

Sadie turned to Debra. "I'll be giving you precise instructions to upload the document to a secure NYPD portal. Follow them to the letter. I gotta make a phone call to get you the link. And by the way, this never happened."

As Donna got started on the new script, Sadie stepped into the alley and pulled out her cell phone. "Rachel, it's Dixon. I need a favor. Are you in front of a compu…scratch that…of course, you're in front of a computer. You're never anywhere else!"

"What do you need?" Rachel asked.

"A little artful sabotage," said Sadie.

"Oh, goody," Rachel replied. "My favorite sport."

"Type in 'sot.org,' " Sadie said. "Let me know when you have the website pulled up."

"Got it."

"Good. Now, scroll to the bottom of the homepage and click on 'SOT Broadcasting.' You'll see a page filled with videos of clean-cut old White dudes dressed in suits and ties."

"Yup."

"I need you to pick one of the videos that has the name Thomas Schmidt as the speaker—it should be about four minutes long."

"They're *all* about four minutes long," Rachel replied. "These guys are nothing if not predictably consistent. Okay, now what?"

"Copy it," said Sadie. "I'm going to be sending you a script. I want you to recite the script into a recorder and adjust the tone and pitch of your speech with that voice enhancer thingamajiggy."

"Thingamajiggy..." Rachel repeated with a laugh. "So that's the new official technical term used by the NYPD?"

"The altered voice has to sound like an older man," Sadie replied, ignoring the sarcasm. "Delete the existing audio track from Thomas Schmidt's video, and then drop in the new script instead—like a voice-over. Don't get too picky about having Schmidt's mouth match the words we're putting in it. We don't have time to make it perfect."

"Oh ye of little faith!" Rachel exclaimed in mock outrage. "Perfection is how I roll. I can play with the sound on the...thingamajiggy... and make my voice sound like...what did you call him? Ah yes, 'a clean-cut old White dude.' By the time I'm done, it won't look and sound like just any clean-cut old White dude. It will look and sound like Schmidt himself is speaking every syllable."

"Excellent."

"I could also make him sound like Donald Duck or Miss Piggy, if you think that might be more effective."

Sadie guffawed. "Tempting, but no thanks," she said. "Do your thing, just do it quickly. I'll get you the IP address of their broadcasting department as soon as I can. Do you think you can hack into it?"

"You know I can, or you wouldn't have called me," Rachel replied.

"Good. Once you're in the system, you'll see a brand new video in the queue. You'll know it by its title. It's called, 'The Bible's Position on Child Protection.' "

"You gotta be kidding me!" Rachel exclaimed. "As if those patriarchal bozos have any interest in protecting the innocent! They're worse than the Catholic Church when it comes to pedophilia!"

"Roger that," Sadie agreed. "Take down that video and replace it with the one you just altered. Keep the new title."

"Oh, Sadie, this is gonna be so much fun!" said Rachel enthusiastically. "I'm looking forward to seeing this alternate script. Too bad I won't be able to see the horrified look on Schmidt's face in real time as he watches himself onscreen. Sorry? Not sorry. Those guys hurt kids—and then they cover for each other. They've got it coming to them, and then some!"

"They sure do, Rachel. Think of yourself as an instrument of karma, my friend, and thank you. Text me the link to the secure upload portal, and I'll have the script sent to you ASAP."

Sadie walked back upstairs to find Donna and Debra still at Mario's computer. "Donna, do you think you could get the Society's IP address from Milton?" she asked.

"Of course," Donna replied. She had just finished the script and was showing it to Deb.

"This is what you thought would not be age-appropriate for me?" Deb asked. "You have no idea what happened to my mom, or why she left the religion, do you?"

"I never met your mom until now," Donna replied, "but let me guess. Was she was raped by an elder in the religion and told to keep it quiet?"

Sadie gave Rachel's secure upload link to Deb, and the new script was on its way.

As soon as Milton finished filming "The Bible's Position on Child Protection," he went back to Fitzgerald's desk on the tenth floor, scrolled through the contact list on his cell, and called the French Pastry Café.

"Are we in business?" he asked.

"We sure are," Donna replied. "All I need from you is the IP address of the Society's broadcasting department."

"Here you go. One...nine..." Milton began.

Just then, Bozz Kruger bolted out of the elevator. As soon as he saw Milton, he headed straight for him with fire in his eyes.

Donna had warned him that Kruger might be coming for him, but this was sooner than he had expected. Kruger must have sprinted to headquarters straight from Mario's Market. Acting nonchalant, Milton held up his index finger as Kruger loomed over him, motioning that he needed one more minute on the phone. "...216 French *crullers*..." Milton emphasized "cruller," hoping Donna would catch on that it was code for Kruger.

"...81 éclairs, and 121 chocolate croissants. Repeat that back to me...That's correct, and please have them delivered to the Society of

Truth's lobby on Columbia Heights. Oh...and don't forget our sympathy discount. Let David, our doorkeeper, know it's for the Fitzgerald funeral service."

"Hand over your phone," Kruger commanded.

"What's going on?" Milton asked innocently.

Kruger didn't answer. He grabbed Milton's cell phone out of his hand, then feverishly scrolled through his photos. He'd expected to find whatever images Fitzgerald had captured of him and Nelson on the loading dock with Silverman's body, but there were none.

Whew! Milton thought. *My Donna—saving my ass once again.*

Kruger then looked at the list of recent calls. Sure enough, the last call had been made to the French Pastry Café. He eyed Milton suspiciously, then redialed the number.

Hearing Milton emphasize the word "cruller," Donna had immediately suspected that Bozz Kruger had gone straight to the tenth floor of headquarters as soon as he had left Mario's, and that he'd gotten there in record time. When her phone began to ring, she tossed it to Debra. "Answer it saying, 'French Pastry Café.' I'd do it, but Kruger knows my voice, and my French is terrible."

"Bonjour!" Debra answered in her best schoolgirl French. "French Pastry Café!"

"I'd like my phone back now," Milton said as he snatched the cell away from Kruger. "If I remember rightly, you're the real estate agent who kissed my wife, and then had the surveillance camera video footage released to the news media..." Milton looked stern, then broke into a wide grin. "I want to shake your hand, brotha!" he exclaimed.

Milton sprang to his feet, then firmly grasped Kruger's right hand and pumped it vigorously. "Ow!" Kruger exclaimed as he withdrew his bandaged hand. "That hurts like a motherfucker."

"Oh, sorry," said Milton. "I had no intention of causing you pain, my brotha—not after the huge favor you did for me."

"What favor was that?" Kruger asked. His hand was still smarting from the vice-grip handshake, and from being seared and blistered by André's knife.

"That stubborn woman was the furthest thing from a godly wife, and I am glad you exposed her true nature for all to see. Her independent spirit has fomented rebellion among young God-fearing Christian women—a very bad example, indeed! I endured her lack of wifely submission for years—too many years. But now I'm free, and I have you to thank for it. Everything happens in the Lord's due time, don't you agree, Mr. Kruger?"

"Umm...yes! Most...certainly," Kruger agreed hesitantly. "I need to ask you something. It's Milton, correct?"

"Yes, but you can call me Brother Chandler," Milton replied.

"Where were you right before the earthquake...*Milton*?" Kruger asked. He was not about to call this man his brother.

"I was here with our beloved Brother Paul Fitzgerald, God rest his soul," Milton replied as he began to repeat the same story he had told Devon Nelson. "We were about to call on one of our members—an older sister who was in the grip of depression. We invited Brother Nelson to come along, but as president, he understandably had important administrative matters to attend to. After the quake, there were no cabs to be had anywhere, so Brother Fitzgerald suggested we reschedule the shepherding visit for another day. I left Paul to go to the dorm to make sure no one was injured there. He stayed behind to check on everyone here at headquarters. Why do you ask?"

Without answering Milton, Kruger turned to walk away.

As soon as he was gone, Milton redialed the French Pastry Café, and Deb picked up again. "Bonjour! French Pastry Café!" she said gaily.

"Monsieur Chandler here," Milton said with a laugh. "You can stop with the French now, but I have to say...whoever you are...well done! Is Madame Donna with you?"

"Oui, oui!" Deb giggled. "Here she is."

"Hi, Milton," Donna said. "I assume Deb handled that the way you hoped."

"It was perfect," Milton replied. "You should've seen Kruger's—I mean Cruller's face. Please tell Deb thank you and that I hope to meet her one day. Did you get the IP address?"

"I did," Donna said. "But now that Monsieur Cruller knows they're expected for Paul's funeral, you should call the actual French Pastry Café and have those desserts delivered. Remember what I said about leaving a paper trail? Sometimes that paper trail is covered in royal icing."

"Got it."

"Did you finish taping the broadcast?" Donna asked.

"Yes, and I stuck around and watched as it was uploaded into the queue."

"That was smart," said Donna. "If they want to accuse you of tampering with the video, you'll have witnesses to confirm you had nothing to do with it."

"Tampering with the video? Is that the bright idea you mentioned?" Milton asked.

"Let's just say we're, ah, *adapting* it..." Donna replied. "The revised version will star Thomas Schmidt himself, but with a twist. We're going to 'borrow' a video he previously recorded, then replace what he said with a different audio. It'll look like lip synching, or a voiceover. We'll pull the broadcast you made and replace it with the one we doctored. Would you like to hear the script?" Donna asked.

"I'm all ears!" Milton replied.

As Donna read, Milton sat back and imagined the words coming out of Thomas Schmidt's mouth:

It took many years to get to this moment. Today, the Society of Truth confronts its own sin—its own unspeakable depravity. Child sexual abuse within the Society is an abomination that has been hiding in plain sight for far too long. Trust has been broken, innocence betrayed.

An in-depth investigation by your Elder Board has laid bare the shocking scale of child sexual abuse within the Society, and the lengths to which our elders—including some of our own elders here at headquarters—have gone to shield abusers. This is not "fake news." We are in possession of both written and electronic records documenting the case files of thousands of Society children who were sexually abused. We also know that countless other accusations have been suppressed or covered up. These heinous acts go back decades, and they continue to flourish in our midst today. Sadly, they can be found in every one of our congregations.

The time has come to hold ourselves accountable. We must formally say to all of you who have been victimized:

We believe you.

We believe you.

The Society of Truth believes you.

We are deeply sorry that you were not protected, sorry that your cries were not heard. We failed you. And we apologize, even as we understand that until trust is rebuilt, all the apologies in the world will miss the mark.

We have outlined a plan to address our shortcomings. The first step in that plan is to compel all elders to disclose whatever information they may have about instances of child sexual abuse—either past or ongoing —to civil authorities. Beginning immediately, elders are barred from keeping any such knowledge confidential—no matter when it occurred. Elders must—I repeat must—fully report all such incidents to the jurisdiction in which they occurred.

But what is the Society of Truth asking of you, our devoted followers? Let this be solemn moment of reckoning. As soon as this video ends, conclude your regularly scheduled service with song and prayer. Do not engage in your usual after-meeting interchange of encouragement. Do not speak with one another about this matter, and do not inundate headquarters with calls and emails. Instead, go quietly home. Turn off your electronic devices. Turn off your phones.

Dedicate the next twenty-four hours to prayer and introspection. Remain in seclusion. Give this day the same honor and respect as the day Jesus Christ, our Lord, threw the corrupt money changers out of the temple. God Himself is asking for your strict obedience in observing twenty-four hours of off-grid silence in deep, gratitude-filled prayer. Trust in the Lord, and honor Him with utmost compliance. Going forward, our Lord will use His Elder Board to begin cleansing and resanctifying His true organization. Soon, we will be back online to offer encouragement, along with a new, enlightened direction. You can access this video on our sot.org website.

"That's fabulous, Donna," said Milton.

"It will be broadcast to all congregations tomorrow at 7:30 p.m. local time, beginning in New Zealand and rolling westward from there. Headquarters won't get wind of it till it's 7:30 here in Brooklyn."

"How in the world is Devon Nelson going to backpedal from this?" Milton exclaimed.

"He'll only have two choices," Donna said. "Either he pretends it was planned, and compares his presidency with the leadership of Jesus Christ himself—like the script suggests. Or he claims that Schmidt, an elderly man with severe Parkinson's and nineteenth-century computer skills—meaning he has none—was fiendishly clever enough to hack into the Society broadcast system."

"What kind of motive could Nelson invent for why Schmidt would do that?" Milton asked.

"Beats me," said Donna. "It doesn't take a rocket scientist to know which one Nelson will choose, and since you're his new right-hand man..."

"And since we figured out how to force him to conclude that I had nothing to do with it..." Milton added.

"It means that he's going to assign you to help him ride herd on damage control. Oh...baby...this is just the beginning!" Donna said gleefully.

"Oh, Donna, there's a new music in your voice, one I haven't heard since we were dating."

"That's because I'm singing on the inside," she replied. "I'm finally listening to my gut. I'd felt so uncomfortable in my own skin for so long. I knew things weren't right—for years. Our marriage wasn't right. Everything in the religion that we lived for every day wasn't right. The kindness was fake, the 'truth' was fake, the love was fake. You knew as well as I did that our marriage had died a long time ago, and yet we'd walk into the congregation as if we were this lovey-dovey couple. It makes me wonder how many other Society of Truth couples fake their happiness, knowing their marriage is dead. I suspect that many wives actually *hate* the men they're married to."

"You're right, of course. I just wish it hadn't taken so long for me to wake up," Milton said.

"Don't get bogged down lamenting," Donna said. "There's nothing you can do about that—it happened. Turn the page."

"I do love you. I love you so much—it aches not to be with you."

"I love you too, baby. I always have," Donna replied softly. "I just didn't love what we had become. It feels good to work at something we both believe in as a real team—no superiority, no domination—just using our gifts, talents, and skills to complement each other. You have to admit...it feels...organic...like this is how it's supposed to be—doesn't it?"

Now that the substitute video had been launched and Zach and the seeds were safely with Aunt Phoebe, Sadie refocused her attention on retrieving her classic T-Bird. In theory, Fonzie was still upstate in the town of Hudson, near Gabby and Rocky's restaurant, the Gabby Abbey, but as she thought back on the raid that had ended with all of them being transported to DEA headquarters in DC, she figured that was unlikely.

"I bet my Fonzie was too big a trophy for Ken Kreighton to resist," she mumbled as she opened the LoJack app on her phone. "That ferret-faced thug thinks he has a new toy, but he's about to find out how wrong he is about that."

Sadie pulled up Fonzie's current location and recent history—as she suspected, the T-Bird had been driven to the DC area, specifically to a Georgian brick colonial in the exclusive Chain Bridge Forest area of Arlington, Virginia.

She immediately made the "okay sign" with her right hand, touching her index finger to her thumb. After putting those two fingers into her mouth, Sadie blew a world-class taxi whistle, much to the earsplitting astonishment of every pedestrian on Old Fulton Street. "Where to, lady?" asked the cabbie who stopped.

"La Guardia," she replied. "Delta Terminal. I need to be on the next shuttle to Reagan National."

"You got it."

Here I come, Fonzie. Mama's on her way! she said to herself. *And, Pheebs, when Fonzie and I get back to the city, I'll be asking you to perform one helluva T-Bird saging—an exorcism of evil spirits. Don't want any leftover icky Kreighton vibes tainting my baby boy.*

CHAPTER 25
BELUKHA

As Min, Greg, and Jacob approached the Sibylline hangar in Tyungur, the ski plane was waiting for them. "Holy moly. Can't sneak up on anyone in that thing," said Greg. The plane was a Pilatus PC-6 Turbo-Porter, a single-engine STOL (short takeoff and landing) aircraft, and it was distinctively painted with an egg-yolk yellow fuselage and bright-red wing and tail. "I wonder if it glows in the dark," he added.

"Laugh if you like, Greg," said Min, "but don't underestimate how versatile it is. The Porter is one of the few planes rugged enough to operate reliably in the highest altitudes of the Himalayas. The skis can be raised or lowered in flight, so we can depart from a standard runway and arrive on ice, and vice versa. It can also be easily outfitted with pontoons to operate as a float plane."

"Those pontoons will be ever so useful on the glacier," Greg replied sarcastically.

"Pbbblllttt," said Min, blowing him a raspberry. "This aircraft is beloved by bush pilots everywhere. It can take off or land in mud, soft sand, tall grass, ice, and snow, and can be used for search and rescue, aerial surveillance, or as an air ambulance. Because it needs so little runway and can operate off dirt strips in the middle of nowhere, it's also a favorite for drug smugglers and gunrunners."

"I'll keep that in mind," he replied.

"And because it's used by the bad guys, it's also used by various customs, border patrol, military, and counterintelligence units. It has room for six people, and it's easy in, easy out," she said. "There are two doors in the cockpit and two large sliding doors on either side of the fuselage, but turn around—see that square in the floor? That's a trap door, and we can open it from up front."

"I bet all our Sibylline gunrunners just loooove that," Greg quipped.

Min and Greg exited the sedan and headed for the aircraft. "My guess is that Ananta, John, and Mireille are in the hangar donning foul-weather gear," said Min. The two took up their positions in the cockpit and began preparing for the flight.

Min and Greg were finished with their preflight checklist well before Ananta and John climbed into the first row of seats. "Ruth sends her regards, Ananta," Min began as she saw Mireille about to step on board, "but what took you so lo—"

Mireille was not alone. Her arm was firmly in the grasp of a mystery passenger whose face was completely obscured by a ski mask. His pistol was pointed directly at Mireille's head. "Take off," he said in a raspy deliberately disguised voice. "Making me wait will have unfortunate consequences."

As soon as the doors were secured, Min taxied away from the hangar and took off quickly. She guided the aircraft past Mount Baida, a snow-covered peak that glistened with ice crystals and rich green vegetation at lower altitudes, then threaded her way through the rocky canyons and icefalls of the Ak-Kem River. Every so often, she caught a glimpse of the tiny bodies of tourists below.

As she began the climb toward Belukha Mountain, she spied a few rugged trekkers who were raising their arms and pointing to the strange red-and-yellow airplane in the sky. No doubt they were thinking they'd missed some kind of guided tour from a company that had the inside track on getting to Shambala, or at least close to it.

Even for a STOL aircraft like the Porter, there were very few potential landing spots on the mountain, but the last time Min had flown Mireille to the glacier, she'd found a good one on an unusually long straight plateau. She planned to set down in this same spot once again, but as she circled doing a low altitude recon of the site, she could see that it was no longer smooth. The flat surface was now littered with large obstacles—they appeared to be ice-covered boulders. Min guessed that they'd been shaken loose during the recent spate of earthquakes, and had tumbled down from higher altitudes.

"This won't work," she said as she circled the glacier once more, looking for something safer nearby.

"Land the plane!" the USF gunman ordered.

"I can't!" Min said. "At least not here. See those big bumps sticking up—it would be bad enough if those were just blocks of ice, but they're solid rock. There are too many of them to avoid, and I don't see an alternative place to land."

"Nice try," the gunman said. "Land the plane."

"Even if we land, it will be impossible to take off," Min said.

"Like I care," said the gunman.

"No way all of us are getting out of this alive," said Min.

"More likely *none* of us are getting out alive," Greg said grimly.

It's not as if this wasn't always a possibility. As protectors of the Sibyllines, both Min and Greg were always aware that they might be called upon to sacrifice themselves in the line of duty. During Greg's time as a USF double agent, getting discovered and summarily executed was a daily possibility. Now, however, the two lovers looked at one another for what they surely believed was the last time. Min wiped away a tear that welled up, as a fleeting vision of a happily-ever-after life with Greg flashed before her eyes.

"I'm only going to say this one more time," said the gunman. "Land the fuckin' plane."

Min set the Porter down as far from the first rock as she could, then tried to weave her way through the boulder-strewn minefield. As she maneuvered quickly left and right, the plane began to fishtail out of control. Finally, one huge rock could not be avoided. The left ski hit it straight on, forcing the plane to cartwheel. After rolling over several times, it finally came to a stop—upside down. The good news was that the fuselage was intact. The bad news was that it was sitting inches from the edge of the glacier. Below them was the seemingly bottomless Ak-Kem gorge.

Mireille was the first to realize that she was hanging upside down in her seatbelt. The crash had forced the gunman's weapon out of his hands and was now resting right below her. Swiftly unbuckling herself with one hand, she kept a grip on the belt itself to avoid landing on her head as she reached for the pistol. "Too slow," said the gunman as he scooped it up quickly.

Just then, the plane slightly gave way, and the busted propeller nosed over the edge. It was clear that the engine compartment would soon follow suit. The situation was precarious. Although Mireille was sure she could take down the gunman, she didn't dare engage in physical combat—the shifting weight would accelerate the skid.

The creaking and groaning of the fuselage jolted Ananta and John back to consciousness. After the initial shock of realizing he was hanging from his seatbelt, John glanced out the window and quickly sized up the situation. "You okay up front in the cockpit?" he asked.

"Not exactly," Greg replied. "Both of us slammed into the controls on impact. I've got a bunch of cuts and bruises, but Minny's slumped over and out cold."

"Leave her," the gunman barked at Greg as he pointed his weapon at Ananta. "You guys, open the doors—both of them. Do exactly as I say, or I shoot the daughter of Jesus fucking Christ."

Even though Greg and John tried to move gingerly, the plane continued to slide closer to the edge. They were keenly aware that they had mere minutes to open the doors and get everyone away from the wreckage before the aircraft plummeted into the gorge.

As the doors slid open, the bitter, frigid wind rushed in and Mireille's body vanished—dematerialized—then reappeared on the glacier. Ananta was not surprised—she had been in telepathic communication with her mother all along. She now used the momentary shock of her mother's disappearing act to grab the gun. Standing in front of an open door, she pointed the revolver at the gunman, then motioned for him to move to the last row of seats. "Sit!" she shouted at him. "Back there!"

Meanwhile, Greg checked on Min once more. He was relieved to find her no longer entirely unconscious, but the bleeding had him concerned. Nevertheless, there was no way she'd be able to get out of the aircraft under her own power. The gunman, he already knew, was fine with that outcome. He had to get her to safety, but how? He suddenly remembered her words as they had pulled up to the hangar in Tyungur. *See that square in the floor? That's a trap door, and we can open it from up front.*

He located the lever and popped the trap door, then pulled Min out of her seatbelt and toward the middle of the plane. As he tossed her up through the trap door, she grabbed wildly at the gunman's mask before landing with a thud on what had been the belly of the aircraft. Greg then jumped up through the trap door himself. Clutching her tightly to his body, he rolled off the fuselage—the two landed together on the glacier.

As soon as Ananta saw that Greg and Min were clear of the plane, she called out to John, "Jump!" Trusting Ananta wholeheartedly, he dove out the open door and landed on his butt on the ice.

Only Ananta and the gunman remained in the aircraft. Huddled together on the glacier, Greg, Mireille, and John heard a gunshot fired inside the plane. Then the plane began to pick up speed as it continued to skid toward the abyss.

"Nooooo!" Mireille screamed.

Just as the aircraft was nosing over, Ananta hurled herself out the door. Instead of landing squarely on the glacier, however, she barely caught the ledge with her hands—there was no way her grip could last for long.

CHAPTER 26
LADDER

John hooked his feet around an ice-covered boulder, then reached out to grasp Ananta's wrist. He pulled the mother of his unborn child up onto the plateau as the aircraft plunged into the gorge. They both fell back, breathing heavily.

"I can't believe I almost lost you," he said.

They were quickly joined by Mireille, who hugged her daughter in a tight, grateful embrace.

"If it hadn't been for Ved, Poonam's son, you would have joined the gunman at the bottom of the gorge," John said. "His gift—the socks with the sewn-on chains—was an act of selfless generosity. I have to confess that when I opened the package, I thought they were the ugliest things I'd ever seen, but they gave me the traction I needed to pull you up. I've never been more grateful for a gift in my life."

"There's a life lesson in that," said Mireille.

"Oh, there sure is," John replied.

"Ananta," Mireille continued, "I have to ask. We heard a shot fired inside the plane just before it...Did you—"

"Did I kill him?" Ananta interjected. "No, Mother, I didn't. He lunged at me from where he was sitting at the back of the plane. His forward motion accelerated the plane's skid toward the edge. The gun went off just before I dove out the door, but it was a random shot. I don't think it hit him."

"Given what happened to him next," said John, "he might have been better off if you had shot him."

"Oh, if it had been necessary, I would have," said Ananta as she patted her stomach. "Not for myself, but for this little one."

Mireille, Ananta, and John made their way to where Greg was sitting on the ice, holding Min's head close to his chest. "How is she?" Mireille asked.

"Minny's alive," he said. "She slammed hard into the control panel and there's a lot of blood. I suspect she may have a concussion, so we'll have to find a way to keep her warm."

"Zhkbb," Min murmured into Greg's parka.

Greg leaned forward to bring his head closer to her lips. "Did you say something, Min?"

"Zhaay. Kubb," she repeated slowly.

"What *about* Jacob?" Greg asked.

"Gun. Man. Plane." Greg could tell that it was a huge effort for her to speak. Even so, her words were barely audible over the howling wind.

"What are you trying to tell me?" Greg asked.

Min lifted her hand to chin level and made a quick fist. Her knuckles grazed her lips, nose, eyebrows, and hairline as she slowly traced the profile of her face. "Mask. Pulled. Zhaay. Kubb," she said weakly as she dropped her arm back into her lap. Then she patted her chest as a tear rolled down her cheek and passed out.

Greg checked her pulse—she was still alive. He looked up at Ananta. "You heard that, right? Do you think she's hallucinating?" he asked.

"No," Ananta answered. "If Jacob is the blue-eyed blond guy who dropped you and Min off at the hangar, it's the same dude. The hangar had already been taken over by the USF when you arrived, and the three of us were at gunpoint inside. After you and Min got out of the SUV and boarded the aircraft for preflight prep, Jacob suited up and put on the mask."

"Shit!" Greg exclaimed. "Jacob was Min's confidant and her protector. They were like siblings. She knew he was acting weird when we left the castle, but I don't think she ever considered the possibility that he might have defected. Frankly, neither did I. The most important question is, when did he switch over to the side of the USF?"

"And how much did he tell them after that," said Ananta. "His cell went into the gorge with him, so we have no way of knowing what he was able to transmit to his USF handlers."

"Probably a shit ton of stuff," said Greg. "He had four hours sitting up front on the way from Quedlinburg to Frankfurt, and another eleven from there to Tyungur. At a minimum, we have to assume that my days as a double agent are over, and that they know the seeds left the castle with us—which means Ruth is in danger."

Whompeta. Whompeta. Whompeta. Greg detected the faint sound of an approaching helicopter. Looking up, he could see a black speck getting ever larger until it finally hovered over them.

An amplified voice from a bullhorn declared, "We're lowering a rope ladder. Come aboard."

"What are the odds it's friendly?" John asked.

"Fifty-fifty at best," said Ananta.

"I think it's a trap," Greg said, "but one of us has a choice. Someone needs to take a good look at the gash in Min's head, and she's in no shape to climb that ladder, which means I'll have to carry her up to the chopper myself...Unless..."

"Unless what?" John asked.

"Unless she goes with you to Shangri-la."

Mireille shook her head. "She'd get excellent care there, but the transition through the energetic field of the gateway would be too much for her. In her current condition, there's no way she'd make it to Shangri-la alive."

"It's settled then," Greg declared. "I'll take her up to the helicopter...if they're USF agents, all I can do is put up a good fight, and Min...well...she's out anyway, so she won't feel it coming."

"Give a signal. If the chopper is Sibylline, give us the peace sign," John said, forming his gloved fingers into a V. "Any other hand sign means it's USF."

While Greg held Min close to him and waited for the ladder, Mireille pulled Ananta and John aside. "If the helicopter is ours, Ananta, only you and I are going on to Shangri-la. John, I'm sorry, but

I'm going to ask you to go with Greg and Min. In the fight that's sure to come, the Sibyllines are going to need you."

"I need him too, Mother," Ananta protested. "Giving birth in Shangri-la will be much safer for our baby, but the idea of doing it alone…"

"Everything has changed," Mireille replied. "We have to assume that the USF was able to track Jacob's position, which means they know a lot more about the location of the gateway to Shangri-la than they did before. We may yet have to relocate the portal, but it is a huge undertaking, and in the meantime, Shangri-la must be defended. It is the only safe place for your pregnancy and for you to give birth, and also for the preservation of the manuscript of humankind's true history. If they destroy the manuscript, no one will ever know the truth about our past. And if they get wind that you're pregnant and know where you are, they will come for the baby."

"I don't want to leave you, my love, and I don't want to leave our child," said John, "but your mother is right. There's no telling how much damage Jacob has done. I must go where I'm needed."

"No!" Ananta cried.

"Besides," he added, "everyone knows that pregnant fathers are completely useless."

John gently separated himself from Ananta as the ladder was unfurled. "I have to help Greg now," he said.

Getting Greg and Min safely up the ladder was not going to be easy —the winds were already strong, and were picking up. The pilot— whoever it was—was doing a masterful job of hovering, and was able to keep the chopper level and stationary. The ladder, however, was whipping around wildly.

John helped Greg securely fasten Min to his body, then grabbed the rope ladder as it danced in the gale. As Greg began to climb with Min tied snugly to him, he turned and said, "Remember, only if I give the peace sign is it safe to come aboard. Understood?"

"I'm scared," Ananta said as they watched Greg making his way up the ladder. "I've never been this scared before."

"Motherhood does that to you," Mireille replied. "Everything is going to change for you—all your priorities and perceptions. You'll be forced to make decisions that you never thought you'd have to make.

You may find yourself having to allow your child to suffer—not only for the greater good of your child, but for the greater good of humanity. And even though you know there is life on the other side of this earthly reality, you will want to do everything you can to preserve your child's physical life—even at the risk of your own, or that of someone else."

"An agonizing choice," said Ananta.

"But as a mother, you'll never hesitate to make it," Mireille declared firmly. "You already found that out for yourself today. You said that you would have shot Jacob to protect your unborn baby—that instinct doesn't change once your child has left the womb. Days ago, I struck Sundara, your brother, to save you, my daughter. Throughout your life, your heart will break with love and burst with love, all at the same time."

Ascending hand over hand, it took all of Greg's strength to make it to the top. Gusts of wind began buffeting the helicopter—only with the help of the copilot was Greg able to maneuver his and Min's bodies into the chopper. "It's getting too dangerous to stick around here much longer," said the pilot. "Whoever's joining us has to come aboard now."

Greg squinted, trying to see who was in the cockpit. The pilot sensed his apprehension and removed her helmet. Long locks of brown hair fell down upon her shoulders. "By the time you arrived at the hangar at Tyungur, the USF had already overpowered our ground crew," she explained. "As they watched Jacob don the parka and ski mask and get on the aircraft with the rest of you, one of our ground crew was able to get us an SOS. We lifted off as soon as we could, not knowing what we'd find when we got here. I'm glad everyone is alive."

"Except Jacob," Greg said. "He went down with the aircraft."

"He was a mentor of mine," she said sadly.

Greg made Min as comfortable as he could on the floor of the chopper. "Where are we taking her?" he inquired. "She needs medical attention."

"The USF is really active right now," the copilot replied. "Their plan to get Jacob onto the bridge to Shangri-la failed, but they know that Ruth and the seeds are in Tyungur. We were able to retake the hangar, but this fight is far from over. I think the best thing is for you to get back to the lodge, make sure Min is stable, pick up Ruth, and then take off as quickly as you can. Figure out where you're going after you get the hell out of Russia. Now, gesture to your gang down there so they know they're safe to come up the ladder."

Greg gave the peace sign from the opened helicopter door—the signal it was safe to climb aboard. John took Ananta's face in his hands. They kissed, tasting the salt in each other's tears. After a final glance into her eyes, John reached for the bottom rung.

"John!" Ananta called out and ran toward him. "Let me hold the ladder, at least till you get started."

"No," he replied. "Your number one job now is to keep our baby safe. I got this."

John almost lost his grip several times before Greg hauled him into the chopper. Once on board, John turned to take one last look at the love of his life, but Ananta and her mother were already gone.

As the pilot battled the winds and veered away from the glacier, John barely caught a glimpse of red and yellow at the bottom of the gorge. A thin column of smoke rose from the wreckage.

CHAPTER 27
RUTH

"Let's get you into bed, Ruth," said Kat. "It's time for you to rest and take your medication. Jacob gave me precise dosing instructions."

Kat walked Ruth upstairs and settled her into one of the lodge guest rooms. "Silly me," she said. "I left your meds in the kitchen."

Kat soon returned with an unlabeled ziplock bag containing six white pills. "Well, that's strange," Ruth said.

"What's strange, Ruth?" asked Kat.

"Min has changed my medication," she declared. "These don't look anything like the ones I've been taking."

Kat's expression turned slightly more serious. "It's to help you rest better," she said.

Ruth peered at the six round white pills in the bag. Two bore the number 648 stamped on them. Two more were imprinted EP 905, and the last two read 54/262. "How many of these am I supposed to take?" she asked.

"All of them," Kat replied. "Jacob gave me precise dosing instructions."

"If Min was going to change my meds, she would have told me," Ruth said. "And I've never had to take six of anything all at once."

"Oh, it's fine, Ruth," said Kat nonchalantly.

"Jacob should be returning soon from taking Min and Greg to the hangar," said Ruth. "Let's ask him when he gets back."

Ruth watched with suspicion as Kat's eyes narrowed and her pupils begin to constrict. This giggly, borderline silly young woman was changing before her eyes. Her warning radar—a highly developed instinct from her childhood in East Germany—kicked into high gear.

"Jacob gave me precise dosing instructions," Kat insisted. "If you're still awake when he gets back, he'll be very cross with me—and with you!"

Again with the "precise dosing instructions," Ruth thought. *She sounds like a ventriloquist's dummy.*

Min, the one person she trusted completely, would be gone for a couple of hours. Before she, Greg, and Jacob left for the hangar, she had insisted on accompanying Ruth to the bathroom. It was the only private place where they could talk, and Min confessed that she already was having doubts not just about Kat, but about Jacob as well. Her words now echoed in Ruth's brain.

Kat took a selfie of the two of us, then immediately posted it on social media. That was reckless during an operation as important as this one. And although Jacob already knew Kat—she was his top combat student —he never mentioned her to me before. And then there's the fact that he's been acting strange ever since we left Germany. Something doesn't add up.

Ruth took stock of her situation—she and Kat were alone in the lodge. *What are the odds of surviving a physical confrontation with Kat?* she asked herself. *Slim…but what are the odds of surviving if I take those pills? None. Slim it is, then,* she decided.

"All right, then, Kat," Ruth calmly replied. She watched as Kat's pupils begin to dilate back to normal. Her shoulders lowered and her face softened.

"I'm glad you agree, Ruth," said Kat. "I'll bring you a glass of fresh mountain water."

"With ice, please," Ruth replied, then thought back once more about her last conversation with Min.

I have to act upon my gut, dearest Ruth, and my gut tells me that the seeds will be safer with me than anywhere near Jacob or Kat. Please trust me, Ruth.

I trust you, Min, just as I trusted Erica Pfeiffer—I mean Ananta,

Easa's daughter, Ruth had replied with a grin. *Turns out I'm an excellent judge of character. Please give her a hug from me.*

Ruth could hear Kat coming up the stairs. To buy some time, she scurried into the bathroom and locked the door. She turned on the water to fill the bathtub and began to sing loudly—an old German song.

Kat rapped softly on the bathroom door, but Ruth continued to sing as if oblivious to the knocking. Her painful shoulder made it difficult to wriggle out of her clothes, but she managed to leave them in a heap on the floor. Then she gingerly stepped into the tub and turned off the water.

Kat was now banging on the door. "Ruth!" she yelled.

"Oh! Sorry, Kat," Ruth called back. "I was running a bath. Have you been knocking for a long time?"

"Yes!" Kat barked. "Why are you bathing? You're supposed to be resting!" Kat's once perky, girlish voice had morphed into that of a drill sergeant.

"I know," Ruth replied, "but it's been such a long journey, and the warm water is exactly what these tired old bones need. I'll be out shortly, my dear."

"Don't be too long!" Kat ordered. "I have work to do...Jacob gave me precise dosing instructions."

Ruth had to think fast. *What do I do now? What do I do now? I'm no match for Kat physically, but what I lack in strength I make up for in sneakiness.*

"Of course!" Ruth replied. "I'll call for you when I'm out and dressed. My dear Kat, is it possible to get some clean clothes for this old woman?"

"Yes, Ruth," Kat answered impatiently. "I'll find some clothing for you and leave it on the bed."

Okay, now what? thought Ruth. *Pretending to swallow the pills won't work. They're tablets, and they'll just dissolve in my mouth. My only option is to make her think I'm unconscious.*

Ruth got out of the tub and wrapped herself in a warm towel. She opened the medicine cabinet above the sink, looking for anything that would help her fend off Kat. She saw a pair of tweezers and impulsively stuck them into her mouth between her bottom teeth and her left cheek. *It's not much*, she told herself, *but it's what I've got.*

After splashing a goodly amount of soapy water outside the tub, she picked up the towel warmer, slamming it hard to the tile floor, and immediately placed it upright once more. She then assumed her position in the midst of the puddle, with her arms and legs splayed out haphazardly.

The sound of Kat's running footsteps quickly followed. "Ruth!" she yelled. "Are you okay?"

Ruth kept her silence as she ruched the towel over her chest to disguise her pounding heart.

"Ruth!" she yelled again. "Fuck!"

Kat summoned up her martial arts training and executed a powerful front thrust kick, striking the door with the heel of her right foot. She aimed her kick just inside the knob, splintering the doorframe and tearing out the lock. As the door flew open, she saw Ruth unconscious on the floor, draped in a towel.

"Goddammit, old woman! Jacob gave me precise dosing instructions. This is not how this was supposed to go. But...Jacob wanted you to sleep, and this will do for now. Let's get you into bed, Ruth."

She keeps saying the same phrases over and over, word for word, Ruth thought. *Something's going on with her brain.*

As Kat dragged her into the bedroom, Ruth made sure she was deadweight in Kat's arms. Because the ends of the tweezers were jabbing into the back of her lower lip, she was generating a lot of excess saliva. Her mouth began to fill, and she felt like she was drowning from the inside out, but she didn't dare swallow or adjust the position of the tweezers with her tongue—she was afraid that Kat would notice.

Kat pulled her up onto the bed and nestled her into the covers. Noticing that the black velvet pouch wasn't around her neck, she immediately went into the bathroom to look for it. Ruth took advantage of that brief moment to hide the tweezers in her right hand and swallow the mouthful of spit.

Kat looked all around the tub and sink and pawed through Ruth's clothes—no bag. "Where is it?" Kat said loudly, even though she was sure Ruth was out cold. "My orders were to get the bag after you fell asleep. This is not how this was supposed to go!"

So far, so good, Ruth thought to herself.

"I must get the black bag. I must get the black bag. I must get the black bag," Kat said, repeating it as if it were a mantra.

She sat on the bed and glared at Ruth, then gave her a hard slap across the face. "Wake up!" she spat.

Ruth let out a muffled groan. "Wake up!" Kat repeated. "I must get the black bag."

Ruth remained unresponsive as she felt Kat's hand on her right cheek. "If you won't wake up, I'll wake you up," Kat said harshly.

Kat's fingers grasped her eyelashes. As she pulled upward to force Ruth's eyelid open, Ruth sank the sharp ends of the tweezers into Kat's head. Although she'd been aiming for her temple, she caught a spot just above her left ear.

Ruth steeled herself for the retaliation she was sure would follow. Much to her surprise, however, Kat fell over onto the bed next to her. Ruth looked at her. Kat's eyes were wide open, but she was definitely unconscious. The tweezers protruded from her head.

A calmness soon embraced Ruth's soul. She stared at the ceiling as her heart slowed and her mouth formed a smile. Her eyes closed. Her heart stopped.

CHAPTER 28
PORTAL

The gusts on Belukha Mountain had become fierce. Mireille struggled to keep her footing as she walked east on the glacier, and hooked her arm around Ananta's waist to make sure they stayed together. Despite being warmly dressed, the biting wind found every gap in their clothing, and they could feel the cold settle into their bones.

A blurry darkness soon came into sight—the women were approaching the opening to the stealth gateway to Shangri-la, the energetic bridge that lay at the edge of the physical world. As they entered, the winds became breezes and the chill abated. A familiar sensation of peace blanketed them. It was as if their bodies were being separated from their consciousness, yet still had form. With each step, the darkness began to give way to a golden glow. Its radiance surrounded and soothed them, calming both their bodies and their minds, until bliss embraced them and filled them with unconditional love.

As they walked, the golden pathway became wider and paler. They began to feel ethereal, and the shapes and silhouettes of others came into view. Mireille and Ananta sensed a commonality with all of them —everyone on this journey felt as though they were all part of one consciousness, yet still individual in character. This was the same dimension where Ananta had found herself when she connected with John in the nonphysical dimension. It was where their child had been conceived.

The women soon reached the intersection on the energetic gateway to Shangri-la where souls who were transitioning from the physical world to the nonphysical world would pause to consider whether to go back or continue onward.

Ruth and Gabby were standing where the paths diverged. Ruth comprehended that her time on earth had ended, but instead of sadness, she was at peace with her departure. She could sense Heinrich's energy not far off amongst all the combined consciousness that existed in the cosmos. She was eager to return there, but needed a moment with Gabby.

"My dear Gabby," Ruth began, "I've had more fulfilment, more excitement, and more appreciation for life in recent days than I've had in all my years until now. It's time for me to go, and I do so with great joy, but I'm a bit saddened to see you on this path with me."

"So am I, Ruth, so am I," Gabby replied. "My son, Zach, misses me terribly, and I had so wanted to be with him to germinate the seeds from the Tree of Life."

"Then go back, Gabby, go back! Your purpose on earth is not yet finished. Your body is still warm, still capable of reigniting with your spirit."

Gabby knew Ruth was right. It wasn't Gabby's time to die.

Mireille and Ananta watched as these two brave women chose their destinies. As Gabby turned to head back up the golden path, Ananta spoke to Ruth. "My dear, sweet, kind Ruth," Ananta said. "What did I get you into? I'm so sorry. I'm so very sorry."

"What do you have to be sorry about?" Ruth replied. "I just took down Jacob's top combat student—with a pair of tweezers!"

Both Mireille and Ananta couldn't help but laugh. "Oh, Ruth!" Ananta replied. "I always knew you had an abundance of hidden talents! Do you remember the day I begged you to be my trusting friend...the day I showed you the secret library at the Society of Truth?"

"I do," Ruth replied. "I remember you telling me how you'd been on assignment there for fifteen years. You said you had no one to trust, and that you needed me to be your friend. You said you chose me because you believed I was pure and kind, but I have a feeling you'd been watching me all along."

"Your intuition is correct, dearest Ruth," Ananta admitted. "I was watching you all those years because you are the last descendant in a very important line of Sibyllines, a line that had stayed pure since the days of Easa, my father. That's why I entrusted you with the seeds instead of carrying them myself—and you agreed to carry them. You became the seed-bearer. If you had steadfastly remained dedicated to the Society of Truth, it would have been a huge defeat for humankind, and for free will. That day when I showed you the secret library, I begged you to make a choice. Do you remember?"

"How could I forget?" Ruth replied. " 'Now it's your turn to choose,' you told me. 'Choose me, Ruth. Right here, right now. This is the one choice you can make right now. There *is* something you can do right now. You can choose me as your trusted friend. We can do the right thing—the *kind* thing—together. Nothing else matters anymore. Nothing except this one choice. All you have to do is say yes. Say yes, Ruth. Please...say yes.' "

"And you did! I was so happy that day!" Ananta replied.

"And you need to be happy now," Ruth said. "Be happy, Ananta."

Ruth began to ascend, but not without some parting wisdom. "Take care of that baby of yours—I can sense your pregnancy."

Mireille took hold of Ananta's hand. The two watched together as Ruth vanished into the cosmos. "Time to go," Mireille said as she guided Ananta forward. "We're headed along a path that leads to a place that exists between the Gangdisri Mountains and the Gobi Desert. It is one of the last remaining unexplored regions on the planet. As you have just seen, my daughter, it can be accessed only by the same gateway through which all beings pass when their time in the physical world ends, and they transition back into the nonphysical world from which we all came."

Mireille lifted her arms and traced the outline of a circle in midair. "Are you ready, my daughter?" she asked.

"I am, Āmā," Ananta replied.

A radiant halo of indigo-colored light appeared before them, and Ananta could see that a portal had opened in the center of it. Mireille led her daughter through it, then it closed behind them...and they disappeared.

[illegible] [illegible] [illegible] [illegible] [illegible]
[illegible] [illegible] [illegible] [illegible] [illegible]
[illegible] [illegible] [illegible] [illegible] [illegible]
[illegible] [illegible] [illegible] [illegible] [illegible]
[illegible] [illegible] [illegible] [illegible] [illegible]
[illegible] [illegible] [illegible] [illegible] [illegible]
[illegible] [illegible] [illegible] [illegible]

[illegible] [illegible] [illegible] [illegible] [illegible]
[illegible] [illegible] [illegible] [illegible] [illegible]
[illegible] [illegible] [illegible] [illegible] [illegible]
[illegible] [illegible] [illegible] [illegible]

[illegible] [illegible] [illegible] [illegible] [illegible]
[illegible] [illegible] [illegible] [illegible] [illegible]
[illegible] [illegible] [illegible] [illegible] [illegible]
[illegible] [illegible] [illegible] [illegible] [illegible]
[illegible] [illegible] [illegible] [illegible] [illegible]

[illegible] [illegible] [illegible] [illegible] [illegible]
[illegible] [illegible] [illegible] [illegible]

CHAPTER 29
THE CARDS

"This way," Phoebe said to Zach, holding the bag of seeds as she walked.

Zach followed her to the back of the store. They walked past the shop's restroom and Phoebe's small office, opposite which was a room with a sign on the door: Reading Room. The door was cracked open, and Zach could see that a candle was its only source of light.

Phoebe led Zach into the room. He had expected to see a small, intimate library, with shelves of books and a comfortable reading chair, but the reality was very different. The room was empty except for a round table with two straight-back chairs. On the table were a deck of cards and an essential oil diffuser.

Zach followed Phoebe through the room and out into a screened-in porch. "I built it myself," Phoebe said. "You're standing on the store's two parking spots in the alley. I don't have a car, and as long as nothing is permanently attached to the building, enclosing them is allowed by the city. The screens are made of black mesh—I can see out, but no one can see in. During the winter, I put up plastic sheeting behind the mesh to keep out the cold. Now that winter is over, I have to take it down. Maybe you could help me with that, Zach."

"Uh, sure." The porch was as crowded as the reading room was sparse. Tables and shelves were wedged in everywhere, and each horizontal surface was covered with pots of exotic flora. There was an electric heater on the floor, and suspended from the ceiling was narrow black tubing—misters that provided fine water spray. Neither the heater nor the misters were on, but the room felt as humid as a bathroom after a shower. To keep the heavy, moist air moving, a fan in one of the high corners was on and oscillating.

Zach was in awe because so many of the plants were familiar. He recognized them because they were the same ones that his mom, Gabby, had smuggled into the country from her excursions around the world. He recognized the smell of perfectly balanced soil and humus, mixed with essential micronutrients. He closed his eyes, taking himself back to the days at the greenhouse with his mom. Phoebe picked up on the melancholy.

"Have you ever had a reading?" Phoebe asked.

"What?" Zach replied.

"A reading. Tarot cards," she replied. "My sister—Sadie's mom—and I were born with a gift—a natural ability to have insight into... well...*things* beyond the obvious."

"You mean you're a fortune teller?" Zach replied skeptically. "So that's what that 'reading room' is for? Sounds a little 'out there' to me."

"That's often a response to what we don't understand, isn't it, Zach," said Phoebe gently. "I suspect there were folks who found your mom's plant-based approach to healing a bit 'out there' too."

"Yeah, they did," said Zach. "They said it was scary and phony—witch-doctor medicine."

"It's the same with tarot readings," Phoebe replied. "Some people are afraid of the cards. They shy away from the idea of 'seeing into the future.' But that's a misunderstanding. Cards don't tell the future."

"So, what *are* you reading then?"

"When I lay the cards out, I'm pretty much reading what *is*," Phoebe went on. "I bypass your conscious mind and tap into your subconscious to find out what truly *is*, and the complex web of possibilities that stem from what *is*. Think of it like tapping into the unseen mycelium fungal communication network in soil—I know you know all about that. Imagine the mycelium letting you know exactly how things currently *are* in the plant world. Wouldn't that be useful to you?"

"Of course, it would," Zach said. "It would tell me what their pH is, and what minerals or nutrients need to be balanced…I could read their hydration levels…It would tell me everything."

"Exactly, and with that knowledge would come an understanding of the range of what's possible from this current state of affairs—which actions would be helpful, and which would be harmful. It's the same with the cards. They merely offer you alternatives, given the *present* situation in your life. And, of course, you always have freewill choice in terms of how you act on what the cards show you."

"Could we do a tarot reading now?" Zach asked.

"I'd love to!" Phoebe said. "But first things first. I'll get these seeds upstairs and into the freezer—like you said—while you go and lock the front door. Be sure to turn the sign on the door so it says Closed. Then come back and take a seat at the table in the reading room. I'll meet you there."

Phoebe returned to find Zach sitting straight up in the chair. "What's the scent in here?" he asked.

"Certain essential oils can open up communication with our subconscious. Right now, I have frankincense, sandalwood, and myrrh in the diffuser. It helps center the mind and expand awareness. Do you like it?"

"Oh yes!"

"Good. Then, it's meant for you. Now, hold the deck of cards in your hand and focus on something that's important to you. Take three deep breaths while shuffling the deck three times. Then spread out the cards and pick the first three cards that you're drawn to."

There was one thing, and one thing only that Zach could focus his mind on, and that was his mom, Gabby. He missed her so much. Picturing her in his mind brought both a smile and a tear. His memory of all the times they worked together in the underground lab dueled with his last image of her, lying dead in the rubble of the bunker doorway. He sighed deeply, then shuffled the cards and pulled three of them.

The first card was the Death card. It pictured the skeleton of the Grim Reaper. The word DEATH was spelled out in capital letters across the bottom of the card.

"Well, that makes sense," Zach muttered.

"Don't assume, Zach," Phoebe cautioned. "Let me do the reading.

The Death card doesn't necessarily mean you're going to die, or that someone else has died. It can also suggest the possibility of some significant changes or transformations."

Phoebe examined the three cards without saying a word. She reached her open hands on the table toward Zach, indicating she wanted to hold his hands. He placed his forearms on the table and rested his hands on hers. She breathed heavily and closed her eyes.

"Where did you last see your mom?" she asked calmly.

"How did you know I was focusing on my mom?" Zach responded.

"I'm receiving a message. Remember, the cards access your subconscious to let me know what *is*. Sometimes, the cards can also access the subconscious of the person you're focusing on, allowing me to know their present circumstances as well."

"Well, my mom is dead, so accessing her subconscious is impossible. The last time I saw her before she died was in the underground Sibylline bunker, right here in Brooklyn. The earthquake caused a doorframe and bunch of rocks to fall on her. Me and Cam had to leave her behind—she told us to go, and to take the seeds and change the world. Her body is still down there..."

Phoebe's eyes opened wide. "Zach!" she exclaimed. "We must go at once!"

"Go where?"

"To your mom!" Phoebe said. "No questions. Where is the entrance to the bunker?"

"Inside Ma-Mario's Market on Old Fulton Street," Zach stammered. "Why?"

"I said no questions."

Phoebe texted Sadie as she led Zach out the back door of the shop:
Call 911! Need an ambulance and rescue equipment—
In the bunker.
Mario's Market on Old Fulton.

Sadie was already on her way to La Guardia on the first leg of her mission to retrieve Fonzie from Ken Kreighton's driveway. "Turn around!" she instructed the cabbie. "I need to go back to Old Fulton Street, where you picked me up."

"Make up your mind, lady," the driver said.

Sadie then punched in 9-1-1. "This is Detective Sadie Dixon,

NYPD," she said. "Heavy rescue at Mario's Market on Old Fulton. Send Rescue 2 and a bus. Tunnel collapse."

Phoebe, Zach, Sadie, and the paramedics converged simultaneously on Mario's. "What the...?" Cameron stood puzzled as Zach approached him. He could tell the boy was extremely agitated. "You said she was dead!" he shouted, repeatedly pushing Cameron in the sternum. "You checked her pulse and you said she was dead! How could you lie about that? I hate you!"

Phoebe grabbed Zach. "Stop!" she exclaimed. "It's not his fault, Zach! Your mom *was* dead."

"But you told me she's alive, Phoebe. Which is it?"

"She *is* alive...*now*," Phoebe replied. "Her heart had stopped and she had no pulse because she was having a near-death experience. But she came back."

"Are you going to show us the way, or are we going to have to find her ourselves?" one of EMTs asked.

When they heard the commotion in the market, Mario and André emerged from the kitchen. André positioned himself in front of the door under the stairs that led to the bunker.

"Move!" Zach shouted.

"What the hell is down there?" another paramedic asked.

Keisha sidled up to Mario and put her arm around his waist. "It used to be a part of the Society of Truth tunnel system, but it got walled off a few years ago," she lied. "I'm ex-Society, so I know. Mario and I...we've been using it as a party space ever since...Haven't we, sweetie..."

"Oh, *cara mia*," said Mario, playing along, "you shouldn't have told them!"

"We have some pretty interesting clients. You wouldn't believe who we get sneaking down there for private hookups," Keisha added. "You know, consenting adults and all that...*Page Six* would pay a fortune if they found out..."

André winked at Keisha as he stepped aside to give the EMTs access to the stairway. Zach led the way down into the tunnel, with Cameron and Sadie following. Debris, dust, rocks, and boulders were everywhere.

"Shhh!" Zach said. "Stop! Everyone stop!"

A faint cry was heard in the distance. "Hello? Is anyone there?"

"Mom!" he cried out. "Mom! I'm here! I'm coming!"

Sadie came up beside him. She'd already figured out that if she didn't give Zach a task to help save his mom, he'd be in the way. "Zach, honey, time go back upstairs and let these guys do their job. The best thing you can do for her right now is make sure the doors are propped open so there's a clear path to the ambulance, okay?"

"Okay," Zach said.

"You too, sir," said one of the paramedics to Cameron.

"He's right, Cam," said Sadie. "Time for you to be a civilian. Back upstairs with you."

A small cadre of Rescue 2 firefighters rushed past them and joined the original first responders in the tunnel. They came with prybars, shovels, axes, hydraulic jacks, a collapsible gurney, a spineboard, body straps, portable oxygen, and a head immobilizer. "Step aside please, and give us room work," said the fire lieutenant.

"I'd like to help dig," Cam protested.

"I can't allow that," the lieutenant replied. "In a rescue, we work as a team. No lone rangers. And if you don't know what you're doing, you could make the victim's injuries much worse—or even kill her. I've seen it happen."

"Upstairs, Cameron Reid," Sadie repeated. "That's not a suggestion, It's an order from the NYPD."

Cam and Zach climbed the stairs back into Mario's. "She's alive! Mom is alive!" Zach yelled as he propped all the doors open. Rocky wrapped his arms around Zach as the two began crying and laughing at the same time. Minutes later, the firemen burst through the doorway with Gabby strapped to the gurney. Zach, Cameron, and Rocky watched as they loaded her into the ambulance and headed off to the hospital, siren blaring.

Sadie thanked the paramedics and firemen, then let out another earsplitting taxi whistle. "You three coming or what?" she asked the trio on the sidewalk. Getting into the front seat of the cab while Cam, Rocky, and Zach climbed into the back behind the plexiglass window, she pulled out her badge and held it up to the driver. "I'm Detective Sadie Dixon, NYPD. The Brooklyn Hospital Center. 121 Dekalb Avenue. Go!"

CHAPTER 30
KAT

Greg carried Min into the lodge and stretched her out on the dining room table. "Consider me your scrub nurse," said John. "Just tell me what you need."

"We've got to get Min stable as quickly as we can, then get out of Dodge," Greg replied. "Before you came aboard, the chopper pilot told me to leave Russia as soon as possible. There's USF everywhere. The Sibyllines are holding the hangar, but who knows for how long."

"Understood," said John.

"This place must have a first aid kit," said Greg. "Find it. I'm also gonna need clean towels, and a whole lot of hot water. Alcohol, too. Where the fuck is Kat? She should know where all this stuff is."

John ransacked the kitchen, then ran upstairs. He burst into Ruth's room and saw Kat lying on the bed next to Ruth. Ruth appeared to be peacefully asleep, but she had no pulse. Kat, however, was alive but unconscious. "Can't deal with this now," he mumbled. "Priority number one is attending to Min."

John went into the bathroom and flung open the medicine cabinet, grabbed the small white first aid kit, then returned to the dining room. Greg opened the box and found a couple of tiny Band-Aids and an eighth of a tube of Neosporin that was several years out of date. "That's it?" he asked.

"That's it," John confirmed.

"My guess is that Russia being Russia, it got harder and harder to replace supplies as they got used up," said Greg. "Either that, or people pilfered stuff out to sell on the black market."

"There's other stuff you should know," said John. "A whole lot of shit went down while we were gone." John took a deep breath before continuing. "I'm not sure how it happened, but Ruth is dead, and Kat's lying on the bed next to her, out cold."

"*What??*"

"Strangest of all, her eyes are wide open and there's a pair of tweezers sticking out of her scalp, just above her left ear," said John. "And someone kicked the bathroom door to smithereens. It's a lot to deal with, I know, but let's attend to Min before we try to figure it out."

"Good call," Greg agreed. "Hey! We left Germany with a black doctor's bag that had meds and dressings to treat Ruth's GSW. Jacob kept it with him all the time, but I don't remember him having it on the flight to Belukha."

"Min changed Ruth's bandages right before we..." John raced away without completing his sentence, and quickly returned with the black bag. "In the powder room," he said.

"This'll work," said Greg. "I'm sure Min knows more about head wounds than I do, but she can't treat herself, and time's a-wasting."

As Greg gently dabbed at Min's lacerated forehead, he noticed that some large shards of glass from the aircraft control panel had lodged in the deepest cut. "Uh, John, this is gonna sound a little weird, but can you get the tweezers out of Kat's head, run them under some superhot water, and douse them with alcohol, and then bring them to me?"

"Sure."

As John eased the end of the tweezers out of the cut, a metallic glint in the wound remained—it looked as if the tip had broken off under the skin. He examined the tweezers, but they were intact. He used the tweezers to grasp a tiny metal object and remove it from Kat's head. "A microchip," he said. "It's a goddamn chip!"

John cleaned the tweezers and brought them to Greg, then folded a small piece of paper around the chip and placed it in his pocket.

"I've done about as much as I can do," said Greg as he finished cleaning the wound. "Let's get her on the couch by the wood-burning stove in the living room. As soon as she wakes up, we're outta here."

As the two men gently set her down, Min's eyes opened and she instantly reached for her forehead. "Welcome back, but hands off!" said Greg. "You're gonna mess up some of my best work."

"What happened?" Min asked.

"That's a much bigger question than you know," he replied. "For starters, we got Ananta and Mireille to the portal. After that, it's complicated, and we still don't have all the answers."

"We're back in the lodge," said Min, "but I see John. He didn't go with Mireille and Ananta? How come?"

"Like I said, it's complicated," Greg replied.

"I'm going upstairs," said John. "What should we do with Kat?"

Greg dug into the doctor's bag and fished out the pair of handcuffs that Jacob had used to secure him to the bench in the back of the delivery truck. "Here," he said as he tossed them to John. "She's not going anywhere until we get some explanations."

"Where's Ruth?" Min asked.

"She's dead, Minny. I'm so sorry..." Greg began. "I know how much she meant to you—to all of us. The world—including those of us who knew her all too briefly—found out much too late what an extraordinary human being she was."

John was overcome with emotion as he saw Ruth lying on the bed. "How I'm going to miss you!" he whispered softly. "You had sass and spirit like no other. No wonder Heinrich adored you." He stroked the side of her face and tenderly kissed her forehead. "But what did you do, and why did you have to do it?"

John cuffed Kat to the bedpost right where she was lying next to Ruth, then returned downstairs. His face was wet with tears. "Ruth passed in her sleep, with a smile on her face," he said. "That feisty old woman..."

"I never thought of her as old," Min interrupted. "And Ruth didn't think of herself that way, either."

"I found Ruth on the bed and Kat on the bed right next to her," said John. "I can't figure it out, Greg. You need to go up there and see if you have any better idea than I do about what happened."

"Aiiiiiieeeeeeeeeeee," Kat screamed from upstairs. "Why am I cuffed to the bed next to a dead body? And why does my head hurt so bad?"

"Stay here and stay down, Minny," Greg ordered. "The only thing holding that gash together is a butterfly bandage and a wing and a prayer. You may need stitches, but that's a skill set I don't have."

He and John then raced for the stairs. Greg entered the room and tried to size up the situation. "This is how you found them?" he asked.

"Yes," John replied. "Except Kat was out cold. You already know about the tweezers."

Kat tried to reach for the spot above her ear where the tweezers had been, but was stopped short by the handcuffs.

"Ruth did this to me?" Kat said incredulously. "That wasn't very nice of her."

"From the looks of the bathroom door, maybe you had it coming," said Greg.

"That's ridiculous," said Kat. "Why would I do that?"

"You expect us to believe that Ruth did it?" said John. "You're the only other person who was here. It also appears that someone took a bath—there's still water on the floor. I'm gonna take a wild guess here and say that was probably Ruth, because she's naked in the bed and her clothes are on the bathroom floor."

"Hey!" said Greg. "If Ruth is naked and her clothes are in the bathroom, where are the seeds?"

"I don't have them," said Kat.

"Shit!" said John. "Do you think Jacob snagged them before we left? Are they with him in the rubble at the bottom of the Ak-Kem gorge?"

"No, they're not," said Min, who'd tiptoed upstairs into the room. "Before we left for the mountain, I assisted Ruth in the bathroom. I'd started getting a really bad feeling about Jacob—and about you, too, Kat—so I persuaded Ruth to let me hold onto them for a bit."

Min reached into the neckline of her sweater and pulled out the black velvet pouch. Then she approached Ruth on the bed and held them in front of her. "Here they are, dearest Ruth," she said. "I still have them, see? You and I would have planted them in the Eden Project under the Weisshotel in Quedlinburg. We would have watched them sprout together."

Min picked up a little plastic bag of white pills that was lying on the nightstand. "Where did these come from?" she asked.

"Aren't those Ruth's pain pills?" John asked.

"Nope," said Min as she looked at them more closely. "648, EP 905, 54/262—phenobarbital, lorazepam, morphine. None of it is what I'd been giving her."

"Kat—" said John and Greg in unison.

Kat's eyes widened in horror. "I didn't kill her, did I?" she asked.

"There's a glass of water by the bedside and there are six pills left in the bag, two of each," said Min. "Depends on how many there were before. How many did you start with, Kat?"

"Dose," Kat responded. "I remember Jacob telling me that Ruth had to receive an accurate dose. Where is Jacob?"

"Jacob wasn't the man we thought he was," Min said. "He was actually USF—or is that not a surprise to you?"

"He forced his way onto the flight to Belukha Mountain," added Greg. "Maybe *that's* not a surprise to you, either. He and the plane went down together. The rest of us damned near went with him."

John reached into his pocket, pulled out a folded piece of paper, and showed Kat the microchip. "What do you know about this?" he asked.

"Nothing," Kat replied.

"I pulled it out of your head," John declared. "It was right where the tweezers were sticking out."

Kat looked at him blankly. "What is it?" she asked.

"It's a microchip," John replied, "but how did it get in your head?"

"This is a mystery we don't have time to solve right now," said Greg. "If the USF intends to take back the hangar, we've got just a small window of time to get out of here. Min, you good to go?"

"Yes."

"Where are we going?" John asked.

"I suggest Min and I take Ruth's body back to her family in Quedlinburg," said Greg. "While we're there, we can gauge how much damage Jacob's betrayal—"

"Don't call it that," Min jumped in. "We don't know what happened to him."

"How much damage the castle sustained after Jacob went over to the dark side," Greg continued. "Is that better?"

"I think it's best if I take the chip with me to Phugtal," John said.

"Saji and her team will analyze everything and figure how it works, what it's connected to, and who controls it."

"Okay," said Min. "You can hitchhike with us as far as Ladakh—you can find your way to Phugtal from there, right?"

"What about me?" Kat asked.

"I still don't know whether you're a villain or a victim," John said, "but you're coming with me."

CHAPTER 31
HARLEY

Sundara followed the Kurgiakh Chu Road that ran beside a river of the same name. The mist was rising in wisps from the rushing water, which was high from spring snowmelt. Sundara stopped several times, not just to hydrate, but to marvel at the breathtaking pastel array—a backdrop of lacy white peaks with delicate watercolor blooms and the light green of the early-spring ground cover in the valleys laid out before him. He drank it all in gratefully.

During his many years as the lord consul of the USF, being grateful for nature's wonders had not been worth his time. As he thought about it, he couldn't remember being grateful for much of anything. Now it was as if he had new eyes—and a new heart to match. "Saji, I left without saying goodbye," he said out loud, "but thank you for putting me right. I hope to say thank you in person soon."

Sundara was nearing the end of the journey back from Cha, and decided to freshen up before his arrival at Phugtal. He found a welcoming-looking homestay in Keylong, just twelve miles from his destination.

Keylong had one small shopping area. Its small grocery, pharmacy, hardware store, post office, bank, and gas station attracted residents and farmers from the nearby countryside. It also had a clinic, and even an animal hospital. It was the Himalayan equivalent of a medieval town square, where people socialized, mingled, and got their business done.

The petite woman at the homestay was overtaken by Sundara's handsomeness and charm. She was older, maybe in her fifties, with big brown eyes. With a dimpled smile and straight white teeth, her dark shiny hair was interwoven with just a few filaments of gray—it was obvious she'd been pretty once.

She offered him a shower and a toothbrush. He hadn't brushed his teeth since the vomit marathon, and was still wearing the same clothes from the fight with his sister and mother. While he napped naked on a narrow cot, she washed his clothes and then laid them nicely folded with his wallet on top. When he awoke and got dressed, he wondered if she had rummaged through his wallet. If she had, everything still indicated his name was Michael Wright, from Manchester, England, born 1976. He checked his cash. It still had 900 US dollars in it. The woman provided him with a meal of flatbread and lentils, glancing and smiling at him as he ate. He literally felt like a new man. When Sundara expressed his gratitude for the woman's hospitality, she told him he could come back anytime. It was obvious she had quite the crush on him. What woman wouldn't?

"Well, Harley," Sundara said as he mounted up, "we're headed for Phugtal. Let's hope they don't shoot, throw rocks or arrows when we arrive!" He had no idea how he'd be greeted—his goal was to find Saji before anyone else found him first.

He had named the horse "Harley" early in the trip. Back in 1905, Sundara was the first one privileged to ride the earliest Harley-Davidson motorcycle. He thought the name for the horse was not only nostalgic, but kind of ironic, and the horse didn't seem to mind.

Sundara was about four miles from Phugtal when he was startled by the sight of a military-style aircraft rising up from the ground. Sundara was very familiar with this particular blue helicopter with its silver emblem on the side—Helzar no longer traveled much, but when he did, this was always how he left home. A daytime departure, however, was out of pattern. On its regular twice-a-year flights, the chopper left at night, but then again, this wasn't the usual time of year for Helzar's visit to Abysses.

"They're panicking and they've called an emergency in-person meeting," Sundara concluded, as if talking to Harley. "The two of us are right here," he said, patting his horse on the neck. "We're so close that we're almost in his rotor downwash. We're watching him leave, and he has no idea—he's not picking up on my energy anymore."

Conflicting emotions overtook Sundara as Helzar's blue helicopter faded into the distance. He hated Helzar and was attached to him at the same time. For nearly 2000 years he had been used as a pawn. He had toiled, strategized, developed, invented, negotiated, manipulated...

True, he'd followed his curiosity into a dark and mysterious cave that had a bizarre creature living in it, and he'd done it on his own when he was seven years old. True, after being introduced to sex, his body began to crave the toe-curling, mind-boggling orgasmic escapades with Helzar. True, his ego had basked in the fatherly-type praise he'd receive from Helzar when mastering advanced training and fulfilling assignments. Helzar knew everything there was to know about operant conditioning.

None of it meant he deserved to have his free will stripped from him because his chakras were damaged by sodomy. Sundara was a true victim of neurologically altered mind control. Even though the core beliefs he was born with remained deep inside him, he couldn't access them—at least not until Saji detoxed him and reversed almost two thousand years of neurological damage.

As soon as her treatment was completed, Sundara's brain reconnected to his core, and his freewill right was restored. More importantly, his core inner being was consciously remembered. In other words, he could recall who he really was—who we all are—beautiful, loving extensions of Source energy in human form. What he was left with, and what he had to deal with now, was the paralyzing guilt about all the corruption and suffering he had caused while being controlled by Helzar.

Hurt beings hurt beings, Sundara thought. *I don't want to feel hurt anymore, and I don't want to hurt others anymore, either.*

The grief and anger were unbearable. He cried so loud that even Harley shook his head. Sundara cried into his hands, he cried toward the heavens...he cried and cried, until it turned into an exhausted whimper.

Just then, a colorful bird perched on the branch of a nearby bush. It had wings of aqua and a bright-orange belly. Sundara crept up to the unusual bird. "What's a beautiful kingfisher like you doing in the middle of the Himalayas?" he murmured to the bird.

The sight of the bird stirred a childhood memory of the bedtime story his mother used to tell him about how she had stowed away on a boat during the massive flood.

With water flooding in from the great Atlantic, and water pouring down from the sky, no one stood a chance of swimming to dry land—there was no dry land. Even those who built boats didn't survive—the rain filled them too quickly and made them capsize. The one boat that was still afloat had a covering. I tried to hang on to the stern of the big wooden watercraft, but it was dark, my hands were bleeding, and I was losing my grip.

I was about to let go when a young woman caught sight of me and mercifully reached out her hand. She hoisted me onto the stern and handed me a piece of raw fish. During the day, she kept me hidden, and after everyone was asleep, she'd sneak me down to the stern where there would be a freshly caught fish in a bucket of water, along with a knife for me to filet it.

The family on the boat never questioned why they were short a fish every day. The woman had convinced them that their god had taken it in exchange for saving their lives—like a sacrifice.

I made a friend in a little bird that would come to me at night—I'd share my fish with him. Oh, how he loved fish! His wings were a beautiful aqua color, and he had a belly the color of ripe tangerines. Then, one day, after the rain stopped and the flood was retreating, I was sitting on the stern watching the moon and stars. My friend the bird came swooping in as usual, but this time he had an olive branch in his mouth. That's when I knew we'd soon be back on dry land.

I named that bird "kingfisher," and to this very day, every evening when the sky turns aqua blue and tangerine orange, I give thanks to my little kingfisher friend who kept me company on that boat and sent me the message that dry land was soon to come, and everything was going to be okay.

"So, you're the little kingfisher who gave my mother a message of good news. Is that why you're here? Do you have a branch of good news to share with me?" Sundara asked.

The bird stayed with Sundara and Harley as they rode toward

Phugtal. Before tackling the hairpin turns on the road leading to the monastery, however, Sundara pulled Harley to a halt. He could see the monastery from a distance, as well as a few monks in their red robes engaged in chores.

He dismounted the horse and gave him a pat. "You're on your own now, Harley, my friend," Sundara said. "I'm sure you can smell the fresh hay and can find your way to the stable from here." Harley understood the signal and began to trot in the direction of the Phugtal stable.

As Sundara was about to set off on foot toward the monastery, the kingfisher squawked and flapped his wings, then perched in a pretty tree. "Where the trees are pretty..." Sundara said aloud. "You don't want me to go to the monastery. You want me to go to the cave where the trees are pretty instead?"

The kingfisher squawked and flapped his wings. "I've never been there by myself, without Helzar, ever," he told the bird.

The antechamber of the cave had changed little since he'd first discovered it at the age of seven. The bioluminescent glowworms on the ceiling were still there, looking like a starry night, as were the stalactites and stalagmites and the sound of slow trickling water from melting snow. A huge rock wall at the end of the cave would have looked to most explorers like a dead end, but Sundara knew better.

He placed his hand on a specific, unmarked spot on a rock. His palm was one of three that the locking mechanism had been calibrated to read—the other two belonged to Helzar and Abysses. The rock began to move, opening up to an immense cavern.

The underground cathedral was dimly lit by what looked like cerulean blue raindrops falling down a darkened window. The light was actually generated by vertically scrolling data on the polished façade of the cavern. Even inch of the walls was covered with computer screen.

It was from this space that the Nephilim controlled the world's commerce. Sundara had spent a lot of time there, steering the banking and monetary system, and world trade.

Occasionally, red blinking lights would appear amid the blue cascade, but Sundara knew that was normal. Insignificant glitches in the world systems were to be expected—the red lights would blink for a while, then disappear as soon as the problem was resolved. Now, however, he noticed that there was one red light that was insistently blinking in concert with other onscreen alert notifications. He touched the red light on the screen to open up its location. It indicated that the issue was occurring with a program called "Quasichip"—a project he'd never heard of. A satellite feed brought up a real-time image of a small lodge located in a remote village called Tyungur. He zoomed in.

"Russia," he whispered.

CHAPTER 32
QUASIES

Sitting in front of the array of screens in Helzar's cave, Sundara peered at the live-streamed satellite imagery from Tyungur, Russia. He watched as a petite Asian woman with a bandaged head exited what looked to be a lodge, walked to an SUV, and pulled it up in front of the door. Two men and another woman soon appeared. One of the men was a tall man with stringy blond hair who was carrying a gray-haired woman wrapped in a blanket.

Sundara recognized them both. The man was John Matthews, the tenth-floor secretary at the Society of Truth, the same man he had hurled headfirst into a rock wall at Phugtal, and the same guy he'd seen on horseback with his mother and sister. The woman in his arms was Ruth Müller, the Society's feisty proofreader. From her ashen color, it appeared that Ruth was dead. Following them from the lodge were a young woman, and a man with dark hair. Sundara noticed that they moved in tandem—were they handcuffed to one another? As they moved, so did the blinking red light on the monitor, but he couldn't tell whether it was tracking the man or the woman—at least not until he tapped the screen.

Name: Katarina Volkov
DOB: 1995
Quasichipped: 1998
Location: Milishka Nursery School

Sundara tapped another blinking red light on the screen and a different pop-up window appeared:

Name: Jacob Hoffman

DOB: 1976

Quasichipped…

"Microchips!" he shouted aloud. "They've been inserting them into people for decades! And this guy Jacob was chipped a couple of days ago in Quedlinburg, Germany. That's over 5,000 miles away."

After a few easy searches, he found Jacob Hoffman all over social media as a mentor for young Sibyllines, and a longtime advocate for the Way of Kyndeness. *How the hell did Helzar pull that one off?* Sundara wondered. *I'm sure it was a surprise to everyone when Jacob turned from kindly Dr. Jekyll into evil Mr. Hyde. And how did he end up several thousand feet below Belukha Mountain?*

"Belukha Mountain!" he exclaimed. "There would be only one reason why the USF would have an agent there." He had expected Mireille and Ananta to exit the lodge at Tyungur, but he now shifted satellite coverage to Belukha Mountain.

Sundara was well aware that somewhere on this icy plateau was the access point to the energetic bridge to Shangri-la. Spiritual seekers all over the world had been going to the mountain for centuries in search of it. So had the USF, without success.

At the bottom of the gorge was the smoldering wreckage of a ski plane. *Mom must've been on her way to Shangri-la*, Sundara reasoned to himself. *Jacob Hoffman…you poor bastard. You were microchipped and assigned to hijack the plane so you could find the gateway to Shangri-la, but even your artificially intelligent Quasichip underestimated my mother. I'm quite sure she's in Shangri-la. So…if John is in Tyungur, and Mom is in Shangri-la, where is Ananta? I would have seen her by now if she was with John, so it looks like she went with Mom to Shangri-la, but why?*

Sundara refocused his attention on the van as it headed for a hangar at a small airfield not far from the lodge. The petite Asian woman exited and climbed into the cockpit of what appeared to be one of the newest long-range Dassaults. She was soon followed by the other passengers who'd been in the van, as well as two maintenance men carrying a large pine box. Sundara assumed that the box contained Ruth Müller's dead body. The blinking red light on the monitor followed the group as they boarded the aircraft.

As soon as the Dassault took off, he shifted his attention to a different monitor. He touched the screen, maneuvered through icons and options, and located Russia's air traffic control system. The jet's flight plan showed it was headed for Ladakh.

"Phugtal," Sundara said out loud. "They're headed back here. Perfect!"

Because he knew Helzar would not be returning soon, Sundara contemplated taking one last look around the rest of the massive grotto, with its gothic oversized furnishings and artifacts from millennia gone by. He remembered the feeling he used to have every time he came here—a feeling of heart-thumping excitement to be with Helzar, mixed with anticipation of being assigned an extraordinary challenge that tested the deepest resources of his mind. He used to find both comfort and stimulation in the smells of the cave, which were a combination of ancient history, earth, and minerals, blended with the musky natural aroma of Helzar's breath and body.

Sundara thought back to the long conversations he and Helzar would have about the past, and all the souvenirs and trophies they had collected over time. The rise and fall of political world powers had all been a choreographed plan involving religion and greed—to them, it was a game. They'd laugh about how his mother and the Sibyllines were always playing defense, never knowing what would come next. Then they'd strategize what that next surprise disruption would be, whether it was a political or religious conflict, a moral issue, or a disease. Free will always had to be factored into how they'd set up their next move because humans had choices, and it was those freewill choices that always got in the way.

On this day, Sundara's experience in the cave was different. There was still a lot of eager anticipation, but for the first time, that feeling was emerging from a different place—a different path. For the first time, the cave felt sinister—menacing and dark. The smell was no longer desirable—in fact, it was nauseating.

Sundara's mind and body were no longer under Helzar's control, and he was making the deliberate choice to use his free will for good. The words of Bodhin, the old monk at the Cha monastery, reverberated in his brain: *Whether you were derailed or launched is only in the belief of it.*

"You were right, my friend," Sundara said. "Revisiting the grotto would only reinforce the idea that I'd been derailed, and that's no longer how I feel or what I believe. I've been launched, and the first part of my mission is to find out what this Quasichip Project is about. I may not be able to affect the Maestros—I'll have to leave that up to my father. But I'm going to take down these two old giants, together with their zealots and disciples in the USF."

He returned to the screen that indicated Katarina Volkov's identity and touched: "Quasichipped 1998." A window opened showing a brief summary of the implantation. Katarina was three years old when she fell on the playground at nursery school—in reality, she was tripped by the USF playground supervisor. She was then taken to the first aid office so the abrasion on her forehead could be looked at. The nurse who treated that wound also inserted the tiny chip above her left ear, and she soon rejoined her preschool classmates. Her parents were told that the wound above her ear had happened when she fell.

Sundara then touched the word "Quasichipped," and there it was. From the project's mission statement to the action summary, it briefly explained the Quasichip program as the antidote to the threat associated with dangerous human independence and free will. A brain-inserted micro A.I. Quasichip, made of twelve hundred electrode filaments, would remotely connect the human brain to the Quasichip Control Panel, where digital commands would be downloaded into the chip. The human brain would obey the command while working and living within the natural environment of everyday life.

If the Quasichipped human brain sensed a threat beyond what it was capable of solving on its own, the chip would automatically power down, causing the human to appear to be in a vegetative state. The human would then be either physically removed from the situation by a local USF team, or left to die.

Children of the Sibyllines were the first to receive the chips. A tiny incision would be made slightly above the left ear to accommodate the chip, which would then be closed as inconspicuously as possible. The entire procedure took about three minutes. Children would be returned to the place from which they'd been taken. With no memory of the incident, they would grow up in Sibylline households.

To all outward appearances, they would become Sibylline adults, but in reality, they were sleeper cells—USF agents in training. As they matured they were obeying a series of commands that would groom them to eventually hold positions in elite organizations controlled by the USF. The first phase would be the abduction and Quasichipping of three-year-old Sibylline children in the United States, Canada, Australia, Great Britain, Germany, and Russia. By the time the first set of Sibylline Quasies reached the age of forty, they would hold mid- to high-level positions in USF organizations in government, religion, and big business. The second phase would begin as Quasichips were inserted in naturally gifted, non-Sibylline children. Phase 3 would involve inserting the chips into exceptionally gifted adult brains. The foremost Sibylline advocates, warriors, and champions would be first, listed by name.

Jacob's name was on the list. The pop-up window that described his procedure showed that it had been an emergency implant in the Sibylline treatment center under the Weisshotel Castle.

Sundara's name was on the list, too. "I should have known that there's no loyalty in the USF," he said aloud, "even at the top. I sure had none—except to the giants, but with the Quasichip, they were going to make sure they never lost control of me, no matter what."

Sundara sighed deeply at the thought of all the centuries he'd spent doing their bidding. "I'm not derailed," he affirmed to himself, taking a deep breath. "I've been launched." Somewhere, he hoped, Bodhin was smiling his very best toothless smile.

Sundara turned his attention back to Katarina Volkov. Both her indicator and Jacob's indicator were blinking, which meant they'd been compromised and powered down. Jacob, he knew, was in a crevasse several thousand feet below the Belukha Mountain glacier. He was dead and his indicator was stationary, but Katarina's was moving! What did that mean?

"It means she or someone close to her still has the chip. They all just boarded the Dassault—where are they going?"

Sundara pulled up the navigational air traffic control panel. The flight plan indicated an approximate arrival time of 6:15 a.m.

"How convenient!" Sundara exclaimed. He knew that it would take them at least an additional ten hours to get from Ladakh to the Phugtal Monastery—more than enough time for him to meet up with Saji before their arrival.

Sundara understood immediately that John Matthews would be extremely skeptical about his transformation. After all, Sundara had tried to kill him. Actually, Sundara *had* killed him—it was Ananta's intercession that had brought him back to life. He'd need Saji as an ally who would vouch for his conversion—or more accurately, his reversion to his true self. If they could convince John, he might even be willing to help brainstorm a plan together, and maybe even connect with his mom and his sister in Shangri-la. In the meantime, though, he needed more intel on this Quasichip Project.

CHAPTER 33
GABBY

Zach, Rocky, and Cameron paced the hospital's waiting room floor, waiting for word on the outcome of Gabby's surgery. They'd lost her once and didn't want to lose her again, but they also tried to be realistic. When the paramedics had brought her up from the tunnel, she'd been pale, almost blue. Hoping for the best but fearing the worst, the trio rode the emotional rollercoaster in the waiting room together—anxiety mixed with hope and bad hospital coffee. Eventually, exhaustion caught up with all three of them, and they fell asleep in contorted positions in the waiting room's hard plastic chairs.

It was many hours before Cameron's eyes opened—someone was nudging his shoulder. "Mr. Abbott..." said the nurse, "you may see your wife now."

It took several moments before Cameron could remember where he was, shake the cobwebs from his brain, and process why anyone might be referring to him as "Mr. Abbott." Once he was fully awake, he bounded out of the chair, startling both Rocky and Zach.

"Only one visitor at a time," the nurse said.

"Zach...*son*..." Cameron said, "why don't you go see your mum first, lad?"

"Thanks...*Dad*," Zach replied, keeping up the pretense that Cameron and his mom were his married parents.

Zach gasped as he entered the room. He was shocked by the array of medical technology that had been deployed to keep his mother alive.

The monitors, oxygen, and tubing—incoming and outgoing—that were hooked up to Gabby overwhelmed him.

"All of this equipment may look a little scary, but it's helping us do our job," the ICU nurse reassured him. "Your mother came through her surgery incredibly well—the surgeon will be in shortly to explain everything."

Zach approached the bed and reached for her hand. "Mom?" he whispered.

Gabby did not respond. "Don't worry, Zach," said the doctor as he entered the room. Rocky and Cameron trailed in behind him. "She's a real survivor, that mom of yours. Her surgery was extremely challenging, but her heart is strong, and her vitals are good."

Zach nodded dumbly in agreement. Gabby was dwarfed by everything else in the room. She looked small and fragile—not at all like the healthy, strong, and confident mother he had known and relied on his entire life. The sound of the equipment, the bright lights, the sterile room, the hospital smell...oh how he wished he could whisk her out of there and take her to their old laboratory. If only he could give her the same kinds of plant compounds she'd used to cure others—like the meds she had given Jen and Cameron after they had been wounded in the shootout that killed Heinrich Müller. She would recover faster and be back to her old self sooner—he just knew it. At the same time, he was overwhelmed with gratitude for the skilled surgical team who'd put her back together.

"I wanted all three of you to hear this together," the doctor continued. "The trauma to her torso shattered her pelvis and resulted in multiple open femur fractures, along with a badly torn artery that required a graft. At times we were more of a construction crew than a surgical team, with all the pins, wires, and plates that were needed. We did have to perform a radical nephrectomy, but many, many people live long and productive lives with only one kidney. She's an extraordinary woman, and I have high hopes for her recovery."

The doctor's tone of voice, along with his faith in Gabby's strong physical constitution, was reassuring. "Thank you so much for taking care of my...my wife," Cameron said gratefully. "Will she be able to use her legs again?"

"In time," the doctor said. "With a lot of physical therapy, I fully expect to see Gabby walking again."

"May I ask what medications you're giving her?" Zach asked.

The orthopedic surgeon was intrigued that such a young man would ask that kind of question. "The nurse will give you a list of her meds," he said, "and these will change as she progresses. She'll be in acute care here in the hospital for some time. When she's ready to start putting weight on that pelvis and femur, I'll discharge her to a rehab facility."

"Thank you, Doctor," said Rocky.

"We'll leave you with her now. Fifteen minutes—that's all you get. I doubt that she'll give you any overt response yet, but we don't know what she can hear or feel. Talk to her in soothing tones and touch her —don't feel reluctant. It can only help for her to know that her loved ones are here supporting her. Just don't be loud or say anything stressful."

Zach didn't waste any time. "Mom," he whispered through tears, "you have to wake up from this. You have to be okay—you just have to. I have so much to tell you, and...and you have to meet Phoebe. She's an old woman just like you—I mean...not that you're old...you're not old—what I mean is that she loves plants and believes in plant medicine, just like you. Phoebe is Sadie's aunt, and she's the one who told me you weren't dead. Sadie took me to see her, and she read a tarot card...and then all of a sudden, she knew you were alive. She saved your life, Mom!"

Rocky's eyes widened in disbelief. *A tarot card?!* he mouthed silently to Cameron. Cameron turned his palms skyward and shrugged his shoulders.

Rocky approached the bottom of the bed and placed his hands on Gabby's feet. "Hey, big sis, don't think for a minute that you can leave me here to take care of our restaurant alone. I've been cooking my brains out with Mario, and I now have bigger plans for the Gabby Abbey—plans that include Italian pastries, calzones, and pizza."

He paused and swallowed, fighting back tears, then walked to the side of the bed, across from Zach. "Gabs," he said as he gently took hold of her other hand, "remember when you told me that there is no other person on this planet better equipped to spread the Way of Kyndeness than a gay man like me? Your words changed me that day. Until then I'd felt so unlovable and so ashamed of being gay, but never again after that. Our conversations over the years have given me purpose. I'm still not whole—I don't know if I ever will be. But...you're the one who taught me that my crazy mix of rugged masculinity and refined femininity are exactly what qualifies me to bring this message of compassion and self-acceptance to the world. I'm a Sibylline because of you. One day, the world can be free of shame—the feeling that we're not holy enough or good enough or lovable enough. You taught me not to hide the truth about myself. You pushed me to be proud of who I am and be honest about it, and...well...you're not getting a pass to leave this world just yet."

The nurse came in to remind them they only had five minutes left.

"Zach, how about we give Cam a moment with your mom," Rocky suggested.

Alone with Gabby, Cameron stroked her face, then softly kissed her lips. "They thought I was your husband," Cameron whispered, "and I let them. I kinda liked it."

He looked at the cannula in her nose, and traced the oxygen tubes across her cheek till they hooked around her ears. Then he fingered a strand of curly brown hair and swept it away from her face.

"Here's something funny...I've never been attracted to women with brown hair—until now. You make brown hair and hazel eyes look like a...a goddess."

He touched her lips.

"I would love nothing more than to be able to taste the kiss of your sweet lips every day for the rest of my life. I've never met a woman quite like you, Gabby Abbott...young in spirit, yet wise in life. It's you who opened my eyes. All I want now is to savor the highs, trudge through the lows, and chase the thrills in life with you. If we...if we can have another chance at life, I want to spend mine with you."

The nurse peeked through the window to Gabby's room and saw Cameron pouring his heart out to his "wife." She decided to give him a few extra minutes, since he was the only one in the room.

Cameron assumed Gabby couldn't hear him, but he spoke to her anyway. "I remember when I was a child, I craved my father's love and attention, but no matter what I did, I couldn't measure up. It was like there was this irrepressible drive to please him, and a constant fear that he'd abandon me—which was akin to death—and I would just recoil at his scolding and criticism, which was all the time. In my childish ways, I did everything within my power to retain his attention and love, desperately trying to keep him from ignoring me, but he knew I was different from him, and I could tell he hated it. I saw how my friends' dads treated them and became increasingly aware that I had to find better ways to retain my father's love. If I couldn't change who I was, I could at least change the way I acted. I could hide my differences from him. But...he knew. He knew all along, and all he wanted to do was to trip me up. It was like he found pleasure in it, and enjoyed punishing me. And yet...I still forced myself to follow in his shoes as a strict and dutiful USF soldier, a man who defended the cause at all costs. There's something about you, Gabby, that made it easy to walk away from it all."

The nurse came back into the room. "I'm so sorry, Mr. Abbott. I know how much you want to be by your wife's side right now, but it's time to leave."

He kissed Gabby—this time on the forehead. He lingered for a few seconds, then finally let go of her hand.

"I'll come get you when she wakes up," the nurse said. "Meanwhile you and your son and brother-in-law really should get some food and rest."

CHAPTER 34
SCHMIDT

It was 7:45 p.m. at Devon Nelson's Society of Truth congregation in Brooklyn. The service was already under way—song and prayer had commenced promptly at 7:30, followed by a short sermon. Nelson had chosen an aisle seat up front. Thomas Schmidt was also there, occupying an aisle seat toward the back. His walker had been stowed to the side by one of the attendants.

To maintain his cover story as Nelson's assistant, and to show other members that he was still a faithful member of the Society, Milton Chandler was in attendance as well. As soon as the sermon concluded, the lights were dimmed in preparation for showing the video. Milton tried to maintain a somber expression, but he was grinning broadly on the inside. He knew what he was about to see, and he also knew how many other Society of Truth congregations had already seen it.

All worship centers followed the same program—the buzz of cheerful mingling amongst the brothers and sisters was quieted when the chairman called on everyone to take their seats. Society meetings were carefully orchestrated to promote a feeling of collegial solidarity, both within each gathering, and from one congregation to another. There was something comforting about knowing that all faithful members of the Society of Truth were having the same worship experience. On any given date, every gathering around the world sang the same song and heard the same keynote speech, after which they all watched the same prerecorded video broadcast from the headquarters in New York.

Milton knew that Donna's "adapted" video concluded with Schmidt invoking God's name and directing everyone to observe obedient, reverent silence. He pictured members blinking in the sudden brightness as the lights came back on, then looking uncomfortably at one another, and especially at the elders. Some of the elders, he knew, would be completely mystified. Others who were aware of instances of molestation in the congregation would be extremely uncomfortable. They'd be apprehensive about doing what they'd been ordered to do—to go to the authorities and rat out the abusers. Then there were the actual pedophiles, who would be feeling angry, betrayed, and intensely fearful about what would happen next. Members would file out silently, drive home, and power down their devices. It was a scenario that had already been repeated from Auckland to Indianapolis—eighteen hours had elapsed since the video's "premiere."

"May we have the lights dimmed, please?" the chairman announced. "The topic of our video broadcast tonight is 'The Bible's Position on Child Protection.' Let us all pay close attention to this fine information from our Lord God."

Everyone applauded as Brother Schmidt appeared on the screen—everyone except Devon Nelson, who turned around, scanning the room for Schmidt and Milton. He made eye contact with both men, giving them a bewildered expression. They frowned and shrugged their shoulders—they were as perplexed as he was.

Schmidt began:

It took many years to get to this moment. Today, the Society of Truth confronts its own sin—its own unspeakable depravity. Child sexual abuse within the Society is an abomination that has been hiding in plain sight for far too long. Trust has been broken, innocence betrayed.

As the video continued, murmurs were heard among the congregation. Children looked questioningly at their parents. Husbands and wives looked wide-eyed at one another. There had never been a video like this before—apologies of any kind from the Elder Board were unheard of, let alone for this kind of ungodly behavior. Many followers of the religion had heard the rumors of child sexual abuse, but they'd discounted them as false, because that's what they'd been told.

Nelson was aghast. He got up and motioned for Milton and Schmidt to meet him in the back of the auditorium, but Schmidt wasn't going anywhere without his walker.

"What the hell is this?" Nelson whispered to Milton. "Is this some kind of joke?"

"I have no idea, my brother," Milton replied. "I'm just as shocked as you are. The brothers in the broadcast department filmed me—not Schmidt. I even stayed after it was finished and observed as they uploaded it. I saw them schedule it to be viewed, like they always do."

The video was finishing up with Schmidt's final words:

God Himself is asking for your strict obedience in observing twenty-four hours of off-grid silence in deep, gratitude-filled prayer. Trust in the Lord, and honor Him with utmost compliance. Going forward, our Lord will use His Elder Board to begin cleansing and resanctifying His true organization. Soon, we will be back online to offer encouragement, along with a new, enlightened direction. You can access this video on our sot.org website.

Silence fell upon the congregation. The elder who was to close the service was a bit delayed in approaching the platform. Once he took the podium, he was at a loss for words, so he simply said, "Please stand, if you're able, and join me in singing song number eleven." After the final prayer, the members walked past Schmidt one by one. To his astonishment, many of them stopped to shake his hand. "Thank you, Brother Schmidt, for having the courage of our Lord Jesus Christ," one said. "Just as Jesus overturned the corrupt money tables in the syna-gogue," said another, "so too you have overturned and exposed corruption that the Devil tried to sneak into the congregation of God." The elder men in attendance, however, glowered at him as if he was the traitor they believed him to be.

Milton and Nelson also received their share of handshakes and praise, but the older men filed past them in stony silence. A young man made sure the projection screen was stowed away and the speaker system was shut down; then he brought Schmidt his walker. Schmidt couldn't wait to defend himself, but by the time he caught up with Nelson, it was obvious that Nelson had come to his own conclusion.

"Should I wash your feet, J.C.?" Nelson snarled.

"I didn't do this!" Schmidt insisted loudly.

"Let's not alarm the others," Milton said softly as he placed his hand on Schmidt's shoulder. "You can't deny that it's you on the video, my brother."

"Schmidt, you have no idea how much trouble this admission of guilt is going to cause for us legally," Nelson said. "What were you thinking? Or more accurately...why *weren't* you thinking? We can't just go 'overturning the tables of corruption' like Christ did, you old fool! Admitting that we turned a blind eye to child sexual abuse will land us in court, and maybe in jail! And if you think the hush money settlements we're paying now are hefty, just wait! Survivors and their families are going to bleed us dry. We may not only go bankrupt, we may also lose our status as a charity! If we have to start paying taxes..." Nelson placed his hand on his forehead, took a deep breath, and then continued, "We have no choice now. The damage is done. We can't un-apologize."

Donna was right, Milton thought. *Nelson didn't have a choice. He went for the righteous "Jesus Christ" option.*

"But...but...you don't understand," Schmidt stuttered. "I was never filmed. I haven't been filmed in a long time. Ask the broadcast department. Someone hacked our system!"

"Right..." Nelson scoffed. "You expect me to believe that you're the victim here? Someone busted through two firewalls, unencrypted our security system, and then was able to manipulate your mouth and your voice on a video using a voiceover that sounds just like you, making it look like you were speaking, but it really wasn't you?"

"Look...I know what it looks like, but I had nothing to do with this. I was never filmed. I'm telling the truth, believe me! Back me up here, Milton," Schmidt pleaded. "You typed the script yourself!"

Milton immediately understood that Schmidt had presented him with a perfect opportunity to cement his position as Nelson's toady and right-hand man. "Yes, I did type the script. I read it before the camera, too. We get it, Brother Schmidt, you were"—Milton paused to flex the middle and index fingers of both hands in the classic "air quotes" gesture—"'never filmed.' "

"Milton, meet me in my office at headquarters," Nelson instructed. "We have to nip this in the bud, or we'll go broke. I have some ideas."

"I'll be there as well," Schmidt said.

"No, you won't," Nelson declared. "You've done more than enough already. In fact, go home and pack."

Schmidt frowned and cocked his head. "I beg your pardon?"

"Schmidt, you are no longer a member of the Elder Board," Nelson declared. "C'mon, Brother Chandler, we have a lot of damage control to do."

Milton stopped Devon as he turned to leave. "Hold on, Brother Nelson," he said. "You have a tag hanging off your pants. Here...let me get it."

Milton grabbed at a small rectangular piece of cloth that protruded from Nelson's pocket. As soon as he pulled it out, there was no mistaking what it was or where it had come from. It was Donna's lacy pink thong. He glowered as he held it up in front of Nelson's face, but said nothing.

CHAPTER 35
SUNDARA

Sundara followed the path from Helzar's cave toward Phugtal—the same one he had taken as a boy. Crouched behind a rock, he saw a monk on the top level and knew immediately that it was Saji, even with her back to him. No one else had such a long gray braid or carried herself with such grace.

Saji was immediately aware that she was being watched, and turned to survey the hills and pathways below the monastery. Sundara stood so she could see him. She acknowledged him, then signaled that she would come to where he was, rather than vice versa. She would explain to the other monks in due time, but not now.

It took a full hour for Saji to descend from the uppermost floor of the monastery to the rock where Sundara was waiting. Saji hurried for no one—especially at her advanced age. When she arrived, they stared at one another for several minutes. "I'm sorry," Sundara finally said.

Saji nodded slowly. What more could he say? Would additional words produce a more meaningful apology? They both knew better. "It's a beginning," she replied. Given all the damage he'd caused over the centuries, "I'm sorry" was enough for now, as long as it was genuine.

Without saying a word, Saji led Sundara to a bench at the three stupas. "I had to leave the treatment room..." he began.

"You don't have to explain," Saji replied softly.

"I don't know where to start," Sundara said.

"How about we start with this recent epidemic of earthquakes," Saji said. "They're caused by the Nephilim, right?"

"Right."

"But how?"

"When I was a kid, I learned to send out an echolocation-based frequency using my vocal cords. The giants can do that, too, but their frequency range is a lot broader than mine will ever be. It's like when an opera singer hits a note that shatters every piece of Waterford or Baccarat crystal behind the bar—except on a global scale. And when they're pissed off, it's epic. As they 'voice' their anger, as it were, it resonates with the earth's frequency, and everything shakes."

"My guess is that this isn't going to get better anytime soon," said Saji. "In fact, it's probably going to get worse now that they know you've...well...changed."

"And before I took off, I didn't get a chance to thank you for everything you did to change me, Saji, so I'm thanking you now," Sundara said. "I can only imagine that I was the world's worst patient at the beginning."

"Pretty close," she admitted.

"If you're willing, I'd like to talk more about what I did when I was under the control of the Nephilim, but I also need your help," Sundara said.

"How about you just tell me what you need help with, and we save everything else for another day," Saji suggested.

"I'd like that," he sighed.

Sundara told her about seeing Helzar leave by helicopter. He then described his return to Helzar's cave, and his discovery of the Quasichip Project there. "They plan to use the chips to destroy free will," he said, "and by the way, a young woman will be arriving here from Tyungur, Russia, a woman who'd been Quasichipped. She is the child of Russian Sibylline parents. Her name is Katarina—"

"Volkov," said Saji. "I was informed that she's on her way—with John Matthews. The two of you will have some stuff to talk about."

"You may have to referee that conversation," said Sundara. "He may not understand that I'm not the man I used to be when I tried to kill him."

"Understood," said Saji. "Katarina Volkov's chip was extracted from a wound above her left ear. The wound was inflicted by a woman named Ruth Müller…”

“The sassy old dame from the Society of Truth?” Sundara said incredulously.

“Apparently, she stabbed Ms. Volkov, a martial arts expert, with a pair of tweezers…”

“No way!”

“And managed to hit the exact spot where the chip had been implanted,” said Saji. “There appears to be no other plausible explanation. John found Ruth Müller and Katarina Volkov side by side on a bed at the lodge in Tyungur. Ruth was dead, and Katarina was unconscious with the tweezers in her head.”

“Unbelievable!”

“It’s unclear whether Katarina is responsible for Ruth’s death. From what we can understand, the chip became deactivated when John removed it from her head. I have an IT team waiting to examine it, and I’ll be examining Ms. Volkov myself. One of my objectives is to determine whether Ms. Volkov has any lingering control effects from the chip now that it’s been removed. Meanwhile, however, your discovery of the Quasichip program clarifies a great deal.”

“We’ll need to create a plan to remove these chips from all the Quasies,” Sundara added.

“How many of them are there?” Saji asked.

“According to what I discovered, there have been about 180,000 chips implanted in children between the ages of three and fifteen. There are another 50,000 or so in older teens and adults forty and under.” Sundara pulled a thumb drive out of his pocket. “I downloaded the identities of all the Quasies,” he said. “This drive has all their demographic statistics—name, date of birth, parents’ names, and date and location when they were implanted. Once we figure out more about Katarina and find out what she knows, we can create a plan to have all of them removed.”

“I don’t know whether that’s going to work,” Saji replied. “Actually, that’s wrong. I’m quite sure it won’t. What you’re suggesting is impractical. You want to take a guess at how we’d convince 230,000 people, including parents of minors, that they have a USF computer chip in their brain, and that it needs to be removed? Even if we could do that, from what you've told me, the program is ongoing—they're continuing to implant more kids with more chips. Adults, too. Do you think you could reprogram or sabotage the system from Helzar's control panel?"

"The program is not only impenetrable, it defends itself. Even if I took a sledgehammer to the central operating system inside Helzar's cave, the Quasi Project wouldn't stop."

"Why is that?"

"Because it's A.I.," Sundara responded.

"Artificial intelligence," Saji said, nodding.

"Yes. Each Quasichip is imprinted with a certain agenda for that particular individual. The chip itself is programmed to learn, gather, store, and remember, and then command—all on its own. When the chip is inserted into a three-year-old child, that kid spends the first decade learning and storing—literally at light speed—downloading enormous amounts of digital information. The next decade is spent processing the information according to the agenda that person is being programmed to perform. The third decade, when the human is between twenty to thirty years old, is when the Quasichip begins making decisions and commanding the human to undertake a variety of tasks. The command could be in the form of a desire to pursue a certain career, or an actual duty, or assignment. From what I can tell, Katarina Volkov is an example. Her parents and her peers thought she was on a Sibylline mission, but what they didn't know—and what she didn't know, either—was that she was starting to respond to commands from her Quasichip."

"In other words," said Saji, "the chip has the ability to learn—on its own—and to decide which command is best for that individual and for the agenda that he or she has been preprogrammed to achieve."

"More than that," Sundara replied. "The chip will make those commands while ensuring its host—the person whose brain it's in—continues to lead an unsuspecting life as well-intentioned Sibylline."

"Which means that the Quasichip is operating independently from the Nephilim control panel," Saji declared. "It achieves digital superintelligence—liftoff, if you will—inside the thirty-year-old Sibylline brain."

"It does," Sundara confirmed. "And that's why deactivating the program is going to be so difficult. Once the Quasichip reaches that level of independence, it's on autopilot. It has a mind of its own, and answers to no one. Those chips can even repair their own glitches."

"Hmmm..." Saji's wheels were turning. "We all knew that A.I. was one of the biggest threats to humanity's free will," she said with a sigh, "but this..."

"There's more," Sundara said. "Guess what professions most of the Quasies in their thirties are in right now?"

Saji shook her head. "It doesn't take superintelligence to guess that. There's only one field they would be placed in at this time—the medical field."

"The first generation of Quasies is now replicating itself by implanting chips into a new generation of children. They use annual wellness checkups, visits to the doctor and hospital, and deliberately created first-aid emergencies—like Katarina Volkov's—to get the child into a secure, private space where the procedure can be performed. The child is coaxed by some young and fun thirty-something Quasi nurse to get weighed, get a sticker, or...whatever...to get them alone for three minutes. Three minutes—that's all it takes. Then the child is brought back to their parent—Quasichipped. The child doesn't remember the procedure, and the parents have no reason to suspect anything is amiss."

"You have to unlock the system, Sundara," Saji insisted. "That's all there is to it. We have no choice. We have to stop this! We're going to need your mother back here."

"I discovered that she—and possibly Ananta, too—went to Shangri-la," Sundara said. "Do you know why?"

Saji remained silent. Like Mireille, she had picked up on Ananta's condition right away, but had kept that knowledge to herself. She had no doubt that this was the reason for the trip to Shangri-la, but it was not her place to tell Sundara about his sister's pregnancy.

"I'll put in a call to Cosma at Shangri-la," Saji said, ignoring Sundara's question.

[illegible] all illustrations is not unusual. It has something to know a... and [illegible] to me that [illegible] they can make another chapter at the [illegible] outline. I say, when you are organizing [illegible] organize almost through typing sites [illegible] be what you said you [illegible] in [illegible]

These make an affordable compared to promoting [illegible] quired in their [illegible] way from [illegible]

So that we have of the [illegible] time, especially place to print this [illegible] paper, only because they would be [illegible] this same chapter [illegible]

[illegible] illustrations of a book is a way of making much [illegible] [illegible] a new generation of images. They use all the [illegible] words especially [illegible] adopt [illegible] and deliberately [illegible] and [illegible] is [illegible] [illegible] is [illegible] book. [illegible] [illegible] what the production can be performed. [illegible] printers can do by some [illegible] and not that [illegible] [illegible] [illegible] developed outlined for audiences [illegible] [illegible] [illegible] first printed the images — things. I think [illegible] a [illegible] bought book no inner terms. He said, [illegible] The said the [illegible] [illegible] the production and the paper. I've put no terms [illegible]

[illegible] writing is sound.

Anyone to inked the way. Sand new surprised that the [illegible] their technical in course. I shall we keep the way of course in [illegible] chapter is a book.

[illegible] surprised that the and [illegible] [illegible] now very [illegible] [illegible] [illegible]. [illegible] [illegible]. Particularly why [illegible]

[illegible] [illegible]. [illegible] surprised that a photo is a book [illegible] him a little a book type the sequence to use. She is [illegible] [illegible] not have a life [illegible] [illegible] there anyone to [illegible] the [illegible] [illegible] [illegible] [illegible] that he say [illegible] about a picture's [illegible]. [illegible] [illegible] [illegible] to announce, said a book [illegible] [illegible] knowing [illegible] [illegible]

CHAPTER 36
FORGET ME NOT

It was raining and still dark in the early-morning hours when the Dassault touched down in Frankfurt with Greg at the controls. While in flight, Min had arranged for a hearse to meet them on the tarmac and take Ruth's body to be prepared for burial. As soon as the hearse had departed, she and Greg had driven straight to Quedlinburg, and into the secure underground parking garage of the Weisshotel Castle, where they were greeted by the Sibylline hospitality services manager. "Welcome back, Min," she said. "It's an honor to have you with us once more. I have a secure guest suite ready for you." There was an uneasy pause before she added, "And welcome back to you as well, Herr Blunt."

"Last time we were here, he was cuffed to a bench," Min said with a smile.

"Last time we were here, everyone thought I was USF, and that my brothers-in-arms were about to storm the castle—literally," said Greg.

"The invasion never happened, but I have no idea why," said the services manager. "I'm just happy that they didn't ruin everything we've built here."

"We—and the castle—have Jacob to thank for that—for better or worse," Min said, touching her bandaged forehead. "When Greg let us know that a USF attack was imminent, we knew that we had to evacuate Ruth and the seeds. What we didn't know was that Jacob had changed sides. Once he tipped off the USF that we were leaving, they came after us instead, even though we were halfway around the world.”

“Jacob was a USF double agent?” the hospitality manager said incredulously.

“It’s complicated,” Min replied. “He wasn’t always on the wrong team, but he was when he died.”

“We don’t know when he defected, but that’s a discussion for another time,” said Greg.

“I want to hear more,” the administrator said, “but for now, only one question remains—food first or rest first?”

“Food!” exclaimed Min and Greg in unison.

The heady aroma of brewed coffee greeted them as they were shown to their table. Sumptuous arrays of the hotel’s signature breakfast foods—pumpernickel bread rolls, nut butters, and marmalades, along with boiled eggs, yogurt, fruit, cheeses, and freshly squeezed juices were set out buffet-style in the bright, elegant restaurant.

“I don’t know about you,” said Greg, “but I can eat a platter of those rolls all by myself.”

“You’ll have to fight me for them,” Min replied with a laugh.

After they had feasted, a castle staff member escorted them down the stone staircase to the Sibylline security checkpoint.

“It’s an honor—and a great relief—to have you back, Min,” said one of the guards on watch. “Your face is your proof of ID, but it looks like we should take you to the treatment room before showing you to your accommodations.”

“He’s right, Minny,” said Greg. “You’ve gotten more mileage out of that butterfly bandage that I clumsily slapped on your forehead than we had any right to expect. Someone needs to clean that wound properly and redress it. And I’m still not convinced that you don’t need stitches.”

The guard escorted Min and Greg to the treatment room. “Wait here, please, Mr. Blunt,” the reception nurse said to Greg. “We’ll have her back shortly.”

Min reemerged minutes later. A fresh—and expertly applied—new bandage was on her forehead. “Stitches?” Greg asked.

“A couple,” she replied. “No biggie. And painless, too.”

When they reached their underground suite, a cozy fire awaited them. Without hesitation, Min headed straight for the bathroom. *Shower or bath?* she wondered. *Bath, definitely bath,* she quickly decided. The hot water steamed up the mirror as Min sank up to her neck in the soaking tub. All the tension of the past few days dissolved in a fragrant cloud of herbal body wash, shampoo, and conditioner as she carefully avoided her wound.

"Your turn," she said as she emerged from the hot, misty bathroom draped in one of the hotel's luxurious oversized bath towels. Her only adornment was Ruth's black velvet bag of seeds that nestled between her breasts.

Greg sized her up as she entered the bedroom. " 'Nothing' looks good on you," he murmured as he pinned her body against the wall and began kissing her lips, neck, and shoulders. "You look edible, and you taste delicious." Min tugged at the towel—it fell away as Greg ran his hands over her torso.

Greg wanted to do more—so much more—but not before he showered away the grime and sweat from the marathon trip to Belukha Mountain and back. Still locked in an embrace, he guided Min to the bed and gave her a gentle push. She fell back onto the mattress, face up. "Don't go anywhere," he ordered, giving her one final, deep kiss. "I'm going to get clean. Then we can get dirty together."

Min turned down the sheets and rested her head on the silken pillow. She closed her eyes and listened as Greg turned on the shower. Nature's white noise—the harmonic thrumming of the water blended with the crackling sounds of the wood fire—amped up Min's sense of romantic anticipation, which was already intense.

Greg stepped out of the bathroom to see Min lying naked with her eyes closed. He paused and stood over her, marveling at her physical perfection—smooth skin, firm small breasts, a tiny waist, and a cute freckle on her right hip. Her breathing was slow and calm. *Sleeping Beauty,* he thought to himself.

He lay down next to her and gently moved a thick locket of hair behind her left ear, revealing two small stitches just above it. *I must have missed that little cut,* he said to himself. *I guess I was preoccupied with the big gash in her forehead and fishing out the shards of glass from the cockpit dashboard.*

He fingered the black velvet pouch, then moved it to one side. He leaned in to caress her nipple, then stopped. The powerful sexual desire he felt was compelling, but he just couldn't bring himself to wake her—they'd been through so much together in the last few days. *There will be other times—lots of them*, he told himself as he reached for the covers and pulled them up over them both.

Min and Greg dressed quickly for Ruth's funeral, and although they were already late leaving the castle, she insisted on stopping at a nursery en route to the graveside service. Greg was exasperated—he was compulsively punctual—but Min told him it was absolutely imperative that she purchase a pot of forget-me-nots.

The old cemetery was dotted with well-worn headstones of the ancestors of local families—men and women who had shaped the culture and history of Quedlinburg over many centuries. When Min and Greg arrived, they could see Ruth's body, wrapped in a simple linen shroud, suspended above a neat rectangular hole in the earth. Her closest family members, along with some of Heinrich's relatives, occupied the chairs that ringed the gravesite.

A large crowd of mourners had gathered behind them—word had spread quickly among the Sibyllines that a great but previously unknown heroine had died in service to the Way of Kyndeness. Many felt compelled to pay their respects to a woman they had never met— Ruth Müller, the longtime proofreader and ghostwriter for the Society of Truth. She had escaped the cult, stolen and safeguarded the seeds of the Tree of Life, and helped expose a pernicious pattern of child sexual abuse. Late in life, she had fulfilled her destiny as the last descendant of the Procula Sibyllines to become a fierce advocate for the Kynde way of life, and had done so at great personal sacrifice. Eulogists praised her, and traditional songs were offered in her honor as Ruth's body was lowered into the earth. Everyone who attended had the opportunity to toss a flower into the grave before the cemetery caretakers filled it with rich, loamy soil.

Min and Greg lingered until everyone else had left. "You ready to go?" he asked.

"Not yet," Min replied. "I know she's not in her body anymore, but

I feel her presence is nearby, and I need to say a few words to her—alone. Could I ask you to wait in the car while I do that?"

"Of course," said Greg. "The two of you shared a special bond. I wouldn't think of intruding on your moment together."

"Thank you," said Min as she rubbed the side of her head.

"Are you okay?" Greg asked.

"I'm fine. Just a slight headache is all," Min responded. "I'm sure it's just that the stress and the sadness of the past few days is finally catching up to me—well that, and the fact that my body has no idea what time zone it's in."

"Take all the time you need," Greg replied as he walked away from the gravesite. "I give good massages, just so you know."

"I'll take you up on that," Min called after him.

As Greg headed for the car, Min lovingly touched each letter engraved on Ruth's headstone.

Ruth Sophia Weiss Müller
geliebte Frau von Heinrich Fimm Müller
Ein leuchtender Stern.
Für immer geliebt.

"A shining star. Forever loved. Never forgotten," Min repeated out loud as she wiped a tear from her eye. "You were all those things and so much more, my dearest Ruth."

Min knelt down, then lifted the pot of forget-me-nots and ceremoniously offered them up to the headstone. "I brought you something, Ruth," she said. "Aren't they lovely? The forget-me-not—*Myosotis sylvatica*—is not only pretty, but has healing properties as well. Right now, however, it's enough that their little blue flowers are beautiful to look at, and they will forever remind me of you."

Min then heard Ruth's voice inside her head. *It was our favorite flower*, Min recalled her saying. *I'm going to plant them on Heinrich's grave so he knows he'll never be forgotten. Please promise me that when my time comes, you'll do that for me, too.*

You have my word, Ruth, she had assured her.

Min lifted a handful of earth from right in front of the headstone, then let the soft, friable soil sift through her fingers. Transplanting the forget-me-nots would be easy, but that didn't mean she would do it quickly. It was essential to be thoughtful and intentional while planting them. This was the fulfillment of her sacred promise to Ruth, and it was not to be rushed.

Before she began, however, she scanned her surroundings to make sure she was truly alone. Her Sibylline awareness and self-defense training was kicking in—she'd sent Greg off to sit in the car, which meant he'd be too far away to respond quickly if she suddenly needed help. Without him nearby, Min would be vulnerable while all her attention was focused on honoring Ruth and preparing the ground in front of her.

Min glanced toward the car. From a distance, Greg looked as though he was staring idly out the windshield, but his mind was in overdrive. He sat behind the wheel, going over recent events. Something was nagging at the back of his brain, and it had to do with Jacob's transformation from Sibylline bodyguard to USF operative. *When did it happen, and how did it happen?* he asked himself. *It couldn't have been at the cottage*, he reasoned, *or Jacob would have easily overpowered Ruth right there and taken the seeds. What I know for sure is that by the time all of us got into the back of the truck for the trip to Frankfurt, he was acting weird...*

Greg tried to recreate the sequence of events in his head. *When Min told Jacob to unshackle me from the bench, he had resisted for the longest time. He had also made a huge show of his Glock 19, patting his holster and waving it around like it was some kind of new toy. What Sibylline does that?*

Then he remembered Min pointing out a scrape just above his ear. At the time, Jacob had shrugged it off as a scratch he got as they were evacuating the castle, but...

"Oh!" Greg cried aloud as a feeling of dread took hold in his stomach. "Oh, oh, oh!" He suddenly recalled that he'd recently seen a wound in exactly the same place—on Katarina at the lodge in Tyungur. *No way that's a coincidence*, he told himself.

Whatever happened to Jacob must have happened underground at the Weisshotel Castle, he concluded. *That means a second USF agent has infiltrated our Sibylline defenses—which explains why I was able to "find" my Walther PPK after I was captured—the spy thought they were helping a fellow USF comrade. Whoever did that is still in place.*

Satisfied that she was alone, Min loosened the forget-me-nots from their pot, spread their roots, and lovingly planted them in front of Ruth's headstone. "They'll reseed, Ruth," she said. "Eventually, both you and Heinrich will be covered in them!"

"Speaking of seeds..." After looking around once more, she removed the black velvet pouch from around her neck and gently opened it.

"I know; I know, Ruth," Min said. "The Eden Project terrarium was supposed to be the perfect environment where these could germinate and grow. And that's where we had intended to plant them—you and me together. That would still be the plan, except who would have thought that Jacob—*our* Jacob—would turn out to be a USF agent? He protected me for many years, so whatever changed him must have happened at the castle. That means we can't plant the seeds there—*your* seeds—the ones that cost you your life—and Heinrich's life, too. It's not safe."

Min paused to listen, channeling her strong connection with Ruth. "What am I going to do instead?" she said to the headstone. "Good question, Ruth! I've decided that since you've been the seed-bearer this whole time, they need to stay with you. Better here than to take the chance that they'll fall in the hands of the USF."

Using her index finger, Min poked six tiny holes into the soil around the perimeter of the forget-me-nots, then dropped one seed into each of them. Leaning toward Heinrich's grave, she plucked some forget-me-not seed pods from the plants in front of his headstone and placed them in the pouch. Then she pulled the cord tight and laced it around her neck once more. "You're right, of course, Ruth," she said. "Those pods won't fool anybody for long, but at least the weight of the pouch will feel right. If any of the bad guys get far enough to remove this pouch from around my neck, the game's over anyway."

Returning her attention to Ruth's grave, she smoothed over the soil where the Seeds of Life were now planted. Min remained perfectly still as a bright-turquoise-and-orange bird landed briefly on Ruth's headstone, then flew off. Only after it was gone was she ready to leave.

Her head throbbed a little as she stood. "Shhh...don't tell anyone, you two," Min whispered as she brushed herself off. "It'll be our little secret. Just you and me," she said. "Forget me not, Ruth and Heinrich. Both of you will remain in my heart forever." Before heading to the car, she quickly rubbed at the stitches above her left ear.

END OF BOOK TWO

ACKNOWLEDGEMENT

I would like to give special acknowledgement to my editor, Kay Diehl. Her vast knowledge, ghostwriting experience, and insight into technical and character nuances shaped my story into colorful and historical beauty that I could not have achieved otherwise.

ABOUT THE AUTHOR

Harper Woods is a pen name. She was born and raised deep in the Motown culture of Detroit, MI, as a devout member of the Jehovah's Witnesses religion until leaving the religious cult in her midforties.

Privileged Secrets, Book One: Seeds of Eden, is her first novel, a fictional narrative based on her own life journey inside the religious cult of her childhood, exiting it, and becoming an advocate of exposing child sexual abuse kept secret behind a veil of clergy protection.

In her secular career, Sherrie Berry is an independent entrepreneur, and a skin care formulator whose expertise in formulation development led her to become the first in history to extract, import, and legalize hemp-based CBD (cannabidiol).

This experience, that has involved regulatory agencies, adds to the rich narrative in this fictional setting. As a formulator, Ms. Berry was also the first to put CBD in skin care and take it through clinical trials with sensational results, as well as nano-size CBD, encapsulating it for time-released effect in both lipophilic and hydrophilic formulations for both oral and topical use. She also invented a 5-in-1 facial handheld device that paired products with ultrasound, ion therapy, laser, massage, and infrared therapy and to liquify crystals for the best conductivity in ultrasound gel.

Sherrie has been featured in *Lioness* and *Locale* magazines and her articles have appeared in *DaySpa* and *Organic Spa* magazines. She has also enjoyed giving speeches and coaching women leaders in public speaking.

www.harperwoodsauthor.com

www.ingramcontent.com/pod-product-compliance
Lightning Source LLC
Chambersburg PA
CBHW010638190726
48289CB00009B/2763

9 781737 411628